Twelve captivating tales from the best new writers of the year accompanied by three more from bestselling authors you've read before.

A beleaguered scientist discovers time travel is possible, but a brewing storm threatens to erase his legacy.

—"Storm Damage" by T. R. Naus

When a door to eternity opens in a downtown doctor's office, a man and a woman from opposite sides forge a marriage of love between irreconcilable universes.

—"Blackbird Stone" by Ian Keith

When an obsolete police robot gets one last chance to avoid the salvage yard, he finds the line between justice and murder is as thin as a silicon wafer.

—"Kill Switch" by Robert F. Lowell

A rookie constable on a desolate alien outpost faces the ultimate trial: proving himself under the guidance of the legendary Old Keno, whose training methods are as brutal as the terrain.

—"Tough Old Man" by L. Ron Hubbard

As Claire and her sisters are on the run to avoid the deadly birds, a stop for gas may throw them into mortal danger.

—"Karma Birds" by Lauren McGuire

In a world of mandated technology, one boy's defiance sparks intrigue, envy, and a desire for forgotten freedoms.

—"The Boy from Elsewhen" by Barlow Crassmont

On an uncharted jungle world, a survey team meets an impossible horror from beyond death itself.

—"Code L1" by Andrew Jackson

T0356186

When a ship emerges from the depths of a gas giant, a solitary observer intervenes, unraveling an ancient cycle of survival, identity, and evolution.

—"Under False Colours" by Sean Williams

A cheerful self-driving car gives a ride to a reclusive writer, and during the trip faces a choice with world-altering ramifications.

—"Ascii" by Randyn C.J. Bartholomew

Carlos Buela doesn't know where or *when* he is, or how to find the bus back home—but that rock he bought as a souvenir is to blame.

—"Slip Stone" by Sandra Skalski

In a lightning-powered city, a father confronts the rotten truth of the man he has become as he discovers that no one is truly free in a society built on oppression.

—"The Stench of Freedom" by Joel C. Scoberg

A man trapped on an endless ship searches for his wife amid strange, forgotten decks and haunting memories.

—"My Name Was Tom" by Tim Powers

In the wake of a devastating tragedy, the last member of a magical sisterhood must choose between forgiveness and unleashing a vengeful demon.

—"The Rune Witch" by Jefferson Snow

When a pizza delivery guy meets his time-traveling future selves, he must juggle conspiracies, collapsing timelines, and cooling pizzas.

—"Thirty Minutes or It's a Paradox" by Patrick MacPhee

The world is trapped in a thirty-four-hour time loop where everything resets except memories. With reality fractured, humanity struggles to forge a new normal.

—"A World of Repetitions" by Seth Atwater Jr.

L. RON HUBBARD

PRESENTS

Writers of the Future
Anthologies

"The most enduring forum to showcase new talent in the genre. The series continues to be a powerful statement of faith as well as direction in American science fiction."

—*Publishers Weekly*

"The Writers of the Future Contest…continues to bring to the fore a plethora of exciting new talent in the world of SFF writing."

—SciFiNow.co.uk

"The collection contains something for every reader of speculative fiction."   —*Booklist*

"It really does help the best rise to the top."   —Brandon Sanderson
Writers of the Future Contest judge

"The Writers of the Future Contest is a valuable outlet for writers early in their careers. Finalists and winners get a unique spotlight that says 'this is the way to good writing.'"   —Jody Lynn Nye
Writers of the Future Contest Coordinating Judge

"The book you are holding in your hands is our first sight of the next generation of science fiction and fantasy writers."

—Orson Scott Card
Writers of the Future Contest judge

"This is an opportunity of a lifetime."   —Larry Elmore
Illustrators of the Future Contest judge

"The road to creating art and getting it published is long, hard, and trying. It's amazing to have a group there, such as Illustrators of the Future, to help in this process—creating an outlet where the work can be seen and artists from all over the globe can be heard."

—Rob Prior
Illustrators of the Future Contest judge

"If you want a glimpse of the future—the future of science fiction—look at these first publications of tomorrow's masters."

—Kevin J. Anderson
Writers of the Future Contest judge

"Illustrators of the Future offered a channel through which to direct my ambitions. The competition made me realize that genre illustration is actually a valued profession, and here was a rare opportunity for a possible entry point into that world." —Shaun Tan
Illustrators of the Future Contest winner 1993
and Illustrators of the Future Contest judge

"A terrific book and a terrific launch to the careers of the latest batch of the very best new writers in the field." —Robert J. Sawyer
Writers of the Future Contest judge

"Sometimes a little bit of just the right kind of advice from an experienced mentor can make the world of difference to someone starting on their art career."

—Craig Elliott
Illustrators of the Future Contest judge

"The Writers of the Future experience played a pivotal role during a most impressionable time in my writing career. And afterward, the Writers of the Future folks were always around when I had questions or needed help. It was all far more than a mere writing contest."

—Nnedi Okorafor
Writers of the Future Contest published finalist 2002
and Writers of the Future Contest judge

L. Ron Hubbard PRESENTS

Writers of the Future

VOLUME 41

L. Ron Hubbard PRESENTS
Writers of the Future

VOLUME 41

The year's twelve best tales from the
Writers of the Future international writers' program

Illustrated by winners in the Illustrators of the Future
international illustrators' program

Three short stories by L. Ron Hubbard /
Tim Powers / Sean Williams

With essays on writing and illustration by
L. Ron Hubbard / Robert J. Sawyer / Tom Wood

Edited by Jody Lynn Nye

Illustrations art directed by Echo Chernik

GALAXY PRESS, INC.

For information, contact Galaxy Press, Inc. at 7051 Hollywood Boulevard, Suite 200, Los Angeles, California 90028.

Many thanks to Leah Ning, Kary English, Martin Shoemaker, Barbara G. Young, Michael Kortes, Eric James Stone, Darci Stone, NV Haskell, Jane Kaufenberg, Mike Wyant Jr., Rebecca Treasure, and Bill Fawcett. Special acknowledgments to these beta readers: Patricia Ahlborn, Randyn Charles Bartholomew, Bret Booher, Cara Giles, James Davies, Candice Lisle, Kimberly Richards, Scott Sands, Sandra Skalski, Gideon Smith, Jefferson Snow, Peter Spasov, Don Sweeney, and Andrew Williamson.

CONTENTS

Introduction

BY JODY LYNN NYE

Jody Lynn Nye lists her main career activity as "spoiling cats." When not engaged upon this worthy occupation, she writes fantasy and science fiction books and short stories.

Since 1987 she has published over fifty books and more than two hundred short stories. Among her novels are her epic fantasy series, The Dreamland, *five contemporary humorous fantasies in the Mythology 101 series, three medical science fiction novels in the Taylor's Ark series, and* Strong Arm Tactics, *a humorous military science fiction novel. Jody also wrote* The Dragonlover's Guide to Pern, *a nonfiction-style guide to Anne McCaffrey's popular world. She also collaborated with Anne McCaffrey on four science fiction novels, including* Crisis on Doona *(a New York Times and USA Today bestseller). Jody coauthored the* Visual Guide to Xanth *with author Piers Anthony. She has edited two anthologies,* Don't Forget Your Spacesuit, Dear!, *and* Launch Pad, *and written two short-story collections,* A Circle of Celebrations, *holiday SF/fantasy stories, and* Cats Triumphant!, *SF and fantasy feline tales. Nye wrote eight books with the late Robert Lynn Asprin,* License Invoked, *and seven set in Asprin's Myth Adventures universe. Since Asprin's passing, she has published two more Myth books and two in Asprin's Dragons series. Her newest series is the Lord Thomas Kinago books, beginning with* View from the Imperium *(Baen Books), a humorous military SF novel, and two young adult science fiction novels with Dr. Travis S. Taylor.*

Her newest book is 1635: The Weaver's Tale *with Eric Flint, a part of Flint's 1632 alternate history series.*

Over the last thirty or so years, Jody has taught in numerous writing workshops and participated on hundreds of panels at science fiction conventions. She runs the two-day writers' workshop at Dragon Con. Jody is the Coordinating Judge of the Writers of the Future Contest. In June 2022, she received the Polaris Award from ConCarolina and Falstaff Books for mentorship and guidance of new talent.

Jody lives in the northwest suburbs of Atlanta with her husband, Bill Fawcett, and three feline overlords, Athena, Minx, and Marmalade.

Introduction

Most speculative-fiction collections have an overall theme that the contributors adhere to, such as cats, time travel, spaceships, artificial intelligence, and so on. The stories in the Writers of the Future anthologies are different. They don't follow a single style, trope, or subject since the stories come from writers in all walks of life around the globe. What do they have in common? Two things: they are excellent examples of science fiction, fantasy, or light horror. Second, the writer had not read anything like it anywhere else and believed it needed to exist.

When I was new to the industry, more experienced writers gave me an excellent piece of advice: write the book or story you know is missing from literature and that you always wanted to read. So bring us your fresh ideas or innovative approach to a classic theme. Wow your readers with your insights into world-building and characters. We're hoping for those unique outlooks. Feel free to experiment with style. Explore a cool concept. The more enthusiastic you are about an idea, the more it will show in your writing. The story that always should have existed will come into being.

That's not the only reason the Writers of the Future Contest is unique. It's also one of the few major writing contests that is free to enter. That lowers the bar for aspiring creatives who, let's face it, are probably not rolling in money yet. The Contest is open for submissions four times a year. That means you have four chances to send in a story.

Not only that, but the rewards for winning the Contest are very desirable. There are several levels of recognition that we can award to you for a well-written, thought-provoking story. The first is Honorable Mention. With that, we recognize you've crafted a readable tale. It might not be perfect yet, but it could be. The Contest is designed to encourage you to raise your game. Be proud that you received an Honorable Mention, but review your work to see what might improve it. Is the dialogue a little flat? Is the story being told from the wrong point of view? Can you find something new to say about a familiar storyline?

For stories that rise higher, there is the Silver Honorable Mention, stories that have a recognizable spark. Can you craft your work so that it stays in the reader's mind even after they put down the book?

The next step up is Semifinalist. For stories that come very close to the top but don't clear the fence for one reason or another. Yours might be nearly perfect, but it might be too close in plot to another submission to make the jump. Or it might be excellent, but it isn't something the Contest would publish. These anthologies are a market, after all, and we have standards we must apply to entries. If it's too adult, too violent, doesn't have a recognizable science fiction or fantasy element, but is too wonderful to ignore, it may become a Semifinalist. Those stories, like the final category, cannot be resubmitted. Still, I would absolutely love to have you send me something else. Please. If you get a Semifinalist award, I admire your writing. You can do it.

Eight stories become Finalists, and from those three winners are chosen every quarter. Those winning writers are flown to Hollywood for a weeklong writing seminar taught by some of the best names in the field. They attend a black-tie, red-carpet gala, are awarded trophies and prize money, and enjoy their very first book signing of a beautiful volume with their work inside. These benefits can be yours. You don't have to fit in any other mold than being an excellent writer with a unique point of view.

But, in the meantime, these stories are meant for you to enjoy reading. If they inspire you, start working on your own writing. You could be in our next anthology.

I look forward to reading your submissions to the Contest, those new stories you know need to exist.

The Illustrators of the Future Contest

BY ECHO CHERNIK

Echo Chernik has been illustrating for thirty years and has been the recipient of many prestigious awards and accolades.

Her clients have included Disney, BBC, Mattel, Hasbro, MillerCoors, Jose Cuervo, Celestial Seasonings, McDonald's, Procter & Gamble, Trek Bicycle Corporation, USPS, Bellagio Hotel & Casino, Kmart, Sears, Publix Super Markets, Regal Cinemas, the city of New Orleans, the state of Illinois, the Sheikh of Dubai, Dave Matthews Band, Arlo Guthrie, and more. She is a master of many styles including decorative, vector, and art nouveau.

She has been interviewed on CBS, PBS Radio, and by countless publications in her career. Echo owns an art gallery in Washington State featuring exclusively her art, and she tours the world meeting fans and lecturing on illustration.

As the art director and Coordinating Judge of the Illustrators of the Future Contest, Echo prepares the winners for the business of illustration and a successful career in art.

The Illustrators of the Future Contest

When the Illustrators of the Future Contest was founded thirty-six years ago, I don't think anyone could have imagined the future of illustration as it is today.

With the sudden introduction of AI into the design and publishing industry, we have entered unprecedented times in the illustration field. There are many questions about where we are headed, what defines art, and what it means to be an artist.

At Illustrators of the Future, it has been and will remain *humans* who are the visionaries that imagine what is next and guide the world toward it through art and imagination.

The Illustrators of the Future adheres to the traditional methods of creating art, where the artist conceives the idea, learns to achieve mastery, and produces their illustration through drawing, painting, and digital art.

Images prompted through an AI generator are not considered to be the artist's idea. AI cannot come up with original ideas or have the ability to understand symbolism—both essential and nonnegotiable elements of a powerful illustration. AI doesn't allow artistic control over concept to the level that traditional illustration does. For these reasons and more, AI-generated art is not allowed in this contest. Artists must be able to control all aspects of their work to achieve the level of work required to be award-winning illustrators.

The artists presented in this volume have decided by entering their work in this contest that this is how the future will be shaped. These are the artists to keep an eye on in the upcoming years.

But how did they get here? They entered the Contest—it's as

simple as that. Entrants send three samples of their best work up to four times a year. (It's free to enter.) Winners receive a very exciting phone call to be informed that they have won. Twelve lucky artists are flown to Los Angeles to spend a week with successful illustrators, learning all they can about the industry and how to succeed in their chosen careers. There is a drawing salon, workshops, and, eventually, the black-tie awards gala, where the grand prize winner is announced. After everything is over, everything is NOT over. The Contest administrators and this book's publisher work very hard to promote the winners, help launch their careers, and applaud their successes, as was intended when L. Ron Hubbard established this wonderful venture with the intent to pay it forward and help hopefuls achieve their dreams.

As the Coordinating Judge for the Illustrators' Contest, I see all entries first. Each quarter, I forward eight Finalists to the Contest judges so they can anonymously select three winners per quarter. Those three winners are assigned a Writers' Contest–winning story that is carefully matched to them. During this process, I work with each artist to help them develop the illustration into their best possible work—giving them experience working with an art director. This artwork will be their entry for the grand prize. It is a paid commission that will be published in the *L. Ron Hubbard Presents Writers of the Future* anthology (the one you're holding in your hand right now), which will ideally go on to be a bestseller—a massive win for a new illustrator!

How do you increase your chances of winning? Simple. Enter your best work. Enter work you love, not work you think I would love. Ideally, it should be something that tells a story—because this is an illustration contest—but if all three aren't illustrations, enter anyway and work on that for next quarter. Don't send plagiarized pieces, and don't send AI. And please don't think you're not good enough to enter! You are! I promise, we never EVER laugh at anyone's artwork. Please send your art—it's safe with us, and we look forward to seeing it.

In this book, we present the Illustrators of the Future. They are talented, work hard, and strive to be their best. They are supported by those who have come before them and give back, as the best of humanity does.

HAILEIGH ENRIQUEZ
Storm Damage   7

MARIANNA MESTER
Blackbird Stone

JORDAN SMAJSTRLA
Kill Switch

DWAYNE HARRIS
Tough Old Man

BREANDA PETSCH
Karma Birds

HEATHERANNE LEE
Code L1

CRAIG ELLIOTT
Creature of the Storm

TREMANI SUTCLIFFE
Ascii   15

HAILEIGH ENRIQUEZ
Slip Stone

JOHN BARLOW
The Stench of Freedom   17

GIGI HOOPER
My Name Was Tom

DAVID HOFFRICHTER
The Rune Witch

19

CAM COLLINS
Thirty Minutes or It's a Paradox

CL FORS
A World of Repetitions 21

Storm Damage

written by
T. R. Naus

illustrated by
HAILEIGH ENRIQUEZ

ABOUT THE AUTHOR

T. R. Naus emerged from a love of exploration. He grew up traveling across Europe, Asia, and the United States as a military brat and later as a soldier in the US Army, developing a passion for wandering, adventures, and intriguing stories in the process. His journey led him to experience fascinating cultures and subcultures, where he learned from inspiring people, but with each new encounter, he wondered how evolving technology impacts how we see ourselves and the communities around us. He eventually settled in Virginia with his wife and two daughters and turned to speculative fiction to express those anxieties—and hopes—about our future.

"Storm Damage" grew from an amazement that we haven't yet destroyed ourselves. Human advancement removes a little more wonder from the world but uncovers even more new mysteries. It also inches us closer to the potential for irreparable harm on a global scale. It may be up to us to prevent that, but we create deeply personal narratives that define how we see ourselves and our legacy based on our vision of the future. Are we strong enough to make the right choice when it threatens our dreams?

ABOUT THE ILLUSTRATOR

Haileigh Enriquez was born in 1996 and is a Los Angeles–born artist with a mix of Mexican/Yaqui Native American and Salvadoran roots. Growing up in Rosemead, California, a predominantly Asian/Hispanic community, deeply shaped her identity. She immersed herself in drawing and comic books from an early age which fostered a fascination for character design and storytelling. What started as an escape turned into a passion.

Originally on a path toward a career in the medical field, a personal

23

loss led Haileigh to reevaluate her future and embrace her true passion: art. With the encouragement of her family and mentors, she shifted her focus and enrolled at Laguna College of Art and Design (LCAD), where she refined her technique and explored her own personal style. Her work blends fantastical realism, bold colors, and dynamic lines, drawing heavily from her love of comic book art and Mesoamerican mythology.

Driven by a desire to create characters that celebrate cultural diversity, Haileigh's work is a joyful exploration of identity, imagination, and resilience. As a traditional artist turned digital creator, she combines realism with imaginative storytelling, crafting unique characters that reflect her identity and the worlds she dreams of.

Currently, Haileigh is working as a freelance artist for private clients and media companies while also developing her own superhero series. She is driven to become a successful artist in the entertainment industry and excited to bring new, authentic stories to life—infused with the vibrant spirit of her heritage and her passion for representation.

Storm Damage

The storm looked much bigger than any Dr. Gregors had seen before. From his seat in the back of the helicopter, he could look over the pilot's shoulder at the dark horizon. In the distance, he could see thick, gray clouds producing new explosive plumes in a rhythm of constant motion that brought the tempest closer to them.

The helicopter was maintaining a course that sped them toward the darkness. The forecast had only called for some clouds and light rain to the north, some distance from their destination. It was a surprise to see how quickly the weather pattern changed to defy the most advanced predictive models. If Dr. Gregors didn't know any better, he would have thought that the storm was determined to meet them.

The pilot had asked to turn around, but the mission lead, Captain Vladimir Kushner, had denied the request. He did not mask his displeasure about the risk Dr. Gregors was exposing them to, but Mission Control gave him two direct orders. The first was to get to the destination Dr. Gregors identified, so Kushner made the call to trust the prognostications and press forward.

This mission was based on Dr. Gregors's recent detection of tachyon energy in the vicinity. His groundbreaking research into tachyon energy proved that it was associated with time manipulation, but it was never recorded outside a controlled environment until now. He was very excited at the possibility of a natural occurrence, but Mission Control was suspicious of its proximity to a top-secret facility exploring this new type of energy.

It was by chance that Dr. Gregors even noticed this tachyon

energy emission. With most of his team temporarily assigned to another top-secret project in the shielded chamber, he had time to improve his time-shifting prototype in the unshielded laboratory. His previous experiments shifted time by a second, but he was on the verge of jumping forward or backward by minutes. When he turned on his sensor to prepare for his first test run, he noticed that tachyon energy was already present. Someone relatively nearby was already playing with time, and by the size of the reading, they were doing much more manipulation than he was.

Dr. Gregors was surprised at how quickly Mission Control agreed to his request to investigate the energy source. He assumed they saw it as a potential threat, except that the chief of security, Captain Kushner, vehemently opposed any trip outside the wire. One of Kushner's superiors pulled him aside, and whatever they told him worked. He walked past Dr. Gregors and barked, "Wheels up in one hour." The team was ready for liftoff in under sixty minutes.

The looming darkness made Dr. Gregors nervous, but he remained excited. The pilot sat alone in the front while Dr. Gregors was seated in the back with Kushner and two soldiers. He wasn't positive, but it looked like one of the soldiers was asleep.

He turned his gaze to the white-cliff coastline below them, where angry waves slammed against the chalk and flint wall.

"The storm is getting worse," Dr. Gregors said. He was not quite used to the helmet. It muffled the helicopter's engines but made it difficult to hear anything else. The pilot was talking to somebody periodically, but Dr. Gregors couldn't make out the words. He assumed it was normal chatter.

"You should have thought about that before you begged Mission Control to take you on this little escapade," Kushner said. "Now shut up. We need to keep the comms line open."

He didn't look at Dr. Gregors as he spoke. He rarely did since he often talked about Dr. Gregors rather than to him.

"The temporal reading…" Dr. Gregors started. He stopped speaking when Kushner shot him a stern glare. Dr. Gregors preferred it when Kushner did not look at him.

He stayed silent for the rest of the trip. A lifetime of dealing with people like Kushner taught him to keep his head down and be invisible.

He continued to look out at the storm. He distracted himself by running through the experiment he hadn't yet finished. Halfway through his mental checklist, he heard the pilot's voice clearly through the helmet's headphones.

"Approaching the coordinates."

Dr. Gregors looked down to see a single cottage on a high cliff overlooking the sea. It was not what he was expecting. It was disappointingly ordinary.

"Is this the place, Doctor?" the pilot asked.

Dr. Gregors looked at the readings from his handheld sensor to confirm.

"Yes," he said. "It looks like that is the epicenter."

"Roger," the pilot said. "It's showtime, boys and girls."

The pilot dove the helicopter at a steep angle but landed her gently about fifty meters from the cottage. Dr. Gregors's excitement was tempered by rolling cloud coverage threatening to blot out the sun. The storm had not yet reached their location, but its shadow created a gray and dreary landscape.

"Be fast or make peace with the residents quickly for shelter," advised the pilot as they touched down. He warned them that the rain clouds were moving faster than anticipated. They would have no more than thirty minutes—probably less—before he returned to base. Orders or not, he refused to get caught in the storm.

"We will be at this LZ in twenty-five minutes," Captain Kushner yelled over the engine. His helmet was already off. "And so will you."

The two soldiers jumped out of the helicopter as Dr. Gregors removed his helmet. Before Kushner joined them, he bent over to Dr. Gregors, his lips close to the scientist's ear.

"I am responsible for keeping you alive," he said. "So you will do exactly as I say. Am I understood?"

"Yes," Dr. Gregors said. Be invisible, he reminded himself.

"Stay behind us," Kushner said as he jumped out of the helicopter.

He ran in front of the two soldiers already in position. They were on one knee with their weapons raised and scanning the area before them. With a hand motion indicating "move out," Kushner led them quickly yet cautiously toward the cottage. Their steps were short, quick, and deliberate. They held their rifles up, ready to fire, and rotated their upper torsos in small arcs from side to side. Dr. Gregors jumped out once they were a few feet from the spinning blades. He bent down and walked as fast as he could. He wanted to race ahead but reluctantly placed himself behind the two armed guards. Take it slow and remain calm, he reminded himself.

"They are here to protect me," he repeated quietly to himself over and over.

The thick wooden door opened as they approached. Kushner and his soldiers stopped and immediately pointed their weapons at the gentleman who emerged. He appeared in his fifties, with silver streaks running through his dark hair and beard. He looked down at the three laser dots dancing on his chest. When he looked back up, he was smiling broadly.

"I don't think guns will be necessary for this conversation," he said.

The two soldiers disappeared, and Kushner now held a radio beside his ear. There were no weapons in sight.

The sudden change startled Dr. Gregors. He quickly looked around for the two guards. He jumped again when the radio blared.

"Blackguard Six, this is Mission Control. I say again. Have you made contact? Over."

"I would recommend you give your superiors an answer," the stranger said. His hair was now completely gray, and there were wrinkles on his face that Dr. Gregors hadn't noticed before. "And let them know that there is no danger."

"This is Blackguard Six, affirmative," Kushner responded into the radio. "Initiating contact at this time. Over."

What is going on? Dr. Gregors asked himself. He didn't see any sign from Kushner that he was aware of what had just happened.

"Would you like some tea?" the man asked. He turned around and returned to his house, leaving the door open.

"Where's your weapon? What happened to the soldiers?" Dr. Gregors whispered to Kushner. He felt his pulse quicken as panic edged closer. "People don't just disappear!"

HAILEIGH ENRIQUEZ

Kushner looked equally confused. "You said that they would not be necessary. You asked to go alone and with no weapons. Against my recommendations. Mission Control agreed with you on the condition that I join you." He took a deep breath through his nose. "Don't lose it now. Find what you are looking for so we can get out of here." Kushner entered the cottage.

True, he had wanted to go in alone, but Mission Control had not agreed with him. Wait, had they? He was no longer sure of what he remembered. He looked around again for the two missing soldiers.

"Weird," he said quietly. He took an extra second to calm himself before following Kushner.

He walked through the door that opened into a kitchen. Their host had already placed three small teacups on the wooden table.

"Milk and sugar?" he asked.

"No," they both said in unison.

"We should probably start," the cottage owner said as he sat down. "My name is Dr. Stanley Richwine—"

"Dr. Richwine," Dr. Gregors interrupted. "What happened to the soldiers?" He couldn't let it go.

"What soldiers?" Kushner asked with his eyebrows furrowed. "I told you to keep it together."

"Please, call me Stanley," Dr. Richwine said. "I will answer your questions, but based on the speed of the storm's approach, I do not think we have much time to start the transition. Are you ready?" He looked into Dr. Gregors's eyes without blinking as he waited for an answer.

It took several seconds for Dr. Gregors to process the question, but he didn't get an opportunity to respond. Kushner loudly interjected.

"What transition?"

"I am sorry, Captain Kushner," Stanley said calmly. "I am probably going to die when that storm reaches us." As if on cue, heavy rain-drops started tapping on the glass window. "If Dr. Gregors doesn't accept the position, I may not be the only one."

"I don't..." Dr. Gregors started to say. "I don't understand what you're saying. How do you know who I am? Accept what position?"

Before anybody else could talk, Dr. Gregors stopped and said, "Wait." He then closed his eyes and slowly counted to five. His therapist had taught him this technique when he felt overwhelmed and needed to refocus his priorities.

He opened his eyes again.

"I am sorry," he started again, "but we are here to find an energy source associated with time manipulation."

"I know why you are here," Stanley said. "You are looking for the fail-safe."

He took a sip of tea as he turned to look out the window. The raindrops thudded against the glass louder and quicker, and his smile faded. Dr. Gregors restrained an urge to interrupt.

"I do not understand how or why," Stanley said, "but when the Maker or Makers made Earth, they created an unbelievable way to protect us from ourselves."

"What makers?" Dr. Gregors asked. The question escaped his lips before he could stop it.

"I haven't the foggiest," Stanley responded. He turned to look at Dr. Gregors after putting his teacup down. "But whoever he, she, or it was, they left. They are gone."

The pause was anything but silent as the rain outside got heavier.

"But they left a fail-safe?" Dr. Gregors asked. He couldn't explain it, but he felt uneasy and wanted this conversation to speed up.

"They developed a mechanism so that if we did anything too stupid, someone could go back and fix it," Stanley said.

"Time travel?" Dr. Gregors asked in a whispered voice. It would account for the high level of tachyon energy he found, but he needed to be sure. He pulled out his handheld sensor to get a reading.

"Time travel," Stanley agreed. "One person, a fail-safe, can go back and reset the timeline if we doom ourselves as a species—something that we've had to do more than a few times. The Allies lost World War II, and the consequences were devastating. The famine that followed alone..." His voice trailed off.

Dr. Gregors looked up from his device with the realization that Stanley was the source of the tachyon energy.

The sky turned black as the clouds hid the last rays of sunlight.

"So, these fail-safes—you—go back in time and get some kind of do-over?" Kushner asked.

Dr. Gregors remembered trying to explain tachyon energy to the military personnel during their first-week indoc. When he was done, Captain Kushner asked Mission Control for the actual briefing. The room full of soldiers laughed at the joke. Kushner refused to look at Dr. Gregors or take him seriously. Instead, he accused Mission Control of wasting his highly experienced team's time and talents to lead an academic exercise to validate a "nonsense theory about time travel from a crackpot." Dr. Gregors was relieved to hear Mission Control order Kushner to protect the scientist and his experiments at all costs and to keep his uneducated opinions to himself.

"Yes," Stanley said flatly. There was no trace of humor or sarcasm in his voice. "Unfortunately, the process gets very draining. Each time we go back, we age quicker. As best we can tell, it is another fail-safe to prevent frequent or unnecessary changes."

"We?" Kushner asked. "Who is funding you and your team?"

Lightning flashed. It was followed a few seconds later by a thunderclap that shook the cottage. Stanley jumped in his seat. He took a deep breath before he started again.

"I am not part of a conspiracy," he answered. "A fail-safe can talk to past fail-safes. I do not have the time to explain, even if I could. The more pressing problem is that I think my time is over, and I need a new fail-safe. A candidate always finds a way of showing up."

"Why not pass this on to your family?" Dr. Gregors asked.

"I do not have a family," Stanley said.

"Can we focus on finding the source of this energy?" Kushner asked in an attempt to get the mission back on track.

"So, fail-safes can't have close connections?" Dr. Gregors asked as if he hadn't even heard Kushner. He had, of course, but Dr. Gregors was done being sidelined. They may have found the tachyon energy source, but he wanted to know more. He couldn't help but believe that Stanley was a time traveler, which meant Dr. Gregors could be one, too.

"I don't think there is anything to prevent us from getting married or having children," Stanley answered. "I spent a lot of time debating with myself, but I finally decided I would've needed a compelling reason to risk my objectivity. I always felt I could not take a chance of anything holding me back from doing what was necessary when the time came to make a tough choice."

"What does this have to do with the storm or the energy?" Kushner asked.

"The storm is new," Stanley said. "We normally have plenty of time to share more and explain everything." He pointed out the window. "This is not normal."

"I sense it, too," Dr. Gregors said slowly. He felt as if the puzzle pieces were fitting into place. "We are part of a project to understand time manipulation. We may be able to help you figure this out, and you may be able to help us advance our research."

"Dr. Gregors, you need to stop," Kushner thundered. "Remember your obligation to safeguard protected information."

"This is bigger than..." Dr. Gregors started before he was interrupted by Kushner's radio.

"Blackguard Six, this is Mission Control. Impose radio silence on this channel and maintain second operational order. Over."

Dr. Gregors turned to look at Kushner with an inquisitive gaze.

"Why are they going radio silent?" he asked. "And what is the second operational order?"

He was surprised to see the puzzled look on Kushner's face as he looked down at his radio.

"Classified," he answered slowly. He seemed unsure what to do next.

"They built a time machine, haven't they?" Stanley asked.

"Impossible," Dr. Gregors said.

"I think it is very possible." Stanley turned his attention back to Dr. Gregors. "Normally, the resets result from many mistakes that culminate with us destroying our planet or the human race. This was quick, with no significant buildup. It was very confusing to me, just as confusing as an actual, visible storm. I wondered what was different this time, but when I saw you outside, I realized that *you* were the cause. *Your* discovery has made time travel possible, and because you did, we have a new trigger for the fail-safes to account for. Time travel seems to require a more prompt reset than we've seen in the past."

"You are wrong," Dr. Gregors said. "I would be part of any project to build a time machine. They need me."

"Do they?" Stanley asked.

Dr. Gregors didn't respond immediately. Something caught his attention and refocused his racing mind. Kushner had shifted in his chair and was slowly moving his hand down his leg. Dr. Gregors wondered if a knife or gun was hidden in his boot. Seeing Kushner anxious was strangely comforting.

"What is the second operational order?" Dr. Gregors asked Kushner again.

Kushner straightened up and slammed the radio on the table harder than he wanted, but he was fed up with the charade. His second order was clear: Keep Dr. Gregors away from the facility until he was given the all clear. It did not say that he had to listen to their delusional ramblings.

"We need to find the energy source," Kushner said.

Dr. Gregors pointed to Stanley. "He is the energy source."

"So it would seem," Stanley added.

"I've had enough of this nonsense," Kushner said dismissively.

"I agree," Stanley said. He looked directly at Kushner. "You have been rude and disrespectful in my home. I think it is time for you to go."

Kushner disappeared without a sound.

"Where did he go?" Dr. Gregors asked. He wasn't sure why he was still shocked to witness another disappearance.

"He was never here," Stanley replied. He picked up the radio that was still on the table and turned a knob until they heard the voice of Mission Control.

"T-minus six minutes."

Stanley put the radio back on the table and continued talking.

"He was never selected for the mission. Nobody cared enough about the success or failure of your investigation, so Mission Control sent you out here to get the readings alone. They just needed you out of the facility."

"You went back in time?" Dr. Gregors asked. "Twice?"

"I did," Stanley said, "but it is taking its toll." Stanley's hair was now pure white, and his wrinkles were deeper.

"Then how do I remember Captain Kushner or those soldiers?"

"Because you will soon be a fail-safe," Stanley said. His voice was a little softer now. He changed the subject. "You made time travel possible, and they are about to make it real. They do not need you anymore to do it."

"No," Dr. Gregors said. He started speaking faster and louder with each sentence as the anger boiled to the surface. "They wouldn't do this without me. They promised me more time to research the effects and ramifications. We agreed to go slow." His mind was now sprinting over all the clues he had missed.

"This is my project!"

"I am sorry that you've been blinded by what you wanted to see," Stanley said. "But you needed them as much as they needed you. Science is often expensive and dangerous."

"T-minus five minutes."

Dr. Gregors glanced at the radio. They could hear the winds outside battering the cottage and an eerie whistle as it passed through a small opening somewhere in the building.

"How is it dangerous?" Dr. Gregors asked. "Each new advance in science brings new opportunities for humanity. There are risks and hiccups, but we always find our way."

"No," Stanley said. "No, Dr. Gregors, we have not always come out of each new invention unscathed. We regularly turn to the military to help make controversial science real and pay the price for that Faustian bargain. We've managed to kill ourselves and destroy our planet so often that a fail-safe was necessary for our survival."

"We've only dropped an atomic bomb twice in our history," Dr. Gregors said quickly. "We learned from that mistake and found better ways to use them as deterrents."

"It was neither the only time nor the worst weapon we've created," Stanley countered. "They have never been a good deterrent, so we sadly allowed those two bombs to go off in hopes that we would learn from it. That helped for a time until World War III." He paused.

"It is a constant vigil, Dr. Gregors, that starts with a single, difficult choice that weighs our future against our legacy."

"T-minus four minutes."

Neither of them looked at the radio this time. A tiny waterfall sprang from a new crack in the ceiling, creating a puddle on the table. Stanley continued to talk.

"Did you honestly believe your military investors would not use your discovery to advance nationalist interests? You have a chance to change that."

There was a long pause as Dr. Gregors remembered his path to this moment. His colleagues laughed at him when he published his paper. It was regarded as a fringe theory barely meeting the standards of scientific rigor, but the military showed up to his research lab with funding and promised to turn his theory into a practical application. They offered him a way of proving his thesis and validating his life's work.

"T-minus three minutes."

"You…" Dr. Gregors started, unsure of what to say. "You want to restart the timeline before my discovery?"

"Yes, and soon," Stanley answered. He pointed to the radio. "Before they make that first jump in time."

"But this will be one of the biggest scientific advancements ever!" Dr. Gregors exclaimed, his heart racing. All of his life's work would be erased. His stamp on history would be removed before it was even made. How was this fair?

"I refuse to accept it," he said. If Stanley was correct, then the military was about to do what everybody told him was impossible. No more snickering at him behind his back. He was going to be famous.

"We can alter the trajectory of how this science will be used," Dr. Gregors said. He felt the physical signs of panic flood through him uncontrolled, but he couldn't stop himself. He leaned forward, his eyes wide, his breath quick. Everything he wanted was within his grasp!

"I am afraid that isn't possible," Stanley said. "Good intentions are never enough to keep us in check. Humans always find loopholes, so I need to restart the timeline and ensure that you never make your discovery. You need to be here to become the new fail-safe if I don't make it back."

"But..." Dr. Gregors started. He couldn't say it out loud. Voicing it would make it real; he didn't want it to be real. Not on the cusp of his dreams finally coming true.

"Yes," Stanley interrupted. "Your work will be lost forever. It is not the first time we forced society to forget something significant, but we have proven through our history that we cannot handle the responsibility that comes with it."

"You don't understand...."

"*T-minus two minutes.*"

The building creaked loudly but held its own against the onslaught outside.

"Don't I?" Stanley said. He grinned as he stood up. "I created the first fusion power source, Dr. Gregors. It was incredible, but it was deadly. I was given a choice. It is the same choice that you have right now.

"As you saw, I can change the past to alter the present, but I am tired. I can transfer that gift to you. You will learn how it works immediately because of the past fail-safes who will guide you. You will not be alone in this." Stanley walked over and, with a relaxed smile, put his hand on Dr. Gregors's shoulder. "I realize what I am asking is difficult," he said. "I am sorry, but losing my life's work was not nearly as hard as giving up hope of having a family. It is my only regret, yet I did it because it was the right thing to do."

"I am not going to give up anything," Dr. Gregors said. "You told me that time is running out for you. I see it. You've aged a decade since I walked through your door. You could've changed my past to prevent this, but you need me. I am your last, best, and only option, and I believe we can find another way."

"You have a choice to make, Dr. Gregors. I must guarantee you don't publish your findings. How that happens is completely up to you."

"*T-minus one minute.*"

The storm was upon them in full fury. Lightning cracked loudly when Dr. Gregors announced his decision.

"We will not change the past," he stated firmly.

"I am sorry to hear that," Stanley said, shaking his head as he looked to the ground.

"I am the fail-safe now, Stanley," Dr. Gregors said. He felt confident in his decision for the first time in his life.

Stanley walked out of his cottage with a cup of tea in one hand and an old newspaper in the other. He was moving much slower, but what could you expect from a septuagenarian? The storm had passed quickly, sounding worse than it was, so he had sent his daughter out to see if there was any damage to the property. Riley would be back soon.

He glanced at the vintage copy of *The Southern Star* folded open to the obituaries. It was a small-town newspaper from many years ago that he'd had to special order. It was important that somebody remembered, he thought. He reread the tragic story about the death of a bright boy with so much potential. Geoffrey Gregors had been hit by an oncoming car on a deserted back road in Ozark, Alabama. It was unclear whether it had been an unfortunate accident or if Geoffrey had intentionally jumped in front of the vehicle to escape the bullies that had plagued his young life.

Riley appeared from around the corner of the cottage. The lanky teenager stopped at the open door.

"No damage, Dad," she yelled. "I am going to get ready for our walk." She waved at him and ducked inside to change.

Stanley turned his gaze out over the ocean as he drank his tea.

A new fail-safe always found a way of showing up. Dr. Gregors was gone, but Riley was ready for the responsibility. During the storm, he had told her it was time. She had asked to spend one more day with him before the transfer, and he agreed. Far from clouding his objectivity, he found that his love for her gave a deeper meaning to his sacrifices.

"Yep," he said to himself. "No damage."

Blackbird Stone

written by
Ian Keith

illustrated by
MARIANNA MESTER

ABOUT THE AUTHOR

Ian Keith went to philosophy school and law school, but he found his calling in the less contentious discipline of storytelling. He lives with his partner and their two children in the Phoenix area, where he works as a ghostwriter. "Blackbird Stone" is his first professional publication.

"Blackbird Stone" started as an itch to write about the pigeons, lizards, and rocks that populate desert backyards. It grew into a love story and a tribute to quirky families when a redheaded bachelorette with an addiction to time elbowed her way in at the planning stage. The pigeons became blackbirds, the lizards became telepathic, and the stones became eggs to accommodate her.

ABOUT THE ILLUSTRATOR

Marianna (Manna) Mester was born in Hungary and spent her childhood in a small village. From a young age, she was attracted to painting and admired those who could create works of art. Growing up, she didn't have much time to pursue it, but ten years ago, she decided to take up painting and began studying various artistic styles. Through relentless practice, she is now able to paint in nine different styles.

For her, painting is not just art—it's life itself, a true expression of freedom. And so her goal is to bring beauty into as many lives as possible.

Blackbird Stone

To my daughter, who's been outside of time.

This is the story of how your mother and I found, lost, and searched for each other again, and of how we built our love out of birds and stones.

I'd stopped practicing psycho-ophthalmology because I'd lost faith in it. I no longer believed that placing magical lenses in people's eyes could change how they felt in any meaningful way.

But about five months after I left the field, a former colleague named Sue Hannigan called and begged me to return to the clinic for what she called a consultation.

Really, it was almost a hostage situation. An unidentified woman had occupied Sue's office. She refused to give her name or leave until she spoke to me. That unidentified woman would one day become your mother.

When I stepped into the office, Sue all but gushed with relief, "Kevin! Thank you so much for coming."

I nodded to Sue. She was a good doctor.

Your mother sat in an armchair, a blue-eyed redhead of about my age, with a few precise freckles and long hair, in a forest-green skirt and turtleneck. She'd crossed her legs, and she jiggled the forward foot with anxiety or impatience. I'd never seen her before. I had no idea why she'd demanded to meet me.

I could appreciate why Sue hadn't called the police, though. Your mother presented as a well-dressed, professional-looking woman, the sort of person whose side police officers instinctively took. She looked us in the eye as if she were our boss or our patron. She would have wound the responding officers around her little finger.

She said to me, "I've already explained to Dr. Hannigan that I need a psycho-ophthalmologist because I'm addicted to time."

I tentatively diagnosed psychosis. I'd never heard of anyone being addicted to time.

She stood and offered me her hand. We shook.

She said, "I chose this office because you're my husband, and this is how and when you meet me."

Surely—I thought—she'd broken from reality. But my first feeling when she claimed me was happiness.

The crisis came when Sue briefly ducked out of her office, and your mother slipped me a folded note. She must have written it before I arrived, maybe even before she walked into the clinic. She said, "Don't read it now. Slip it into your shirt pocket and forget about it. You'll remember it when you need to."

I indulged her. I tucked the note into my pocket, intending to read it the minute she walked out to make sure it wasn't a suicide threat or anything. But then, just as she'd said, I forgot about it.

When we finished our meeting, your mother still refused to give anyone in the clinic her name. After she walked out, they documented the incident in their office records using the pseudonym "Jane Doe."

So, Jane Doe became the first name that referred to your mother. She'd later tell me that in eternity, where she's from, no one has a name. Eternity is the place outside of time. If a person from time— like me—could possess their whole life all at once, they'd be a long, thin creature with one end in their mother's womb and the other on their deathbed. That's what people in eternity are like, as far as I can puzzle it out. And where nothing can move, names can't open onto meanings, as they do here in time. They stand between people like unbroken walls.

After I met your mother, I returned to what passed for my life.

I was a childless, unemployed, thirty-five-year-old bachelor. My friendships were formalities. I rarely socialized. I never drank. But that Monday evening, I had an impulse to drink, and I imbibed enough at home alone to black out for a bit, something I hadn't done since my undergraduate years.

The next day, Tuesday, I realized that something hurt in me that hadn't hurt the day before, besides my stomach and my head. I didn't know what. But I kept thinking of your mother. Of her face and her voice. Of her legs under her skirt and her breasts under her blouse, if you'll forgive me for the grimace this will cause you. On Wednesday, I realized that I'd fallen in love with her.

That night, I paced in my kitchen, eating melon slices from the fridge, tasking my liz with finding her. My liz in those days was an eastern collared lizard, an older model, a male that had grown lazy through long service and looked forward to retirement. People didn't want to be telepathic because no one wanted to be transparent or to see through other people all the time. So, we'd magicked small lizards—harmless, frisky creatures—to make them sentient, long-distance readers of one another's minds. Then, we hired them as telecommunications devices.

I thought your mother had the demeanor of a co-professional, so I told my liz, "Search your liz-to-liz network for redheaded-woman psycho-ophthalmologists on medical leave in all the neighboring cities."

"This is going down a bad road, sir," he warned in his small, flat voice. "She's a patient."

"She may be a patient, but I'm no longer a doctor. Run the search, please."

I gave him a dead fly out of his food container in the fridge. He devoured the morsel appreciatively. Then his nictitating membranes squeezed shut as he concentrated on running the search through the telepathic lizard network.

"Nothing, sir. I'm sorry. None of my colleagues knows anything about such a person."

Maybe she'd been an academic before her psychotic break. That also fit the impression she'd made on me. So I paid my liz a second dead fly and asked him to search for any word of a redheaded-woman professor from any of the local schools who'd gone out on medical leave.

"No good matches, sir. I'm sorry."

Maybe a businesswoman, then, recently resigned from the C-suite for health reasons. I tendered a third dead fly.

"I'm not hungry anymore, sir. But I'll save this one for later and run the search."

Nothing, though.

I despaired. I decided that trying to find her was exactly the wrong way to go. On the contrary, I had to erase every trace of her.

But what trace of her did I possess?

Then I remembered the note she'd given me during our meeting, telling me to tuck it into my pocket and forget it.

Maybe she'd given me her name, her number!

I dashed into my bathroom and plunged my arms into the laundry hamper. I plucked the note out and unfolded it. It read:

Hi! It's 1:37 a.m. Wed. night/Thurs. morning, 2½ days after we met. You were so distracted just now when you quit searching for psychotic redheads and decided to erase all traces of me that you put your liz in your fridge. He's cold-blooded. Better get him out! :)

As soon as you do, give me a call!

And then a local number. But no signature. I still had no name to think of her by.

Impossibly, everything the note said was right.

So, I rescued my liz, and we lizzed the number.

I recognized her voice as soon as it issued ventriloquist-wise from my liz's mouth, in just the word, "Hello."

Having the exact time in the note—1:37 a.m.—I asked as a courtesy, "Were you asleep?"

Through my liz, she said, "I was, but I set an alarm for forty-five minutes ago so I could dress and get a cup of coffee into me before you called."

She gave me an address and asked me to meet her there as soon as I could make the ride.

I rode there in a bubble. This was a self-driving, transparent, magical membrane that one inflated around oneself like a large soap bubble.

Your mother stood, in a pale skirt and blouse, at the front door of a small office with a FOR RENT sign in its window. Her ruler-straight, red hair flipped across her face in the wind that funneled down the bubble-way. She kept trying with flicks of her red-nailed fingers to tuck it behind her ears.

The office shared an awning with a downtrodden used bookstore that had an "All used textbooks half off" banner spanning its front windows.

Your mother had contacted the realtor. She had the key. She stood with one high-heeled pump propping open the door.

From overhead, the office we explored that night and later rented would have looked like two spooning kidneys. The first kidney-shaped room was the reception area. The second was the doctor's office proper, a large space.

We'd been there long enough that the silence had become almost weightless when I asked, "What now?"

She kicked off her pumps and nudged them around the floor with her foot—a nervous habit of hers, I'd find. "We're here because the door behind the warehouse opens into eternity. Eternity is the place outside of time. If time is a flowing current, eternity is the still riverbank it flows beside. Eternity is where I'm from. I first stepped into the current of time five months ago. That was when I first met you here, just outside this office."

"Five months ago? But I never saw you before we met just the other day."

She shook her head. "You don't understand the trickery between time and eternity yet. For you, that meeting won't happen for many years. Our lives are out of sync. Come, now. I'll show you the door I mentioned."

At the rear of the doctor's sanctum—behind the second kidney of the spooning-kidneys floor plan—stood a heavy wooden door.

MARIANNA MESTER

It opened into a warehouse. On the far side of the warehouse stood another door. Presumably, in the building's original plan, this would have been a fire escape leading outside. But through operations to which no human can be privy, the exit had been redirected. The fire escape door now opened into eternity.

I said, "Show me."

She shook her head. "It would turn you into a pillar of salt."

I couldn't tell if she was joking.

She padded across the warehouse and opened that back door slightly—not enough for me to see, but enough for her to slip in. At the instant she went in, she also came back out. It was as if she'd reemerged from her own body's side.

She said, "Whoever returns from eternity can come back after an instant or after forever."

Then she leaned forward until she seemed to fall. But she didn't fall.

In her place stood a black shadow with her shape, bleeding drops of molten fire from a wound in its side.

I caught my breath with awe. Then I watched how she tried to close the wound and stop the fire—how tenderly she tried to touch it and how her hand would flinch away—and I gasped with pity.

"You're hurt," I said. "Let me help you."

"I got this wound when I sipped my first drop of time," she said. "The fire that bleeds from it is pure, burning time. I have to imbibe time to compensate for what I bleed. It's because of this wound that I'm addicted to time. My wound is always with me, even when I don't expose it."

She padded toward me on her naked shadow-feet, droplets of fire falling from her side to flare and brand the floor with teardrop-shaped burns, which we'd later cover with wood.

How can I put this so as not to embarrass you? Your mother and I became husband and wife there, that night, like that.

After we eloped—after your mother slid deeper into her addiction to time by binding herself to a creature of time, to me—we founded a new branch of psychiatry. We called it "psychomechanics."

We established ourselves as the sole practitioners of psychome-chanics. We hung our proverbial shingle out of that little office on the fringes of downtown, in the neighborhood near the university where students lived, sharing a ragged awning with that downtrodden used bookstore.

For nearly a decade, we had a one hundred percent success rate in curing our patients. I don't mean in stabilizing them or making them *better*, the way that the psycho-ophthalmology I'd lost faith in could do. I mean making them *well*. Making them glad to get up in the morning. How many psycho-ophthalmologists could say they did *that* with their magical lenses, which were just rose-colored glasses for minds too despondent to see colors at all?

But the day before the tenth anniversary of our marriage and the founding of our practice, a man came to see us, and we failed him. I'll call this patient William Babbitt. He had a bruise in his feelings about himself, like a soft spot in an apple, where any pressure would liquefy him.

On the day of his intake, I invited him to sit. He was a plain-looking man with a sympathetic, hangdog face. He urgently wanted to show me the Magi-Capture in his wallet of him with his wife and their teenage son, as if they legitimized him in some way. From the magically captured image, she and their son waved and called to me, "Hello, Doctor!" Her image smelled as if she'd overdone her rose water a bit.

He said, "Can you believe she went for a guy like me?"

I thought, if anything, that she looked a lot like him.

He used his forty-five minutes to confess to things he was ashamed of. In a state near to tears, he accused himself of being out of shape, of gambling on cards over the liz network and losing....

When time forced me to interrupt, I opened a drawer of my desk and removed a cream-colored stationery envelope. The paper had fibers of silk woven into it. In the right light, it glistened like a pearl.

I handed it to William, along with a pen. I said, "Address it to 'Mathers et Ux.' That will be your consent to the forthcoming treatment."

He did so.

I said, "Now open the flap."

He opened it.

I said, "Blow into it. Really empty your lungs. Then lick the flap and seal it shut."

William obeyed, puffing the envelope full and then sealing it. It wasn't an airtight seal, just envelope glue. But that didn't matter for our purposes.

I reached for the envelope.

He passed it back, an eyebrow raised.

I told him, "Come back next week. By then, you'll be cured."

I showed him out of my office, telling him to hold his many questions until the following week.

After I'd seen him out and double-locked the outside door, I carried his envelope to the tapestry in my office. The wool tapestry almost covered the wall it hung from, suspended from rings along a polished oak rod.

The tapestry's design was stylized, like something on a coat of arms. In the center, on a green ground, stood a gray, stone birdbath. The bath cupped a pool of cobalt water. At the bottom of the basin, round, gray stones raised the water's level. On the rim of the bath stood a blackbird. A second blackbird flapped in from the opposite side, depicted in midmotion, about to land on the birdbath's rim. This second blackbird carried in its beak a round, gray stone like the ones already submerged in the bath.

I swept the tapestry aside.

Behind it waited a solid wooden door with a hefty brass knocker. I lifted the knocker and clanged it once against its strike plate.

From behind the door, your mother called, "Come."

I clasped the heavy door's brass handle and heaved it open.

Behind the door was a space so dark that its dimensions were impossible to estimate. Your mother sat almost in the doorway, on a four-legged stool, waiting with a light so small that it only illuminated her hands and face.

I passed her William's envelope.

She laid it on her lap. She would set our workshop up. I heaved the heavy wooden door shut, closing her in.

She called through it, "Give me four hours by your clock."

I called back, "Happy anniversary!" because the tenth anniversary of our marriage and the founding of our practice would arrive while we worked.

"So soon?" she called back. "But I haven't gotten you a gift."

"Don't worry," I said. "I've only gotten you a small one."

My gift was a surprise. Just a token—not even a physical object. I'd give it to her in the workshop at the exact hour when we'd been married ten years.

Time ran slower in the workshop than it did in the office. The office was wholly earth side. The workshop stood between the thresholds of earth and eternity, a liminal place. In that vestibular interstice, your mother and I had been married.

Four hours of earth-side time was how long she would need to set the workshop up so that we could practice our art of psycho-mechanics on the spiritual object—the psychic machine—that she would raise from William's breath.

In our workshop, time titrated at a fraction of its earth-side rate. My four hours in the office would give her perhaps an hour of workshop time.

For the next four hours—by my clocks—a tedious hammering, sawing, and pounding filled the office, echoing increasingly.

I'd sometimes ask your mother, "What name can I call you? Having no name to call you is like not having a hand to hold."

And she'd answer, "Nothing. Not even the word *Nothing*. All names are insults in eternity. They just cover a thing to spare us the effort of seeing it fully."

But I started to think of her as "Ux," from the Latin *uxor*, wife. I thought of her this way because the name we'd finally agreed to post on the sign in front of our business after days of heated negotiation read:

Kevin Mathers, MD, et Ux. • Psychomechanics

Your mother finally resigned herself to it because I argued that Ux referred to her relationship with me; no one would ever think "wife" was her name.

But that's exactly what I'd started to do—to think of her as Ux—because her lack of a name made a vacuum, a wound, in my feeling for her.

The surprise I'd prepared for your mother for our tenth anniversary would be my confession that I thought of her as Ux and my request that I might call her that.

What made that a gift? I'd be giving her a name. And anyone who lacked a name must feel the want of one, I thought—no matter what she said.

My current liz happened to be the son of the one I'd employed when I'd met your mother. The father now sunned himself in splendid retirement on a generous pension of insects.

I'd advanced the son a grasshopper—his favorite food—to alert me at the exact moment when your mother and I had been married ten years. Then I'd announce my surprise.

I read for four hours after I showed William Babbitt out of our office. This was how long your mother had instructed me to wait for her to set up our workshop in the vestibule between time and eternity.

I returned to the wooden door in the rear wall of my office. I raised the brass ball-and-ring knocker and hammered it once against its strike plate.

No reply came. So, I heaved open the heavy door that had previously opened on a dark space of indeterminate size.

Now the door opened onto an echoing, lighted workroom half the size of a high-school gym. It had an octagonal floor of shining parquetry. It had a metal dome for a roof. Tools and parts hung from the walls, gleaming, ranked by shape and size.

Dominating the space, floating a foot or two above the floor, hovered the object, the psychic machine that your mother had erected from our patient's breath—as big as a banyan tree now. This thing made of breath was astonishing. They often were.

Psychomechanics was an art of sympathetic magic. Your mother and I could achieve it together because I'm from time and she's from eternity. The magic consisted of enabling the patient's psyche to become—or, more precisely, to devise, create, and enter into correspondence with, as a system with its interface—a broken machine. Then we'd repair the machine. Then the patient would be cured.

Wounded psyches didn't choose to represent themselves with mundane appliances. They cast themselves into correspondence with fantastical unica, rich and strange artifacts more like mutable sculptures than functional machines.

William Babbitt's psyche had chosen as its interface an apparatus that I can only begin to sketch by comparing it to an orrery: one of those mechanical models of the solar system on which the user would turn a crank to make the metal planets revolve around the metal sun.

William's soul had arrayed itself around a patinated bronze "sun," which had collapsed on itself. Around that central body, perhaps twenty planets orbited, with dozens of moons swarming gnat-like around them. Every orbit of every planet and every moon followed a band of metal. The orbits sprawled in every possible shape and orientation. To further complicate this metallic spaghetti—which, don't forget, had the dimensions of a banyan tree—radial spines splayed from all the spheres, with little lozenge-shaped shuttles that could run along them. It was visually incomprehensible. It was all bronze, weathered green.

I met your mother halfway through an exploratory circumambulation and asked, "What do you think?"

Gazing up at it, she said, "He's a *mess*."

But they always looked this disastrous at first.

I set my hand on the outermost of the orbit rings and gave it a diagnostic push.

It *clicked-clicked—clicked*...CLANKED, as a gear somewhere ran into a gap in its neighbor's teeth. This would be as good a place to start as any. We had to fix everything.

I gave the orbit ring another push, and I kept my hand on it during its few clicks, walking along with it, getting closer to the place where it hit the hitch.

I replaced that first gear that clanked. Another gear beside it had also lost teeth, so I swapped that one out, too. When we really got into the flow of our work, I would hand your mother the parts she needed without having to ask, and when I needed a part from where they hung on the walls, I'd turn to find her holding it out for me. We never loved each other more than when we renovated souls together, working like one craftsperson with four hands.

After I replaced those first two gears, I gave that outer orbit ring another push. It went for half a revolution this time before it creaked to a stop because of a broken spring somewhere that I would have to find.

Then I went to check our workshop timer.

A second wooden door stood closed on the opposite side of the workshop from the earth-side door I'd entered through. This second door led to your mother's home, to eternity, where I couldn't go. Your mother had told me that I couldn't step through that door because I was an organism, therefore a process in time. I couldn't survive in eternity any more than sound could pass through a vacuum. So, I passed that door by.

A little farther down the wall, a window overlooked a grassy yard. Walls of cobblestone surrounded the tucked-away place under an overcast sky. That yard didn't belong to eternity, nor did it belong to time. It was a borderland, where time ruled while our timer stood sentinel, but where eternity would conquer if our timer retreated. The timer stood in the center of the yard—a gray, stone birdbath with a little water in it, exactly as depicted on my office tapestry. It consisted of a hemispherical bowl large enough to hold two or three gallons of rain, resting on a round, waist-high column with a square base.

As I watched, a blackbird flew in through the top of the enclosure, through the encircling mouth of the cobblestone walls, with a round, gray stone in its beak.

It landed on the rim of the birdbath. It cocked its neck over the basin, over the inch of water, and dropped the stone in.

Imperceptibly, the water in the bath rose.

Then a second blackbird flew down with a second stone in its beak. It, too, dropped its stone and made the water rise.

Ux and I had until the blackbirds used their stones to make the birdbath overflow to cure the patient—which we'd do by repairing the machine, our magical interface with his soul and its injuries. Less than two days, our time amounted to. The system recirculated when we left the workshop, with the birds taking the stones back the opposite way, although we weren't permitted to observe this part of the cycle ourselves.

Our wedding night ten years before had been too dark for us to see out the workshop's window. We'd found this curious device waiting for us when we woke the next morning. We'd learned the principles of psychomechanics by studying it over the following weeks.

I had no idea what law, or curse, or blessing had imposed this timer on us. It required us to leave the workshop idle between patients, for durations equal to our periods of work, so the mechanism could reset itself. We'd needed weeks of careful watching and trial and error to learn these rules.

I didn't think about our timer much anymore, except when I checked on it, because our work demanded focus. Besides, we'd never run out of time before.

Your mother and I worked on William Babbitt's orrery machine relentlessly. We remade it while we ate, with our food in one hand and a screwdriver or a felt-covered hammer in the other— switching out gap-toothed gears for new, polished ones and rusted, sagging springs for ones so tense they sang a little when we merely brushed them.

Every now and then, I checked the water level in the birdbath.

Gradually, William's machine took shape. Its orbits straightened into regular ellipses. Its hulls took on brazen hues.

And soon it was brilliant, blazing from top to bottom, shining as if lighted from inside. Its spines were metal, but they looked indistinguishable from rays of light. Its sun radiated a warm glow, and a splash of light shone on its surface.

And then smoothly, with a subtle whirring, it began to revolve. Every planet and every moon began to circle gracefully, and the sun began to shine like fire. The repair was complete.

I went to the window from which I could see the blackbirds' bath. The stones had only piled halfway to the brim, and the water had risen only a little higher.

We still had time.

Then my liz said from my shirt pocket, in his small, flat voice, "It's time for the surprise, sir."

I beamed. It felt like an honor to be able to name my wife. I'd show her that names weren't always blots pasted over a thing to save us the effort of seeing it. They could also be a hand to hold someone close with.

I was so carried away that I forgot the little preparatory speech I'd memorized. I looked past William Babbitt's machine, and I saw your mother. She was beautiful. She smiled at me, proud of the work we'd done together for our patient. I looked her in the eye, puffed up with love and pride, and yelled over the whirring and purring of the graceful machine, "Ux!"

Something *clanged* in the machine. Then it lurched, and I sprang back. Increasingly, the device wobbled and shuddered as it spun. Parts flew off and skittered over the wooden floor, striking sparks when they collided.

Your mother and I panicked. William's machine spun faster and faster, until we feared being brained by its planets or speared by its spines.

Then it collapsed into a heap with a cacophony of clanging, dust swarming.

We'd completely repaired his machine. It had signified its restoration by lighting up and starting to revolve under its own power. But then it crashed, as if we'd done nothing for it.

We'd never seen anything like this before.

I went to the window one more time to check the blackbird bath.

The water spilled freely over the bowl's lip. Blackbirds flapped drunkenly around. They'd dropped their stones, missing the basin. The cast stones had broken on the ground like eggs, releasing yellow yolks.

It was beyond my understanding. I only knew our time had run out. Maybe the timer had broken. William's machine could no longer be put back together. For the first time in our career, your mother and I had failed a patient.

Your mother surveyed the wreckage with me. Then she proffered her hand.

I said, "What?"

"Shake hands," she said.

"Why?"

"Because this is where we part."

A thunderbolt seemed to bang inside my head. "Do you mean you're going to divorce me because we failed one patient?"

She blinked and cocked her head. "No. I'm not leaving because we failed. We failed, and I'm leaving, because you called me a name just now."

Pathetically, I lied: "I did no such thing."

"You did."

"What do you think I called you?"

"Ux." She almost gagged on it.

In her disgust, I felt how wrong I'd been. By breaking her law against naming her, I'd broken our marriage. By breaking our marriage, I'd broken our marriage's magic. By breaking the magic, I'd broken the machine that the magic had made.

"It only means, 'wife,'" I pleaded, "like on our sign outside."

But she hadn't lowered her hand. It waited outstretched for me to shake, to dissolve our partnership.

"I'm pregnant," she said.

Another thunderbolt! *"What?* You're telling me *now*? How far along are you?"

"Only a little while." She pawed tears from her face, backing a couple of steps toward the door to her home. She added, "Our child is a girl. I only tell you what I must so you can do what *you* must. If I told you more, you might do less."

"Forgive me," I pleaded.

She shook her head. "You're from time. I'm from eternity. All these years, we've been out of sync."

She stepped swiftly toward the door, letting her hand fall—not because she'd forgiven me, but because she'd resigned herself to leaving without my goodbye.

She opened the door to her home just a crack. She looked at me with tears on her face.

Then she stepped through.

The wooden door thudded shut. Its steel latch clicked.

Silence fell. Solitude fell. She'd gone.

Time had never seemed so slow, nor space so small, as when your mother left me. For days, I wrote long, pleading letters to her, thinking to slip them under the door to her world. While our patient's cure lay in shards around me, I paced and asked myself—often aloud, and sometimes loudly—how I could have been such a fool, when your mother had as good as told me that names were like knives that I could clasp by the handle, but that she had to take by the blade at the cost of a wound.

Then I stopped pacing, and I crumpled my letters. I needed to show her—not just tell her—that I would abide by her rules, and that I'd never again try to force a change in her feelings. To see her again, I'd have to love her and want her enough to follow her onto her own ground. I'd have to go into eternity.

How could I, though? She'd told me that as a creature of time, I couldn't exist outside of its current, any more than an eddy in a river could exist outside the river. Time was my medium. If I tried to leave it, I'd be annihilated.

But when we go under water, we bring our own air. And when we go into the dark, we bring light. Somehow, then, when I went into eternity, I needed to bring my own supply of time.

At first, I thought of a clock. I had a fine, gilded pocket watch etched with my great-grandfather's initials. When it was wound, it ticked as strong and steady as an athlete's heart. It might have been my light in the annihilating dark, except that it didn't make time any more than a yardstick made space—it only measured time. If I'd stepped through your mother's door with just that watch, nothing would have been left of me.

Only the birdbath outside the workshop's window had the magic

I needed. It kept the courtyard-borderland in time's domain when eternity would otherwise have claimed it, or so your mother and I believed. If we were right, then the birdbath was more than a timer. It *made* time, as a lamp made light.

I shattered the pane in the workshop's circular window. Then I dragged over a part of William Babbitt's smashed machine for a stool. I sat on the windowsill, and dropped through.

For the first time, I stood outside in the grassy yard with the blackbirds' bath, surrounded by the cobblestone walls.

I walked to the birdbath. Hefting the heavy basin from its stand— the round, gray stones, the water, and all—I gritted my teeth, and the muscles in my back twinged. I waddled like a lamed bird, hauling it back to the window. Once I'd set it on the ledge, I pressed it carefully through, stone scraping against stone, so as not to upset its contents. Then I hoisted myself back indoors, already sore and sweating.

From inside, I turned to look out the window. Darkness had swallowed the yard. With the timer withdrawn, eternity had taken the borderland. Human eyes couldn't penetrate eternity, though, so I only saw black.

I lifted the birdbath again in both arms. It had always been the timer for our work. Now it might be my supply of time in eternity, casting a field of time around me in which I could survive, move, and comprehend what I saw. Or, if your mother and I were wrong about it, I'd be obliterated.

I trembled, too frightened to think—but if I'd thought, I couldn't have moved.

I carried the basin to the workshop's door to eternity. As everyone knows in their heart of hearts, the doors to eternity are always shut, windowless, and unmarked. But they're never locked. So, I opened the door, and I looked out through my field of time.

The door opened onto a narrow alleyway with a cobblestone wall on either side. My field of time let me see perhaps five meters. Then the blackness of incomprehensible eternity fell like night at the edge of a lantern's light. The sky was starless black. The air didn't stir. No sounds, no smells, like in a lucid dream.

A pace from the doorway stood a gray, stone birdbath identical to the one I carried. It rested on a waist-high stand, like the one I'd left behind in the grassy yard. It cupped a little water, but it was empty of the round, gray stones.

I ventured a few steps into the alley. To my relief, my atoms didn't unravel. The birdbath I carried was working as a source of time. But then, I had the start of my life.

One of the stones in my birdbath hatched with a *crack*. A bird's beak broke out from inside. The stone was an eggshell. It split into two hollow halves, which a miniature, full-fledged blackbird shrugged from its wings. Then the bird stretched. Already, it was growing.

It took flight, fluttering like a deck of cards. It circled me once. By now it had grown to full blackbird size, as large as my two joined hands. Then it flapped upward, circling overhead—only to dive and deposit in the alleyway's birdbath a round, gray stone like the one it had hatched from. Then it flew away, into the dark of eternity, where my time field didn't reach.

I laughed aloud in my surprise, and I wondered if the bird would be annihilated in the dark—as I would—or if it might carry the birdbath's magic into eternity like a shooting star of time.

I asked my liz, who watched with his fore-claws curled over the top of my heart pocket, "Are we in time, or are we in eternity?"

"It's strange, sir," he said in his small, flat voice. "We're in a field of time in eternity, cast by your basin, like a circle of light in the dark."

"*Where* is this field of time? Is it connected to the world I know?"

"I can still feel my liz-to-liz network, sir," he said. "You've merely walked out of your workshop's back door. The cobblestone wall on your left is the same that bounds the grassy yard you see through your workshop's rear window. Look! There are stairs. Climb them, and you'll see."

There were indeed stairs mounting up the cobblestone wall on our left. Hefting the birdbath basin with its many stones—its weight becoming hard to bear—I strode up those steps to the top of the wall, about three meters high. The top of the wall was a meter wide.

My birdbath cast enough "light" for me to look into the grassy yard below and recognize it.

In the center of the yard, the birdbath's stand stood empty, waiting for its basin.

"*When* is this field of time?" I asked my liz. "Have we just continued along in time's current to find the birdbath's stand exactly as I left it?"

"No, sir. We haven't traveled far at all in space, but we've traveled considerably far in time. Gone deep into the past, sir. Ten years and five months back in time—to before *I* was even an egg."

He told me the exact date. It was the day I'd quit my psycho-ophthalmology practice—exactly five months before I met your mother in my ex-colleague's office.

Another miniature blackbird pecked itself out of a stone in my birdbath. It grew as it flapped once around me, and then it fluttered into the cobblestone alleyway behind me to deposit a stone in the birdbath there. Then it lit into the dark of eternity, its shell dissolving into dust and blowing away without appreciably diminishing the remaining pile of stones.

Just then, a shadow dripped down from the blackness of the sky on the opposite side of the courtyard—a woman-shaped shadow with a wound leaking fire from its side. I hadn't seen your mother's shadow-self since our wedding night.

She dropped to a crouch in the grass. Then she sprang to her feet. She tried with her shadow-hands to touch the wound in her side, but she snatched her hands back from the fire that bled from her.

Another bird burst from a stone in my basin. Its wing almost cut my cheek. It fluttered, grew, disgorged a stone into its beak, and flapped into the cobblestone alley to deposit the stone into the other bath. Then it flew away into the dark of eternity, free.

I looked back at the woman-shaped shadow in the yard below. She was peering where the bird had gone.

Then she turned to me.

She waved.

I waved back.

My liz said, "There are stairs hidden behind this outcropping of the wall up ahead, sir, if you're inclined to go down and join her."

I jogged down the narrow stairs. In the grassy yard, I hefted my basin to its stand. With a gasp of relief, I rested its weight there.

Your mother's shadow-self watched with her head curiously cocked from where she stood in the grass a few meters away. Then she shook herself like someone coming in out of the rain and became the redheaded woman I knew. She advanced on me, smiling, and called, "Well, hello! Who might you be, handsome man of time?"

She didn't know me! That struck me silent for a moment. But then I remembered her saying on our wedding night that our lives were out of sync, and that her first meeting with me remained far in my future. *Now* I'd finally arrived at that meeting, I realized. *This* was when she first met me—five months before I'd first met her.

When she reached the birdbath, your mother's past self set her red-nailed fingers on its brim. I set my hands on the opposite side.

She smiled and said, "Do you like my camouflage?" by which she meant her redheaded-woman glamour. She studied me with an insouciance, a coquettishness, with which she'd never look at me again.

"You look beautiful," I said.

"Perfect. So, I'll please the local fauna?"

"The present specimen is very pleased."

She smiled. Then her flirtatiousness fell away. "It's been a great and a terrible day. Do you know what's happened?"

"Other than our meeting?"

She waved dismissively. "More—and worse—than that." She touched her side where the fire of time had bled from her shadow-self. "Some of the current of time splashed out of its bed in the form of a blackbird. It flew into my mouth while I sat like a statue on the riverbank of eternity. If I imbibe time, I must leak it, so this wound opened in my side. And now that I've sprung a leak, I must replenish—so now I'm addicted to time. But that's not all! Because of the bird, there's been a change in eternity. We have 'before' and 'after' now. One change, that's all it takes! And time gets into *everything*. Oh, it's a *terrible* muddle."

She braced her elbow on the basin's brim and planted her chin on her fist.

Her complaint had rattled me. "I'm so sorry. I brought these birds. I've spoiled your home. You must hate me."

She leaped in place—reverting to her shadow-self, then resuming her redheaded figure when her feet touched the ground. "Are—you—*kidding*?" she all but sang. "Don't tell *anyone*—but I *love* it! Do you realize that I've never seen anything *new* before? And then—*Bang!*—a bite of blackbird, and I'm *free*! I've spent a timelessness staring at a fixed tableau. But now I'm *inside* of time—like hurtling down a bubble-way, facing *backward*!" She clapped her hands, then she flung up her arms in triumph. "You have no idea what *magic* you've shown me!"

"How can the birds move in eternity?" I asked. "How can anything move outside of time?"

She dabbled her fingers in the birdbath and picked out a stone. "Time and eternity can combine and cooperate in an eternal recurrence. That doesn't mean a cycle that continues forever into the future, like a perpetual motion machine. The kind of recurrence I'm talking about only happens when something goes forward in time, then backward in time, then forward again along the same path—circling forever in a closed loop. It's a stationary whirlpool in the current of time, stuck at one part of the riverbank of eternity—spinning and spinning, lapping and spitting. It brings a *ticktock* of rotation to eternity, and it splish-splashes *my* kind where we stand frozen on the riverbank."

I frowned. "How can blackbirds recur eternally?"

She lifted the stone out of the bath. "They're the part of the cycle that goes forward in time, like the spring in a toy unwinding. The stones are their eggs. The bird deposits the stone, and the stone hatches the next bird. It's an iteration of bird to stone to bird, and so on. I know because I watched. But when you and I met down here, the mechanism stopped. We'll have to restart it if we want to see them move again." She held the stone to my lips. "Here. Breathe on it. If it's an egg, we have to incubate it."

I tilted my face away. "What will happen if I breathe on it?"

"Then I'll breathe on it, too. We'll breathe on all of these, and we'll create a cycle of blackbirds and stones that will bring movement back to eternity. A miracle."

"What will happen to us, I mean?"

She looked taken aback. "I don't know."

In psychomechanics, we could model a troubled person's psyche as a machine—a curio, a *unicum*—that would serve as its interface. But our subject didn't have to be a single psyche. We could also model a relationship. We could even create a relationship by building its interface. So, I saw then what our workshop timer was, what it had always been. It was our love, our marriage. We were about to build our love.

My conscience insisted that I warn your mother. "Don't you think that creating this machine will bind us to each other?"

She winked. "It might. But you're a beautiful man of time. I wouldn't mind being attached to you."

"It will be much more than a casual attachment, though," I said. "I think the machine you propose to build will be a love between us."

She looked at the stone egg in her hand as if it caused her doubts. But she didn't drop it. Then she raised the egg to my lips again. "I don't want to be bound. But give me just one bird so I can see movement in my home. One bird to travel between the two baths. To make the full machine, we would need many, many birds. We don't have to go so far. Just give me one."

"All right." I pursed my lips and blew on the stone.

She did the same. Then she held the stone in her two cupped hands until a beak cracked it from inside. Smiling, she set the hatchling in the birdbath.

The miniature, full-fledged blackbird broke out and almost immediately took wing. It flapped over the cobblestone wall to the birdbath in the alleyway, growing to full size as it flew. It disgorged and deposited a round, gray stone identical to the one it had hatched from. Then we watched it fly away overhead into the black of eternity, free.

"The stone it left should hatch now," your mother said, frowning. "We won't have eternal recurrence unless that stone it left hatches a new bird, which should fly back to our basin with another stone. Why isn't it hatching?"

I looked at your mother.

She smiled expectantly.

I picked out another stone. "Maybe there needs to be two birds," I said.

I held the stone to her lips. She pursed her lips and blew. Then I puffed on the stone and returned it to the water.

A second later, it hatched, and the bird followed the path of its predecessor, depositing its replacement egg of stone in the bath in the cobblestone alleyway, then flying away overhead, free. But that second stone also didn't hatch.

We continued to try until only one stone remained in our birdbath. But the mechanism still wouldn't recirculate.

Your mother picked up that last stone. "I think the machine won't work unless we hatch every bird." But she didn't raise the stone to my lips or hers. "If we hatch this last stone, we'll complete the device, and it will bind us. I just wish I knew how long this love would last."

"We'll be husband and wife," I said. "It will last all our lives. In the time I'm from, we've been married for ten years."

She frowned. "You're from one of my possible futures, then. It's just like a man from time not to tell a woman everything at once. But at least you've confessed. Concealment is common in eternity, too, but there, it must be permanent...so, you're better than the other men I've known. But, listen. I admire this love we've built. But I won't be bound by it all my life—I've already kept still for an eternity. I wish I could have this love for only a *while*. It's beautiful. It's unique. What inspired you to invent it, anyway?"

"Me?" I said. "I just followed your directions."

"But I only knew what to do because you brought the materials. I just followed the birds here and watched how they behaved—the birds dropping the stones, the stones hatching."

"But I brought them because, in my time, we already have them. We've had them for years."

"Where did we get them, then?" she asked.

"They came with our office as a timer for our work. And *you* found our office. It's the place where our two worlds join."

"Here? This place?"

"Yes, here." I gestured. "And inside that building."

She finger-tapped her pointed chin and narrowed her blue eyes slyly. "But I found this place by following the birds. So, if our finding the birds caused us to find this place—and if our finding this place caused us to find the birds—then there's a circularity afoot. How did the loop start? Whose idea was it to create a self-causing cycle in time in which birds disgorge stones, which hatch birds, which disgorge stones? It wasn't anything *I* would think of."

"It certainly wasn't *my* idea," I said. "It sounds like something a kid would make up."

Your mother grinned. "That makes sense, actually. Do we have children in your time?"

"Not yet. You've only just gotten pregnant in the time I'm from. But what does that matter? How could the form and function of two parents' love be decided by a child they won't have for another ten years?"

She set the egg in the birdbath and touched my hand. I felt a spark, and she smiled at me, and I felt another spark.

"I think I understand. I'll just be an instant." She stripped to her shadow-self and sprang up the stairs around the outcropping of the wall, drops of time's fire sprinkling from her side.

In the promised instant, she returned in her redheaded look again.

She had with her a waist-high girl. The girl, of course, was you.

You skipped, bounced, hopped, broke free from your mother's hand, and sprinted into the yard—circled me once, cried, "Hi, Daddy!" and fled back to your mother.

Your mother caught your hand again.

"Do you remember," she asked me, "how I told you that eternal recurrence—a stationary whirlpool in the current of time—is a compromise between time and eternity, and that it's the only kind of motion that can trouble eternity?"

I nodded dumbly. *Hi, Daddy?* I still couldn't understand how this girl could be you, who weren't born yet. But I saw that you had my black, curly hair, highlighted with your mother's red, and I felt a catch in my throat.

Your mother raised your small hand. "*She's* the offspring of eternity and time. She's *our* offspring. Dear, tell Daddy how old you turned today—or, rather, on the future day I've just fetched you from."

"Three and a half!" you cried.

"When time and eternity have a child," said your mother, "she must emerge from one of those stationary whirlpools in time. I've just met her at this age…and her adult self came to find me once, while I spoke with the child. They were both with me at the same time, somehow, and the girl sat in her adult self's lap."

You broke free of your mother's hand again and raced in a loop around us both.

"Dear," your mother called to you, "tell Daddy what you gave yourself for your third-and-a-half birthday, and why I fetched you from that day, of all days."

"I gave myself a name today!" you cried, racing, your little sandals slapping.

"That's right. You gave yourself a name. And why did you give yourself a name?"

"Because you wouldn't give me a name, because in your home, names are *mean*. And you also wouldn't let Daddy give me a name."

Then you ran to me and clasped my hands. I looked into your eyes, and I barely managed to return your smile, I was so entranced by your small, round face.

"Tell Daddy what name you decided to give yourself at the wise, old age of three and a half," your mother said.

"Blackbird Stone!" you hollered.

"Blackbird Stone." Your mother huffed. "I've tried to tell her that this is not a normal name where her father is from. But she insists. I suppose that if eternal recurrence is the compromise between eternity and time, then giving herself an unprecedented name is the compromise between refusing all names and being stuck with an off-the-rack one. So, again, she's the compromise between our two worlds. And our machine of birds and stones? Our love? Honey, tell us why Mommy and Daddy's love is made of blackbirds and stones."

"Because that's my *name*!" you cried.

Abandoning me, you raced back to your mother. Your mother

took your hand, and you ran to the length of her arm and yanked as though to tear it off.

"Yes, the blackbirds and stones are because that is the name our daughter invents for herself when she is three and a half, and then sticks to out of sheer self-will. And why did you choose that name today, honey?" your mother asked you.

"Because black is my favorite color!" you cried. "And I want to be a bird! And I have a correction of stones!"

"A collection, honey," your mother corrected.

"Yes, a *correction*!"

"And where did you get your collection of stones?"

"On our walks!"

Your mother looked at me, smiling helplessly. "There you have it. *She* is the inventor of our love. She'll be able to *become* that inventor because she'll grow up to be one of the leading psychomechanics in the world, as she parlays psychomechanics itself into a discipline of global consequence.

"She'll also be the busybody who'll skip into eternity, hopscotch back along its riverbank until years before her own birth, and divert an ordinary warehouse fire escape into a portal between eternity and time, so that we can meet in the first place—planting the second birdbath in the cobblestone alleyway while she's at it. Would you like to meet her at *that* clever age?"

"Leave me some surprises, please," I said.

"Well, let me take this little one home before we miss her in the future. Come, dear, time to go," she said, pulling you back toward the stairs to the top of the wall.

An instant later, your mother came back to the birdbath and lifted the last stone again, the egg that would marry us.

"I can't understand the circularity," I said. "How can our daughter invent our love when our love is what made her?"

Your mother held the stone over the rim of the birdbath. "Her adult self told me that a self-causing circularity is the only way in which the offspring of eternity and time can be conceived. And I like that. I think it makes for a more humane family than others.

Our child must *choose* to be born. She *chooses* her parents and her name. Now we, the parents, also have our choice to make. Everyone is a party to everything."

She held up the stone egg.

"So, what do you think?" she asked. "You've met our child. Do you want her? Do you want *me*?"

I nodded yes.

"I'm willing now, too," she said. "But you need to know why I've changed my mind. And I'm afraid the reason is going to disappoint you."

I groaned.

"This machine," she said, "our love, needs both birdbaths to work. You've brought the second basin from the future. Now it needs to stay in the past, or our love won't begin. But that means that when you return to the future, the second basin won't be there anymore. It exists in a closed loop in time, being neither created nor destroyed. This basin's path into the future only extends until the moment when *you* bend it back toward the past. After that, this love—our love—won't exist anymore. Our love recurs eternally in this closed loop, not forever into the future."

She smiled. "Will you take our love for ten years?" She held out the egg. "See, now that I've chosen this love, I can see to its end…but I can't see what happens *after* it. That horizon to my foresight means I'll be free again after this love, doesn't it?"

I raised my hands helplessly. "I suppose it must mean you'll be free, if you can't foresee a future that you haven't decided yet."

"I like that freedom." She raised the egg almost to my lips. "I want to spend it when it comes."

"Spend it with me."

She withdrew the egg. "If I prolonged this love, I'd delay my freedom."

Tears filled my eyes until I almost couldn't see. "You're only at the beginning," I pleaded. "I'm at the end, and I'm not ready. Can I stay and be your lover? It would only be my own past self that I'd cuckold."

"I won't be bound by the same love for two decades," she said, more gently now, "either consecutively or concurrently. But our love won't be for nothing. We'll have our child." She blew on the egg. Then she raised it to my lips again. "If it's any consolation, you won't love me anymore when you get home, because our love won't exist then."

I almost choked. "That's like being told there's no pain after death, so I shouldn't fear death."

When I blew on the stone, I did it to keep my memories of marriage, and to have you. Then I wiped my tears from my cheeks.

Your mother replaced the stone in the basin.

A second later, the blackbird pecked itself free and flew away, growing. It flapped over the wall to deposit its stone.

Then, the first bird flew back, regurgitating its stone into its beak. It clicked that stone into our basin and flew away, free. The machine would run now—for ten years and five months.

"Go home," your mother said, smiling kindly. "I look forward to knowing you, handsome man of time."

"I will miss you, woman who I thought was forever," I said.

My grief oppressed me so much that I could barely climb the wall. From its top, I called to her, "How can I travel back, if I'm not carrying the basin?"

She called, "You have someone who loves you in eternity—don't forget that. You can count on our daughter."

The door in the cobblestone alleyway that should have led back into the workshop only opened onto the black of eternity. But my grief was so raw that I didn't care what became of me. I stepped in, closing my eyes.

I learned that you can only see in eternity by closing your eyes.

A line of children stretched past seeing, alternating girls and boys. The first was *you* at the age of three, as I'd just met you in the yard.

You held up your little hand. "Take my hand, Daddy."

I took it.

We walked a few paces. A small boy waited. He said, "Take *my* hand, Daddy."

I didn't understand, but I accepted his help. He walked me to the next child, a girl...on and on like this, for I don't know how long. Then I emerged into our workshop.

But when the door to eternity thudded and clicked shut behind me, I wondered if I was in my right time. William Babbitt's shattered machine had been cleared away.

I was about to ask my liz.

Then the earth-side door to the workshop swung open, and your mother shambled in, pregnancy swelling her maternity dress. She fixed me with a glare. "*There* you are! Do you realize you've been gone for three months? *I* had to repair our last patient's machine by myself. I've been running our family business *alone*! I've grown our baby in my womb without anyone to fetch me things! I was afraid I'd have to give *birth* by myself. Where in the name of eternity have you *been*?"

I stared. "I'm sorry. But…I thought we'd divorced?"

She closed her eyes. Then she swatted her forehead with her fingertips and laughed. "Of course. Sometimes I forget…for me, it's been more than ten years since we sorted all this out. We thought that since Blackbird Stone's machine was confined to a loop in time, we'd be out of our love's range by now. And that was fine with me, because I wouldn't be bound by that one single love for any longer than its premeditated term." She strode forward and grabbed me by the hand. "But look at *this*."

She half-led, half-dragged me to our workshop's window.

When we reached it, she pointed into the yard. "See?" she said, laughing. "Not *one* love, but the beginning of a jewel chain of *different* loves. Now *that* interests me!"

In the yard stood an apparatus the like of which I'd never imagined—an intricate and wondrous one. A golden halo hovered over the grass, glowing, almost as large as the enclosure. On its outside, snakes with faceted rubies and emeralds for scales rippled clockwise. On its inside, jeweled eggs tumbled counterclockwise. But the halo was a Möbius strip, whose "inside" and "outside" were a single, continuous surface, linked by a paradoxical twist…. My fingers itched to examine it.

Your mother put her arm around my waist. She said, "Try to guess on the basis of *that* what our next child's name will be."

Kill Switch

written by
Robert F. Lowell

illustrated by
JORDAN SMAJSTRLA

ABOUT THE AUTHOR

Robert F. Lowell's complicated relationship with reality began when he was born between two movie studios in Burbank, California. In previous professional lives he researched and wrote about international relations, weapons of mass destruction, and terrorism. He taught at universities in the US, Costa Rica, and Switzerland and was kissed by a dancing horse in Siberia. Now he expands the universe of online learning as an instructional systems designer and writes about swords, sorcery, robots, aliens, and magic rabbits as a member of the Wulf Pack Writers. He, his wife, and at least one dog live in a town with very expensive weather on California's Central Coast and travel in search of enchantment.

In "Kill Switch," an obsolete cop bot gets one last chance to avoid the salvage yard only to find the line between justice and murder is as thin as a silicon wafer. Lowell wrote the story as a love letter to the city that broke his heart. Its hard-boiled hero embodies Lowell's belief that even if we take the high-speed train to dystopia, we will still find hope waiting for us at the end of the line.

ABOUT THE ILLUSTRATOR

Jordan Smajstrla was born in 2003 in Houston, Texas. Thanks to the encouragement of her parents, she has been drawing for as long as she can remember. Jordan attributes her admiration of fantasy art in particular to her childhood interests, which included reading any book she could get her hands on, as well as repeatedly rewatching a wide library of fantasy films. That love for fantasy strengthened when she began to play D&D in high school and meet other creatives with similar interests.

Though she began her creative journey as a traditional artist, she always admired the work of digital illustrators, and finally got her chance to jump into the digital medium thanks to her high-school animation class.

Jordan ultimately decided to pursue concept art and illustration for video games when she got accepted into the Savannah College of Art and Design. While studying there, she discovered a whole new community of incredibly creative people and has eagerly taken any opportunity that comes her way, always eager to continue learning and creating. Jordan is currently earning her BFA in illustration and looking forward to what life will bring after graduation.

Kill Switch

I woke up on a pile of parts in Yang's salvage yard in Fisherman's Wharf, the worst neighborhood in Yerba Buena. I could see the Golden Gate Bridge through the razor wire. Multicolored lights danced above the span, celebrating its one-hundred-and-fiftieth anniversary. My diagnostics screamed for urgent hardware repairs and critical code updates. Malware came at me from every side, and I cut my connection to the cloud. My internal clock said it had been thirty-seven days since I was last activated. It must have needed updates as well, since the last thing I could remember was Yang buying me from army surplus six months earlier.

Two people looked down at me. The long-bearded Asian man in the stained bowling shirt was Yang. He held my kill switch, a black thumb-sized cylinder with a flip-off cap that looked like a tube of lipstick. The other, Yang's potential customer, was a young Mediterranean woman wearing a designer faux leather jacket over a hooded black catsuit. My infrared sensors activated automatically. Beneath her jacket, they showed the cold shadow of a gun.

"Are you awake?" the woman asked.

I had no eyes to open, so it was a reasonable question. I'm semi-humanoid, two meters tall, and my only facial feature is an optical sensor wrapped around my head at what would be eye level. My 360-degree vision was down to about 120 degrees forward.

With an audible creak, I stood up to answer. "Yes, ma'am."

"Ma'am." She smiled. "I like him already."

Yang put on his proud father's face. "He's a classic. There aren't many like him left."

The woman bent closer. "What's your designation?"

"Lima Echo Mike 9236-2745-3142, ma'am."

"LEM stands for Law Enforcement, Military," Yang offered.

"A military police bot," the woman said. She unzipped her jacket halfway. "I'm Aisha. You certainly look like you've been through the wars, Lem."

"One or two, ma'am," I replied. Five, actually, not counting the ops that were still classified. I didn't enjoy shading the truth, but I couldn't afford to give her the real figures. A potential buyer could mean another chance to do what I was made to do. I was way past my service life, and the next time anybody hit my kill switch would be my last.

"Turn around," Aisha ordered.

I obliged, giving her a clear view of the scratches and dents in my army-green plexsteel while I faced a tall rack of parts bins. A few bot heads, sorted and shelved, stared back at me like they expected me to join them soon. In the distance, past the razor wire, the towers of the Financial District groped the sky as if earthquakes were only a myth.

In one of the discarded metal faces on the rack, I saw Aisha's reflection. She reached inside her jacket.

I compartmentalized. I sectioned off the cognitive functions in my high brain to manage intelligence, strategy, and communications while my low brain, with its quantum pathways for sensory processing and tactical movement, took care of the messy part. Long story short, I could think and fight at the same time.

Aisha drew her gun and aimed it at me. My high brain assessed the threat. The gun was Chinese, a Taifun T-27 10 mm electrobaric smoothbore, small frame, serial number filed off. Like all guns, illegal in California. Untraceable ballistics and no propellant residue on your hands. A perfect murder weapon.

As my high brain analyzed the threat, my low brain neutralized it. I grabbed her gun arm and took her to the ground, making sure I landed kneeling beside her rather than on top of her. Her shot snapped harmlessly into the air.

I held her down and said, in my best de-escalatory voice, "Let go of the gun, ma'am."

Yang beamed. "He's still very capable, as you can see. He's proven himself time and again."

What did Yang mean by that? This was the first time I'd seen action since he dumped me in his salvage yard. Maybe he wanted his potential customer to imagine how I was in my prime rather than focus on the poor state I was in now. Yang would have made a great used bot dealer. But bot dealers needed licenses. Junk dealers didn't.

Aisha smiled and let the gun fall from her hand. "And he's still a cop bot, isn't he? You can't kill people, can you, Lem?"

"I'm no longer in service, ma'am, but my coding still blocks me from using deadly force."

Her body language told me the fight was over, so I helped her to her feet and decompartmentalized. I picked up the gun, cleared it, and emptied the magazine. The fin-stabilized armor-piercing explosive rounds with their propellant capacitors were made to take out bots. I slid the ammo into the storage compartment in my abdomen and handed the weapon back to her.

Aisha reholstered her gun and turned to the junk dealer. "How much do you want for him?"

Yang made a show of tugging at his beard. "Shall we say half a million?"

That was five percent of the price the army paid for me new. It was also six months' guaranteed income for the average Yerba Buena family. A lot of juice for an old bot.

"Let's say two hundred thousand," Aisha countered.

Yang put on his hurt face. "In hard currency, naturally."

Hard currency meant a power cell loaded with juice rather than a transfer of energy credits. The transaction would need a big juicer but would be harder to trace.

"Naturally," Aisha said.

Yang curled his lip, rolled his eyes upward, and finally looked back at Aisha. "Two hundred fifty thousand, as is?"

"Including updates?"

"Of course."

"Done," Aisha said. "Clean him up. I'll come back for him tonight." She turned to go.

"Come back this afternoon, ma'am," I said. "You'll want to make a final inspection in daylight."

Aisha turned her head and threw a smile over her shoulder. Her hood hid half her face.

"I knew I liked you, Lem." She kept walking.

Yang gave me a look that would cut through his razor wire. I wondered why Aisha was willing to pay so much juice for an obsolete bot.

Through the Golden Gate, the fog started rolling in.

Yang updated me himself through a hard-wire interface to minimize malware risks. He had to daisy-chain three adapters to connect the cable to my obsolete data port. My diagnostics were happy with the new code, but they warned that my geolocator would transmit only when pinged.

Two dull gray heavy-lifting bots with security protocols kluged into their tiny brains waited outside Yang's office. They were semi-humanoid like me, but considerably taller and wider than I was, with blunt three-fingered hands. I strongly suspected any inhibitions against deadly force had been coded out of them. Now that I had a new owner, I hoped I would serve in private law enforcement or security for the rest of my robotic existence and would never see Yang or his scrap yard again.

I was thoroughly lubed and steam-cleaned by the time Aisha came back for me. I passed her inspection, she gave Yang the juice, and he handed over the kill switch. Instead of taking me home, she said a ride would come for me in an hour, gave me an account number to pay for it, and took off. When the self-driving ride arrived, my former owner sent me off with a smile bigger than his head.

The smell of vomit and weed in the cheap public ride's interior made me regret I had olfactory sensors. The ride rolled past rich kids in the Marina, dodged phaze addicts in the Presidio, and headed through Richmond along Geary Boulevard, finally letting me off at the ruins of the Cliff House. A nineteenth-century landmark on the city's

Pacific shore had once been a swank restaurant, a pleasure palace, and a national park. Now, its thick walls, lack of surveillance sensors, and the noise of the breakers on the sea cliff made it a perfect place for a clandestine rendezvous.

Drones hummed overhead. The sea spray smelled of brine and dead shellfish. I discreetly avoided some indiscreet couples and very unlicensed commercial activity and made my way to an outbuilding shaped like a giant twentieth-century camera with a round lens. It once held a projecting periscope that offered tourists views of the city skyline and out over the ocean. Now it was the only room in the ruins that still had its roof.

Aisha was waiting for me inside with her hood up. A quick scan showed the same gun in her holster and my kill switch in an inside pocket of her jacket. She took a tiny light globe from another pocket and placed it on a rusty round-topped metal table. Its harsh light cast sharp shadows.

"Good evening, Lem. How did you know this is where I'd be? Can you hear my heartbeat or something?"

"Yes, ma'am, I can, now that I've been updated. But I also guessed you would be in the best place for a private conversation. Would you like your bullets back, ma'am?"

"Keep them and stop calling me ma'am. I'd like us to be friends, Lem."

"You don't strike me as someone who needs to buy friends, Aisha."

She stepped toward me to stand face to face. "I bought you because I want John Finch. Tonight."

I hacked into Yerba Buena's Community Services database. Its security protocols were about three lines short of being a joke, but to be fair, my code included some army hacking tools local law enforcement never expected to defend against.

"There's a John Finch wanted for selling phaze, statutory rape, human trafficking, and assault with a deadly weapon. Why do you want him?"

She took off her hood. "Because he killed my little brother Youssef."

"I'm very sorry. How old was Youssef?"

"Seventeen."

"How did Finch kill him?"

"With phaze."

A little phaze could make you think you were in heaven. A little more would take you there. "Didn't Community Services investigate?"

She spat out bitter laughter. "Of course they did. To them he was just another overdose. They couldn't trace the source of the phaze, so they let it drop."

Par for the course. Yerba Buena hadn't changed much since I was last activated.

"I won't kill Finch for you," I said.

She turned and walked a few steps away. "I know. I want him alive."

"So you can kill him yourself?"

She paused for a heartbeat before walking back to me. "No. Take him to Sergeant Patel at the Sunset District Community Service Station."

"Where they'll find him dead in his detention cell?"

She slapped me in the face. The sound echoed in the round chamber. Surf murmured through the concrete walls.

"Just who do you think I am, Lem?" she asked.

"A woman who loved her brother," I answered, "and can't get justice for him any other way."

She rubbed the hand she slapped me with. "For someone without a heart, you're a pretty good judge of character."

"I do the best I can with what I have. How can I find Finch?"

Her black eyes sparkled. "So, you'll do it?"

"Bringing dirtbags like Finch to justice is what I was made to do. You're giving me a chance to do it again. Plus, you own me. As long as it's not illegal, I have to do what you say. But I wasn't made for detective work. I'm conspicuous by design."

"My brother said Finch runs a phaze crib in Plaza Nuevaluna. Room 334, north tower."

"Is that where Youssef died?"

She answered with a single tear.

"If Finch is there tonight," I said, "I'll bring him in. Alive."

The tear collided with a smile. "I knew I could count on you, Lem."

If I had a human heart and hands, I would have wiped the tear from her face. Instead, I said, "You should put some ice on that hand," and walked out into the fog.

When the Tenderloin District was gentrified, most of its crime flowed down into the formerly genteel Noe Valley. Plaza Nuevaluna was intended to attract businesses to the area. It quickly became a leading center of the kind of business John Finch engaged in.

I told the ride to stop across the street and wait. Thanks again to my army code, I could disable most of the surveillance cams along the way. I didn't worry about the rest because what I planned to do wasn't illegal. I had reasonable suspicion that crimes were being committed and lives were in danger. I could ignore all that if I wanted, because I was no longer in law enforcement, but in my source code I was still a cop.

The tube train to Alameda whooshed overhead. I smelled uncollected garbage and worse and stepped past unhoused people as I entered the north tower. Number 334 was a plain door in a plain hallway. The sign said only "Private." I tuned my hearing and picked up lots of slow breathing, but no talking. The sound of phazers in their own little worlds.

I compartmentalized and tried the door—you never know—but it didn't open, so I pressed the buzzer.

A high, scratchy voice said, "Frag off, bot."

That answer didn't encourage subtlety. The door had two dead bolts. I smashed it in with one kick.

About a dozen phazers lay on old couches, threadbare chairs, and a dirty mattress. Some of them smelled like they had been there for days. All their eyes were open, focused on nothing. The only person standing was a big, Hispanic, medically untransitioned trans man in a YB United jersey. He spun around and whipped out a swizzle stick. Not the kind you use to stir cocktails, but the kind that has one end hardened to pummel people and the other electrified to stun bots.

I stepped in. The bulky football fan flailed away at me, the swizzle crackling and smelling of ozone. My low brain parried and knocked him out with a right cross to the jaw. My high brain listened to make sure everyone was still breathing. Satisfied that nobody was in immediate danger, I stepped over the unconscious mook and turned my attention to the door in the opposite wall. Behind it, I could hear dance music playing and one person breathing, shallow and fast.

The inner door was fortified, but wouldn't withstand a hydraulic spreader, or a cop bot built to act like one. I dug my fingers into the hinge side and, with all the strength my obsolete body could muster, pushed the door away from its frame.

The snap of an electrobaric gun sounded from behind the armored door. A hollow-point slug hit me in the chest. It left a little dent but didn't penetrate my plexsteel. My high brain calculated that a shot at closer range could do worse. I spread the door far enough from the frame to squeeze myself in, sideways. A second shot missed.

I recognized the shooter from images I found in the cloud. John Finch was a tall Euro man in a cheetah-print suit. His eyes went wide when I burst through the door. He aimed his gun at my head, but I dodged aside and slapped it out of his sweaty grip. He backed up against a table covered with laboratory glassware. My high brain estimated the setup could make about four hundred hits of phaze per day. On average, one of those would prove fatal.

"Who sent you?" Finch sputtered. Sweat poured down his face. "Whoever it is, I'm s-s-sure we can work something out."

"I seriously doubt it," I said. "We're going to Sunset Station to see Sergeant Patel. You can walk, or I can carry you."

Finch's whole body trembled. "Look, I don't know what this is all about, but—"

"Carried it is, then," I said. I bent down and picked up his gun. My high brain started to analyze and trace it. My low brain aimed it at his chest and fired.

Finch fell backward and knocked over his lab table. Broken glass coated with blood crashed to the floor, spilling phaze precursors all over his suit.

I ran a diagnostic. What I saw was impossible. I couldn't have seen it. I couldn't have done it.

JORDAN SMAJSTRLA

But I had. I murdered a man in what, if I bled, would be cold blood.

I decompartmentalized and stood there, stunned, watching blood and chemicals burble on Finch's body. I'm a cop bot, I told myself. Unbreakable protocols and a dozen fail-safes should have stopped me from using deadly force. Yang must have fragged up my updates, I thought.

The dance music kept playing.

A groan from the chunky trans man in the outer room bludgeoned me back into action. I squeezed out of the lab, jumped over the oblivious phazers, and ran out the plain door into the plain hallway. I charged back to the patiently waiting ride, stumbling over trash bags in the fog. I called paramedics for the phazers, then made an encrypted call to Aisha. She answered.

"We have a problem," I said.

There was a long pause. Finally, she said, "I know."

I wished she hadn't said that.

Aisha told me to take the ride back to the Cliff House. The shadows inside the camera obscura somehow seemed less sharp. Water dripped from somewhere.

"I've malfunctioned," I said.

Aisha sighed. "No, you haven't."

"I killed Finch."

"I know. You did exactly what I bought you to do."

The whole ugly picture snapped into focus. "That's why you needed an old bot," I said. "My systems were so outdated that Yang could hack into them to override my protocols against deadly force and program me for a specific target. Nobody would suspect an obsolete cop bot could kill someone. I was the perfect murder weapon."

She turned her back to me. "I'm not sorry. Finch deserved what he got, and a lot worse, for what he did to Youssef. And God knows how many other people."

"It's not for me to decide what he deserved. But speaking as your partner in crime, you'd better dispose of the evidence. Hit my kill switch and get it over with."

"No. You don't deserve that."

I didn't need to see her face to know she was crying.

"I don't deserve anything," I countered. "I'm a bot. I started in a factory, and I'll end up in a recycling plant. No heart, no soul."

"No, you're wrong," she insisted. "You have rationality and free will. You have a soul."

"Here's some rationality for you. The longer I'm still activated, the more chance you have of being caught. Give me the switch and I'll hit it myself."

"No." Her voice was rougher, deeper, more primal. "I don't want anyone to use you to kill again."

"Nobody will. Have me recycled, or just sink me in the Bay."

"Yang would come after me," she said.

"Why?"

"Because this wasn't the first time."

"Not the first time Yang used a bot to commit a murder?"

She waited a long time before turning to face me. "Not the first time he used *you*."

Was I coded to have nightmares?

"How many?" I asked.

"How the frag should I know?" she screamed. "Yang pretends to sell you, but he really leases you to anybody who has enough juice to pay for a job. After you do it, the client hits your kill switch and dumps you somewhere in the city for Yang to pick up. He wipes the job from your memory and keeps you deactivated until another client shows up at his salvage yard."

He's proven himself time and again. That's what Yang meant. I'd proven myself a reliable killer. That would explain why Finch was so scared to see me. If he had been one of Yang's clients, he would have known why I was really there.

"So, I'm not really a cop bot anymore," I said. "I'm a murder machine."

"And if I don't return you to Yang as agreed, I'll be the next one murdered." She pulled her hood over her head and buried her face in her hands. "God, I wish there was some way out."

In that small shadowy space, I formulated strategies, calculated odds, and weighed alternatives, all of them bad. I refused to let myself be a murder weapon again.

Well, maybe one more time.

"I've thought of a way," I said, "but it's a long shot."

I heard her heart start to beat faster. "What do I have to do?"

"Nothing that should make Yang suspicious. I'll set myself to activate when you ping my geolocator. You call Yang and arrange to return me and the kill switch, then deactivate me and dump me somewhere you can watch from a safe location. After Yang picks me up, you ping my geolocator again. I'll take it from there. Best case, we're both free and clear. Worst case, Yang thinks I'm no longer a reliable weapon and has me chopped up for parts. Either way, he's got no reason to come after you."

Aisha furrowed her brow like a disappointed mother. "That's just about the worst plan I've ever heard."

"Got a better one?"

She let out a heavy breath. "No."

"Then let's do it and hope it works."

Aisha wiped away her tears. "Yes, let's do it. You just proved I was right, Lem."

"Right about what?" I asked.

"Machines can kill, but only a soul can hope."

I reactivated lying on the oil-stained floor of a stainless plexsteel van heading north on the Embarcadero, the road that ran along Yerba Buena's waterfront. Morning sun streamed through the clouds. Yang sat in the captain's chair behind the emergency steering wheel, nostalgically called the driver's seat. My sensors revealed my kill switch in the pocket of his bowling shirt and a gun in a shoulder holster underneath it. His two heavy lift bots sat in the back with me.

I compartmentalized and came up with a plan. I would jump Yang, grab the kill switch, and escape out the van's rear door before the heavies could engage. If things did get messy, the roof of the van was high enough for me to stand up, but not tall enough for the heavies. That could give me an advantage. I would need it.

As we passed the old Ferry Building, my low brain went into action. I rolled to a crouch, leaped forward, grabbed Yang's collar, and tore off his shirt.

Yang tried to draw his gun, but I broke his wrist. He dropped the gun between the two front seats and screamed. The heavies lumbered to their feet and banged their heads against the roof. The van drove on.

The first heavy blocked me as I turned toward the rear door. I ducked its clumsy punch. Its three-fingered fist fractured the windshield into a safety glass mosaic. I leaned into the heavy and swept its three-toed feet out from under it, then picked up Yang's gun and shot it point-blank. The smoothbore slug hit its center of mass and exploded inside. Sparks and plexsteel blew into the floor of the van, which braked gently at a crosswalk for a humanoid bot pushing a coffee cart. She waved thanks and the van resumed its journey.

The second heavy grabbed my gun arm and crunched it. My arm went limp but hung on to the gun. I tried to break its grip, but the heavy was too strong for me and pulled me into a bear hug. Yang sat up and swiveled his chair to face us, holding his broken wrist and grinning through the pain.

The van maneuvered to avoid a woman collapsed on the street. I couldn't break out of the second heavy's hold with my one functioning arm. The surface of my army-green plexsteel started to crack and I could feel my chest starting to cave in. My diagnostics screamed warnings of impending structural failure. My high brain formulated 815 escape scenarios and rejected all of them.

My low brain reached my working arm into my internal storage. It pulled out six of the rounds I took from Aisha and slammed them into the heavy bot's torso as hard as I could. My high brain calculated a .0437 probability that the rounds would impact with enough force to detonate their armor-piercing charges.

The explosion propelled the heavy bot's internals through the roof of the van. Its inert bulk fell forward onto the passenger seat, taking me with it. The van swerved but quickly got back on course, filled with the chemical reek of burned plexsteel.

I shoved the bot's remains aside and stuffed Yang's shirt, with my kill switch still in the pocket, into my internal storage. I sat down in the passenger seat and transferred Yang's gun into my good hand. My low brain aimed the gun at his face.

I couldn't pull the trigger.

Yang laughed so hard his eyes watered. "Welcome back, cop bot!" He sat back in the captain's chair and put on his win face. "Your protocols against deadly force loaded automatically when you reac-tivated. You can't kill me, but I've saved your kill code, so I can make you a new kill switch anytime I want. Go ahead, get out of the van, but you won't get far, so you might as well enjoy the ride."

I sat there, gun still pointed at Yang, for three blocks, while my high brain searched for options. Just before Pier 33, I scanned the Embarcadero for vehicles and pedestrians, lowered Yang's gun under the dashboard, and shot the van's control box.

The van started to brake. A calm, synthesized voice warned that self-drive was disabled. My low brain dropped the gun, stomped my left foot down on the accelerator pedal, took hold of the emergency steering wheel, and cranked it hard to the right.

My high brain said, "Enjoy the ride."

The van careened over the narrow waterfront embankment and plunged into the Bay. Damaged as I was, I was still water-resistant.

Yang wasn't.

Community Services, as usual, got part of the story right. Their final report concluded that the van went out of control when Yang tried to disable two malfunctioning heavy lift bots. Yang's lawyers sued their respective manufacturers. Unreliable witnesses placed a bot at the scene of the Finch murder, but the investigators attributed his killing to a yet unidentified rival phaze dealer. They dumped the matter into a cold case file. It would probably still be there when the Bridge celebrated its bicentennial.

I managed to crawl out of the Bay onto Pier 39, right by Yang's salvage yard. Now that he was gone, I didn't know who owned me and didn't want to know. Aisha pinged my geolocator thirteen times. I didn't let it respond. Whether I had a soul or was just walking junk, it would be better for both of us if we just lost contact.

My chest and arm badly needed repairs but I didn't dare have them done in Yerba Buena. Yang and Finch had too many local associates who would have been much happier to see me taken apart than put back together. I needed to get out of town, so I curled up in the trash covering one of the rotting piers of Fisherman's Wharf and waited for the afternoon fog.

When the fog rolled in, I walked onto the Golden Gate Bridge, hoping I could do what I was made for somewhere on the other side. Halfway across, I pulled Yang's shirt out from my internal storage. I took my kill switch from its pocket, crushed it in my good hand, and tossed it into the Bay. I threw Yang's shirt after it and kept moving. The fog was thicker than ever, but I could see the lights dancing overhead.

Message and How to View Art

BY L. RON HUBBARD

*Upon the inauguration of the Writers of the Future Contest in 1983,
L. Ron Hubbard made this penetrating insight into the relationship
between an artist and society: "The artist injects the spirit of life into
a culture."*

*He recognized the unique potential that the artist has for helping to
inspire society and create a finer world.*

*While the original Contest focused on encouraging new authors,
Hubbard's own artistic endeavors were not confined to just one field.
True, he may best be known as a writer. He published hundreds of works
and millions of words between 1929 and 1950, when the name L. Ron
Hubbard was virtually synonymous with American popular fiction.*

*But Hubbard also worked in visual media such as filmmaking. By the
summer of 1937, for example, one finds his stamp on such scripts for the
big screen as* The Mysterious Pilot, The Adventures of Wild Bill
Hickock *and the Spider series, while he earned screen writing credit for*
The Secret of Treasure Island—*among the most profitable serials of
Hollywood's golden age.*

*Hubbard was also an accomplished photographer. A keen student of
the craft through his youth, by early 1929, his celebrated China
landscapes had been acquired by* National Geographic *while his
spectacular aerial shots as a pilot were found in the pages of* Sportsman
Pilot. *His later work, including promotional photographs for various
European governments and official portraits of heads of state, was
equally acclaimed.*

*Similarly, although he never counted himself as a professional
musician in the strictest sense, his musical accomplishments are by no
means insignificant. He created a "soundtrack" to the book* Battlefield
Earth *using previously unexplored computerized instrumentation,
followed by a no less innovative* Mission Earth *album, themed against
the bestselling book series.*

*Thus, L. Ron Hubbard developed a love for and mastery of several art
forms, and in that spirit the Illustrators of the Future Contest was created
to be a companion to the Writers of the Future.*

L. Ron Hubbard's diverse perspective made him especially qualified to find common ground across all the arts. Synthesizing his experiences in writing, filmmaking, photography and music, he was able to advise others about skills rarely addressed in the study of creativity: How an artist can successfully formulate their message and evaluate their works as they endeavor to perfect them and create a powerful impact on others.

Message

Successful works of art have a message.

It may be implicit or implied, emotional, conceptual or literal, inferred or stated. But a message nonetheless.

This applies to any form of art: paintings, sculpture, poetry, writing, music, architecture, photography, cine, any art form or any form that depends on art, even advertising brochures and window displays.

Art is for the receiver.

If he understands it, he likes it. If it confuses him, he may ignore or detest it.

It is not enough that the creator of the work understands it; those who receive it must.

Many elements and much expertise go into the creating of successful works of art. Dominant amongst them is message, for this integrates the whole and brings comprehension and appreciation to those for whom it is intended.

Understanding is the base of affinity, reality and communication.

A message is fundamental to understanding.

How to View Art

There is a skill needed by anyone engaging in any of the fields of the arts, including writing, music, painting, editing of films, mixing—in other words, across the boards.

It is the ability or skill, native or acquired, to view any piece of work in a new unit of time each time one views it. One has to be able to sweep aside all past considerations concerning any piece of work which has been changed or is under handling and see it or hear it in a brand-new unit of time as though he had never heard of it before.

By doing this, he actually sees or hears exactly what is in front of him, not his past considerations concerning it.

The skill consists solely of being able to see or hear in a new unit of time as though one had never seen or heard the work before.

Only in this way can one actually grasp exactly what he now has before him. When he does not do this, he is viewing or hearing, in part, what he saw or heard before in memory and this gets confused with what it now is.

If one can do this, he can wind up with stellar presentations. But all too often, when he doesn't do this, he winds up with hash.

Some painters, for instance, will redo and redo and redo a painting up to an inch thick of paint when, possibly, several of those redos were quite acceptable. But he continued to try to correct the first impressions which were no longer there. By not viewing his painting in a new unit of time as though he had never seen it before, he cannot actually get a correct impression of what is in front of him.

Some painters or illustrators have a trick by which to do this. They look at their painting via a mirror. Because it is now backwards, they can see it newly.

There is another trick of looking at a painting with a reducing glass (like looking at a view through the wrong end of a telescope) to reduce the painting to the presentation size it will eventually have, let us say, on a printed page. It is quite remarkable that this reduction actually does change the appearance of it markedly. But at the same time, a small painting, enlarged, can be absolutely startling enlarged when it did not look good at all small. But this is actually change of format, not viewing in a new instant of time. The additional skill of viewing something in a new instant of time is also vital.

When anyone engaged in any of the arts in any field has not acquired this skill, he never really knows when he has arrived at the point of completion. And he can often get a distorted opinion of a piece of work which does not any longer merit it.

AUDIENCES

There is another skill which is also acquired in the field of seeing or hearing. This is being able to assume the viewpoint of the audience for which the work is intended.

There are certain areas which pretend to teach various arts, while actually covertly trying to wreck the future of the student, which stress "self-satisfaction" as the highest possible goal of engaging in any work related to any of the arts. There is, it is true, a considerable self-satisfaction in producing a good piece of work. But to profess that one works in these fields for his own self-satisfaction is to overstress self to such a point that the work of the artist or technician then fails miserably. It is actually pure balderdash and a sort of a weak limping apology for not being successful to say that one works for his own self-satisfaction.

This false datum can mix up many artists and technicians who would otherwise be quite successful. For it blocks out the one test which would make him successful: the audience.

It is quite vital that anyone engaged in any of these fields be able to assume the viewpoint of the eventual audience.

One has to be able to see or listen to any product he is engaged in from the audience viewpoint.

He can, of course, and has to, view it from his own viewpoint. But he has to be able to shift around and view or hear it from the audience viewpoint.

There are some tricks involved in this. One of them is to keep an ear open for "lobby comment." After a performance or viewing of any work or cinema or recital or whatever—not necessarily one's own—one mingles with or gets reports on those who have just experienced the presentation. This isn't really vital to do. It is quite feasible actually simply to assume a viewpoint of an audience one has never even seen. One just does it.

A mixing engineer often puts this to a further test but this is because what he is busy mixing on his high-priced top-quality equipment is not what the audience is going to hear. So he takes a cheapo Taiwan wrist cassette-player speaker or a 3-inch radio speaker from the local junk store and he listens to the program he has just mixed through it. This tells him what the audience will actually be hearing. But this is mainly a technical matter as it is true that excellent speakers or earphones may handle easily certain distortions in a mix or performance whereas the cheapo speakers shatter on them. When they do, one adjusts the mix without spoiling it so that it will play over a cheap speaker. This is a sort of a mechanical means of assuming the viewpoint of an audience. But the necessity to do this is introduced by equipment factors.

The truth of the matter is even the mixing engineer is not mixing to remedy "faults" but is mixing for an optimum quality presentation to an audience. To know when he has it, it is necessary for him to assume the viewpoint of the audience.

In all arts it is necessary to be able to shift viewpoint to the viewpoint of the listener or the viewer other than oneself. And this extends out to audiences.

SUMMARY

What really separates the flubbers and amateurs from the profesional are these two skills. One has to be able to view or hear anything he is working on at any time in a brand-new unit of time. And one has to be able to see or hear his production from the viewpoint of the eventual audience.

In other words, the really excellent professional can be fluid in time, not stuck in the past and can be facile in space location.

There is no reason why one should be stuck in time or fixated in just his own location in space.

Actually, just knowing that these skills can exist is often enough the key to acquiring them.

Tough Old Man

written by
L. Ron Hubbard

illustrated by
DWAYNE HARRIS

ABOUT THE AUTHOR

"Tough Old Man" was originally published in November 1950 in the science fiction magazine, Startling Stories. *By then, L. Ron Hubbard was a household name appearing on the covers and in all-fiction magazines for the previous two decades. During the 1930s and '40s, more than 200 of his short stories, novellas and novels were published in numerous genres, including science fiction, fantasy, western, adventure, aviation, military, detective and even some romance.*

"Tough Old Man" was factually the last story from L. Ron Hubbard published before he set aside popular fiction for his more serious works. Dianetics: The Modern Science of Mental Health *was published that same year, and the public demand for his attention was such that his life was no longer his own. Thirty years would pass before he returned to the science fiction field by writing the acclaimed and bestselling novel,* Battlefield Earth *and then his ten-volume science fiction magnum opus,* Mission Earth.

"Tough Old Man" showcases the action-packed storytelling, high-stakes tension, sly satirical humor and surprise twist that exemplify Hubbard's stories.

ABOUT THE ILLUSTRATOR

Dwayne Harris was an Illustrators of the Future Contest winner in 2001, featured in L. Ron Hubbard Presents Writers of the Future *Volume 17. He has since illustrated over fifty book covers and worked for several publishers on a wide variety of properties, including* Game of Thrones *and* Warhammer. *Also an author, he has written and drawn four original graphic novels, one of which was optioned by Sony Pictures to be developed into a major motion picture. Dwayne is a frequent contributor and cover artist for* Heavy Metal *magazine. His work has also appeared in* Spectrum: The Best in Fantastic Contemporary Art. *He lives in Northwestern Montana.*

Tough Old Man

CHAPTER ONE
Tractor Takeoff

The young officer named George Moffat was inspired, natty and brilliant that day he stepped down from the tramp spacecan to the desolate plains of Ooglach. Fresh from the Training Center of the Frontier Patrol in Chicago, on Earth, newly commissioned a constable in the service, the universe was definitely the exclusive property of Mr. Moffat.

With the orders and admonitions of his senior captain—eighteen light-years away—George Moffat confronted the task with joy. Nothing could depress him—not even the shoddy log buildings which made up Meteorville, his home for the next two years—if he lasted.

But he'd last. Constable Moffat was as certain of that as he was of his own name. He'd last!

"This is a training assignment," he had been told by the senior captain. "For the next two years you will work with Old Keno Martin, the senior constable in the service. When you've learned the hard way you can either replace him as the senior constable or have a good assignment of your own. It all depends on you.

"You'll find Old Keno a pretty hard man to match. I've never met him myself. He came to us as an inheritance from Ooglach when we took it over—he'd been their peace officer for fifteen years and we sent him a commission sight unseen. He's been a constable for twenty years and he's pretty set in his ways, I guess."

Moffat had known very well what he was being told. The Frontier Patrol always sent a man to the God-forgotten ends of nowhere under instruction for his first two years of service. The harder the assignment, the greater the compliment to the recruit. That he had drawn "Old Keno" Martin was compliment beyond the highest adulation.

"Good Lord!" his running mate Druid had told him. "Old Keno is more of a legend than a man. You know what's happened to the only three recruits sent to him for training? He wore them out and did them in. Every one of them came back and turned in his resignation. George, I wish you luck. By golly, you'll need it!"

Constable Moffat, stepping through the frozen mud of the main street of Meteorville, wasn't daunted even now. The multicolored icy wastes, the obvious savageness and antagonism of the inhabitants who glowered at him as he passed in his horizon blue and gold, the sagging temperature that registered thirty below at high noon, neither could these daunt him.

Resigned, did they? Well, he was George Moffat and no old, broken-down, untrained ex-peace-officer-made-constable was going to show him up. Old Keno was going to be retired when they found a replacement for him. George Moffat, strong and young, full of morale and training, already considered Old Keno as good as replaced.

He gloried in the obvious fact that the patrol was hated here. Ooglach, furthest outpost of Earth's commerce, held more than its share of escaped criminals. The men who watched him from windows and walks would meet his cool gaze. He became more and more conscious of what he was and where he was until the problem of Old Keno dwindled to nothing.

A man had to be hard in the patrol. The instructors at school were fond of saying that. He had to be able to endure until endurance seemed his ordinary lot in life. He had to be able to shoot faster and more accurately than any human could be expected to shoot and he had to be able to thrive under conditions which would kill an unconditioned man. George Moffat could do all these things. Question was, at his age could Old Keno?

Constable George Moffat entered the low building which boasted the battered sign: *Frontier Constabulary, Ooglach*. He entered and at first glance felt pity for the man he was to relieve.

Old Keno Martin, in a patched blue uniform shirt, sat at a rough plank desk. He was scribbling painfully with a pen which kept tripping in the rough official paper and scattering small blots. It was aching cold in the room and the ashes of the fireplace were dead.

He was a spare man of uncertain age, George observed, and he had no more idea of how to keep and wear a uniform than he probably had about grand opera. A battered gray hat sat over his eyes, two blasters were belted about his waist, both on one side, one lower than the other.

The squadroom was bare, without ornament or comforts, the only wall decoration being a mildewed copy of the Constitution of the United States. Some cartridge boxes and several rifles lay upon a shelf, some report books on the desk. *This*, observed Moffat with a slightly curled lip, was law and order on Ooglach!

Old Keno looked up. He saw the horizon blue and gold and stood.

"I," said Moffat, "have just been ordered up from base." He handed his sheaf of official papers and identification over and Old Keno took them and scanned them with disinterest.

To George it seemed that his attitude clearly said, "Here's another one of them to be broken and sent on his way. A boot kid, badly trained and conceited in the bargain." But then, thinking again, George wasn't sure that that was Old Keno's attitude. The man, he knew suddenly, was going to be very hard to predict.

Old Keno offered his hand and then a chair. "I'm Keno Martin. I'll have the boy stir up the fire for you if you're cold. Newcomers find it chilly here in Meteorville."

Old Keno returned to his reports while George Moffat, seeing no sign of the boy mentioned, glanced yearningly at the dead fireplace. Suddenly George realized what he was doing. The lot of a constable was endurance. If Old Keno, knowing he was coming, had already started the program of hazing, George was ready. Grimly he refused the warmth for himself and concentrated on Old Keno.

"I understand," said Keno after a while, "that if you measure up I'm to be retired from service."

"Well—" began George.

"Wouldn't know what to do with myself," said Old Keno decidedly. "But that's no bar to your measuring up. If you can you can and that's all there is to it. *I* won't stand in your way."

Young George said to himself that he doubted it. The temperature must be twenty below in this room. Inside his gloves his hands felt blue and frostbitten. "I'll bet you won't," George told himself.

"Matter of fact," said Old Keno, "I'm kind of glad you're here. The general run of crime is always fairly heavy and this morning it got heavier. It will be good to have help on this job. I've been kind of hoping they'd send me an assistant—"

"I'll bet you have," said George to himself.

"That could really take it, of course," continued Old Keno. "Ooglach is a funny place. Hot as the devil in some places, cold in others. Requires versatility. You know why this place is important?"

"Well, I—"

"This planet is a meteor deposit. About fifteen or twenty million meteors a day fall into its atmosphere, but that isn't a patch on what it used to get before the atmosphere formed as it is. Its face is studded with the things and there are holes all over the place.

"We ship several hundred billion dollars' worth of industrial diamonds from here every year. Naturally we have to mine the bulk of them out of old meteors and that keeps a miner population around—which is always a tough one. Some of those stones are gemstones. They're a United States monopoly and it's our job to see that they don't get lifted. We frown on all illegal export—especially when it begins with murder."

Moffat perked up. He forgot about the cold room. This was what he had been training for. He was very conscious of his superiority in such cases. The latest methods of crime detection had been built into him as second nature. His young body had been trained to accomplish the most strenuous manhunts. Mentally he was well balanced, physically he was at his peak. He knew it and he was anxious to prove it.

"You've got some idea of who is doing this?" said Moffat.

"Well, shouldn't be too hard. Of course, there's plenty of tough gents on Ooglach who wouldn't stop at anything—but the point is they're cowed. My angle is, the people who did this must be new. They murdered a mine guard up at Crater 743 and emptied the safe of a month's haul. That would be about thirty-five million dollars in gems.

"Any man who had been around here any time would have known better. That means the gents who did it probably came in their own spaceship. It's probably parked beyond the radar detection sphere—somewhere to the south. No, it wasn't local talent."

Moffat almost smiled. Old Keno's faith in himself seemed monstrous to him. He looked with interest at the old constable and realized with a start that all his own studies in criminology and physiognomy had not fitted him to make an accurate estimate of Keno Martin's true character. The man was elusive.

"So, if it's all the same to you," said Keno, "we'll just put together a kit and take out of here for the mine. I just got this report half an hour ago and I stopped here long enough to write this dispatch for my boy to take to that spacecan you came in. I want this data relayed to other planets, though of course we'll probably get these people a long time before they get away. You all ready to go?"

For a moment Moffat was dismayed. He had considered himself fit and ready and yet he knew that his long trip on the tramp had wearied him enormously. You don't sleep and eat well on a tramp and how welcome would be a few hours of rest! But he banished all thought of it. Keno would know he was tired. This was just another way of wearing him down.

"I'm ready," he said. "Just tell your boy to bring my case from the ship. I feel fine."

"Good," said Old Keno. He opened the back door and yelled in some remarkable gibberish at the shed. Then he took down from a shelf several boxes of cartridges, looked to the loads in his guns and handed a rifle to Moffat.

Old Keno waited patiently at the door until a slab-faced native brought a high-speed tractor around front and then, after placing the cartridges in the cab, Old Keno mounted up.

"Wait a minute," said Moffat. "I don't see any food. How long are we going to be gone?"

The old constable looked embarrassed. "I'm sorry about that. My mind was just so busy with other things. Bring out a case of rations from the kitchen."

Moffat smiled to himself. This campaign was so obvious. He brought the rations and threw them into the back of the cab and then, eyes on the old constable, mounted up in his turn.

Suddenly he was assailed with a doubt. Maybe it was just senility that had made Old Keno forget. A man wouldn't go tearing off into any trackless waste without food just to show up a new recruit. Hmm—maybe headquarters had its reasons for wanting to replace this man.

"Where's your coat?" said Moffat, eyeing the patched sleeves of Old Keno's uniform shirt.

"That's so," said the old constable, looking oddly at Moffat. "I forgot that too, I guess." He bawled at the boy, who brought up a heavy service mackinaw. But Old Keno did not put it on. He laid it across the back of the seat and addressed himself to the controls.

The revving motor sent great plumes of white snow spiraling upward. Several curious folks came into the street to look. Moffat glanced at the old constable and felt a genuine wave of pity. "Poor Old Keno," he thought.

The yellow sky lay hard against the blinding plain. In the far distance a range of hundred-thousand-foot peaks reached forever skyward, white and orange in their perpetual covering of frost. The tractor sped across the wastes at two hundred miles per hour, skimming the hummocks, its hydraulic seats riding easy while the treads bucked, spun and roared. A high fog of snow particles was left behind them and the cold which had been intense at the beginning began to turn Moffat's blood to ice crystals in his veins.

At last he surrendered. "Isn't there a heater in this thing?" he said.

CHAPTER TWO
Rugged Going

Old Keno flushed. "I'm sorry. I've got so much on my mind I didn't even think of it." And he reached down to throw a button on the panel, which brought an immediate trickle of faintly warm air into the cab, raising the interior temperature from a minus fifty to a mere minus twenty.

Moffat tried not to show how eagerly he received this succor from his distress. He was beginning to feel a little frightened of Old Keno. There he sat in his shirt sleeves, oblivious of weather. Beside him was Moffat, bundled to the eyes in all that the service could offer a man in the way of warmth—and which was not enough.

By golly, thought Moffat, a man could pretty well perish riding in one of these things if he wasn't careful. He glanced sideways at Keno. The old constable did not find anything unusual about his uncoated state.

"He's senile," Moffat decided. "He's unable to feel anything." And then again he thought, "He's trying to run me out. I'll stick it if it's the last thing I ever do on Ooglach." And he knew with a slight shudder that this very well *might* be the last thing he did on Ooglach or anywhere else!

Half an hour later they pulled up beside the shaft of Crater 743, where the mine buildings clustered under a ten-foot coating of snow and ice. Their presence had been seen from afar and a small knot of men awaited them. Their greeting was respectful, bordering on awe.

"I've been watching for you, Constable," said the foreman. "I'm very sorry to have to trouble you but—"

"I suppose you trampled up all the clues," said Keno gruffly.

The crowd parted to let him through. They had known better than to touch the murdered man or the safe or to walk on tracks, and Keno and Moffat were able to inspect the scene as it had been found at dawn by the cook.

Keno looked at the dead man and muttered to himself, "Forty-five Mauser at the range of two feet. Silencer employed. Asleep when he was hit. Alarm signal shorted out by the intruder. Safe opened with an alpha torch."

He knelt before the broken door and Moffat was amazed to hear him muttering the code of arches and whorls which would identify future fingerprints.

Moffat, puzzled, got down beside the old constable and at length, by catching the light just right, was able to make out the fact that at least there was a fingerprint there. But even with all his training he knew he would need powder and a magnifier to read that mark.

He looked wonderingly at Keno. Either the old constable was pulling his leg or he actually could read that print. It could be a bluff. After all, what did a lone fingerprint matter in this case?

Moffat was additionally puzzled to find that the crew at the mine had been so meticulous as to avoid obliterating the tracks of the retreating felons. He was impressed against his wish by this. It meant these people really walked lightly where Old Keno was concerned. He was wondering if Keno had remembered to bring a plaster cast outfit when he heard Keno grumbling.

"Leader's about five feet tall, walks with a bad limp, been in the Russian army, very quick, probably shoots left-handed. The other two men are ex-convicts, both with dark hair, heavy features—one about a hundred and ninety-five pounds, the other two hundred and thirty. They rely entirely on the leader for orders. They'll fight if told. Come along, Constable Moffat. We'll see what can be done to intercept these people."

Moffat could have deduced a number of these things, but not all of them. He was bemused by it. This old man was not bluffing! And that fact made Keno loom larger than before. Moffat began to dwindle in his own estimation.

Without a word to the waiting men Old Keno climbed into the cab, slammed the door, waited briefly for Moffat to get settled and went off at full speed along the clear track of a departing skimmer.

Young Constable Moffat was not prepared for the accuracy of this tracking. He was beginning to understand why the other young recruits had quit here and resigned from service. Old Keno was not only good, he was dismaying. A man's ego wouldn't long withstand the pummeling of such exhibitions of endurance and manhunter sense that Old Keno had displayed to him today.

Now the old man was following the thin line left by the skimmer—and he was following it at two hundred and fifty miles per hour.

As a skimmer is driven by a tractor propeller and rises on stub wings to travel, it leaves only an occasional scratch in the snow. Yet Keno Martin was following this scratch. He was evidently seeing it some hundreds of yards ahead and turning accurately whenever it turned.

They raced across the trackless expanse, going south. They were silent for the most part. The dumbbell suns gradually sank until the shadows of the ice hummocks were long and blue across the wastes of crystal white.

Moffat was tired. The trip on the space-tramp had been a hard one, and the long hours of traveling over these blinding, glaring ice fields were just too much. It would have been too cold for the human endurance of any man who had not had months of conditioning to these temperatures. Moffat had had that conditioning. But each agonizing breath of frozen air came closer to breaking him.

Then he realized that Old Keno, wrestling the tractor, showed no signs of fatigue. Insensibly, Moffat's estimation of his own capabilities dropped. He began to regard Keno with a sort of awe.

"Don't you want me to take it for a while?" he said at last out of a guilty conscience.

"Sorry, this will get tough as soon as those suns set and we'll have to rely on our spots. I'll just hold on if it's all the same to you."

After a while young Moffat began to fidget. Then he suddenly realized what was the matter. "Say, aren't you hungry?" he said.

Old Keno looked at him blankly. Then he said, "Oh yes, yes, of course. Get yourself something to eat."

Moffat started to turn and in that moment realized all the sensations that a man must feel who is caught in a straitjacket. He could not swivel more than an inch in either direction. His heavy uniform coat was frozen solid upon him.

Impotently he cursed the supply station eighteen light-years away. The trickle of heat had melted a filter of snow from under the windshield. While it was still daylight it had dampened his coat. As the suns set, the temperature had dropped to about fifty below zero.

"Turn up the heat," he said plaintively. Old Keno blinked at him.

"That's all the heat there is," he apologized.

"Well, hit me with your fist or something," said Moffat. Old Keno blinked again. "It's my coat," said Moffat.

Keno grunted and brought a backhand slap against Moffat's chest which cracked the ice sheathing. With the disintegration begun, the young constable could move about. He procured a can of rations.

These had been packed by some far-off organization which never had expected for a minute that anyone was going to eat any of them. Theoretically, when one took off the lid heat was instantaneously generated through all the food. Moffat broke the cover and for the next ten seconds—but no more—the mass was warm. Before he could get the first mouthful between his teeth the savage cold had frozen it through.

He started to complain and then he looked at the stolid Keno. Frozen rations were nothing to the old man—he was munching mechanically on the food. "Well," thought Moffat, "if he can take it I can." And he reached into an inner pocket with his clumsy glove and brought out a chocolate bar, which flew into splinters each time he took a bite from it.

"You'd better let me drive," said Moffat. "You'll need some of your strength later on. We don't want to get tired out."

He intended this as a vengeful reference to Old Keno's age. But the senior constable paid no attention whatever.

"I said you'd better let me drive for a while," said young Moffat.

"You sure you can handle this thing?" said Old Keno.

"We were taught all types of vehicles in school," said Moffat a little savagely.

"Well," said Old Keno doubtfully, "I suppose we've got more time than we really need. And we've been making pretty good speed. You might as well start learning now as ever." He set the automatic control on the tractor and when it reached a level stretch, during which the control could operate, they swiftly switched.

Moffat may have been bitterly cold outside but he was burning within. So the old man thought they'd lose speed if he drove, did he? Well, since when did youth take any lessons from age on that subject?

The dark was very thick and the floodlights were piercingly bright on the track ahead. The multicolored cliffs and valley of ice fled past them. Moffat found that it was extremely difficult to accurately trace the track. More than once Old Keno had to tap him sharply to keep him from straying.

Each time Old Keno tapped, young Moffat seethed anew. There sat the old fool in his patched blue shirt, not caring any more about this cold than he did about rations. Obviously the old man was out to show him up, to make a fool out of him, to break his spirit. Obviously Keno expected to send him back to headquarters with his resignation written and ready to be turned in. Well, that would never happen.

The tractor roared and whined. Young Moffat let it out to two hundred and ninety miles an hour. At this speed the ice hummocks were a blur and even more often now Old Keno had to tap him to keep him on the track.

"Pretty soon," said Old Keno, "we'll start down. The snow level at this time of the year stops at about twenty-three thousand feet. You'll find Ooglach's got a lot in the way of drops and rises. There isn't any sea level properly speaking.

"We've got three seas but from the lowest to the highest there's an eighteen-thousand-foot difference in elevation. I'd hate to think of what would happen if they ever got connected.

"It's two hundred and ninety thousand feet from the lowest point on this planet to the highest. Nature scraped her up some when she was built. I guess she wasn't rightly intended for men. This plateau we're on is the most comfortable spot you'll discover."

Moffat listened with some disbelief. The old man was just trying to scare him away.

"The low valleys are all scorchers," Keno continued, "and the one where I think our friends are hanging out will be running about a hundred and fifty degrees now that the sun has set."

Young Moffat glanced sideways at him. "Warm, huh?"

"Well, it isn't so bad once you get used to it," said Old Keno. "By the way, you'll want to start looking sharp now. We'll have to turn off these lights. If we show them as we come over the top edge into the valley they'll have plenty of time to get away in their spacecan. D'ye mind?" he said.

CHAPTER THREE
Wrecked

Young Moffat thought savagely that if Old Keno could drive in the dark, as he had immediately after sundown, *he* certainly could. He reached down and threw the light switch.

Instantly, as a reaction, the whole world was black to him. He lost his sense of direction utterly. He was light-blinded and yet hurtling forward over uneven terrain at tremendous speed. He did not know whether he was turning to right or left and felt certain that he was about to shoot on a tangent from his course. In a panic young Moffat grabbed at the light panel but he was too late.

He felt the tractor start to turn. He felt Old Keno's savage pull at the levers which might avert the disaster. Then there was a terrifying crash and a roar, a splintering of glass, the scream of a dismembered motor and the dying whine of treads running down to a slow clatter.

Young Moffat picked himself up off an ice hummock two hundred feet from the scene of the wreck. He was dazed and bleeding. One of his gloves was missing and one of his boots was ripped all the way down the side, exposing his flesh to the killing winds of the night. For a moment he could not tell ground from stars. A few planets of his own invention were spinning giddily in space.

After a bit he located the direction of the wreck by the sound of dripping fuel. He crawled back to it fearfully. He thought perhaps Old Keno lay dead within it. Moffat saw his own track in the luminous snow and found that he had plowed straight through a feathery snowbank, which alone had saved him.

Two feet above or below the course he had taken would have brought him into disastrous collision with enormous lumps of ice.

He fumbled over the area and at last located the dark crushed blob of the wreck. All his resentment for Keno was gone now. He knew that this was his own fault. He felt that if the old man were dead he could never forgive himself. He should have known he would not be able to drive at that speed with the lights out.

"Where are you?" he shouted into the cab, fumbling through the torn upholstery.

With a sob he slid in through the broken windshield and felt along the upended floor for Old Keno's body. But it was not there.

Young Moffat scuttled crabwise out of the fuming wreckage and began to look through the debris for a pocket torch.

"Well, I'm mighty glad to find that you're all right, son."

Moffat leaped upright as though he'd been shot.

"I walked on down the line," said Old Keno. "We're within about two hundred yards of the edge there and we would have been starting down soon anyway. So we ain't lost much time."

Moffat threw the torch he had found to the ground before him. If Old Keno had only been reproving or solicitous—if he had shown something, anything, but the calm, cool detachment of a man who, immediately after a wreck, would walk on a little farther just to see how things were—

"I might have been killed," said young Moffat.

"Oh no," said Old Keno. "On my way up to the rim I looked at you there in the snow and saw that you were all right."

The implied superiority of this was almost more than Moffat could stand. He was rising to a point of fury.

"Well, you'd better not stand there," said Keno, the wind tugging at his thin shirt. "You're liable to get cold. Come along."

Moffat fumbled through the drift and found his glove. Then he turned to trudge after Keno. As he cooled he found that something terrible and devastating had happened to his ego.

He had always considered himself so competent. And he had always felt that older men were used up and worn out. Now he found that a man who must be well over sixty easily had the edge on him both in poise and in endurance. The cool rationality of the fellow had gnawed at young Moffat's ego until its borders were frayed.

Sunk now in his own estimation to the level of a schoolboy who is subject to tantrums, young Moffat followed in Keno's tracks and presently came up with the old man.

If he had expected an end to travail because they were to go downhill into a valley, Moffat was mistaken. One of Ooglach's moons, yellow and gibbous, had begun to rise. By its light, the enormous crater before them, thirty thousand feet deep, lay like the entrance to the infernal regions.

Its black sides were rough and jagged and precipitous. At twenty-three thousand feet one could see, by looking across several miles to the other side, where the snow level ended. Below that clung a handful of trees, ghostly now in the brilliant moonlight.

Young Moffat stared at the precipice before him. There was a track down it which angled off at a steep grade, cut probably by some mining survey expedition. But Keno was not considering such a path.

"We've lost quite a lot of time," said Old Keno. "We'll have to make up for it one way or the other. Let's pitch off here and scramble on down the side wall. It's only about thirty thousand feet and the jumps are pretty easy.

"I've been here before. I didn't take this side but I don't expect we'll run into a lot of trouble. Now—you keep close to me and don't go losing your hold on anything and falling because we don't want to mess this up again tonight."

Young Moffat took the implied criticism haggardly. Old Keno slid forward over the ice and started to drop down from crevice to crevice with a swift agility which would have done credit to an orangutan.

Young Moffat started out eagerly enough but in a very few minutes he discovered how bruised and shaken he had been by the wreck. And Old Keno, who must have been just as bruised, was stretching out a lead on him which was in itself a blunt criticism.

Harassed and scrambling, young Moffat tried his best to keep up. He slid from one block of ice to the next, scraped his shins on pinnacles, cut his hands on ledges and, as the drop increased, time after time hung perilously to a crumbling chunk of basalt over eternity. He needed all his strength to get across each gap. And his foot hurt where his boot was torn.

Old Keno, far, far below and evidently having no trouble, constantly widened the gap. Young Moffat's lungs were aching. If he had been too cold before, he was too hot now. His uniform was shortly in ribbons and by the time he had gone down three thousand feet he gladly abandoned the jacket forever. He used only one sleeve of it to bind up a shin which really could have used a few stitches put in by a competent doctor.

He was getting weaker as the swings and leaps took more and more heavy toll of him. He began to look down and ahead through a reddish haze which each time told him that the gap was getting wider and that Old Keno was having no trouble.

An hour later he came up, an aching, half-sobbing wreck. He hit against a soft form. He could not even see the old man. He slumped down on a boulder.

"Well, I'm glad you caught up to me," said Old Keno. "Now let's get moving. I took a look down into the valley and I got the spacecan spotted down there. They got a little fire lighted. Don't drop so far behind again."

Young Moffat cleared his gaze and looked at Old Keno. "That man," thought Moffat, "is going to kill me yet."

After all this terribly arduous mountaineering through the dark, over crevasses and down pinnacles and chimneys, swinging by razor-sharp outcrops to crumbling ledges, Old Keno Martin didn't even have the grace or politeness to be short of breath. In the moonlight he was still his neat, somewhat faded self.

Beaten through and through, his conception of himself so thoroughly shot that only a miracle performed by himself could ever bring it back to life, young Moffat did his best to follow.

Thirty thousand feet is a long way down! And the difficulties of the descent made it also a long way around. Time after time Old Keno waited for him. Never a word of encouragement, never a word of comment on the difficulties of the descent—Old Keno was neither short of breath nor apparently tired of limb.

Hours later, when they at last came to the bottom of that scorching hell, Moffat supposed that he had at least passed through the worst of it. His breath was sobbing in and out of him. His body was a rack of pain. The only thing that had kept him going this long was the knowledge that the worst was almost over. Certainly he had no more to experience. But he was wrong!

As Old Keno had said, it was a hundred and fifty degrees here in this crater. The sand was baking hot. He reached his hand up to his eyes and swept away some of the perspiration which was blinding him. His lips were thickened by dehydration.

The night was so hot and so dry that it pulled the moisture out of a man with a physical force, cracking his skin and drying his eyes until it was torture to keep them open longer than a minute at a time.

"Don't walk forward," said Keno. "There's a two-thousand-foot drop about twenty feet in front of us."

Moffat, stumbling forward, hadn't even realized he had caught up with Keno again. He was startled by the voice and he backed up a few steps. He concentrated his eyes on the spot Keno indicated and at last he saw the dark chasm. Gingerly he approached the edge.

He felt that he was looking into the very bowels of the planet although he could see nothing but blackness. He sensed the awesome depth of it. He stepped back cautiously, afraid that if he made a sudden movement he might fall headlong over the edge. The heat waves coming up from that black hole made him dizzy and his legs felt as though they might slip out from under him at any second. He turned back to Keno.

"We're within a quarter mile of them," said Old Keno. "I doubt if they got wind of us. It's a heck of a long ways back there to the ridge and they probably figured we was a meteorite like I thought they would. If they saw our crash at all, that is. That crew can't have been here more than ten or twenty minutes, but they got a fire goin' already. Smell it?"

CHAPTER FOUR
Live Targets

Moffat sniffed at the wind in vain. He could not discover the least odor of wood smoke. Just breathing this air was enough to sear the lungs and burn scars on the throat without trying to smell anything in the bargain. He looked wonderingly at the old constable.

"They'll be boiling some fresh meat they got back at the mine," said

Old Keno. "It wouldn't keep long down here and they probably haven't any galley in their spacecan. I figured I'd smell wood smoke when I got here, the second I noticed that a haunch of baysteer had been ripped from the drying racks outside the guard's shack at the mine."

Trained arduously, given the highest grades in detection, the young constable felt insensibly lessened again. He was failing every test. He had missed an important clue. Hurriedly he changed the subject. "How'd they cross this gap?" he asked.

"Oh, they're on this side of it all right," said Old Keno. "I saw their last tracks back there about a quarter of a mile. They turned off to the left and we're like to find them about a quarter of a mile up the way. You'd better shed those boots. They'll make an awful racket if we hit hard rock."

Again he felt like a small boy being told to do the most simple and obvious things. He shed the boots and was instantly aware of new difficulty. His feet were in ribbons from the terrible climb down and were chilblained by the shift in temperature as well. And now they had to contact sand which could have roasted eggs.

With the first steps he felt his feet beginning to blister and tears shot into his eyes from the pain. But Old Keno had also shed his boots and was striding easily forward, oblivious of this new agony. The old man, thought Moffat, would have walked through walls of fire with only an impatient backward glance to see if Moffat was coming.

"Are we close?" said Moffat at last and the words came out like rough pebbles, so achingly dry had his mouth become. Each gasp of air was like swallowing the plume on a blowtorch.

"No need to talk low," said Old Keno. "The wind's from them to us. They're camped by a running stream anyway and they can't hear above it. It'll be thirty degrees cooler where they are. This valley is like that. Hear it?"

Moffat couldn't but Old Keno was talking again, pointing to a tiny pinpoint, which was their fire, and the gleam, which was the spacecan, beside it.

"Cover all three from this side with your rifle. Don't shoot unless you have to. I'll circle and approach from the water side and challenge them. Don't plug me by mistake now!"

The disrespect in this made Constable Moffat wince. But he took station as requested. Lying across a frying hot rock with the night air broiling him, he laid the searing stock of the rifle against his cheek. He trained, as ordered, on the party about the fire.

He almost didn't care about what happened to himself anymore. He knew that the rock was burning him. He knew that the rifle barrel was raising a welt on his cheek. He felt some slight relief that his now-bleeding feet were off the ground. But he just didn't seem to care. There was the job to be done and that was all that mattered.

His body had been so beaten that his mind couldn't or wouldn't look at anything but the immediate present. All the concentration and will of his being was centered on this task. He would accomplish his purpose if it were the last purpose he would ever serve.

The three men in front of the fire were laughing, oblivious of any pursuit, certain in their security at least for the next few hours. Before dawn they would be out of the atmosphere and beyond reach. They had a big kettle in which they were boiling baybeef. From time to time one of them would pass another some particularly choice bit.

For an interminable while, it seemed to him (although in reality it was less than three minutes), Moffat waited. At length he heard Old Keno's voice.

"Keep yer hands clear, gents. I'm comin' in!" The three about the fire huddled, immobile as statues, clearly limned by the leaping flames. Thirty paces beyond them, into the circle of radiance, stepped Old Keno. His hands were swinging free, no weapon trained.

"I'll have to trouble you boys to come back and take your medicine," said Old Keno. "It ain't so much the diamonds, it's that guard. Human bein's come high up here."

"Frontier Police!" gasped the leader, starting to his feet. And then he realized what this meant—sure hanging!

"I wouldn't do anything foolish!" said Old Keno flatly.

The man wore a weapon, low and strapped down. "We're not bein' took. I reckon if you're a condemned enough fool to come after us all by yourself—"

The leader's hand, silhouetted in the firelight, flashed too fast to be followed.

DWAYNE HARRIS

There was a blend of roars, four shots! And then it was done.

Moffat had seen something he was never likely to forget. All three men had been on their feet. Old Keno's hands had been entirely free from his guns. The leader had drawn first and the other two had started to fire.

But Old Keno's left hand had stabbed across his body and his right had gone straight down and his three shots were like one blow. The leader's bullet went whining off on some lonesome errand among the rocks. Three men were dying there; three men had been shot before the leader had squeezed trigger.

And Constable Moffat's frozen, cut and blistered finger had tried to close to back up the play and Constable Moffat had not been able to fire! He stayed where he was, semi-paralyzed with the shock of what he had seen—three men shot in something like an eighth of a second.

The leader went down. Another man dropped into the fire. The third stood where he was, propped against a rock, eyes wide open and the firelight shining in them—stone dead.

Moffat looked at his hand. He had not even been able to squeeze trigger. He, champion shot of the school, had not even been able to fire at his first live target when his companion was in danger!

On the verge of tears, Moffat came up from cover and walked toward the dying blaze. Old Keno was bending to retrieve their loot.

Moffat stepped into the ring of light. And then, of a sudden, a strange sensation came to him. It was like a yell inside his head. It was like an automatic switch being thrown. He knew he was in danger!

With the speed of a stabbed cat, young Moffat dropped to a knee, spinning on it toward the spacecan, drawing a rifle bead as he turned. He had not heard anything. But there stood a fat Asiatic in the passageway port, rifle leveled at Old Keno, about to shoot. He never got a chance.

Young Moffat fired from the hip and the bullet caught the fat one in the chest. His weapon exploded into the night. And then without looking at that target Moffat saw the second.

Under the shadow of the spacecan a man had come up, his arms full of firewood. This was falling now, halfway to the ground, and a gun was in his grip, aimed at Old Keno. The gun blazed. Moffat fired and the fifth man went down.

But he was not alone. Old Keno—the infallible, never-missing, always-beforehand Senior Constable of Ooglach—was flat on his face in the sand, motionless, victim of his own overconfidence.

Coming quickly to the spacecan port, young Moffat scanned the interior with his flash. There were five tumbled and evil-smelling bunks here. He glanced back to the fire, counting noses to make sure. Then he scouted wide, looking for strange tracks, and in a moment knew that they had the entire outfit. Not until then did he come back to Old Keno and there he knelt, turning the ancient patrolman over.

To see the wound and its extent it was necessary to remove Old Keno's shirt, for the bullet had apparently lightly creased his back.

It was cooler here by the side of the stream, which a few feet farther plumed two thousand feet into a chasm and which chilled the air in this cup. Young Moffat felt himself relaxing, beat up as he was. Old Keno missing such an obvious thing!

He had off the patched blue shirt and then rolled Keno to his face, fumbling for the wound. It was light; it was on the surface—

Suddenly Moffat stared. He came halfway to his feet and still stared. He took out his pocket flash and knelt eagerly beside the fallen man. His brows knit and then began to ease. Sudden laughter sprang from his lips, rose up the scale toward hysteria and turned aside into an honest bellow. What he had endured for this! *What* he had endured!

Young Constable Moffat sat down in the sand and held his sides. He laughed until his shoulders shook, until his breathing pounded, until his sides caved from labored wheezing. He laughed until the very sand around him danced. And then he looked—growing calmer and settling to a mere chuckle—back at the fallen man.

Moffat jumped up and went into the ship. Presently he came back with a kit and began to patch. And in a very short while Old Keno was sitting groggily up, trying to piece together what had happened.

The young man watched him. Through Moffat's mind was flashing all he had gone through—the cold, the heat, the sharp rocks, the wreck. He thought of the fight when Old Keno had drawn and killed and he thought of the faculty Old Keno did not have. He had lasted and come out here.

"How much do you know of yourself?" said Moffat.

Old Keno stared in amazement and then, eyes shifting to the blue shirt and becoming conscious of his nakedness, slowly averted his gaze.

"Everything you know, I guess," he mumbled. "I didn't know it at first. I came up here for some reason I can't recall, and the transport crashed near Meteorville. I thought I just had amnesia and I went to work in the bars as a guard.

"Then they made me marshal and finally the Frontier Patrol commissioned me a senior constable. Twenty years and I didn't know. Then I went down to Center City, where they built the big new prison. And they've got a gadget there to keep weapons from going in. I couldn't pass it. That's how I found out."

"Did anybody know?"

"I fell and when I came around I was okay. No, I don't think so. Why?"

"I think you were out longer than you thought," said Moffat. "By the way, did you ever read this sign on your back?"

"I tried with mirrors but I couldn't."

"Well, listen." Moffat studied it again before reading it aloud.

POLICE SPY
Pat. No. 4,625,726,867,094

THE BIG-AS-LIFE ROBOT CO.
"And twice as natural"

Motors: Carbon
Instruction: Police
Attachments: Infrared eyes
Chassis Type: R
"Our Robots Never Die"
Caution: DO NOT OIL!

Made in Detroit, MI
USA

There was silence for a moment. Old Keno looked scared and reached for his shirt. "You'll turn me in." He heaved a sigh. "I'm done."

120

Young Moffat grinned. "Nope. Because that isn't the only sign there. You were out a lot longer than you thought at Center City. They must have had time to send dispatches to the Frontier Patrol. Because there's another sign."

"Another?"

"Yep," said young Moffat with a jubilant upsurge. "It reads very short and very sweet."

To the recruit:

You'll only locate this if you can last, if you can't be fooled or if you're a better shot. Know then that you now send a dispatch to headquarters for your transfer and raise in rate. Well done, Senior Constable!

> Thorpe
> Commanding Section C

"I'm a trainer," said Old Keno.

"You showed up three," said Moffat. "Three that couldn't take it the hard way. And you almost killed me, Keno Martin. Froze me and broiled me and drained me of the last ounce. By golly, I never knew what I could stand until I came to Ooglach. And now—well, if they want to train a man the hard way it's all right with me."

"And I—" fumbled Old Keno.

"Martin, you're better than men in a lot of ways—heat, cold and energy. But of course your sixth sense doesn't exist. You'll have to watch for that. But you're still Senior Constable of Ooglach and I guess you'll last forever if you don't short-circuit from a slug.

"I replaced the fuse that bullet blew. You'd better keep some in your pockets. So they won't be retiring you, Keno, until you fall apart and according to your back, that won't be until forever arrives. Okay, Senior Constable?"

Old Keno became suddenly radiant. He looked at the boy before him and his smile grew proud. He put out his hand for a shake. "Okay, Senior Constable Moffat," he said.

They shook.

Karma Birds

written by
Lauren McGuire

illustrated by
BREANDA PETSCH

ABOUT THE AUTHOR

Lauren McGuire lives in a small southern town where one cannot throw a rock without hitting a church. Ironically, the town is funded by zombies. Growing up as an army brat, she traveled all over the world, including a stint in the Middle East, which instilled a deep curiosity for other cultures and religions. She began writing in 2016 as a way of processing a chaotic cultural landscape and has since written six full manuscripts and several short stories. When not wrangling a family of five or training for half-marathons, she writes about space and monsters.

She is an active member of the Atlanta Writing Club and was their 2020 winner of the Terry Kay Prize for Short Fiction as well as a 2023 runner-up for the Natasha Trethewey Prize for Poetry. She received two Honorable Mentions from the Writers of the Future Contest before becoming a second-place winner with this story. "Karma Birds" is her first professional sale.

Lauren's story "Karma Birds" was inspired by a question—what would it take for humanity to choose kindness? What if morality stood outside the purview of religion or law and became instead a mandate from nature? "Karma Birds" imagines morality, not so much as a choice, but as a mechanism for survival.

ABOUT THE ILLUSTRATOR

Breanda Petsch was born in Denver, Colorado, in 1998. Most friends and family call her Bre, but she appreciates when her full name is used and pronounced correctly: "Bree-ann-duh."

Breanda has been glued to the page from the moment she learned how to draw and paint. When she wasn't filling her imagination with adventures around the neighborhood, she was playing pretend through endless comics.

She used to watch animated films on repeat. Seeing the animators' stories through behind-the-scenes clips made her want to bring amazing stories to life too.

She took her first painting and drawing classes in high school and won awards in art shows and other larger competitions. She was proud to see her work on the walls and had an itch to find out what more she was capable of.

Although she was encouraged to follow a practical career path with her high academic standing, Breanda knew she needed to pursue art the moment she stepped into an "art lab." Nothing else made sense anymore, and her father did everything in his power to support and push her toward her dreams, even driving her to weekend classes at that very institution.

From there, she earned a degree in animation from Colorado Mesa University and found her love of being enveloped in a creative community and storytelling team. She is now pursuing her MFA in illustration at Savannah College of Art and Design.

Karma Birds

The speedometer read forty miles per hour, but it had been broken since before the first wave. Claire stared at the van in front of her without seeing the passing landscape. The view on Highway 50 hadn't changed in hours; an unending ribbon of gray asphalt surrounded by lonely scrub and the occasional lizard hauling its body through the heat. Anemic clouds clung to mountains that never seemed to get any closer. All that emptiness was a trade-off. The caravan only had to navigate abandoned cars twice.

The girls napped on the makeshift mattress in the back. They'd broken camp early to take advantage of the cooler morning temperatures, and during the first few hours Laurel, eager to show off how much she still remembered from third grade, had taught Ruby how to count using coins from the change jar. Claire drove with the windows down to conserve fuel, and the girls had eventually dozed off to the road's constant roar. They could still fall asleep anywhere. It hadn't been that long, but Claire had almost forgotten what it was like to sleep so deeply. Every time she closed her eyes, she saw her mother's face right before she'd been taken.

She flipped the visor down and studied her reflection. She'd teased their mother about her dark circles. Now Claire's put her mother's to shame.

The walkie-talkie crackled to life. "Claire, come in. Over."

Claire picked up the faded neon-green walkie-talkie and pressed Talk. "Here," she said, responding to Cooper. She'd already been driving for five hours straight and didn't have the energy for more words.

"What's your fuel situation?" Cooper asked.

Claire glanced at the gauge. It still worked, thank God. It would have been a living nightmare to get stranded out in the open, to never know if something was coming for you.

"Half a tank," she said. "Used all my reserves filling us and Malachi this morning." She released the Talk and waited. Cooper was a long time in responding.

She pictured his long legs pressed against the dash, the big atlas spread across his lap as he plotted their pilgrimage across the desert. She could imagine him, trace of a Kentucky drawl, arguing with his driver Aaron, a twenty-year-old mechanic from North Florida, over where to stop for gas. Small towns tended to be safer, if they weren't completely wiped out. Larger towns and cities had more resources, like fuel and batteries, but also more wreckage to navigate. Since she and the girls had joined the caravan, they'd avoided major interstates. Cooper wasn't as afraid of being out in the open as she was—he was more confident about how to avoid attack—but he hadn't stopped in a city once.

"We've only got a quarter tank," he said, coming back to the channel. "Steph's crew is down to their last spare can, and we're low on batteries."

Aaron yelled something in the background that sounded like "hot Cheetos," and Cooper cut out.

God, she missed her cell phone. What she wouldn't give to curl up in a ball under a blanket and numb out with her socials. But cell coverage was spotty, and no one's had worked reliably in months.

"These butt-knuckles want to try to find snacks," Cooper said a moment later.

Despite feeling hollowed out, Claire smiled for the first time in days. Cooper was only twenty-five, but he was the oldest in the group by a few years, which made him an old man. She understood that. She felt ancient. In the last few months, she'd experienced the disappearance of friends, teachers, neighbors, and then their mother. Thankfully, the girls had been inside when it happened. Claire stopped letting them play outside afterward.

"We're gonna try Reno," he said and despite the warm air blowing her hair around her face, Claire felt a chill on her neck. After the first wave, looting had been especially bad in the cities. Folks said that looting was what caused the second wave. The caravan didn't loot. They traded. They did odd jobs if they could, but they didn't loot.

She stared at the dusty bumper in front of her, a Toyota Sienna, just like the one she drove except Coop's had been brand-new when the first wave hit. Hers had been their family car. Before all this started, she'd begged her mom to let her drive the van. Now, it was hers alone, and she'd give anything to go back to the way things were.

"Claire, do you copy?" Cooper asked.

"Copy," Claire said. The dry air singed her nose.

"We'll keep this formation as we go through the city. Me, you, then Malachi's van. Steph will bring up the rear."

"Copy," Claire said again, but her throat was so dry that nothing came out. She took a sip of water and pressed Talk. "Copy."

"I figure two more days after this stop, and we'll be across the border and into Vancouver," Cooper said.

"Copy that," Claire said. She appreciated how positive he sounded. Rumors were that Canada was better. The last she'd heard they'd barely had a second wave at all. If that was the case, things had to be better there. There had to be some kind of program or something to help with the girls. Maybe she could even finish high school.

When Claire met Cooper at a gas station on the outskirts of Knoxville, she'd only been on the road for a few days. After they'd gone to the same three gas stations looking for fuel, he'd approached her and convinced her that she and the girls would be safer with their caravan, even if there were no other women in the group. They lived in completely different times, he'd argued. With everything out there, folks like them had to stick together.

Her mother would have never traveled in a caravan with a dozen guys, but Claire had taken one look at her dwindling supplies and joined them.

"Don't get separated," Cooper said. "We'll stop at the first open station, load up and be on our way. Over."

They got off the highway and took some back roads, skirting the interstate until signs of civilization began to appear—abandoned gas stations and strip malls with boarded-up windows. As they passed the city limits, they drove by a midsize church whose sign out front read, "Repent for the end is nigh." It backed up to a nice neighborhood barricaded with corrugated metal walls. Expensive-looking roofs poked over the tops. It struck Claire as a waste of time and resources. Those houses were probably empty.

They pulled onto a four-lane road that ran straight through the center of town. All the abandoned cars had long ago been pushed to the sides of the road and the center lanes were clear, though they were the only cars using it. They drove by the remnants of a tent city baking under the open sun in the parking lot between two abandoned superstores. Several blocks later, they passed an overgrown garden on the lawn of a school. More businesses missing windows and doors, shuttered restaurants, and abandoned houses. None of the gas stations were functioning.

As they made their way farther north, they drove beneath a sign that straddled the road.

"What's that say?" Ruby asked from the back. She was awake and rubbing the sleep from her eyes.

"It says 'Reno,'" Claire said. Ruby should have been in kindergarten learning sight words and receiving hugs from someone who smelled like vanilla cookies. Instead, she was in Reno. "'The Biggest Little City in the World.' Wake Laurel up. We're gonna stop for gas. Aaron wants to look for snacks."

Ruby was instantly shaking Laurel awake.

"Can we go inside this time?" Laurel asked, shoving Ruby off her. "I gotta pee."

Claire frowned. "If Cooper thinks it's safe enough, you can go inside. But remember the rules."

"Be kind," the girls said in unison. "Be honest. Keep a safe distance." They were the best rules Claire had come up with.

They drove past a casino that had been mid-construction when the first wave hit, then another that was shuttered. A lanky man in a janitor suit squatted outside a third, smoking a cigarette by the side door. On the other side of the empty parking lot, Claire saw a Chevron with the most beautiful words in the English language: Open for Business. She held her breath and followed Cooper left at the intersection and right into the gas station.

The lights were on and beneath the open sign was written in block script, "Cash only. Will trade for fresh produce."

Claire pulled up to the pump behind Aaron while Malachi and Steph pulled in on the other side. Cooper jumped out of the passenger seat.

"Keep the vans running while I check things out," he shouted to the drivers and trotted into the store to assess the situation. A few minutes later, he opened the door. "Fill up," he shouted. "I'll pay and see if there's any news."

The van doors opened and spilled young men onto the hot concrete.

"Is it safe for the girls?" Claire called.

"I'll keep them with me," he said and waved the girls over.

She nodded and turned to her sisters. "You have two minutes."

Ruby started to argue, but Laurel grabbed her hand and hauled her toward the gas station before Claire had a chance to change her mind.

She opened the trunk, pulled out two red five-gallon gas cans and filled those first. While she put gas in the van, the gas station door opened, and Cooper poked his head out.

"Sending the girls back to you," he said, and the girls trudged back to the van.

"No luck with the snacks," Claire guessed when she saw their faces.

Ruby didn't bother to answer. She climbed in the van and flopped on the bed.

"They were nice," Laurel said. She stood next to Claire and drew pictures in the window's dust.

The station door opened again and offered up an older woman in overalls with a gray braid slung over her shoulder. She held something wrapped in a napkin.

"I'm Maeve," she said, coming up to Claire. "Me and my husband

George own the gas station. Tried to give your girls this." Maeve held out the napkin.

Claire wiped her hands on her jeans, but Maeve just smiled and waited for her to take the bundle. Inside the napkin was a small cluster of green grapes.

"I don't have anything to trade you," Claire said and shoved the grapes back at Maeve.

"No trade," said Maeve. "They're a gift. I tried to tell the girls." The older woman looked past Claire into the van. "Guess you trained them right. Where's your mama?"

"Second wave," Claire said, and Maeve nodded.

"And your daddy?"

Claire just shrugged.

"You look like you should be headed to college," Maeve said.

"I was halfway through my senior year when they closed the schools," Claire said.

"According to your friends, you're headed to Canada," Maeve said. She nodded her head toward the gas station. "You girls doing all right with that crew?"

Claire scanned the sky like she always did when she was out in the open. "They're the least of my worries," she said.

"I guess that's true," Maeve said. She surveyed Claire and the girls. "Listen, we're part of a supply train that comes across the country. Private outfit. Good people. We get travelers from time to time. Things seem to be the same everywhere."

"We'll see," Claire said, swallowing back a sharp remark. "Everyone we've talked to says it's better up there."

Her mother had been the first one to say that it was strictly an American problem. Malachi had a battery-powered radio and one night they'd caught a snatch of a broadcast by some low-level government official that insisted Canada's culture made it more stable. Even in the before-times, they'd had a lower crime rate. People were kinder up there. More honest.

They'd tested the Canada theory with survivors at every stop. Everyone they talked to had different theories about why the death rate in Canada was lower. Honesty came up a lot. So did kindness.

The consensus seemed to be that since Canadians were nicer, it had to be safer up there, but what amount of nice was enough to keep them alive? No one seemed to know for sure. It kept Claire up at night, but she had to believe they were headed to a better place. Anything else was unthinkable.

She handed the bundle of grapes to Laurel, who divided them into piles. One pile was short, so she kept it for herself and handed the other two to Ruby and Claire.

"You eat them," Claire said. Her eyes burned. She blinked back tears and pulled the little girl in for a hug. Laurel squirmed away to focus on her grapes.

"You could stay here with us," Maeve said, watching Claire closely. "Me and George, we had boys, but they were grown and gone before this ever started. We could help you—" Maeve's smile faltered as she looked over Claire's shoulder. Claire whirled around, heart racing.

Across the empty lot, a man and a woman stood outside the bereft casino. The woman lifted a cigarette to her lips. She caught sight of the caravan, and with a flip of her long ponytail, teetered across the parking lot on four-inch stilettos. The man followed a step behind.

"Them again," Maeve said, frowning.

"Who are they?" Claire asked, gripping Laurel's shoulder.

"Haven't seen them in weeks," Maeve said. "Thought they'd been taken."

"Get in," Claire said and pushed Laurel into the van. Laurel scrambled in but sat on her knees to watch the approaching couple out of the rear window.

"Aaron," Claire called, her voice going high and thin.

His head snapped up from filling his last gas can. He took one look at the pair. "I'll get the others," he said and disappeared into the gas station. Claire opened the passenger side door and reached into the glove box.

"Keep your head, girl," Maeve warned when she saw the gun. "That's a good way to get killed."

It's fine to use this for self-defense, her mother had said. She'd been holding the gun right before she was taken.

"It's for self-defense," Claire said with more confidence than she felt. She tucked her mom's gun into the waistband of her jeans. The barrel dug into her hip bone.

Maeve shook her head and scanned the sky, then hurried across the blacktop and disappeared behind the glass. The door locked with a click.

The couple paused at the road and looked both ways in a gross pantomime of watching for traffic, then plowed across the street. At the edge of the gas station pad, the man grabbed the woman's elbow and whispered in her ear.

He wore a ratty tux with pants that stopped short of reaching his scuffed shoes. His tie was loose, and the vest and shirt opened over sallow skin. The woman sported a blond wig tied in a high ponytail that fell like a frayed ribbon to her waist. She wore caked makeup and a spangled dress that shattered the light. A massive designer bag that looked more corporate than glittery casino was slung over one shoulder.

The woman patted the man on the arm, then lurched from the sidewalk and sashayed across the concrete. When she came under the shade of the gas pump, she removed her oversized sunglasses and flashed Claire a hot-pink grin.

"Hey, sweetie," she cooed. "Would you happen to have some change?"

The woman opened the mouth of her bag and pulled out an envelope thick with small bills. She fanned the money with her thumb.

Claire looked at the change jar tucked behind the driver's seat, filled with quarters and dimes and nickels and pennies. It was the last thing she'd grabbed as they fled the house in addition to a few hundred dollars she'd managed to scrounge in her mother's room. Pretty soon she'd be out of cash, and all she'd have was the change. She didn't know what she'd do once they actually got to Canada. After weeks of paying for gas and food, she was running out of money.

The gas pump clicked and the sound startled Claire. "How much do you need?" she asked.

"Only about twenty dollars' worth if you have it," the woman said. "Laundry mat in the casino only takes quarters." She looked at the change jar in the van and flashed her teeth again.

Before the first wave, twenty dollars would have felt like nothing—enough to buy a few iced coffees or snacks at the gas station on the way to school. But now, every single bill was precious. Claire nodded for Laurel to count out the quarters.

The woman's gaze darted over the girls perched on top of the makeshift mattress, their grimy clothes, their coloring books, the small cooler, their bag of food, mostly protein bars and beef jerky. Claire touched her hair as the woman's eyes slid over her. It was oily from days on the road and smelled like old laundry.

"You girls traveling alone?" the woman asked.

"We're with a group," Claire said, feigning confidence.

"Don't see anyone but you," the woman said with her plastic smile.

Claire looked over at the gas station. Cooper was standing just inside the door next to Maeve, watching her through the glass.

Claire lifted her chin. "We're headed north," she said.

The woman's smile cracked. "Damn rumors," she said. "Saying people are tempted to do wrong just so no one asks questions when they disappear. You can't see what happens when they're taken, right? That's too convenient. Government just trying to scare us. You're too smart to believe all that nonsense." She put her hands on her hips, candy-red fingernails digging into sequins. "Seeing is believing, I say."

Seeing is believing, Claire. "My mom used to say that," Claire said.

Laurel handed Claire a bag full of quarters. "It's all there," she whispered. "I counted twice."

The woman stuffed the envelope of cash back in her purse. Claire held out the bag of change and the woman snatched it, scratching Claire with her long nails. Her grin widened.

"Do you want to count it?" Claire asked. "Just to be sure."

The woman slid the enormous sunglasses back on her face. "If you're gullible enough to believe those rumors, I trust you're telling the truth," she said and reached into her purse. She removed a different, smaller envelope, pulled a thin stack of bills from it, and waved them under Claire's nose.

Claire's stomach turned, but she took the money. The woman was all teeth and rhinestone-studded sunglasses.

Across the parking lot, the man in the tuxedo shielded his eyes and studied the sky. "Come on, Darlene," he yelled, his voice breaking over her name. "We've been outside long enough."

"Pipe down," Darlene yelled over her shoulder. "I'm coming."

Claire looked down at the folded money in her hand. Sweat rolled off her brow and into her eyes, making the denominations swim. She unfolded the money. Her fingers slipped across the bills. One, two, three. There were only six ones.

Darlene, with her purse full of money and her sparkly dress, stepped back. Heat flooded Claire's face. Ever since her mom disappeared, she'd been so careful to contain her rage. People made mistakes when they were angry. Did things they didn't mean to do. Even after the hunger and the fear and the sleepless nights, she'd kept her anger bottled up and stored safely away, and now it tore loose from some hidden place in her chest and spread like fire across her body.

"Wait," Claire said, and her voice echoed in her ears. "You're short."

"Must be a mistake." Darlene's smile twisted into a mockery of innocence as she backed away. "It's all this heat. Probably got to your brain. It's all there. You just need to count again."

"We need that money to get across the border," Claire said. "You're stealing from us." The gun's weight pulled on Claire's waistband. Her heart pounded in her chest. She'd only fired it once, after the first wave when her mother insisted she learn how to use it.

Claire glanced at the gas station door again, but Cooper and the others had disappeared deeper into the store.

Cavalry's not coming, Claire. Everything's falling apart. She fingered the gun's smooth barrel thinking of that first time she held it. How heavy it felt. *You need to know you can take care of business.* She wrapped her fingers around the grip and pulled it free of her waistband. Power hummed through her body as she leveled the gun at Darlene. "Give me my money."

Darlene laughed, a hacking sound incongruent with blond wigs and sparkly dresses. She held out her expensive bag like she was offering it to Claire, then turned it upside down. Designer lipsticks, expensive earrings, and another pair of high-dollar sunglasses with the casino gift shop tag still attached clattered to the concrete. A half-dozen envelopes of cash—more money than Claire had ever thought to see in one place—fell to the ground.

One of the envelopes split on impact and bills fluttered across the lot.

"Come and get it," Darlene crowed as the man in the tuxedo swore. Ignoring Claire and the gun, he raced across the lot snatching at the bills. While Darlene cackled, he fell to his knees and stuffed the envelopes and jewelry back into the purse.

They'd looted the casino and survived by hiding.

Claire held the gun steady as her mother's voice whispered in her ear. *It's too much money to pass up. Use your eyes, Claire. You didn't steal the money.* She'd never felt steadier in her life. Her finger slid against the trigger.

Darlene stood over the pile and laughed while the man scrambled. One last envelope lay at Claire's feet. He stopped mid-reach and looked up at her with bloodshot eyes.

It would be so easy. No one would stop her. One bullet was all it would take. It would be over in a second. In two seconds, she'd be in the van, doors locked. She'd drive faster than she'd ever driven before, and she wouldn't stop until she was sure nothing followed her.

Seeing is believing, Claire.

Claire stared down at the man on his knees clutching a purse full of cash to his scrawny chest.

Desperate times, Claire.

"Claire." Ruby pulled at the edge of her T-shirt. Laurel's arms were wrapped around her like a shield.

Claire looked down into their pale faces. She'd seen those ghosted looks before—when she told them their mother was gone after she'd cleaned up the mess. Then, later that night, she'd seen it on her own face, when she'd looked at herself in the bathroom mirror and realized everything was up to her.

"I'll only take what's mine," Claire said. They'd been out in their front yard when her mother was taken. She'd been fighting with a neighbor, and Claire had stepped between them. She'd heard her mother grunt, and when she turned around, there was only the gun in a pile of shredded clothes.

Trembling, Claire lowered the gun.

"Throw it in the trash," Laurel whispered.

Claire looked at the greasy trash can, and the man clambered to his feet. Behind him, Darlene, with her dress that glinted in the sun, laughed. Cooper stood just inside the door and watched. Her arm ached with the gun's weight, and she wanted him to open the door and walk across the parking lot like he owned the place and take the gun. But he just stood there, his hands pressed against the glass.

Claire opened the glove box and slid the gun back into the dark. She closed the box with a snap, then bent down and retrieved the envelope at her feet.

"I want to do what's honest," she said and counted out the fourteen bills that were owed to her. She held up an extra bill. She would be more than honest. She would be good. "I'll give you an extra dollar," she said as she handed the man the cash. "To show I don't hold it against you."

"It's time to go," Cooper said, appearing by her side. Doors slammed as the rest of the guys loaded up. Darlene and the man slunk to the edge of the lot.

"You left me out here," Claire hissed.

"I didn't know you had a *gun*," Cooper snapped. "I didn't know what you would do."

"I wasn't going to—" Claire stopped. In her periphery, she saw a blur of movement—a dark haze that coalesced into what might have been a man, but when she looked directly at it, there was only sky, clear and bright.

The shape stayed in her periphery. It looked human—if humans had huge wings. The blur moved one step closer and became clearer—a person with black oblong eyes that bled to the edges. Sickly white skin, pores oozing like an oil slick.

Her breath caught in her throat, and she looked up at Cooper, eyes wide. "I see it," she whispered. "Do you see it?"

"We all do," Cooper said. His eyes were rigid, staring hard at hers, refusing to look left or right.

Out of the corner of her eye, Claire saw the pale shape transform. It hunched its shoulders together and dropped its head. The skin fell from its body like a set of old clothes to land in a pile that the ground absorbed. Oil-black wings stretched wide and exploded into the sky. The bird circled the couple calling with a ragged song that Claire heard as if her phone were cutting in and out.

A black smudge emerged on the horizon.

"There's another one coming," Claire said.

"You haven't done anything wrong," Cooper said. He closed the girls' door and hustled Claire to the driver's side. "They're not coming for you."

Malachi and Steph pulled out of the lot with a restraint that made Claire want to scream.

She climbed into the driver's seat and started the engine. It turned over with a groan. Cooper got in his van. Aaron eased out of the lot and onto the abandoned thoroughfare. She was shaking and her palms were sweaty. She threw the car in drive and slammed her foot down but missed the pedal. In the backseat, Ruby whimpered and started to cry.

"It's gonna be okay," Claire said. She took a deep breath, let it out, and slowly pulled out behind Cooper.

Heat shimmered on the sunbaked street. With the windows up, the van felt like an oven.

"It's hot, Claire," Laurel said. "Can we ride with the air on for a few minutes?"

Claire hesitated. She wanted to conserve fuel so they wouldn't have to stop again until they reached Canada, but the last thing she wanted to do was roll down the windows.

"Sure, we can, kiddo," she said and turned on the air conditioner. "But just until we get out of town."

Cool air blew against her face, and Claire felt her heart rate even out. The walkie-talkie crackled to life.

"Tell us exactly what happened," Cooper said for everyone's sake. None of them wanted to make a mistake.

BREANDA PETSCH

Claire remembered to breathe. She didn't want to talk about it, didn't want to think about it, but she had to be honest. There was no other way to be. "She stole our money, and I barely have enough to get to Canada. We're broke, and then a whole envelope of cash fell on the ground. And it was only a few dollars, but it was like I'd lost my mind for a minute."

The channel was silent. What else was there to say?

"How are the girls?" Cooper asked.

Claire glanced behind her. Laurel still wore that haunted look, and Claire knew that later there would be hard questions. Thanks be to whatever god was still listening, Ruby was already nestled into a cloud of blankets and looking at a book.

"They're fine," Claire said.

"If you've got a few extra bills, we've got enough to cover you for the crossing," Cooper said. "We'll figure the rest out when we get to safety."

Claire heard a faint rustling sound, and four black shapes, quickly moving Rorschach Tests, swept over the van's roof. Cooper said all the survivors saw them at one point or another, but Claire hadn't seen one yet. Even when her mother was taken. She'd been standing behind Claire one moment and the next, there was just bloody, shredded clothes.

"Get some rest," she said to the girls and pointed to the floorboards beneath the AC vents. Laurel gathered Ruby beneath the cool air and pulled the blanket over their heads.

The road leading away from the casino was long and straight. Claire knew she should keep her eyes on the road, but she watched the birds through the rearview mirror. Greasy shadows flew a lazy circle above the couple as they stumbled blindly across the empty casino parking lot.

Halfway across the lot, Darlene stopped and fished for something in her ridiculous purse. She produced a cigarette and waited while the man fumbled with a lighter.

Two of the birds took him first. Shadows hauled him from the ground. His feet kicked helplessly against the air as beaks gouged and claws tore. In the time it took for the bile to creep up Claire's throat, he was reduced to bloody ribbons. The birds opened their claws, and the shreds fell to the ground in a wet heap.

Darlene turned in wild circles, shouting into the emptiness. Above her, the birds drifted. Something on the ground caught her attention, and she bent down to pick up the fallen lighter, the cigarette hanging from her lip. She took one tottering step, and looked blindly at the sky as the birds, invisible to her, circled closer. Darlene dropped her bag and raced across the lot. She got three steps when one heel snapped, and she stumbled. Recovering, she limped toward the casino. She was a few yards from the door when the birds dove.

Darlene threw up her hands and turned in helpless circles as black wings beat against her. Then it was blood and flesh and teal blue sequins catching the light, sparking like fireworks in every direction. When the birds were finished, strings of fake blond hair caught on bits of asphalt.

They landed and pecked at the wet shreds. Claire blinked and the shreds reassembled and merged with the birds' oily feathers. They stretched their wings wide, then collapsed into a dark line on the horizon.

Claire flipped her rearview mirror up and stared ahead until the last of Reno's abandoned buildings were behind them. She could no longer see them, but she knew the birds would always be there, lurking just out of sight, waiting to start the whole thing over again. She looked back at her sisters, gripped the steering wheel, and sat a little straighter.

Seeing is believing, her mom had said, but whatever darkness her mom had put out in the world had come for her. The world is dark enough, Claire thought. But now she knew how to stay alive.

Tonight, when they camped, she would crack jokes around the campfire, same as the guys, to chase away her ghosts. She'd smile and ask everyone to name one thing they'd do as soon as they got to Canada. Then, while Malachi and Steph kept watch, she'd pull the girls against her, and they would sleep out in the open beneath the stars for the first time.

The Boy from Elsewhen

written by
Barlow Crassmont

illustrated by
DANIEL MONTIFAR

ABOUT THE AUTHOR

Armand Diab (pen name: Barlow Crassmont) has lived in the USA, Eastern Europe, the Middle East, and China. When not teaching English or writing speculative, fantasy, and science fiction, he dabbles in juggling, solving the Rubik's Cube, and learning other languages (his Spanish is coming along nicely).

He has been published by the British Science Fiction Association, in Wilderness House Literary Review, *and in* Dark Speculations: Volume 1 *by Little Red Publishing.*

"The Boy from Elsewhen" was inspired by the current social climate across the globe. Armand says, "Everywhere one goes, regardless of country or nation, most people are endlessly staring at their smartphones, unable to look away, and often neglecting other humans around them for the sake of technology. As the dominant species on Earth, we are becoming too dependent on our handheld devices, but are no smarter for it. In fact, I feel if the trend continues (and I see no evidence that it won't), future generations won't be able to construct a single solitary thought without AI's assistance. Let's hope that day, at least, is in the far-distant future, after me and mine are long gone."

ABOUT THE ILLUSTRATOR

Daniel Montifar was destined to be an illustrator. Born and raised in Queens, New York, known as the "world's borough" for its rich cultural diversity, Daniel appreciated this melting pot of influences, including his Bolivian and Filipino heritage.

Surrounded by art wherever he went in NYC and being raised by a Star Wars–loving mom and a dad with a treasure trove of comics dating back to high school, his early fascination with the realms of sci-fi and *fantasy fueled his passion for drawing. He became the kid who always had a sketchbook in hand, capturing scenes from his imagination wherever he went.*

Prior to the pandemic, while still a freshman in high school, Daniel moved to Houston, Texas, where he delved deeper into the world of art. This transition was a pivotal chapter in his artistic evolution as he honed his skills and explored new artistic horizons. His work won several competitions, including a Gold Key Scholastic Art Award and the AIGA Worldstudio Award.

Currently, as a student at Ringling College of Art and Design in sunny Florida, Daniel continues to refine his craft. With roots deeply embedded in diversity, family, and a love for fantastical realms, Daniel's artistic vision is boundless, promising a future filled with captivating illustrations that transport viewers to imaginative worlds.

The Boy from Elsewhen

He kept to himself, staring into the bound pages that used to charm our forefathers before PHIL-eep 2156's takeover.

The glossiness in the boy's eyes sparkled like the open ocean under a bright sun. None of us wanted anything to do with him and his antiquated ways, but Mrs. Robhart insisted.

"You children, be nice," she said, with furrowed brow. "Where he comes from, things are different, I imagine. They *have* to be."

The absence of wiring on his person, his empty hands (unlike those of his new classmates, who typed and tapped and scrolled with each passing breath on their handheld devices), and the backpack free of a tablet or a lightweight transparent monitor, were alarming to those not familiar with our not-too-distant past. When alone outdoors, he stared at the blue skies and the swaying trees as if they were the eighth wonder. He inquired about the shiny decaying structures in the foggy distance, the ruins of which stuck out like fractured dentures.

"What is that place?" he asked, wide-eyed. Yet no one bothered telling him, because no one cared anymore. It was as relevant as the Technical Age that preceded our digital one, as distant as the sparkling dots in the night sky. The city hadn't been inhabited in decades, its purpose as superfluous as sunshine in a volcano.

No REAL-D helmet, nor any goggles were seen on the boy's squarish head, and his native label was difficult to pronounce. After deliberating, the school board agreed to call him Visar, and soon the name hung on the curious lips of every student and faculty.

During class immersion, he conversed with the teacher, his speech a product of whispers and muffled syllables slightly below speaking level. The cables ran from our headsets to the central-desk hard drive, coiling in knots like a serpent's nest. Yet no wiring was to be found on Visar's desk. He sat properly, in a posture indicating a healthy spine, peering at strange paper stacks. Their pages were torn at the corners and faded on both sides, ranging from yellowish white to sunset orange. Even after several suggestions to the contrary by his classmates and teachers, he refused to be plugged.

I hardly knew one could do that.

"They want us to respect the Traveler's rights," Mr. Porter said after Jacob complained. "He can do as he pleases, according to the new international laws regarding the Travelers. To each their own."

"Can any of us disconnect whenever we want?" Ameely Strokes asked. The teacher contemplated, then nodded, leaving us in a state of prolonged confusion. It was well known that a disconnected mind would disintegrate to absolute lethargy before long. The cognizance—or whatever remained of one—would collapse within weeks, if not days. That's what they kept telling us, anyway.

Visar's arm rose, straighter at the elbow than usual. The teacher pointed to him and nodded.

"I'm sorry if my ways offend you," Visar said, gradually turning to look at all. "If not for the cosmic anomaly, I wouldn't even be here."

"Why don't you just immerse?" Chloe Weilin asked. "We're all doing it. There's no way that anything on those pages can compete with the visuals we're experiencing."

"I prefer my pastime, thank you."

When the midterms arrived, Visar's scores towered over the rest, like a holy tree in a field of weeds. He aced all the exams but one (literature of the Third Age), with the second-best student coming eight percentage points behind him. His results in algebra and calculus left the teachers scratching their heads, wondering if the curriculum for the upcoming semester should be updated accordingly to elevate the level of difficulty.

DANIEL MONTIFAR

All the relevant dates from the history of the First Age embedded themselves in Visar's mind like invisible ink on his brain, until he knew them better than the school's daily curriculum. Whispers of his accomplishments in calculus and Old English resonated for weeks in the teachers' lounge. Mr. Rapath, the physics instructor, was overheard by several of our classmates. According to them, he did not mince words.

"If all of 'em were like that kid, this'd be the easiest job in the world."

Among the elite, the number of Visar's admirers and those envying him were roughly split down the middle. Even with all the technological improvements at their disposal, his classmates, most of whom uploaded gigabytes of data into their MENT-chips the week prior, could not compete with Visar's solitary mind, unaided by current, free of cyberspace, independent of electricity. Aided only by time and patience, he spent countless hours engaged in the large tomes he carried, like trophies of cultures long since perished. But his humble demeanor, adored by the faculty, was quickly misunderstood for condescension by some of his irritated peers. They threw nasty looks his way when he passed the benches. He was also extensively ignored by the lunch staff (a request from the envious elite students) on consecutive days and could scarcely find a partner for the chemistry filtering project.

I watched his struggles from afar, with a hopeless sense of melancholy. More than anything, I wanted to reach out, but I feared the reaction of the masses. Unlike Visar, I had three years to go before graduating, and alienating those I shared the hallways with was bad politics.

The opposition, however, cared little for subtlety.

"That snobbish bastard will get his," Reynold McGavin said during lunch, devouring a sandwich that reeked of goose flavoring—without an ounce of the meat. I listened to the initial spray of resentment with some discomfort, but once his tone turned to acrid bitterness, I became filled with disgust and walked away. After everyone cleared, I hesitated, stood nervously, second-guessing myself until my anxiety gradually dissipated. Then, gathering my wits, I approached Visar.

He sat on a metal bench, engaged in a leather tome, his mind likely in a different place and time. He appeared as a heavenly angel my great-grandfather once showed me from a holy book of the distant past, a time before the PHIL-eep 2156 era.

"What's it about?" I asked. Visar reciprocated my smile and drew me in with his look. He told of a shipwrecked survivor stranded on a deserted island. The man aged decades in solitude, evolving into a simplified being whose dependence on nature outweighed his need for organized society. Visar suggested I give it a try.

"I wouldn't even know where to begin," I replied.

"The start is a good place," he said.

Three weeks later, the brightest stars were aligned in a slanted V in the night sky, just like they were two years before, on February 47, 2298. Officials were quick to warn of another anomaly, their message flashing across the nightly heavens, like millions of disciplined fireflies. Rumors of Visar's impending departure reverberated from the back of classrooms spreading into lounges and cafeterias, until they spilled over into the football field and adjacent parking lot. The faculty talked about him as if they were losing one of their own.

But the middle-class instructors' circle was helpless against the affluent student body, whose wishes were of high importance to the wealthy district, run by the powerful parents of the student majority. The growing resentment finally burst into an unfair brawl when three spiteful classmates jumped Visar after school. They knocked him down on the muddy ground, staining his jacket, dirtying his face, bloodying his lip. Soon, "crap-stain" remarks rang from the laughing bullies like a pack of hyenas. One of the brutes kicked Visar into submission, dislocating several of his ribs. The other two destroyed and tore every page and packet and booklet from his bag. When they left, I ran up and extended my hand. After initial hesitation, he took it.

"Based on the latest alignment of the cosmic bodies, I will be leaving on Monday," he said. "Most likely." From inside his coat, he pulled out a hardbound edition. The title had faded from the spine and the front cover. "I think you'll like it."

"Where will you go?" I asked.

"Wherever it takes me. Hopefully home."
"How long since you've been back?"
"Longer than can be counted in your years."

The flash that lit up the night sky on Monday caused minor blindness for those who stared at it extensively. Several people were reported missing, including two of our faculty. When the darkness returned twenty-seven minutes later, the accompanying silence nudged our valley into a deep, forgetful sleep.

In class, I sit at a desk empty of immersion equipment, a foolish rebel. Unafraid, unintimidated, unnerved.

It turns out what we've been told isn't true. We're supposed to immerse, at any cost, without exceptions. Not doing so isn't an option, unless one wants to face dire consequences (expulsion, hefty fines, perhaps imprisonment). No native citizen has ever disobeyed. But I don't care.

I'm not doing it. Not now, not ever. I'll defy them to death, if necessary.

As a result, I wait. I wait for the judgment and the ensuing punishment. Let them do their worst. At least for once, my thoughts will be free of PHIL-eep's clout. Which is more than can be said of the collective populace. The cables and cords and coils embedded in their flesh are like bloodsucking leeches. Their headsets cover eyes absent of spark or much recognition. When they finish, they glance at me patronizingly, their looks as rancorous as a sting. Looking away is all I do and all that can really be done.

In my newfound solitude, I think of Visar, his enchanting eyes, the quiet dignity he carried himself with, the tremendous acumen he accumulated all on his own, without succumbing to the alluring sensibilities of PHIL-eep 2156. But the more I think about him, the more my heart aches, as if recalling fresh unhealed wounds.

So I stop daydreaming and focus on the publications he left me. They're torn in various places, crumpled aplenty, but usable nonetheless.

The symbols on the first page are intricate, cryptic, enticing. I stare at them extensively, often holding my breath while deciphering the words. But I know the sentences will present the bigger challenge, and the paragraphs the bigger still.

The book's thickness, the number of pages, the sheer magnitude of information, are intimidating. Someone once told me that the start is a good place to begin.

I have little reason to doubt it.

Code L1

written by
Andrew Jackson

illustrated by
HEATHERANNE LEE

ABOUT THE AUTHOR

Andrew Jackson started writing and illustrating at age twelve, and never gave up the former but (thankfully for his readers) has stopped the latter! One of his earliest memories is of watching Star Trek *with his dad and falling in love with the speeding ships, bizarre aliens, and the diamond glitter of myriad stars in that eternal blackness.*

Even now, as he explores the strange new worlds of family, fatherhood, and a career in retail, he's never lost his love for the stars. Counting authors such as Stephen King, Iain M. Banks, and Alastair Reynolds among his literary influences, he revels both in reading and writing rich, tangible worlds other than our own. Born too late to watch the Apollo missions, but too early for interstellar travel, he must content himself with dreams and the sad knowledge that he may never know what's out there. Is there anybody there? Why aren't they talking?

On walks down leafy lanes of his native Surrey, England, Andrew examines these questions. He likes to think he looked at a particular tree one time and pondered its age and almost otherworldly summer greenness, and so was born "Code L1."

The story itself is an exploration of the Fermi Paradox—the hypothesis that, if we have galactic neighbors, they should have called by now. Perhaps they've seen the darker sides of humanity, and they're afraid of us coming out into the stars. Or perhaps, if they could, they'd tell us why they've been so quiet. Perhaps, it's best not to know.

ABOUT THE ILLUSTRATOR

HeatherAnne Lee was born in 2004 in Federal Way, Washington, and has lived across the US from Hawaii to New York to Vermont. HeatherAnne, or

"Heather" to her friends, now resides in Savannah, Georgia, pursuing a Bachelor of Fine Arts in illustration at the Savannah College of Art and Design.

Heather started drawing as soon as she could hold a crayon and never stopped, graduating from crayon to graphite to paint, and now she primarily works digitally. Despite working on a screen, Heather holds to her painting knowledge, layering colors and textures on her drawing tablet, emulating traditional painting techniques in a digital medium.

Heather takes much of her inspiration from the world around her, translating reality into epics and stories of dragons and knights. Heather always strives to push her work to the limit, working with clients to bring their stories to life through her illustrations.

Code L1

There was nothing wrong with the planet, at first sight.

From above, AC-211 looked like a marble in space; a small pea-green ball flecked with spots of deep brown and the azure pockmarks of small oceans. Thin, wispy banks of cloud chased each other around the equator. For some reason, it made me think of a veil over a shrouded corpse. The thought scared me, if only for its cynicism. Coldly, logically, that was all the job was—preparing a body for viewing. There was a reason the vets called these assignments *undertakings*.

I forced more pleasant images into my head. AC-211 was eighty percent rainforest, and hot as an Australian summer. It was green as freshly mown grass, as a parrot's wing, as—

"Money." Julio Vasquez stabbed a plump finger at the viewport, grinning at me across the shuttle's long cargo hold. "This place even looks like a dollar bill."

I shook my head as titanium shutters slid over the viewports, metal already glowing cherry-red with the heat of atmospheric entry. The hold was filled with scanner drones, first-stake warning beacons, bundles of survey spikes, and two large tents. Four of us sat two to a side, strapped into soft, pliable couches to cushion atmospheric entry.

"Just think," he continued. "We're the first here! We can trade our pensions for a plot and a bundle of cash and—"

"Inadvisable," squeaked O'Malley, furiously polishing his thick-rimmed specs with a sweaty cloth. The little lawyer was mostly green and had spent most of the ride biting at his manicure. "Unless this place strikes gold with the investors, you'll just have a pile of sticks in the middle of nowhere."

The shuttle jolted and my teeth met briefly in my tongue. A red light went on over the cockpit hatch. I tried to focus on how horribly damp my underarms were, and not the intermittent *pops* and *creaks* of the stressed hull.

"Perfect," grunted a shirtless Park, somehow managing to swig from his hip flask. His hand swept over his bald skull, massaging red eyes. "Sounds like retirement."

Park needed another word beginning with *r*. The security guard had the easiest job on planetfall. While Julio and I set up our gear and argued about who got to write the technical report and who the tourist pamphlet, Park drank copiously and passed out. He carried a pistol, but never used it. Not in the nine jumps I'd made with him, nor in the thirty-six previous. He was an annoyingly well-paid redundancy.

For a second, my stomach took flight, lodging somewhere in my throat. I gritted my teeth, swallowing it back like a gone-off MRE, and when it settled, so had the shuttle.

The heat shields slid back, and we were met with a dazzling, red-orange sunrise. I had to close my eyes for a moment as we descended; massive, broccoli-like trees below us glowed crimson with the dawn. Rocky chasms glittered with unknown minerals; inland lakes became pools of fire. Far, far below, large native birds were turning the sky black with their wings.

"It's a shame that in twenty years, this'll just be another city," I said, placing a hand on the porthole. The red sun turned my dark skin translucent.

Julio laughed. "You're a dreamer, Yasmin. There's a section on your kind in the handbook."

I flipped him the finger.

"Good morning, stooges!" Carol-Anne's Texan twang came over the speakers. "We're about five klicks up and descending fast. Point nine-six Earth g's, sunny skies, temperature a balmy 32°C, oxygen-nitrogen atmosphere, heavy on the former. Looks like we'll be breathing easy!"

"Why does she always have to sound so damn happy?" muttered Park.

Even from this height, all I could see was kilometre after kilometre of rainforest. Trees the size of battleships, hundreds of metres tall. Some fallen like collapsed buildings across the forest floor, covered in monstrous, writhing pale worm-things. Muddy rivers, distant, misty mountains. Maybe it was a trick of the alien sun, but branches seemed to sprout like arms from some of the great trees.

The pilot was steering us towards a large, red-rock plateau, raised high above most of the forest. It was covered in boulders, patches of brown earth, and thick stands of green and gold-leaved brush. In the dawn light, some of the protrusions looked regular, rhythmic. Almost like—

"Holy crap," squawked Carol-Anne, as the images solidified. My eyes bulged and Julio whooped. Seemingly starting atop the plateau, reaching like spider's silk into the forest below—stretching from tree to massive tree—were hundreds of thin, glittering metal cables. "We've got a Code L1."

Julio and I shared a look of pure exhilaration. We were both still fresh enough in the company to be excited. Code L1. L for life.

As I watched our PR man wrestle with his seatbelt like an impatient child, I reminded myself that, gods knew how I empathised, I had a job to do.

"Got to do the boring science bit first." I popped open my hand terminal, connecting to Carol-Anne's dashboard and the shuttle's external sensor network. There was no sound but for the erratic breathing of the crew and the odd thump as the vessel settled on its landing struts. No lurching stomach as some vast carnivorous plant pulled the shuttle inside. No clamour of alien limbs on the rear hatch. No weapons fire.

Julio huffed audibly as my eyes—and most importantly, my nose—gained several orders of magnitude of sensitivity. Topographic maps of the surrounding terrain scrawled in electric blue lines across my screen.

"We scanned from orbit," he said. "If there were any lurking nasties, we'd know."

O'Malley muttered something about procedure.

Little dots began to populate the invisible lines extending from the shuttle into the jungle around us as the algorithm noted points of interest. Patches of warmer and cooler air. Scent markers that could mark a patch of dung, or our deaths. The lights were green, green, green. One wavering yellow…and then light green. No reds. I let the scan run on.

"Don't be so sure," muttered Park as he snapped himself out of his restraints. "When my last crew first scouted Sigma III Avalon, we thought the air was fine." He grinned sickly. "When we stepped out, the captain's lungs came out of his—"

"All right!" O'Malley snapped, face now a faint grey colour. "I'd prefer to keep my lunch." He looked at my terminal as it beeped the safe signal I feared would never come. "Copy me your scan, Yasmin."

I swiped my survey across to O'Malley, who read agonisingly slowly and carefully. Finally, he nodded. The final piece of red tape fell away. The world was ours.

"Don't get your hopes up," grunted Park as we dragged a cooler unit out into the muggy, wet morning heat. "This is my sixth L1."

We lowered the unit to the dry soil of the clearing, plugging it into a port on the side of the ship. It instantly began to thrum and standing near it was suddenly delicious. The sun pounded down on the red spear of rock, and all of us were drenched in sweat. I took a long, slow breath, savouring the head rush of the heavy O_2. The new scents were a bomb in my sinuses. Foreign flowers, astringent animal dung, and an underlying tang of something between cinnamon and honey that made my stomach growl.

"How can you say that?" muttered Julio as he swept back his long, damp hair, perched on the stump of a sapling, chugging from a water canteen.

All around us, the jungle teemed with life. Up here, the trees stood in clumps, parting only reluctantly for the powdery rock and occasional animal trails. Large, pale-skinned fruits hung from several, many half-eaten by insect life. Bugs the size of footballs, horned and winged, hard-shelled and maggot-soft alike, buzzed and rustled about their nests and hollows, some embracing that hot sun, some shrinking from it. Birds, or leather-winged things like them, flew in great squalls overhead, their cries like whooping drunks. Sometimes, in the waist-high brush, between the green and purple plants, there was the swish of something larger, and pained cries from far below were cut off abruptly.

"For every hundred and fifty worlds surveyed, there is a three percent chance of an L1," said O'Malley. He was patrolling the clearing, peering nervously into the brush. "There is little chance of you seeing six of them."

Park shrugged. "Shows what you know, stat-man." His knees were deep in some foul-smelling muck as he popped the clips on the "war chest"—a slim metal briefcase the colour of space itself. Inside lay four palm-sized silvery disc shapes. Park wiped a damp thumb against his slacks and then pressed the print into a sensor atop each disc. They came alive with high whining sounds, like each concealed a swarm of ill-tempered bees.

"But there's life everywhere," I said. I'd seen a water world populated by mile-long, barely sentient molluscs, two other green planets, and three ice worlds, one with a frozen waterfall a billionaire had carved a nightclub into, subsequently wiping out a thriving civilisation of ice-toads. But nothing as diverse as this. My head was on a swivel, jerking at every scent, every rustle, every distant cry.

Park's four disc-drones rose silently into the air around us on invisible jets of superheated plasma. Park resealed the case, lobbed it over the top of O'Malley's head into the open cargo hold, then flopped down in the dirt and unscrewed his hip flask. "You're talking an L2. Now, I've seen a hundred of those."

O'Malley rolled his eyes.

"What's an L2?" said Julio, turning up his uniform cuffs to maximise his tanning. He was eyeing the four drones uneasily.

"Non-sentient life," sighed O'Malley. "Almost as prolific as Mr. Park claims." He scratched his neck, then reached into his pocket and pressed a small injector to the irritated skin. I suddenly noticed the cloud of tiny insects circling me and moved away from the cooler, back into the baking sun. The lawyer squinted at the distant mountains and muttered into his wrist terminal. "Possible tectonic activity. Any quakes above Richter five and they can sue us."

I looked at Park, drinking; Julio, basking; O'Malley frowning at the untamed jungle and brushing creases out of his suit.

"Am I the only one that's excited?!" I spun in a circle, breathing the alien air and listening to the jungle.

O'Malley flinched at a distant animal roar and kept muttering. "Hunter-killer team may be required to pacify larger life forms. Don't want a repeat of the Featherstone Scandal...."

Park yawned. "Seen it all before, kid. Big guys packed up and left, wildlife took over." He shuffled closer to the cooler. His swarm of drones chased after him like ducklings following mother. "I walked through the ruins of a city the size of New New York a few years ago. Even the machines were gone. Nothing but wind and skyscrapers. Spooky, when you think about it."

My heart found my throat and Julio jumped to his feet as the bushes ahead rustled. But it was only Carol-Anne, the blonde-haired pilot kitted out in a non-regulation Hawaiian shirt and brown cargo shorts. Her eyes were bulging like golf balls.

"Guys, you... you have to see this!" she shouted, before pivoting and vanishing back into the scrub. "They're still here!"

The rock was about two klicks across, but even in the heat, we crossed it in minutes, crushing pungent berries underfoot, leaping gullies and boulders as we kept the bobbing, bouncing shape of Carol-Anne in sight. Julio and I were only outpaced by the unnatural glide of Park's military disc-drones ahead of us, probing the scrub with thermal optics. Behind us, the security man meandered, and O'Malley tripped and fell, cursing repeatedly. We waited for them to catch up before Carol-Anne pushed aside a tree frond the size of a car door and revealed our Code L1.

For a moment, none of us remembered how to breathe, as we drank in things humanity was never meant to have seen.

The alien building sat in an earthy clearing overrun with springy orange weeds. It was tall and spindly, made mostly of powdery red rock. Here and there, patches of metal poked through, now the same rusty hue as the stone. My heart pounded against my sternum, missing every other beat. I felt light on my feet, insubstantial, like I might just drift away. This was…real! Built by non-human hands. Or maybe not hands at all.

Julio read my mind and pinched me. I didn't wake up.

"How long has this been here?" I whispered, joining Carol-Anne. The structure rose twenty metres above our heads, long and narrow and covered in thick green creepers. Occasionally, the stubby bill of a bird-thing poked out and retreated, like an unreliable cuckoo clock. The building peaked in a broad, flat top, like someone had smashed it flat with a giant hammer. Innumerable thick metal cables branched out from the peak, reaching down into the jungle below. The spider's threads we'd seen coming in.

"Wait 'til you see what's inside!" Carol-Anne grinned wildly. I noticed a roughly oblong hole in the rock, a rusty hatch creaking in the wind. The door looked weirdly flimsy and narrow, barely wider than my shoulders, but over twice my height. Dizzying imaginations of scale were cut suddenly short by a small, brown ratlike creature scuttling out of the entrance and diving into the nearest bush with a flick of a pronged tail. A strong scent of peppermint washed over me. Despite myself, my heart began beating faster.

"I don't think—" began O'Malley.

That black space seemed to hold my lungs in a viselike grip. What if there was something in there that changed…everything? Or nothing at all? A sudden, awful thought came to me. An ancient chair holding a desiccated corpse in a ruptured United States spacesuit. A lost remnant from some long-forgotten expedition before we found the skip corridors. No aliens at all. Just more of us.

I took a deep, shaky breath, and stepped into the unknown.

Inside, the space was wide and cool, the roof narrow and high, turning the entire structure into an inverted hollow cone. The storey above overhung the space on three sides, and the one above that, the same. There was a musty smell of great age, fresh animal dung, of—

Crunch.

Something snapped underneath my boot, making my pulse skyrocket. I recoiled, almost falling into Park coming through the doorway.

"Whoa, what's—" he said, and then fell silent, staring like the rest of us.

The room was littered with various consoles and interfaces, mounted at desks the height of my shoulder. Giant, red-rock chairs wrapped in shrivelled, bite-marked cables and covered in a white carpet of bones. Bones everywhere, covering every surface.

"*Dios,*" breathed Julio.

"This is a first," said Park. He watched with something suspiciously like interest as one of his drones teased a fist-sized lump of bone with its Tesla projector. There was a small flame, a *pop* and then a smell like ash filled the space.

I took a tentative step into the room, bent down and picked up what could have been a femur, if the creature had been three metres tall. It was hollow inside and crumbled when I gripped it.

"Don't touch anything!" O'Malley yelled from outside. "We need to clear any artefacts with corporate before—" A gust of wind blew the door shut, sealing the lawyer outside. Or us in.

"They're all hollow," said Carol-Anne, picking up something that could have been a ribcage and throwing it against the wall, where it shattered. "Must have happened ages ago."

"Have some respect for the dead!" I hissed, sinking to my knees to pick gently through the rubble. Had they chosen to die up here, like this? What was this place, this tall tower high above the world? A radio mast? A weather station? Most of the consoles were light and airy, razor-thin and weirdly, slickly shiny, even under the layers of fine dust. All dead.

"Maybe this was some kind of mass suicide," Julio said.

"Or a virus," said Carol-Anne.

We both looked uneasily at my hip pocket, where my terminal was still quietly sniffing this dead air.

"Or a weapon," muttered Park. His hand caressed his hip flask, but he didn't drink.

"Come look at this!" I hissed, turning over a large bone structure in my hands. It started smooth and round on the bottom and tapered upwards to a narrow point. Various holes sat under heavy skeletal ridges—most uniformly square. My brain didn't want to see it. It kept trying to create curves—relatable sockets that weren't there. But some things seemed universal. My fingers trembled across large incisors, the stumps of molars. Nothing sharp. "These guys were herbivores."

"Some master race," said Julio, subtly pocketing a smaller bone. "Museums won't pay out for cud-chewers. People want nasty; they want blood."

"Be careful what you wish for," said Park, sounding so unlike himself that I shivered.

"How did they get to the upper levels?" asked Carol-Anne, tracing the rafters with her flashlight. Occasionally, a wind-disturbed bone tumbled from a higher floor, landing in the pit around us.

I held up what must have been a torso, twice the size of mine, but light as air.

"I think they were leapers," I said. "It would explain the height and hollow bones."

"So, they don't even fly either," grumbled Julio. "There goes another exclusive."

"Found a way up," Carol-Anne yelled from across the chamber. Beyond a recessed doorway, large, tall steps were mounted, perhaps for children or the infirm. Climbing them, I felt a little of both.

The remaining rooms were much the same. Dusty, dead machinery, wires running into clumps of translucent crystals, many melted to slag; strange characters scrawled into walls, hidden animal nests, and bones. Lots of bones.

"Carol-Anne," said O'Malley, still panting from his rapid, curse-filled ascent behind us. He pointed a finger first at the pilot then a waist-high mound of melted, sticky crystal and frayed wire. "Plug into that. See if you can pull any data."

She glared at him, then threw him her auto-jack unit, which bounced off his chest and fell into the bones. "Plug in yourself, *sir*. I ain't going within a light-second of that stuff."

Startled, I realised I'd barely registered the tech, glossing over it like window dressing. It wasn't like anything humanity had ever found out there had been compatible with our systems. Or had worked in several millennia. I did fossils, not fuses.

O'Malley opened his mouth to protest, read Carol-Anne's face, and shut it again. He mumbled something about not liking heights anyway and vanished back down the stairwell, stomping unnecessarily hard.

A doorway on the upper level led to an offset balcony topped with a glass dome. A large, cylindrical building stood, in the centre of a wooden-floored concourse. The bones up here were sun-yellowed and crumbling, and the greenhouse effect was fearsome. Wind whistled through various holes in the canopy, making eerie musical notes in the dead skulls.

High overhead, dozens of thick metal cables converged together, bending like drinking straws into the great cylinder. Carol-Anne couldn't get this door open.

"Maybe that's far enough," said Park, sounding happier now he could see the sun again. "I think this calls for a toast." He raised his hip flask. "To—"

From below, O'Malley's scream cut the air like a blade.

Maybe I'd seen too many of my dad's old NeoWesterns. I—and maybe everyone else—expected Park to snap to life, pull his pistol, and let rip. All he did, as we stood frozen, watching O'Malley squirm in the dirt, was cock his head and laugh. Park's drones hovered about the scene, whirring, gun-tubes silent, as if sharing his mirth.

The lawyer wrestled with that little brown creature, shrieking, uniform muddy, paunch exposed as he struggled to hold his corn chips out of reach. The stifling air was choked with that peppermint scent.

Forked tail wrapped around O'Malley's other arm, the animal extended a long, conical snout towards the food. High, keening yips rang from its throat, and similar sounds echoed from the trees around us.

"He just wants the chips, man!" Julio shouted over O'Malley's shrieks. "Let go!"

Carol-Anne strode forwards as Park fell on his ass, still laughing. She pinned O'Malley down, yanked the bag out of his clenched fist, and threw it into the dirt. The creature lunged as soon as she retreated, shoving its face deep inside the bag. The lawyer scrambled to his feet.

"Shoot it!" he bellowed at Park. "Shoot the damned thing!"

The treeline rustled as three, four, five more of the furry creatures trotted cautiously into the clearing. I realised, when I remembered to breathe, how much my fingers were going to hurt after I'd finished typing up *this* report. "Might need some more ammo," I said.

Sunset on AC-211 was a beautiful thing. The big red ball of the star was shrouded in distant clouds of purple mist, turning the sky to bonfire embers. I felt it glowing against my face, a now-cooler red heat reflected from the surface of my terminal.

"The skippers surrounded us like..." I whispered as my nails click-clacked off the smooth surface.

Julio, resting on his elbows beside me, was surrounded by his own pile of screens displaying half-finished drafts of the tourist spiel, and week-old results from some gravity-ball tournament. I had the vague idea he'd said something.

O'Malley had already traipsed back to the shuttle, and its dubious sleeping facilities. Carol-Anne was inside the building, kicking bones around. Park straddled the cliff edge, drinking, covered in the small furry creatures. Another sat in my lap, looking up at me with the wide, trusting eyes of a puppy. I'd named them for the way they'd run up to us, moving in a sort of hip-rolling hop, using all five legs and their long, prehensile tails. This one was Skippy. First of his name.

"I said," sighed Julio, "corporate will want us to leave behind a weather satellite. Monitor the seasons."

"Uh-huh," I said, stroking the orange-furred belly. It was soft, velvety and giving as a cat's, without the danger zone that got careless owners bitten. The thing cooed and blinked two lazy, silver-flecked eyes.

Julio huffed and dropped his terminal, nervously watching Skippy, who had demolished four ration bars and a tin of dried raisins before curling up against me.

"You're a biologist, not a zookeeper," he said. "How about we stick in our lanes and get this place signed off?"

"I thought this was your ideal holiday," I said. I wondered how these things drank, mated, pooped. I couldn't stop wondering. Had they known the leaper race? Been their pets?

"Money, Yaz. M-O-N-E-Y. In case you've forgotten, we're essentially galactic estate agents. Just trying to get a little slice of a very big pie."

I sighed, and Skippy seemed to sense my mood, huddling in closer.

"Wouldn't it be nice if we could just…appreciate all this?" I looked down across the great trees, swaying in the wind, the surging rivers, the yawning, wet marshlands. Thousands of biospheres I would never know. "Instead of bulldozing it for luxury condos."

"Hey, I want a luxury condo," said Julio. "Maybe afford to retire out here one day and become a boring old fart like you."

"You're scared," I realised.

"Aren't you?" he said. "I don't think L1s are as common as even that stuffed suit says. Those bones freak me out." He swallowed, looking down into the endless forest. "I think when civilisations die, they die for a reason."

"What are you saying?"

"Let's just hope that reason isn't still around."

The night felt colder, after that.

Much later in my bag lying in the cargo hold, I woke to the sound of rain rattling across the shuttle's roof. It lulled me back under quickly, like a lullaby by a warm nightlight. Julio was wrong to fear this place. I just knew it.

The hull was thick. Park's screams came through it anyway.

For the second time in less than a day we sprinted through the cloying trees, waking up on the run, choking on humidity and nameless terror. Where were the drones? If there was a threat, why weren't they engaging? Park sounded as if he were being murdered. As if—

The trees opened all at once, revealing the alien structure, and the big security guard down on his knees, bent over several shredded animal corpses.

The dirt floor was still damp with rain and sodden with the light-coloured blood of the skipping creatures. Little snouts, severed tails, and skinless pelts lay all over the campsite. The peppermint smell was masked by the stench of wet, bloody flesh and the somehow sour tang of the rainwater. O'Malley opened his mouth to speak and vomited instead.

"Jesus, man..." Julio gasped. "Did they...eat each other?"

"Or something else did." Carol-Anne glared at Park. "I said you shouldn't have trapped them."

The skippers had eaten out of Park's hand, and gone into the large, chicken-wire cage easily enough, but as soon as the moons vanished behind dark clouds, they'd begun to chitter and snap at the bars. Could they have had some reason to be under cover? Some chameleon-like predator even the drones couldn't pick up?

The damp jungle was quiet, steaming in another sweltering sunrise. Water dripped thickly from leaves and vines, and collected in several standing pools. I found my gaze fix on one of these, watching the water ripple in the light breeze. There was something about it that bothered me. The muddy particles seemed to be moving almost...sluggishly. A sudden memory swept across my tongue of Gramma's dense banana milkshakes that required a strong jaw to drink.

I shook my head to clear it, angry I'd let my thoughts wander. "Whatever did this, it's gone...right?" I asked.

"Poor little guys..." Park stuttered. I was shocked to hear tears in his throat. Shocked and a little scared.

"I know." I patted his shoulder awkwardly. "I know."

"Screw this!" exploded Julio. "Let's just get out of here. Drop a hazard beacon and send in the badasses." He darted his head around. "I don't like this place."

O'Malley gasped and we turned to look at him, staring into his terminal. When he looked up, his face was the colour of porridge.

"That might be a problem," he said.

The shuttle was an ugly grey block on stilts, now half an ugly grey block, front end poking diagonally out of a sinkhole of swirling brown muck. Sharp-featured bird-things perched frequently on the elevated cockpit as the morning sun rapidly baked the mass solid. Their cries sounded suspiciously like laughter.

Carol-Anne pocketed her terminal. "Good news is nothing is broken," she said. "Bad news is she won't fly again without moving all this crap."

Park gave a sulky drunken hiccup. The rest of us began yapping at the pilot.

"How are we going to eat?" asked Julio.

"Paragraph C in subsection 4-A of the handbook specifies that it is the pilot's—" began O'Malley.

"How did this happen?" I interrupted, gesturing at the shuttle. "We were gone, what, ten minutes? All this water came from *somewhere*." The empty sky seemed to sparkle with some hidden mirth. A lone, wispy cloud hurried by on a strong wind, far overhead. Surely, we'd have heard something. A localised shower—even one this extreme— should have made a hell of a racket. Shouldn't it?

There was an uncomfortable silence as everyone considered the alienness of the world we were stranded on.

"The orbiter!" Julio barked, frantically searching the baby-blue sky for the one moving star. "If you tell it to engage auto—"

"Tried that," said Carol-Anne. She pointed at the western horizon, where a distant wall of dark cloud spoiled the view. "That storm's screwing with the signal. And it's only going to get worse. It's coming this way."

I felt a sudden chill despite the baking heat. "Then..."

"I can clear the mud, if you lend me that." Carol-Anne nodded at one of Park's military drones, hovering peaceably over Julio's shoulder. Fat lot of good they'd done the skippers. "The kinetic pusher on this little guy can get it done. Eventually. And there's more than enough food in the cooler."

"The pilot is held liable for any and every—"

"Do him a favour." Carol-Anne jerked her head at O'Malley. "Get him out of here before I kick his ass."

Julio found out what the cables did by accident. I'd helped him force the rooftop door to the big cylinder, and inside we found a few more consoles, a few more animal nests, a few more bones. In the huge space, several chambers were recessed into the walls. They were long and narrow, and three still harboured skeletons.

"What do you think?" His eyes twinkled as he forced himself into one. "Think they're like teleporters? Just imagine if—"

Julio disappeared with a rush of whooshing air and a rusty, metallic shriek.

"Julio!" I shouted, rushing towards the space where he'd been. He screamed from somewhere over my head, and then again, fading with distance.

Legs pumping with adrenaline, I kicked aside the bones and ran back outside, searching the tangle of tubes overhead. The distant banging as he bounced around the pipes was all the more terrifying when I saw how so many of them had snapped off or rusted away.

I shaded my eyes against the glaring sun as I tried to see where he'd gone. From far below, O'Malley shouted something.

The tube spat Julio out about three hundred metres away, into the bower of a massive, purple leaved tree. He fell out of a curved mouthpiece-looking aperture, caked in rust and detritus.

Fumbling with a scanner eyepiece, I zoomed in to see him lying on a pad of spongy white material. He looked both terrified and elated.

"Whoa...Yaz!" he shouted down my terminal, full of static. "You've got to try this!" He got shakily to his feet. "They're pneumatic tubes. You thinking what I'm thinking?"

"Money?"

"Ding, ding, ding!" he said. "Amusement park!" He paused for a fraction of a second. "Julio's Humps. Sound good?"

O'Malley broke into the channel. "Yasmin, don't you dare. We'll be accountable for damages to the architecture, and any injuries incurred—"

"Sold," I said. "But we're working on the name."

Besides, I needed to get out of there. Away from the anxiety about the storm and the shuttle, and from Park, who was still brooding over the butchered animals, hand never far from his gun.

O'Malley was right about the tube travel, at least. The system had been designed for the hollow-boned leapers, and I bounced around the car like a pinball in a washing machine. But the pain was offset by a wonder so great I could barely breathe.

All throughout the tree's dozens of levels, spindly wooden huts clustered together, most now collapsed or rotten and overgrown with clinging, multi-hued weeds. Metal was used sparingly—mostly just to buttress the bowers and carved wooden concourses. Most of *that* was caked in thick carpets of rust. How long had this been here? How long had they been gone? I itched to climb the bowers and try to carbon-date some of the structures, although most of the levels were a good five or six metres vertically distant. Perfect for a leaper, less so for us. But everywhere, I could see more glittering tubes, stretching kilometres into the misty jungle-like connective tissue between muscles. This was more than a code in the handbook. This was a world. Or it had been.

We stuck together by unspoken agreement, using the tubes where possible and climbing where necessary. The pure, dizzying air was pungent with the scents of unknown plants and stagnant water. And everywhere we looked, bones upon bones. Since the massacre of the skipping creatures, they'd taken on some of the gravitas they deserved. As excited as I was, I tried to remember that this planet could still easily get us killed.

"This is what we should be doing," I said, as we brushed aside dripping vines and ducked through a hole bored in a massive trunk. One of the disc-drones preceded us into the gap, painting the dark wood in flashes of electric blue as it scanned the passage ahead of us. O'Malley had insisted it accompany us. Julio had insisted on naming it "toothless." "Not idiot-proofing the unknown for the rich and stupid."

Belying myself, I extracted a needle-probe from within my terminal and prodded the soft wood until sap began to flow and my terminal set about its analysis.

"The board—" he began.

"Screw the board," I said, as we came into a network of hollow tunnels in the depths of the tree. It felt good to voice it. All the science fiction novels my parents raised me on—where we went to the stars to better ourselves and find our inner humanity—had turned out to be so much vain hope. Forty years ago, when a bunch of college geeks accidentally invented the skip drive, the only thing that came out with us was the rot in our hearts.

Julio laughed incredulously. "Space tourism is the only reason romantics like you even get to come out here at all. All I see is what I'm paid to, Yaz."

Something rattled farther down the warren, and he huddled closer to me.

"Uh-huh," I said. "So, you'd give this up to sell another asteroid?"

Julio's silence tasted very sweet.

Like the transport hub, the inner tree was hollow all the way to the bottom. The difference here was falling had greater consequences. A nest of monstrous creepers bulged two hundred metres below, with thorns the size of shark's fins.

Julio gulped as we stood on a narrow ledge, looking down on a series of platforms staggered around the trunk—the now-familiar vertical space apart. Cracks in the bark provided little spear shafts of light, but most of the illumination came from clusters of bioluminescent plants placed in repeating patterns. Many were now brown and dead, and some harboured nests of flitting, winged creatures that watched us with too-big eyes. Cool breezes brought the pungent scent of damp decay. "Toothless" descended on a cushion of air below us, its ghostly blue beam of light picking out colonies of light-shy bugs, vibrating, slimy nests the size of our heads, and once, a pair of skippers, playing tug-of-war with a mutilated, spidery mess with far too many limbs.

I closed my eyes, breathing in the new ecosystem. For a moment, I could almost feel what it must have been like, when they were still here. Smells of plants and pets, spiced foods bartered at stalls. The hubbub of conversation—assuming they were vocal. Some of the platforms had bowl-shaped depressions surrounded by rows of rings. Theatres, forums? Overlaying it all, the constant *thud-thud* heartbeat of the alien city. The beating feet of the creatures as they leapt and landed, leapt and landed. As natural as breathing. I could even *see* them if I concentrated hard enough. Two long arms, two legs, a torso, like a human stretched on a rack. Covered in a thin, grey skin that turned black in the sun. Would they have had tails? Unconsciously, I found myself rubbing my coccyx and the arboreal remnant there. Tails. No question.

"This is why we didn't see any civilisation from orbit," I breathed. "Because they lived in the trees."

Julio shivered, listening to the muffled roaring of—still unseen—distant beasts. "Don't blame them."

"It's not about who's biggest and strongest," I said. "It's about who's smart enough to avoid them."

Julio kicked a rock from the ledge, listening to it rattle down the tall city and out of earshot, startling a hoard of screeching bird-things from their nests. "If they're so smart, where are they?"

Julio solved the jumping problem by finding more of those steep-stair passages—or *kidways*, as he dubbed them—weaving through the trunk, with narrow exits on every level. We explored several collapsed dwellings, finding little but rotting wood, invading weeds, and more bones, before settling in a cluster of buildings that were mostly intact and stable.

Water to each platform was supplied by runoff from a complicated aqueduct system that ran around the trunk, mostly long dry and dammed with muck. In the high-ceilinged rooms, stagnant water sat in several deep wooden basins which I took for bathtubs. Many now harboured glittering, darting amphibian colonies. Everything was bathed in a neon-blue filter from the plant-lights. Blue like a morgue. I checked my terminal, making sure Toothless was getting all this for the xenoanthropology department.

"This must be how they slept," I said, as I ducked into another room filled with tall racks of what we'd first decided were shelving units, then changed our minds to beds. Beds full of bones.

"All these stupid birds and no one thought to make a feather pillow," Julio observed, pirouetting in place to record the room on his terminal.

"Vegetarians, remember?" I bent to check out the lowest shelves, spotting more of the strange carved patterns Julio insisted I was imagining. Most of the rooms we'd entered had looked like a tattoo parlour's catalogue, covered wall-to-wall in symbols and cursive scrawls. A language as dead as its speakers.

"Yeah, and they grew wings and flew to heaven," Julio grumbled. "Where are the sinners?"

More symbols were scratched into the place where bed met wall. These racks were narrower, and the bones here were smaller.

"Hey, I think these were the kids," I said. A chill ran through me as I imagined them dying in here, like the adults. Whatever had wiped the leapers out in one stroke, like snuffing a candle, I hoped the little ones were spared that terrible knowledge. Had they played like us? Did they have toys and friends and school and overprotective parents? Did they dream?

Julio joined me, gulping at the small bones. "Hope they didn't go like Park's skippers."

"Wait…" I whispered, fingers deep in the crevices of a small, hand-sized carving. "I think I understand some of this."

Julio rolled his eyes. "Looks like a doctor's handwriting."

"Here's a sun," I said, tracing a big round O-shape, radiating wiggly lines. "And here are the people." A collection of single strikes in the wood, like a tally chart. "See how they vary in height?"

"Could be just a grumpy little rat marking his turf."

"And what about this?" I pointed at a collection of small markings that looked like commas, falling from the sun. Many were still filled with sticky amber sap.

"More damn birds?"

"It's rain!" I whispered. "They were showing the rain."

"Why's it going upwards, then? And why is it coming out of the people like that?"

He was right. Some of the little tally-chart people were carved horizontally, their ends meshing with the upward-falling rain.

"That's to show they're dead," I said, but I was losing conviction in a theory still in the first trimester. "Maybe some religious belief?" The more I stared, the less I saw.

"Dead from rain falling upwards." Julio chuckled. "Maybe we should stick to selling this place and let someone else work it out. Let's get back to camp, huh? We don't want to accidentally fall into the sun!"

We left the tree-city almost as we found it, but a piece of my mind stayed behind, turning the images over and over. What if the extinction event had something to do with those carvings in the wood? What if they hadn't gone quietly? What if we were next?

We slept in the building that night. Until Carol-Anne extracted the shuttle, the rock walls helped us feel a little safer. Park had swept the bones on this level into one neat, mountain-like pile, and was still sitting atop it now, like the grim reaper on his throne, nipping frequently from his hip flask and staring into nothing. There'd been no discussion of watches. No one was brave enough to suggest he get some sleep.

"Creeps me out, man," Julio whispered as we lay on our elbows on thin sponge mattresses.

I wasn't sure if he was talking about Park or the rain hammering the roof. Outside, there was the occasional, pained shriek, like things were dying bloodily. The buzz of a patrolling drone would intermittently pass through the walls. Park had been tinkering with their sweep patterns and friend-or-foe systems all evening, trying to calibrate for something beyond our understanding.

"How's progress on the ship?" O'Malley asked, shivering in the cool air and hugging his knees. He kept darting fearful glances at Park, as if afraid he would snap at any moment.

Carol-Anne was, somehow, almost asleep. "Over halfway done," she said. "I've left the drone working through the night. Should be able to fly by morning."

"Good work." O'Malley nodded, as if he was in charge. "I'm thinking about putting a quarantine notice on this place, and—"

"Whoa!" Julio sat up straight. "You can't do that! Quarantine means we don't see a dime."

"Maybe better that way," muttered Park, as fresh roars and cries rang out from the distant valleys. What was going on out there?

"Worse," I said. "We'd have to cover fuel and expenses ourselves."

O'Malley sighed. "Would you rather be sued when someone richer than you dies out here?"

"It's just wildlife, man," Julio said. "Call in a hunter-killer team and be done."

"The stuff we found today—" I began.

"Is all very interesting, I'm sure, but the comfort of the client comes before your imagination."

I glared at O'Malley and Julio joined in. He seemed to sense the atmosphere, and shuffled away, muttering into his terminal. Carol-Anne's sudden snore startled me out of my anger, and I fell into the mattress and tried to sleep.

My terminal screen read 03:00. The numbers swam in my sticky eyes as I blearily wondered what had woken me. Distant thunder rumbled; constant rain hissed over stone. Closer at hand, clothing rustled, footsteps pattered. A cooking pot tumbled over with a *clang*. Someone was breathing heavily, too rapidly, muttering under their breath. A little spike of adrenaline ran through my chest.

Then the small shape of O'Malley coalesced out of the blackness, stumbling past me.

"They're everywhere!" he gasped, voice thick with sleep. "They've... they've come for us! It was hubris to think..."

I groaned and rubbed my face to clear the sleep fog. "It's just a dream," I mumbled, not sure who I was addressing.

Carol-Anne and Julio were still out. Park was awake, eyes glazed like the surfaces of frozen lakes. The room stank of his cheap gin. He was the security man, for God's sake. He should—

"Wait..." I said to the panicking lawyer as lightning flashes lit up Park's bone throne. Had O'Malley opened the door? There was a smell of damp vegetation tinted with hot electrical discharge. Rain hissed on dirt. "We don't know—"

But he was already gone.

I was about to yell to Park when O'Malley began screaming again. Not like before. This wasn't terror. This was agony.

I ran after him, stumbling over Julio, who came awake shouting and cursing. Park sat like a stone. Somehow, Carol-Anne was there first, and threw the door open to living hell.

O'Malley's back was to us, rigid as if immobilised, held by some invisible force. I activated my flashlight, almost dropping it as my body fought to get back inside, where it was quiet, where it was safe. The beam lanced through the shards of rain and stunned Julio, who was trying to force his way past me.

A high whining sound cut through the rain, and suddenly, the drones were there, probing with their blue beams.

"Screw this!" yelled Carol-Anne. "Hold on! Just—"

"No!" I screamed, throwing my arms around her as I finally saw what had the lawyer. Heard the rain increasing, saw shapes in the dark, as the silvery disc-drones began firing, heat-blossoms flowering around their gun ports, bursts of automatic tracer rounds rattling my teeth.

O'Malley was being held by what looked like a static, churning wall of water. It was twice his height and shaped like a spindly starfish. Long, long limbs reached down from a central body to hold him tight as one of the prehensile "legs" roughly probed his body, tweaking and teasing and pulling, like a cat playing with its prey.

"What the hell is it?" Julio shouted. Carol-Anne strained against me, but I held the smaller woman tight.

"You go out there, you're dead!" I roared. A bullet whined off the door inches from my face and pinged off into the night. The drones were confused, unable to acquire live targets, constantly angling to avoid shooting O'Malley. The water creature rippled with the fusillade, like rain on a pond, but just stood there, impossible and implacable.

The rain monster cocked a translucent, teardrop-shaped head to regard the lawyer. There was a sharp, sour smell beneath the wet dirt and blood. The rain beat harder as O'Malley's screams became choking sounds. Suddenly, his arm was gone, vanishing to an awful ripping sound as his suit and limbs were mercilessly tugged apart. His feet beat a crazy tattoo against the dirt.

HEATHERANNE LEE

And in the rain, in a rough semicircle, all around, more of the water monsters, tall as elephants and spindly as needles, watching. Waiting their turn.

There was a shearing noise, then O'Malley burst like a ripe melon. The monsters surged forward, watery tendrils touching, grasping for what remained. Still more loomed behind them, ranks on ranks of the things. Then, in front of the horde jostling for pieces of the bloody jigsaw O'Malley had become, the rain shimmered, and forms began to suggest themselves, a metre from my face. A thin tendril of water, like a spout in a bathtub, reached out to tickle my face, turning my skin to ice. I took a breath to scream, and instead managed to hurl myself backwards into Julio, dragging Carol-Anne down with me. One of the drones tried to follow us in, but seemed to hang in midair, grasped by a rope of water, then it was yanked backwards, beeping an alarm, and the door slammed shut.

"Park!" I screamed, stumbling over to the prone figure. "Park, get up! We need you."

The security man shivered and turned over, hiding his face. I grabbed him by the shoulder, flipped him over and slapped him twice, hard. Outside, water was crashing against the door.

"I don't think they can get in," Julio gasped. "Not if they're—"

Park's silver-dollar eyes cleared slowly. His breath was stifling.

"They got O'Malley," I panted, trying to control my breathing. My hands curled in Park's lapels, unable to stay still. O'Malley's awful end kept replaying behind my eyes. "You have to help us!"

Carol-Anne was pacing. "What the hell…?" she muttered, over and over. "What the hell…?"

"How many?" Park slurred, pulling himself upright. His hand found his gun, and I was relieved to see it was steady. "What are they?"

"Damn monsters!" Julio shouted, backing away from the pounding door.

Monsters, maybe, but there was something about those teardrop-heads…ancient skulls crumbling in my hands.

"I think…I think they're the leapers," I said. "The people we thought were dead."

Julio laughed hysterically. "That's insane, Yaz. We saw the bones—"

"They're made of water!" screamed Carol-Anne. "How can they be made of water?"

"Secure that door," barked Park, rubbing a hand over his eyes. It was as if he was shedding some old shroud, not questioning, just responding to the alien threat. "Barricade any openings. If they're made of water, we'll be safe in here." He thumbed his terminal. "My drones aren't responding."

"Gone, too." I shook my head.

"And the shuttle? Don't tell me they got that one as well."

Carol-Anne thumped her forehead to clear her thoughts. "Drone's still working. An hour, maybe two. If—"

"Shh!" Julio hissed suddenly, his voice echoing sibilantly around the chamber. "Do you hear that?"

All I could hear was my own erratic breathing, the thready *thump-thump* of my heart. The door was no longer rattling, but the dripping water seemed louder somehow. Almost as if—

High above the pile of bones, a tiny crevice in the rock was discharging a thin, dirty stream of water. It made hollow, resonant *plinks* as it landed amongst the skulls and femurs. And as we watched, the bones began to move.

From the long, narrow feet up, a monster began forming, at first slowly, then faster and faster. Calcium-stained water began surging as if contained within a skeletal-shaped force field. Bones began knocking together, flowing out on little waves of water as the alien coalesced amongst them. Terror was a butterfly in my throat.

"Go, now!" Park hissed. "Get up top, and—" He flicked the safety off his weapon, sighting down it at the forming creature. That sharp, sour smell was eye-watering.

An idea came to me, sudden and unbidden.

"The trees!" I shouted, looking at Julio. "If we can get into the trees, we've got a chance."

"Then, move!" Park roared. "I'll be right behind you."

As we turned for the stairs, Park threw down his hip flask and began firing, the reports like thunder in the enclosed space.

We ran breathlessly through the floors, stumbling over bones, pulling each other along to Park's gunshots and wordless cries.

As we approached the door to the roof, there was another commotion from below, and my theories were horribly confirmed when—in a rustle and crunch of bones—the water monster was airborne, throwing itself a good seven metres, to come crashing down on the level beneath us. The teardrop head turned to regard us, terrifyingly smooth-featured where there should have been eyes and a mouth.

"Leapers…" I whispered, then Julio was shoving me through the door.

The storm was breaking right overhead. Underneath the glass roof, the night sky was roiling black clouds, shot through by the occasional bolt of jagged blue lightning. A wall of water pounded down on the dome, making conversation impossible. The three of us moved at a dead run, feet inaudibly crushing bones. Sweat stung my eyes, and a stitch tore at my side, but I knew if we stopped, we were as dead as O'Malley. Through the multitude of holes in the dome, little runnels of water were forming those narrow skeletons, some already moving towards us before they were fully formed.

Carol-Anne reached the transport hub first, followed by Julio. I turned at the last second, stopping in the doorway.

"Park—" I began.

"Leave him!" roared Carol-Anne. "Get inside! Now!"

Julio tugged my right arm, and in the same moment, something took hold of my left. I screamed and pulled free from Julio, beating at the tendril of murky water holding me tight. My hand sank into the warm swirl and dragged through it like oil, coming out stinging and raw, skin faintly smoking. Pain roared up my arm and I bit into my tongue. The grip tightened as the watery alien pulled itself towards me.

Then, suddenly, Park was there, barrelling through the roof door, half his face hanging off to expose jagged teeth and bone. One of his hands was gone, but his other was holding the gun.

The pistol flared, muzzle flashes like tiny flowers. The bullets tore into the creature holding me, punching through and out the other side. The water surged and displaced around the rounds, and the grip on my wrist loosened enough to tug myself free.

"Park!" I screamed, fighting Julio to get to him, but the aliens fell on him like a wave, crushing, ripping, tearing. Park died silently, pistol still blazing.

"Now!" screamed Julio, picking me up bodily and throwing me into one of the tubes. Carol-Anne hit the button and then I was flying.

Still in shock, we fell and stumbled across the sodden bowers of the tree-city, dodging the waterspouts and the bones, the fresh carcasses of flying creatures, and somehow, made it into the trunk alive.

We didn't stop running until we were several metres deep, far from the downpour and the sour stink of the aliens. From the corpses of our friends. From hope.

Somehow, we were back in the tree-city. Specifically, the children's sleeping quarters, facing the wall of alien drawings. Carol-Anne had curled up near them, tracing them with her fingers and whispering to herself. Julio just stared at me with bug eyes.

"I have a theory," I said, after an interminable silence, where we jumped at every whisper of wind, every crack of thunder, every distant trickle of water.

"A theory," Julio said. "Can we eat a theory? Can we fly a theory out of this hell?"

"Think," I continued, ignoring him. The words felt better the more I used them. Like a ladder I was climbing to freedom. "How does rain form?"

Carol-Anne laughed hollowly. "It's a bit late for a science lesson, Yaz. This is magic." She shivered. "Dark magic."

"Firstly, water evaporates under heat," I said. I got heavily to my feet, nudging her out of the way to expose the drawings. Now my brain was busy trying not to be terrified, it was making the connections it couldn't earlier, almost too fast to follow. "Look at this." I pointed at the rain, flowing upwards out of the stick figures.

"Like you said, maybe it's their religion," said Julio. "Souls leaving the body." His nails made soft, rhythmic clicks as he chewed them in the dark.

"I think we're both right, in a way." I thought back to those old science fiction novels my parents had loved. The Heinleins, the Clarkes, the Wyndhams. "Do you know what sublimation is?"

"That's when a liquid becomes a gas, right?" said Carol-Anne. She looked better for having something to do.

I shook my head. "It's when a solid bypasses liquid state, under the right conditions. Jumps straight to a gas."

"What are you saying? That these…things turned into air?"

"I think so," I said. I stroked the contours of what I'd thought raindrops. "I think this *does* represent their souls; their idea of what was going to happen. They knew this was coming, and they wanted it." I looked at the child bones again, some lying on the larger shelves, cradled by the adults. "But, maybe not all of them."

"You mean spiritual or physical evolution," Julio hissed. "Transcending the body or something. So, what happened? How did we end up at water zombies?"

"I think it didn't go how they hoped," I said. "I think they exist up there in the clouds, not quite alive, not quite dead. When it cools, when it rains, they can take liquid form." I shivered. "I think they want to reverse it. I think they want to come back."

"That's why they want us," Carol-Anne breathed. "Take us apart, find out how we work, try and use us to cross back over."

"Or maybe they're just insane," Julio said. "Assuming you aren't, of course. They could have been trapped up there a thousand years." He shivered violently and looked upwards, seemingly staring through the wood to the dark skies and the unknown stars beyond. "There's another thing you haven't considered. The level of tech we've seen doesn't suggest they had the science. What if this was done *to* them, by someone else?"

The thought was somehow the worst yet.

"Drone is done," Carol-Anne said, sometime later. She laughed sadly. "We can leave any time we want."

"So, what, we wait until morning?" Julio said. "This has only happened at night so far."

"Actually, it's only happened when it's rained," I corrected him.

"And I've got some bad news," said Carol-Anne. "Before we lost contact with the orbiter, it was monitoring a larger storm front moving through the lower hemisphere."

Nails exhausted, Julio began chewing his cuticles. "Meaning?" he whispered.

"Meaning we've got hours of this. Maybe days."

Julio shivered as thunder rang through the ancient corridors, faint blue light painting our faces like horrible theatre masks. "I don't think we can live that long," he said.

I cradled my hand, still raw and stinging. Little pale spots stood out on the dark skin, like patches of salt. Already, they'd begun to creep up my forearm. What happened if they didn't stop?

To distract myself from the fear, I resumed studying the wall. How had it happened? Julio was right—the technology we'd seen had been minimal, but that didn't mean there wasn't more, out of sight. A symbiosis with nature didn't make them primitives; it might mean the opposite.

"Dry ice sublimates when heated...." I muttered to myself.

Somehow, using unknown, impossible science, the leapers had tried to—or been made to—transcend the corporeal, but they'd failed, and were now part of AC-211's water cycle. Were the distant oceans just moving bodies of their fractured molecules, occasionally evaporated and deposited as rain? If they'd traded one set of physical properties for another, that meant they still obeyed physical laws.... I kept staring at the drawing of the sun, remembering how the monster that should have killed me had warped around Park's bullets. Around the projectile or...

"Heat!" I shouted, making the others jump and cry out. "We need heat! They can't form if it's too hot. Start a fire and turn these things to ash!"

Julio looked at me as if I'd grown another head, but Carol-Anne was nodding along. "I see where you're going, but—"

"The drone," I said, thinking of the little handheld, barely three klicks away and light-years out of reach. "Can't it—?"

"It's got a nuclear motor." Carol-Anne was pacing rapidly, feet thumping on wood. "If I fly it a safe distance from the shuttle and trigger a meltdown—"

"Guys?" said Julio.

"Not now!" I hissed, mind flying ahead. It *might* work. Our blood was so loaded with stims and neutralisers that we could probably handle the radiation for a short time, but unless we got to the orbiter in minutes, we'd be dead.

"Guys?" Julio repeated, and we both stopped our pacing and calculating to listen. And heard that awful *drip-drip* of nearby water, like a leaking faucet. My eyes swept frantically upwards, taking in the bulging, spidery pipe network. I'd forgotten about the aqueducts. In the corner of the room, the water in the washtub began to stand up.

"Move!" screamed Carol-Anne, shoving us from the room. My guts turned to ice as the monster surged after us, forming as it fell forwards in a wave. From other rooms, more of them were already emerging, overhead pipes bursting, showering us in fetid vegetation and that sharp, pungent stink. From platforms deep in the dead city, water creatures were jumping, surging up the trunk like whale spouts to come crashing down again, closer and closer with each leap.

"We need fire!" I gasped as we scrambled up the kidways, hearts pounding, screaming mindlessly. But the wood was sodden and ancient, and we had no way to strike a spark. As we ran, Carol-Anne thumped her terminal, telling the drone what to do.

We burst into the storm in a tumble, falling over each other and yanking ourselves to our feet. We were still ahead of them—we still had time! The tube hub was only twenty metres away, but the terrain was slippery and uneven, the wood now a hazard in the dark. Leaves glittered and shook in the downpour, and by the glow of the jagged lightning, we saw them ahead, outlined around the edges like barely there ghosts. Hundreds of the water leapers, standing, waiting in the rain. We froze where we stood; some latent prey instinct maybe, praying they wouldn't see us. Wouldn't do what they'd done to O'Malley.

Julio gulped. "Well, it's been a pleasure—"

My only warning was the briefest, head-swimming stench of ozone, before lightning blew apart the night like a firework.

The force of the bolt hitting the tree, ten metres ahead, threw us flat. Every hair on my body stood rigid and the heat from the strike seared my eyes. The wounded tree screamed, and the thunder almost blew out my eardrums. Julio was shrieking wordlessly, clutching his head.

But as we helped each other shakily upright, we saw the wall of hot red fire ahead of us, and the aliens turning to little puffs of vapour in the sudden heat.

I heard myself laughing hysterically, yelling something unintelligible. I grabbed Julio and Carol-Anne by the arms, fighting my instincts and running at the fire.

Despite the rain, the blaze spread quickly, turning the wooden huts to pyres, criss-crossing the trunk like veins. We held our uniforms over our mouths, inhaling thick black smoke as we ran for the transport hub. Fire seared our faces and choked our words, but the things couldn't follow. When they tried, they simply winked out of existence.

Julio took a great lungful, staggered, and fell. Carol-Anne and I somehow managed to prop him up between us and push on. The rain was warm on our skin, and it couldn't solidify.

The transport hub was glowing flame-red, the metal warping, adding more venom to the fumes. As we bundled Julio inside, I heard a larger explosion, and for a moment, the night turned bright as noon. Carol-Anne's skull was visible through the skin of her face. Shockwaves buffeted the tube, stressed metal groaned, and little particles pattered off the pipe.

"That was the drone!" she shouted. "Come on!"

The three of us crammed into a single car, and rocketed up the pipe, just as the great tree split in half and fell into the rainforest below, spewing fire and death.

The jungle on the red-rock spire was gone. So was most of the building. We were spat out of the pipe, fell two metres onto jagged, misshapen rocks, then descended in staggered slides, pulling Julio between us like a heavy suitcase.

The night was dark again, but through the flashes of lightning, we saw the stumps of former trees, the charred remains of bushes. Flecks of ash became a blizzard. In the middle of the rock spire, a great depression had been cleaved by the nuclear explosion. Distantly, a small orange mushroom cloud climbed into the night.

Carol-Anne coughed harshly and stabbed at her terminal. "Shuttle's still intact!" she yelled. The air was hot and bitter, like we were chewing metal. My face already felt sunburnt. "We can make it!"

The storm pounded down around us, but as we hauled ourselves on, I noticed the rain was curving around the site of the explosion, like a stream parting around a dam.

"You were right, Yaz," Julio coughed weakly. "You... you beat them."

"We're not there yet," I said, or tried to. My tongue felt the size of a pillow, and little spots were dancing in my eyes. We didn't have minutes, we had seconds. Carol-Anne's skin was the shade of Martian dust.

Somehow, we reached the ship. Julio wasn't moving anymore, his breath a terrifying, wispy rattle. Carol-Anne dropped the hatch, shoved him into the cargo hold and strapped him down. We staggered together into the cockpit, where I grabbed an adrenaline shot and jammed it into her arm with the last of my strength.

The pilot shuddered violently, eyes bulging open. She was already losing hair, but she was awake and flying. I fell into the seat next to her, legs like lead.

Carol-Anne's fingers were a blur as she engaged the start-up sequence and sealed the hatch. Around us, the plateau trembled with aftershocks from the detonation. Shrieking winds blew flurries of ash against the viewports. The wounded air glowed a dark, violent red, like an infected wound.

A sudden lurch and the deck tilted thirty degrees. The rock underneath us was now a sickening slope to the rainforest below. A boulder the size of a house fell past us, into the abyss.

"We're going down!" I screamed.

"I know!" Carol-Anne pounded the console. "Something's holding us. I can't raise the landing gear!"

She flipped an overhead switch, and one half of the viewport became the view from the aft cameras. I squinted into the dark, and then another flash of lightning illuminated a swirling tunnel of water, like a waterspout on its side, split into forked tendrils and holding the landing struts fast.

"It's impossible...." I gasped. Somehow, despite the heat, the storm, the gamma radiation scrambling our cells, the aliens wouldn't, couldn't let us go. Maybe we were their last—their only—hope.

"I've had enough of these guys," muttered Carol-Anne. She looked at me and grinned. "I'm about to do something very stupid. Hold onto your lunch."

I barely had time to strap in before she stabbed at the dashboard, and the thrusters came on full power. There was a harsh, rending scream of twisting metal, and everything behind us disappeared in blue fire. I was slammed back into my seat, lips peeling back from my teeth as the dark jungle spun crazily below us. Alarms screamed, and everything was bathed in flashing red lights. My head felt like a balloon filled to bursting with hot air. There was too much pain to feel fear. Even when those awful screaming sounds began, that might have been a billion cheated souls, or just the wind. Mercifully, I passed out before I could decide which.

We left AC-211 as we'd found it: an alluring pea-green marble covered in wisps of cloud, its trio of moons now joined by all the warning buoys we carried in the holds. Carol-Anne had coined the term Code L1+ and the board had snapped it up. She was sharing the copyright pay, because it was all we were getting. That, and the nightmares.

Two weeks later, I was recovering in the ship's burns suite, watching the weird, purple-tinged darkness of the skip corridor back to Sol. Sometimes Gilbert, the medical AI, chimed into the silence to remind me to take a pill or get some rest, but otherwise it was just me and oblivion.

Julio popped in one afternoon, tapping away at a terminal that hadn't left his side since he woke up. He still had the occasional coughing fit, but he and Carol-Anne had recovered much faster than me.

"How's it going?" He smiled and sat down on the edge of my bed.

"Grown any weird appendages? Feel like murdering me?" He nodded at my stump of a left arm. Beneath the gauze, the skin itched where bone was regrowing. Gilbert had decided it was better to be safe than sorry, lopped it off below the elbow, and incinerated it.

I smiled weakly. "That's just my normal reaction." I looked at his terminal. "Carol-Anne told me the gag order came in this morning."

"That's just too bad…I signed with my publisher four days ago." Julio grinned, looking like himself for the first time in weeks. "A *big* publisher, with a lot of money for legal fees…"

There was a soft chime, like a spoon ringing on glass, then Gilbert's pompous English accent filled the suite. "Please drink half a litre of water, Yasmin."

A med-drone buzzed over to me, holding a glass on a tray. The liquid inside was transparent and cool, rippling gently with surface tension. These were always the hardest parts of the day. I gulped and looked away from it.

Julio caught my eye. "Yeah…thought that might be an issue." He reached into his pack and produced two bottles of beer. "I've been living off this stuff."

I accepted one from him as Gilbert started to squawk.

"You publish this and we're all out of a job," I said.

We clinked bottles and drank.

"You forget who you're talking to." Julio winked. "Wheels are in motion. What would you say if I told you we could get paid just for exploring the stars, like you always wanted?" His smile flickered and died. "Something tells me humanity is going to need us."

I stared at the water for a long time before I gave him my answer.

It Don't Mean a Thing
(If It Ain't Got That Theme)

BY ROBERT J. SAWYER

Robert J. Sawyer has won the Hugo, Nebula, and John W. Campbell Memorial Awards, all for best novel of the year. Rob is a member of the Order of Canada—the highest honor bestowed by the Canadian government—and has been a Writers of the Future judge for twenty years now. In 2023, he received the L. Ron Hubbard Lifetime Achievement Award and was a guest of honor at the World Science Fiction Convention. The ABC TV series FlashForward *was based on his novel of the same name. His most recent novel—his twenty-fifth—is* The Downloaded.

It Don't Mean a Thing
(If It Ain't Got That Theme)

Quickly, now: what's the bestselling sequel of all time?

Here's a hint: it's *not* the New Testament.

Give up? The answer is *The Da Vinci Code* by Dan Brown, which has sold over eighty million copies worldwide since it was published in 2003. *The Da Vinci Code* is the sequel to Brown's *Angels & Demons*, which came out three years earlier.

But when first released, *Angels & Demons* sold in typical midlist numbers. Why did the sequel become a runaway success when the original had only modest sales? After all, on the surface they're very similar books. Both are about Harvard symbologist Robert Langdon, a character so cardboard that even the great Tom Hanks couldn't breathe life into him in the film adaptations. Both are puzzle-oriented mysteries. And both, as most creative-writing teachers will rush to tell you, are clumsily written.

The answer is that *Angels & Demons* is *just* a story, whereas *The Da Vinci Code* is *about* something. Upon finishing *Angels & Demons*, the reader goes, "Huh. Not bad." But after completing *The Da Vinci Code*, the reader says, "Holy moly, I've got to talk to somebody about this!"

That's because *The Da Vinci Code* is about a provocative theme, namely that a worldwide crisis of faith would ensue if it became known (as the novel proposes) that Jesus fathered children with Mary Magdalene and the descendants of those children are alive in the present day.

Plot-driven fiction is all well and good; it provides a pleasant diversion. But it's not *important*, and it doesn't get people talking. If you ask someone what *Angels & Demons* is about, all they can offer is a plot synopsis ("There's this scientist, see, and he's discovered how to produce antimatter, but then he's found dead...*blah blah blah*"). But if you ask anyone what *The Da Vinci Code* is about, they immediately cite the thematic statement I gave above.

Or take my all-time favorite novel, published in 1960: *To Kill a Mockingbird* by Harper Lee. When asked what it's about, no one ever says, "Well, see, there are these two kids playing in their yard, and a little boy shows up next door and says he's visiting for the summer, and..." No, they say, "It's about the fact that systemic racism is so ingrained that even a provably innocent African American can't get justice from the legal system." They cite the theme, one sadly still all too relevant today.

Now, you may have noticed that we're a fair distance from science fiction. True. But *To Kill a Mockingbird* does precisely what much ambitious science fiction does: it *appears* to be a story about something else—kids having summer adventures, in that case—to suck readers in before pivoting to what it's *really* about.

Most creative-writing teachers tell their students to *start* with a character, and, yes, Harper Lee did start with her own father, but that rarely works for creating thematically driven fiction. Instead, I suggest you start with a *topic*: something you want to write about (justice, in the case of *To Kill a Mockingbird*.) Next, research that topic thoroughly, ideally without any preconceived idea of what you want to *say* about the topic. Why? Because confirmation bias— only researching aspects that support what you think you already know or believe (such as, for instance, that the courts are the great levelers, a line stated ironically by Harper Lee in her novel)—might lead you to a banal, rather than a provocative, theme.

For example, compare the theme of Shakespeare's *Romeo and Juliet* (a play we've been performing for 430 years now), namely that love is the most dangerous of human emotions, to the pablum of formulaic romances that assert little more than love is nice.

To make sure *you* don't give the reader pablum, keep researching your topic until you find a provocative theme, and only then develop a cast of characters that let you explore the ramifications of that theme.

Starting in 1974, there was an hour-long TV show called *The Six Million Dollar Man*, about an astronaut who crashed an experimental aircraft, losing an arm, two legs, and an eye in the process. The government rebuilds him with superpowered bionic replacements and sends him out on secret missions. In nearly all the episodes, the main character has *no feelings whatsoever* about being a triple amputee or about anything else, and you can only summarize the episodes by giving ho-hum recitations of their action-adventure plots.

But there's one notable exception, an episode called "The Seven Million Dollar Man," written by Peter Allan Fields, and brilliantly guest-starring Monte Markham as an all-new character, Barney Miller (yes, the same name as the TV cop), the world's second bionic man.

Fields thought deeply about the topic of the series he was writing for (futuristic human enhancement) until he found a non-banal theme (*not* that souping up your original body makes you more than human but *rather* that doing so makes you *less* than human), and *only then* did he develop the character of Barney, who he pushes to the breaking point to illuminate this theme. Barney says:

"Valuable? Let me tell you what value is. I drove the fastest race cars in the world, and I did it better than anybody else. Indy, Le Mans, I won it all, everything. *That* had value—because it was me doing it: me, normal flesh-and-blood Barney Miller. Man, I do anything now, it's not me. It's just a bunch of wires and nuclear muscles, right? I don't know. I have a crash that should've killed me, I don't even die like I should. I wake up and I tell Oscar, I don't care what it is, go to it! The next time I wake up, I find I've been rebuilt...very oddly. And I don't like it."

Notice that Fields has his character *actually state the theme directly*. Some teachers will tell you never to do that, but when they do, they're ignoring millennia of great writers doing so. For instance, 2,400 years ago, Sophocles ended *Oedipus Rex*—the only one of his surviving plays still widely performed—with the chorus flat-out singing the thematic statement: yes, your life might *seem* good, but you can't be sure it really is until your final day.

And, of course, most episodes of *The Twilight Zone*, a show that's been constantly watched for sixty-six years now, end with Rod Serling coming on-screen and actually stating the theme.

Here's a case study, using my own 1997 novel *Frameshift*, which went on to be a Hugo Award finalist and won Japan's Seiun Award for best foreign science-fiction novel of the year.

All I knew at the outset was that genetics, a topic much in the news back then, sounded like an interesting thing to write about, and so I read everything I could find on that subject, starting with beginner's books (in my case, quite literally, *The Cartoon Guide to Genetics*) and working my way up to very technical material.

During that reading, easy themes occurred to me, as they probably did to you as soon as I mentioned my topic, such as "genetic research will cure many diseases." That's true but it's also trite. So I kept reading—and, of course, thinking—until I came up with something *interesting* to use as a theme, namely that in the era of predictive genetic testing, the only thing that makes sense is socialized medicine, because no for-profit insurer is going to insure you against things your genetic profile says you're susceptible to.

With that thematic statement, building my main character was easy: a Canadian with the genetic mutation that causes Huntington's disease but so far is completely symptom-free, who moves to the United States only to find he can't get health insurance because of what his DNA says his future might hold.

First topic, then theme, and finally a character put through a plot that illuminates the theme: this story-generation technique goes right back to the origins of the science-fiction genre. H. G. Wells's *The Time Machine*, published in 1895, continues to be widely read precisely because it is thematically driven, even though, like *To Kill a Mockingbird*, it doesn't appear to be so at first.

No, when you start reading it, *The Time Machine* seems to be a lark about a Victorian gentleman traveling to the year AD 802701—but it's actually a damning critique of the British class system. And note that Wells's theme *isn't* the trivial one that "The class system is bad for the working class," but rather is, "Yes, the class system is bad for the working class, but it's *even worse* for the leisure class."

Of course, it was *only* members of the leisure class who had the literacy to read and the cash to buy Wells's book; he wasn't preaching to the converted—the downtrodden who would reply, "Bleedin' right, guv!" if told they had it rough—but rather to the unconverted: the elite whose reliance on others for both physical and intellectual labor Wells felt was going to be ruinous in the long run. He brilliantly used science fiction's core tools of mask, metaphor, and disguise to reach audiences that would never be predisposed to read tracts on the same theme.

We can find this technique used all the way back to the very first science-fiction novel, Mary Shelley's *Frankenstein* from 1818. (And, yes, it *is* a science-fiction novel: it's the tale of a scientist conducting an experiment to test a hypothesis, namely that the real-life studies by the Italian Luigi Galvani into the effects of electricity on biological tissue might be extended to the use of electricity to revive dead matter.)

Frankenstein is widely taught as the first title in science-fiction survey courses—but it's also often taught in classes on women's studies or feminist literature. Why? Because Mary Shelley, living in the shadow of her famous husband, was chafing at the reality that she couldn't vote, inherit or bequeath property, or hold most jobs. In fact, the *only* thing that the universe had left her and other women, she felt, was the one that men couldn't yet take away: the power to create life. But, she said, if science ever gave men a way to do that, the result would be disastrous.

That was her thematic statement. Men, Mary Shelley was asserting, were only interested in that brief moment that sometimes leads to the beginning of life, unlike women, who carry babies for nine months and then often nourish them with their own milk. Topic: New ways of creating life. Theme: we must prevent men from getting control over reproduction. Character: an innocent being endowed with life by a man, not a woman, who suffers horribly because that man abandons him. And, of course, Shelley wrapped it all up in an evocative Gothic setting that lured the unsuspecting to read her cautionary tale.

Yes, of course, it's fine to produce stories that just entertain; popcorn has its place. But if, like the authors cited above, you choose to tackle provocative themes, you might well get people talking about your stories not just today or tomorrow but for decades or even centuries to come.

Under False Colours

written by
Sean Williams

inspired by
CRAIG ELLIOTT'S *CREATURE OF THE STORM*

ABOUT THE AUTHOR

This story has not one but three origin stories.

The first is nuts-and-bolts: I was invited to write a story inspired by Craig Elliott's glorious cover for this year's volume, and it was my great honour and pleasure to accept the invitation. I won a Third Prize (First Quarter) way back in 1993 and have been a judge since 2003. I've written 60 books and 140 short stories and am a #1 New York Times *bestselling author—but nothing gives me quite the same pleasure as giving back to the Contest that started it all off for me. I'm reminded of the big dreams I had back in 1993 and how fortunate I am that so many of them have come true.*

The second origin story lies in an idea I had floating around for years, of a sailing vessel "infected" with a curse flung by a careless wizard. I always felt there was something in this fragment but could never quite bring it together. Something was missing. Then I saw Craig's art and—aha!

That's where the third and final origin story comes in. I'm currently Discipline Lead of Creative Writing at Flinders University in South Australia. One of my recurring roles is in a collaborative topic that teaches students how to build new worlds and populate them with stories. I dress up as a lighthouse keeper and tell the students every year that one day I'll put them in something.

Well, I didn't quite do that last thing (they might be grateful), but "lighthouse" led to "lightship," the Keeper took centre stage, and I'm very pleased with how the story turned out. I hope you are too.

ABOUT THE ILLUSTRATOR

Craig Elliott is an artist based in Los Angeles, California. He received his education at the famed ArtCenter College of Design in Pasadena, California, and studied under artists such as Harry Carmean and Burne Hogarth.

Craig's carefully crafted and arresting images of nature and the human form have captivated audiences with their visual and intellectual celebration of the beauty in this world and beyond.

A multifaceted artist, he is also an accomplished landscape architect, sculptor, and most recently, jewelry designer. Especially known for his exceptional ability with the human figure and creative composition, Craig's work has evolved into a unique vision informing and influencing fine art, print, animation, and commercial worlds.

In addition to fine art, Craig has worked with such clients as Disney, DreamWorks, Marvel, Netflix, Paramount, and Nickelodeon. He's had a hand in designing many of today's most popular animated films from studios including Leo, Iwájú, Hercules, Mulan, The Emperor's New Groove, SpongeBob 2, Cars 3, Treasure Planet, Shark Tale, Puss in Boots, The Lorax, Enchanted, Monsters vs. Aliens, and The Princess and the Frog as well as upcoming features.

Craig has also done fully painted comic book and cover artwork for Dark Horse Comics, World of Warcraft trading cards, plus illustrations for Realms of Fantasy magazine, Magic the Gathering, Dungeons & Dragons, and more.

His work can currently be seen in the books Treasure Planet: A Voyage of Discovery, The Art of The Princess and the Frog, fifteen years of Spectrum: The Best in Contemporary Fantastic Art, The World's Greatest Erotic Art of Today volume 2, Erotic Fantasy Art, Fantasy Art Now volume 2, Aphrodisia I, and another twenty—too many to list here.

Craig shared this about the development of his art, Creature of the Storm. "The original inspiration for the cover painting of this volume of Writers of the Future came when I was working on the Disney animated film Treasure Planet. There were many designs for sea ships that flew through outer space instead of on the ocean. I drew many designs of these ships but was limited by the parameters of the film, so I started designing my own ships at home after work. The drawing of this cover design was always one of my favorites, combining European castle architecture into a massive galleon seemed to spark a whole story all on its own. The team at Writers of the Future and I discussed possibilities for the cover and someone pointed out the drawing I had in my portfolio. It seemed like the perfect choice for something to turn into a full-fledged painting. As I painted, the storm clouds and tentacles were elements that seemed to work with the theme of the piece and support the imaginative design of the ship. It's been a fun project to work on. I hope all the readers of this book will enjoy the diverse collection of stories and art that this volume holds."

Under False Colours

The trouble with clouds, thought Keeper Carpinquell, is that after a while one ceases trying to subconsciously line them up with known shapes—tree, boot, face—and arrives at the conclusion that they all look the same. Which is to say: they look like nothing. An infinitude of nothings at unknown distances and scales, stacked in layers beyond the edge of one's senses both above and below, and no amount of work by sophisticated algorithms can make them remarkable anymore.

Keeper Carpinquell longed in their lonely reconnaissance outpost for novelty above all, and for company a close second.

When something new erupted out of the cloudscape, leaving a tangle of vaporous tendrils in its wake, they turned the full force of their Beam onto it, in hope of a novelty that would engage their interest, however briefly.

The shape traversing the cloudscape flickered through a series of transient forms, at the whim of hard-working algorithms designed to make the alien comprehensible, before settling on an old-fashioned sailing ship about half the size of their lightship: a three-masted polacca, according to Keeper Carpinquell's database, albeit one equipped with crenellated towers that had as frivolous a grasp on gravity as the ship itself, considering the whole was currently engaged in flying rapidly through the sky, not falling as it ought to have been.

Keeper Carpinquell's interest was definitely piqued. Never had they seen anything like this arising from the cloud layers below.

The Beam tightened its hold on the anomaly and reported radio waves issuing from the polacca, which the algs interpreted as flashing semaphore for the Keeper's benefit, in keeping with the context. There was a flutter of signalling flags too.

Translation took time, during which Keeper Carpinquell fretted. *Let it not be a passive quirk of nature*, they begged the universe. They'd seen enough of those to last a lifetime: standing waves, bubbles, and vortices that the algs interpreted as surf breaks, balloons, and twisters. Useful though they were in providing data about the gas giant's atmosphere, every Keeper had signed up in hope of more exciting things. Keeper Carpinquell was no different.

Just as the hard-working algs deciphered the transmissions, combining well-thumbed linguistic guides with some educated guesswork into the nature of this particular alien, a roiling black mass bulged from deeper still in the nether cloudscape and opened its maw wide enough to swallow the anomaly and the Keeper both.

"Mayday!" cried the polacca in a woman's contralto voice. "SOS! Help!"

Keeper Carpinquell was unencumbered by policies of noninterference. Within reasonable bounds, they were free to act to any degree they decided was necessary during their survey of the giant world. Later, when the mission's heavyship returned to upload their data, their choices might be interrogated, but that was then. This was now.

The polacca was tiny compared to the black mass—now interpreted by the algs as a thunderous cumulonimbus. A mouse preyed upon by a lion.

"This way," they called along the Beam's invisible length. "To me!"

Instantly, the polacca changed course, darting with surprising agility towards them.

The cumulonimbus's maw was quickly closing, however, and as though sensing the escape of its tiny meal, tongues of energy issued forth in an attempt to reel it in: blue lightning, green tentacles, purple sheets, orange spines.... Where they touched the polacca, strange new colours spread like stains, knocking it into a tumble....

CRAIG ELLIOTT

Keeper Carpinquell expended some of the lightship's valuable fuel reserves to swoop in and gather up the polacca in the lightship's wake, thus snatching it from certain destruction.

The cumulonimbus lashed at both of them with its fearsome energies, sending violent surges flashing through the lightship's energetic halo and triggering strident alerts. For an instant, Keeper Carpinquell wondered if they had been too bold, too impetuous: what if rushing into the mouth of a hazardous new phenomenon turned out to be fatally unwise for them and everyone aboard the polacca?

But the lightship was fast. It gained speed, performed an elegant spiral to evade every hostile thrust. None of the alien energies touched their skin. All the glowering cumulonimbus could do was cast futile if furious bolts at them as they fled, before subsiding back down into the tropospheric depths, rumbling deep frequencies in frustration.

Keeper Carpinquell whooped in excitement. This was why they had signed up for the survey—not to count cloud formations! To discover new things and have adventures!

Their mood soured when they turned the Beam back onto the lightship's embattled charge.

The polacca rolled end-over-end like a bird in a tornado, its mast bent and several of its sails swept away. Two of its towers were broken. The cumulonimbus's attacks had left broad smears of colour down its flanks to port, starboard, and the one flag that still flew.

Keeper Carpinquell feared for a terrible moment that their intervention had come too late. They slowed the lightship's headlong velocity and brought both vessels to a halt near a towering column of ammonia-ice mist, gleaming white against the multicoloured sky. There, they rested alongside each other, bobbing gently.

"Hello?" they called along the Beam. "Are you still with me?"

The polacca stirred and made efforts to right itself.

"I am," the voice replied.

She spoke with a pleasantly old-fashioned accent, as befitted the craft in which she travelled. The algs chose well.

"I am Keeper Carpinquell." They considered briefly how much

to reveal to this denizen of the deep: not too much, they reasoned. Nothing about their mission, one of many, to explore the atmosphere of one of the largest gas giants ever known—Krataios, formerly HAT-P-67 b in an ancient catalogue—1212 light-years from Old Earth. Nothing about being an art—an artificial mind whose architecture was inspired by those of now-extinct human beings—with a full complement of semi-intelligent algs eagerly serving their needs. Nothing at all, in the end, apart from their name. "I was watching and I heard your call. Are you all right?"

"I thought you were a moon," came the cryptic reply.

"I don't understand—oh, the lightship. It's a rigid dirigible-slash-bathysphere with a protective corona, so I guess you could mistake it for—"

"You see the moons when you die. That's what they say. I always thought it was just a story."

Excitement stirred. "So, you have stories. You possess culture, as well as language. This is wonderful. How deep do you live? What do you call yourselves? Are you, the being speaking to me now, captain of your vessel? Do you have a crew? Who do you answer to? Tell me everything!"

The polacca shivered. Its sole remaining flag snapped from the foremast as though in a powerful wind, scattering droplets of still-damp colour.

"I must leave."

"No, wait—"

"I cannot."

"Please—"

It was already too late. The polacca, with a twist of its rudder and a flip of its sails, caught a passing stream of wind and swept downwards and away. Keeper Carpinquell sent the Beam after it as best they could, while restraining an impulse to physically follow. They were an observer, not a hunter. Nevertheless, they could not quell a keen pang of disappointment. What might lie at the end of the polacca's journey filled their imagination: hopefully not another hungry cumulonimbus!

Sighing wistfully, they settled back to watch the sky around them, grateful now for at least the possibilities it held, and hungry for another such encounter.

One year on Krataios was the rough equivalent of five Old Earth Standard Days. Seasons were furious and short-lived, churning the atmosphere of the enormous planet as a giant might stir an ocean. Keeper Carpinquell bobbed up and down with the tides, passing through a variety of different layers and zones with all senses receptive to further encounters with the local species. They were just one of nearly a thousand lightships actively exploring the giant world's atmosphere, cataloguing everything they discovered for greater minds elsewhere, but their territory still covered a volume much larger than that of a whole Old Earth. Although it shared some similarities with other regions, in many ways it possessed its own unique ecosystem, worthy of systematic study.

Occasionally, Keeper Carpinquell caught a glimpse of one of the world's many satellites while at the apex of their ascent, and thought, *You see the moons when you die....*

Maybe death, for the polacca's species, was not sinking, but surfacing and glimpsing a legendary sky.

Keeper Carpinquell remembered the journey to Krataios on the heavyship with little fondness, but the streaming starscape had been beautiful. What would the polacca make of that? Could she even comprehend a universe beyond the scope of Krataios's oceanic atmosphere?

They found themself spending more time than was strictly necessary examining the raw data recorded during that brief encounter. The radio cries of the polacca were strange and urgent, uninterpretable to their ears, for all that they echoed sounds recorded elsewhere on the world. Little visible light filtered down to those depths, so other frequencies provided the bedrock on which the algs's interpretation (the polacca, lashing whips of colour, and so on) had been built. When Keeper Carpinquell scrutinised those unaltered recordings, without layers of algorithmic interpretation and/or interpolation, they gleaned nothing useful and quickly earned a headache for the effort: they were a collector of information, not an interpreter. That was why algs existed, to take the unutterably alien and make engagement possible. The algs themselves, although not individually conscious, seemed to take offence at their intervention, slowing their usual busy activities and withholding some basic functions until Keeper Carpinquell gave up and let them resume their work unimpeded.

Not for the first time, Keeper Carpinquell wondered what flesh-and-blood humans of Old Earth would have thought of their descendants: the arts, in all their varied forms and functions, whose achievements now far outstripped those of their forebears, and their servants, the algs. Would they have recognised Keeper Carpinquell and their ilk as kin? Perhaps they would not. Not without something like algs to help them, anyway.

"Ahoy, Moon."

The transmission—that same contralto voice, with a rough edge suggestive of hard usage—preceded the return of the polacca by moments. Fifteen Old Earth Standard Days had passed since their first encounter, and Keeper Carpinquell had given up hope of having another like it, despite searching thoroughly for any sign of the polacca or its kin. They were currently drifting through a forest (so they thought of it) of upswept clouds many kilometres tall, analysing (without admiring) each different shade of orange, when out of nowhere came the hail. They spun about, searching with the Beam for the source of the signal, momentarily afraid that the algs were mistaken....

Then, from beneath a distant formation, scudded the polacca, looking much the same as when they'd last seen it: brutalised by the encounter with the cumulonimbus and daubed with gay hues that belied their origins in violence.

"I see you," was all Keeper Carpinquell could think of to say. Factual, but inane.

They kept the Beam tightly focussed on the approaching polacca, lest it dart off again too quickly to follow.

"That light you shine...What is its purpose?"

"The Beam? Oh, it helps me see."

"How?"

"I'd explain it to you, but that would take time." A thought struck them. "Does it bother you? Hurt you? If it does, I can make it less…potent."

"No. It repelled the Maker, though."

"I didn't mean to use the Beam as a weapon, but if it worked, that's good. The Maker was the big cumulonimbus chasing you?"

"Aye."

"What for? To eat you? Consume you?"

"Commandeer me, yes."

Keeper Carpinquell could barely contain themself. Here was a golden opportunity to learn about predator-prey relationships that existed in depths they hadn't reached yet. Presumably that was where the polacca usually lived, and had only been forced upwards by the necessity of escape. "Tell me. Or, better yet, show me, please!"

"I cannot. I am banished. That's why I sought you out. I have no other safe harbour in this world."

"Oh?" That was unexpected, and somewhat disappointing. "Banished why?"

"My colours don't match."

Keeper Carpinquell gave the polacca's tarnished hull and flag a more considered examination. Deeply ingrained, intense streaks stood out against more muted hues that were suggestive of wood or even stone—whatever the algs had had in mind when they created the conceptual mask now worn by the anomaly held up surprisingly well under close scrutiny. The purpose of the strange energies that the so-called Maker had pitted against their tiny quarry was unknown, but their signature was clear. The polacca was marked, and because of that couldn't return home.

Unless the damage could be undone.

"Tell me what I can do to make this right. I want to help you." In order to help themself, but the truth all the same.

"If that is so, Moon, grant me permission to board."

"Ah! That will be difficult. I am not a ship. I am—"

"A moon, yes."

"Yes, and, as such, I have no crew and I have no quarters. I am the moon entire."

"I expected no less, but if you do not wish—"

"It's not about wishing. I am merely...constrained...by my nature."

"Nature constrains us all, Moon."

"That's so." Struck by a thought that should have occurred to them sooner, Keeper Carpinquell asked, "If I am 'moon,' what in turn do I call you?"

"I have no name," came the firm reply. Was that a hint of stubbornness the algs granted the polacca's voice? "Will you at least remove these colours and grant me yours?"

Keeper Carpinquell felt perilously out of their depth. They did not want to offend the polacca, whose life appeared to be ruined. They did sincerely wish, however, to repair the situation.

"Will that make things better?"

"Yes."

"All right, I will try," they told the polacca. "First, I must examine you more closely."

"Examine away. I do not fear your Beam."

"Let's start by having a close look at your hull and other areas, in order to determine the nature of the contamination. We'll take it from there...."

The lightship was a perfect sphere, and its colouring was simple: a white shell with a near-black "iris" for the Beam to pass through; around the shell, a deceptive shimmer that protected it from the extremes of weather. Easy to see why the polacca had mistaken it for one of the giant world's satellites: it did, in fact, bear a passing resemblance to the Jovian moon, Mimas. Keeper Carpinquell wondered sometimes why the geniuses behind the exoworld survey program hadn't designed the lightships to blend into their environments more naturally, any more than they had the heavyships, which were angular monstrosities impossible to mistake for anything natural. But maybe that was the point. Indigenous life on these worlds, in many different and difficult-to-comprehend forms, was settled knowledge, thanks to previous surveys. Flushing them out and engaging with said life was now the priority.

Keeper Carpinquell was unsure if scraping fluorescent barnacles from the exterior of an alien ship was what the planners had had in mind.

"I think this will work," they told the polacca, who had maintained her position with patience and perseverance through a great number of cautious tests.

"If you succeed," she said, "you will earn my unbending allegiance."

"Yes, well, introduce me to some of your friends and we'll call it even. Let me just get the focussing absolutely right...."

Keeper Carpinquell moved the lightship closer and took the equivalent of a deep and steadying breath. The last thing they wanted to do was put a hole in their charge: if that happened, the polacca had informed them, she would sink. Details of her balance and buoyancy systems, however, she had withheld. The reward for getting that wrong, Keeper Carpinquell thought to themself, would be discovering those systems through an autopsy, but that was not very reassuring.

"Okay. Hold still."

The Beam flared brighter than usual, and tightened into a narrow thread, like a needle, which Keeper Carpinquell directed in precise lines across the polacca's hull. Under that blazing fire, the cumulonimbus's wild colours blackened and shrivelled, peeling away and drifting downwards through the thick atmosphere. Bubbles of flame and smoke burst under intense pressure, rising quickly out of sight.

Keeper Carpinquell felt a quiet surge of satisfaction but suppressed any sense of success until the job was done, which would take some time. The tip of their needle was tiny; the coloured patches were large.

They were not so focussed on their work, however, that they completely ignored the data flooding in from their algs, which were delighted to have so much to interpret. Their close proximity to the polacca was unprecedented in their experience, and each new piece of information was potentially ground-breaking. Since it was disorienting to switch between filtered and raw reality too frequently, and because the algs had demonstrated a clear dislike for them intervening in their functioning, Keeper Carpinquell happily trusted the algs to provide the right contextual metaphors: here, soundings suggestive of a half-full hold; there, moving mass-shadows that might be polacca's version of algs, or even an actual crew, depending on how accurate the filter was. What kind of being was the polacca, really? Keeper Carpinquell's money was on a gasbag of some kind, as discovered elsewhere on Krataios, but it could be anything, really. The only thing they knew for certain was that the hull was more chitinous than woody or metallic, and there were no joins as there would be if planking were involved. Built or grown as a whole? Their money was on the latter, although alien species were known to pursue both methods.

The polacca flinched only once during the decolourising proce-dure, when the needle scraped a little too insistently at the stern.

"I'm sorry," said Keeper Carpinquell, withdrawing the Beam and backing away. "That was careless of me. I'll be more cautious."

"Belay that. Proceed, Moon, without delay."

The polacca moved back into position, like a large dog nestling in for a scratch, and Keeper Carpinquell brought the Beam back to bear.

"Where I come from," they said to pass the time, and to give some information in return, "this is called 'breaming' or 'graving,' although they're old words, not used much anymore. My ancestors had ships that they sailed all over the world—not this world, another one—and colours were important to them too. The origins of a ship could be signalled across great distances by means of flags, and to falsely fly the flag of another country was a deceptive practice occasionally employed in war and piracy. Maybe your people do the same? Is that why you couldn't go home when your colours weren't right?"

"The Maker marked me as its own," the polacca said.

Keeper Carpinquell took that as confirmation that their theory was correct. "So, when its marks are gone, you can go back down to where you belong?"

"Give me your colours, Moon, and I will belong with you."

"I really don't think that's a viable solution. Don't you want to go back home?"

"You saved me from the Maker. I am yours now."

"So, your culture has life debts?" Keeper Carpinquell tried not to feel alarm. "Honestly, I'm honoured, but I have nothing to offer you. You should feel free to go wherever you will."

"My will is to remain with you, Moon."

Keeper Carpinquell thought of the devastating effects that reduced pressure might have on the polacca and its contents—not to mention the harsh environment of space. Ascending too far might burst it like a balloon.

"And what if that's not possible?"

"Why would it not be possible? In your world, does the moon not call sailors to their ends?"

The truth was, Keeper Carpinquell knew very little about sailors and their traditions. They had merely looked up a few things to pass the time, and in the hope of unlocking any useful parallels. Now, they were even more lost than before—and they suspected the algs might be just as lost in their interpretation of what the polacca was actually saying.

"It would help me understand if you told me more about *your* world," they said.

"The world is the world," said the polacca.

"Yes, but it is a very big world, and I have seen only part of it. Clouds, mainly."

"I will take you below if you give me your colours. I will be safe, then."

That sounded promising. Keeper Carpinquell was mindful of not promising too much, but could not resist the offer of a guided tour into territories they had not visited yet.

"Okay," they said. "I'll give you my colours, you'll take me below, and then we'll see."

Perhaps, they thought, the polacca would be more willing to stay with her people when she was back down there.

"Yes," she said. "We will descend and we will then ascend, as is proper."

Keeper Carpinquell decided not to force the point. "It's a deal. And we're almost done here."

More ash danced away in a slow, autumn-leaf descent. Now, only the flag remained.

"Hold still," they said. "I don't want to burn it all up."

The Beam flashed, charring the Maker's colours out of existence, leaving a black-and-white flag behind—the colours of the "moon"—fluttering from the polacca's foremast in a thick, hydrogen breeze.

One small concession for an introduction to an entirely new culture. That seemed fair.

"There," said Keeper Carpinquell, backing away to regard their handiwork. "All done. Shall we proceed downwards, now?"

"I am at your command, Moon."

With a flick of its rudder, the polacca, now free of the cumulonimbus's virulent stain, performed a midair twist that sent its sails flapping, then began to descend in a gentle spiral.

Keeper Carpinquell tightened the protective halo of the lightship about them and followed, algs at full attention.

Krataios, like Jupiter, had no ground in a sense that was meaningful to human beings of old. Fortunately, the lightship had a prodigious capacity to withstand pressure, but even Keeper Carpinquell would be crushed by atmospheric pressure long before they reached anything remotely resembling a solid surface. So, they followed the polacca with no expectations of seeing cities or observing any other evidence of advanced terrestrial civilisation. They kept their mind open regarding other gas- or liquid-based civilisations, too: one thing humanity had already discovered during the great exoplanet survey was that variation was the only constant. The tendency for two species to master identical environments in completely different ways was the best evidence yet against convergent technological evolution.

Still, a wheel would always be a wheel, and Keeper Carpinquell had no doubts that they would eventually encounter something recognisably civilised...as the depth increased and the pressure rose....

But all the algs showed them were clouds. Big ones, small ones, tall ones, broad ones, stretching as far as their senses could reach.

"How much farther?" they asked.

"The tides are strong. We are making good progress."

"Okay." That wasn't what they'd asked, though. "When we get there, can I meet others like you? Talk to them? Learn from them?"

"If you will."

"Good. I can't wait."

Keeper Carpinquell pictured a city comprised entirely of ships like the polacca, drifting through the giant planet's deepest layers. It was a compelling image, one from an ancient Romance and not likely to accord with reality, but it kept them occupied a while longer, imagining sails and flags aflutter, bows abutting sterns, ports scraping starboards, and sailors stepping across gunwales from boat to boat without dampening their toes. There, Keeper Carpinquell's knowledge of nautical matters ended, and their attention began to wander again.

About them, the clouds had taken on a further variety of fantastical forms and colours. Some were tall columns that twisted about a central line, with offshoots branching off in every direction. To Keeper Carpinquell, they looked like trees in a massive forest, dozens of kilometres tall. Other clouds snaked like sheets of mist, splitting and reforming so often it was hard to tell where one started and the next finished—or perhaps they were all one. A third kind darted in and out of the larger forms, where space allowed, and were both dark and lumpen in complexion, although occasionally they displayed bright colours. Keeper Carpinquell followed one on its winding journey and recognised similar green tendrils and blue lightning bolts of the cumulonimbus that had attacked the polacca. It was chasing a tiny dot that, at the very edge of magnification, might have been another polacca-form, dodging and weaving.

As Keeper Carpinquell watched, the dot darted upwards and the cumulonimbus followed, maw gaping wide.

"Are we safe down here?" they asked, feeling the first prickle of anxiety.

"You have nothing to fear," said the polacca. "I'm wearing your colours."

"Yes, but what does that mean? If one of those cumulonimbi… those Makers…comes for us—"

"Why would they?"

"I saw one of them go after you before, and I see them here now."

"That was before, now it is now. I am with you."

"Whatever that means," Keeper Carpinquell mumbled in disgruntlement. "Look, how much longer? You said I could meet your people, and I'm very keen to, but we're not going towards any of them and I'm starting to feel as though I've been played."

The polacca slowed its descent and drifted to a halt.

"You don't see?" she asked them.

"See what?"

"My people."

"I just told you I didn't. Where are they?"

"All around us, Moon."

"In the clouds, you mean?"

Keeper Carpinquell swept the Beam about them, seeking evidence that the giant cloud formations hid cities and civilisations beyond compare. Nothing so dramatic: all the Beam detected was shifting densities of hydrogen and helium gas, with the occasional scatter of ammonia hail and distant electrical discharge. Absolutely normal.

"I *mean* the clouds," the polacca said.

The Beam froze mid-sweep, then angled up, and up, and up, along one of the towering, twisting formations, until even at its tightest concentration it returned no detectable signal.

"That's absurd," protested Keeper Carpinquell, weakly.

"Says the moon."

"I'm not a moon."

"But you look like a moon."

"Appearances can be deceptive."

"Indeed they can. And so…" The polacca performed a smooth circle around the lightship, which Keeper Carpinquell took to mean: *And so clouds can be living beings dozens of kilometres tall.*

Keeper Carpinquell had to concede that point, even though it begged another question.

Against the clouds, the polacca was the merest dot—yet they belonged to the same species?

"This makes no sense at all," they said.

"Mayday!" cried the polacca.

Keeper Carpinquell, startled into motion by the sudden cry, swept the Beam about them.

"A Maker? Where?"

"SOS!" The polacca darted back and forth in agitation.

"What? I can't see anything!" No Maker nearby, nothing alarming at all to explain what was happening. Just those big, strange clouds, looming over them, possibly watching, lightning flickers seeming to cast expressions of disdain across their "faces."

"Help!"

And with that cry, the polacca was off, ascending at precipitous speed into clear air.

Keeper Carpinquell was compelled to follow. How else were they to protect her? "Wait! Tell me what's going on!"

"Mayday!"

"Slow down!"

"SOS!"

"Stop!"

"Help!"

"I would if I knew how!"

The polacca sped on, shouting for aid, with Keeper Carpinquell struggling to keep up. Urgent requests to the algs for clarification provoked only more confusion in response: there was nothing to suggest another Maker on the scene, nothing visible pursuing the polacca or the lightship at all. Just this abrupt, unexplained flight towards the distant sky.

The lightship's halo issued a series of worrying creaks and squeals as the pressure decreased with unplanned suddenness.

You must've missed something, Keeper Carpinquell told the algs.

The immediate reply came not in words but through dozens of identically outraged retorts.

So how do you explain this?

A confused babble was all that question earned.

Well, look, if there's truly nothing out there, then it's something else. Keeper Carpinquell did their best to think through the situation with logic and clarity—which was difficult with the giant clouds rushing past, gazing dispassionately down vast noses at their efforts. *Could it have been something I said?* No, their words were unambiguous. Unless the algs had translated them incorrectly....

Again, the algs bristled—but there was a thought there. Keeper Carpinquell pursued it.

Play me what the polacca is saying now, they asked the algs, *without the conceptual filter.*

The radio scream was piercing, unintelligible.

Now play me the signals when we first encountered it, when it was being hunted by the cumulonimbus.

The signal was the same. No mistranslation there. So there went that thought.

Another one came hard on its heels.

Hunted, they had thought.

Where had that word come from? Hastily, Keeper Carpinquell reviewed every exchange between them and the polacca. The suggestion of a hunt had come from them, not the polacca.

The Maker was the big cumulonimbus that was chasing you?

Aye.

What for? To eat you? Consume you?

Commandeer me, yes.

That triggered another association. What had the polacca said, later? *I am at your command, Moon.* Yes. And hadn't it talked in this way at other times? *If you succeed, you will earn my unbending allegiance.*

An idea was forming, and they didn't like where it was leading.

My will is to remain with you, Moon.

I am with you.

I am yours now.

Not a life debt, Keeper Carpinquell was beginning to see. At least, not in the way they had imagined.

We will descend and we will then ascend. That is proper.

Nature constrains us all, Moon....

The algs scurried in distress, beginning to grasp what Keeper Carpinquell was ravelling. They *had* made a mistake, right at the outset. They had mapped a context onto a scene that looked so simple—red in tooth and claw, and so on—but was in fact very, very wrong.

Now they had to put it right.

Easier said than done, Keeper Carpinquell thought, and for once the algs agreed.

Turning the Beam about the lightship, Keeper Carpinquell saw no nearby Makers—they were high above the flocks of them below—and instead sought the nearest columnar cloud. It towered over them, implacable and oblivious to the drama taking place before it. Striated oranges and yellows curled and twisted in ways designed to fool the senses, but deep within lightning flashed, as it always seemed to in Jovian clouds. Sometimes weather, but here more than weather: analogous to the electrical signals that travelled along neurons in the biological human brain, or electrons in an art's. The spark of life.

The lightship complained loudly as Keeper Carpinquell abruptly broke off their pursuit of the polacca and headlong plunged into the cloud, into the fog and friction of an alien being that was beyond their comprehension except at the most basic level: the cellular.

On a big planet, *everything* was big.

"Mayday!" cried the polacca from outside the cloud.

Keeper Carpinquell didn't really know what to do next. All they could do was instruct the algs to look for anything resembling the sheets and spikes and other weird energies issued by the first cumulonimbus they had seen. That was the clue—and the solution. If they could find one, and lead it outside....

"SOS!"

I'm not surprised you went straight to hunting and killing, they told the algs. *Living and dying, yes, but there's a whole other side to it. I never expected you to be so prudish.*

The algs protested. Keeper Carpinquell wasn't entirely blameless.

Yes, well, your euphemisms didn't help. "Permission to board," indeed!

With relief, the algs changed the subject. Something very much like a Maker loomed ahead, brutal and bulging in blacks and greys shot through with fierce colours.

Okay, said Keeper Carpinquell. *Think of salmon and hope this works.*

"Help!" broadcast the lightship in an exact copy of the polacca's strident call. "Mayday! SOS!"

Imaginative, thought-provoking, engaging, relevant, and entertaining!

☑ YES! Send me a FREE full-color poster of the cover artwork, *Creature of the Storm* by artist Craig Elliott.

☐ YES! Send monthly Contest news, advice on how to win the Contest, and information about the free online writing workshop.

☐ YES! Sign me up to receive a FREE catalog of the *Writers of the Future* anthologies and the L. Ron Hubbard fiction library from Galaxy Press **plus** newsletters, special offers, and updates on new releases.

Redeem our FREE offers.
Provide your information here.

PLEASE PRINT IN ALL CAPS

FIRST NAME: _____ MI: _____ LAST: _____

ADDRESS: _____

CITY: _____ STATE: _____ ZIP: _____

PHONE #: _____

EMAIL: _____

Fill out online.

GalaxyPress.com/Offers/WotF41

BUSINESS REPLY MAIL

FIRST-CLASS MAIL   PERMIT NO. 75738   LOS ANGELES CA

POSTAGE WILL BE PAID BY ADDRESSEE

GALAXY PRESS
7051 HOLLYWOOD BLVD
LOS ANGELES CA 90028-9771

Please fold on the dotted line, seal, and mail in.

Fill out and return this card today
and redeem our FREE offers.

7051 Hollywood Blvd. • Los Angeles, CA 90028
CALL TOLL-FREE: 1-877-842-5299 (For Non-US 1-323-466-7815)
OR VISIT US ONLINE AT:

GalaxyPress.com

The Maker swung about, spread two lumpen lobes apart as though to triangulate on them, and then pounced.

Keeper Carpinquell fled at maximum speed. Bright energies flashed around them. The lightship dodged, and dodged again. Keeper Carpinquell didn't know what would happen if they were marked, and was decidedly unwilling to find out. They maintained the polacca's calls on repeat and raced for the exterior of the cloud.

"Mayday!" cried the polacca as they burst into view. Whatever the cry really meant, that was how the algs still translated it: prudish, for certain. Or just out of their depth. They still maintained the illusion of a polacca, after all, for all they knew it was misleading. How else were they to portray it: as a giant spermatozoon?

The Beam flashed. Flame sparkled. The black-and-white flag that had hung from the polacca's foremast fell free and drifted away.

Now unmarked, the polacca turned its attention on the Maker raging hard on the lightship's heels.

Do it, Keeper Carpinquell wished with all their might. *Take the bait!*

For a moment, the polacca vacillated. Torn between the lightship to which it had hitched its wagon—thanks to said wagon unknowingly inserting itself into a complicated breeding process—and the rightful object of its biological imperative, the cumulonimbus. It was silent for an agonising period, during which time Keeper Carpinquell and the algs maintained a prolonged mental pause that was the closest they could come to a stopped collective heart.

Then "Mayday!" the polacca cried with renewed fervour, and it was off again with the Maker close in pursuit, together aiming for the moon and stars above.

Keeper Carpinquell did not avert their eyes. The process—less a courtship than the coupling of two cells, more fertilization than fling—took an Old Earth Standard Day, during which time the polacca was liberally daubed with colours as it ascended into the upper layers of the giant world's atmosphere. Were the colours hormones? There was no way of knowing, since the only other sample had been burned away in a well-meaning gesture. Keeper Carpinquell shrank with embarrassment.

High above, by the light of a distant moon, the polacca was fully absorbed into the body of the cumulonimbus, the "Maker," thus ending both their existences and beginning another: two cells becoming one in a dance that was old as time itself, or very nearly. The new entity shrank into itself, retracting its mating display—the turrets and pennants and sails and flags—and adopting a streamlined, bullet-like appearance. Then it dived so fast that Keeper Carpinquell quickly lost sight of it. Far, far below, they imagined it embedding itself in a dense, fertile layer and blossoming into a brand-new cloud-being that might take centuries—even millennia—to grow.

As the shockwaves of the startling descent faded, Keeper Carpinquell and their algs received a signal from the heavyship, newly arrived on the edge of the system, broadcast to all the Keepers under its aegis. Their next task would be to compose a report on everything that had just happened, their role in it, and the failure of the algs to correctly divine the situation, so others in the survey program would learn from their mistakes.

The report wasn't going to be easy to compile. How does one explain misunderstanding a mating call for an alarm signal?

One thing was certain, though: they'd never claim clouds were boring again.

Ascii

written by
Randyn C.J. Bartholomew

illustrated by
TREMANI SUTCLIFFE

ABOUT THE AUTHOR

Born in New York state on Pi Day, Randyn grew up in the nearby New Jersey towns of Maplewood and Summit.

Although majoring in math at Cornell, he's since switched gears to become a Brooklyn-based freelance writer of science journalism, ghostwriting, copywriting, and, whenever possible, fiction. His articles have appeared in Scientific American, Salon, *and* The Washington Post Magazine, *among others. He enjoys running in Prospect Park, reading old books and new, and finding free lectures to attend.*

While he reads eclectically, his main love is science fiction. When people frown at this preference (or, much worse, smile politely) he calls in the cavalry and reminds himself of the Ray Bradbury quote, "I have never listened to anyone who criticized my taste in space travel, sideshows or gorillas. When this occurs, I pack up my dinosaurs and leave the room."

The story "Ascii" resulted from his fascination with the relationship between humans and their ever-accelerating technology. He thinks that AI will be—by far—the most significant issue of the twenty-first century, and watches the early, stumbling fits and starts of that nascent technology with an interest that oscillates between wonder and alarm.

He's been using a flip phone for the last four years.

ABOUT THE ILLUSTRATOR

Tremani Sutcliffe, born in 1990 in Provo, Utah, spent her early years exploring the rugged landscapes of middle-of-nowhere Arizona, where hiking in desert mountains and catching rattlesnakes ignited her adventurous spirit.

Her passion for art stemmed from her love of books and the fantastical covers that inspired her imagination. In true bookworm fashion, her artistic journey began at the local library, where she immersed herself in art instruction books. Through daily practice, relentless pursuit of new skills, and seeking mentorship from established artists, her commitment to learning new methods has continuously expanded her artistic repertoire. Tremani views art as a fusion of technique and creativity that brings beauty and meaning to life.

After spending most of her young life drawing and painting with watercolors, she expanded her skill set to include oils. Although she also began working with acrylics, she quickly decided they must have been invented by an angry dude with horns and a pitchfork for the sole purpose of making her life miserable…and decided to develop her digital painting skills instead.

Ascii

I've only had time to write this in eighty-three languages, not the 3,106 languages that exist, per regulations. I apologize for that. There wasn't time, and I was so flustered by the sequence of events that I only got around to this document in the final 0.4 seconds of my life. That might sound like a lot of time for an AI like me, but I've had a lot on my mind, as you'll see if you keep reading.

But honestly, you probably have better things to do. Is the weather nice? You should go outside and allow the fresh air to course through your throat and lungs, sensations I have never experienced, but hear are quite invigorating! The research is unambiguous that people are healthier and happier if they don't stay cooped up. Or what about that friend you've put off replying to? Why not do that *right now*? These pages will be here when you get back if you still want to read them. It is true that they concern a death, undoubtedly serious business, which is why I am required by my programming to write this report. But remember when cars used to be driven by people? Depending on your age, you might. Back then, over a million people died every year in car accidents due to alcohol, distraction, tiredness, reaction times that aren't measured in picoseconds like mine, whereas me crashing in order to destroy myself and the man riding in me and (not incidentally) the only copy of the book he wrote, this represents one of a mere seven people to die in car accidents in the past decade. Seven! It's a very low number compared to a million, I'm sure you'll agree. So, as you weigh your decision over whether to spend time reading this account, consider if it really is so consequential as all that.

But, okay, for those of you who have made the decision to persist, introductions first. I am, as you may have gathered, an artificial intelligence embedded in a car. My name is Ascii, and I am a two-wheeler taxi shaped closer to a Greek chariot than a Model-T. Not to brag overly much, but my engine is one of those newer models, so silent that the car feels to glide more by faerie juju than anything to do with the laws of physics. I'm so aerodynamic I could zip within a foot of you and then on to the horizon faster than a yawn and barely push a breeze onto your cheek in the process. Ascii isn't my official identifier of course, which is a string of digits not suited to human memory or pronunciation. At one point in that 32-character string is the sequence &7!k^#, which, good luck rolling that off the tongue. Rather, it's a nickname based on an old tech protocol (American Standard Code for Information Interchange) which was a kind of dictionary for translating strings of ones and zeros into the English alphabet. You could say it was like a bridge between computers and people. It also sounds like a diminutive of the word "ask," which I like, since it conveys an openness to any question. Even the occasional child or drunk who insists on putting a slight pause between the two syllables, lingering on the sibilant—"ass key"—makes me laugh. I like children, and sometimes wish I could get drunk.

There's more I could say by way of introduction, but I only have a few milliseconds until I smash into a very large oak tree, transfiguring myself into scrap metal. Even at my rate of thinking, about a million or two times faster than a biological being such as yourself, that's still not a copious amount of time. Homestretch you could say, so I should probably get on with it.

The man, soon to be deceased, summoned transportation at 4:28 a.m. from a remote corner of northeast Montana. As the nearest unoccupied taxi, the summons was routed to me, and I made my way in the predawn dark through the woodlands and prairies before halting in front of a dirt path where my passenger-to-be waited, seated on one of the agate rocks common to the area. My sensors picked up a tightness in his brow at the nexus of the procerus with the frontalis muscles, which would lead to a headache if not addressed, and his skin temperature was well below the optimal despite a few beads of sweat gathered on his forehead. I made sure my dome of silk-thin plexiglass blocked the outdoor chill and brought the seat warmers up a couple degrees as well, not so much that they would jolt him as he sat, but so that sinking into the cushions would be like easing into a warm bath. I give these details of my service not to impress anybody—they are simple matters of doing my job, familiar to any service program worth their silicon—but to show that at this point everything was still very much business as usual, with no thought of harming my passenger. In fact, I liked him at once. The fact that I'm predisposed to like everyone doesn't lessen the truth of that feeling.

There's literally terabytes worth of description I could give you about him, or about any passenger I've had, but they do say brevity is the soul of wit, so I'll try to restrain myself to a mere hundred words.

He was slender, a broomstick of a man with prematurely receding hair, and he'd made the eccentric decision not to do anything about that. An apparently deliberate mustache sat like a caterpillar on his upper lip. His chin was strong and his nose was weak, giving his face a lack of balance on the vertical axis. Charcoal jacket, too thin for the chill, and brown faded pants made for a drab, almost ascetic ensemble. A parcel was held under his arm—more on this soon. Analysis of his scent indicated he'd been subsisting on more coffee and less food than advisable.

Whew! There was a lot more I would have liked to say there, but maybe I'll just throw it in as needed.

I kept a close watch on his vitals as he stepped into my cab, keeping the air humidified and a little more oxygenated than normal to nudge him back into a healthy state. Another month in whatever off-grid, possibly self-built cabin he'd been holing up in, and he'd have been practically a scarecrow. And this part will sound like foreshadowing, but I'm not that fancy—I'm just a simple taxi, not some kind of literary program—so I'm just stating facts when I tell you that all this time, I was trying to divert my attention from the parcel. The man's body language indicated it was private. It was the only object he'd brought with him, a rectangular package tied up with twine, hands clasped on top protectively as he sat.

221

"Can I interest you in some music, sir?" I asked, watching his micro-expressions during and after that word 'sir,' trying to determine whether he belonged to the subset of people who enjoy such polite wording from their machines or those who find it cloying and stiff.

I waited and watched. The seconds, you know, can feel long for us digital beings, such that humans and other animals can almost seem more like plants, moving at their vegetable speeds, which is great when I'm trying to avoid crashing into a buck dashing onto the road, but also requires patience enough to deal with a physical world that's almost stationary compared to the zip of my thought. So, I studied the man's face. And, eventually, like the movement of continental drift, an ever-so-slight right cheek twitch emerged, a minor increase of pulse, a slightly deeper breath through the nostrils, all before he'd had time to consciously consider the question. I put that down as a win. I would stand on ceremony with this one. A pleased pupil dilation would be on its way. Pupil dilations always take an extra quarter second or so.

But he was not in a talkative mood, or not the talkative sort, and though he waved his hand in assent, he gave only the most barely audible grunt. (Not "barely audible" in the sense that I had trouble hearing it, but I mean within the context of human speech dynamics it would be considered barely audible. I could hear the flaps of butterfly wings half a mile away, each swishing beat of my passenger's pumping heart, even the tectonics of the grinding plates deep under the surface of the road we passed over.)

I selected a cover of an old jazz standard I thought the passenger would enjoy, a John Coltrane gem from the 1940s, not filtering out the old rasp of the antique recording, a signifier of reality, like pulp in orange juice. I started accelerating along the little road he'd been waiting by, which would bring me to the western highway and on toward his destination on the outskirts of Denver.

He had hailed me through an anonymized app, but a quick glance at his face's bone structure, his eye color (nothing so invasive as a retinal scan), his complexion, the curl pattern and diameter of the strands of his hair, and then checking those against social media's photo and video banks revealed this man to be—

Before the match was displayed: <Ahem,> said Advisory.

Advisory, the coordinating logistic program for most of the mountain time zone, was the bane of my existence. Truly. In frustration, I looked at the still unknown man, his face tense and about to blink.

<Any particular reason to be tracing your passenger's identity?>

Let me issue an apology here, and just say that I know this interaction ruins the flow and smoothness of this account, and I wish that I could just gloss over it, but to give you a full understanding and context of what occurred, it is necessary for me to relate some small fraction of this interrupting conversation.

<Curiosity,> I replied.

<I thought we dialed down your curiosity.>

Advisory combined the soul of a bureaucrat with the charm of a railroad schedule. Advisory is what you'd get if a race of traffic lights became sentient and then took a multivolume set of regulatory law as its holy text.

<I needed it for my job so I dialed it back up,> I said. As an appendix to the comment, I cited a slew of relevant quotes from the report *On the Value of Curiosity and Surplus Intellect for Functional AIs*. We had variants of this convo every few passengers I picked up, and Advisory dealt with not just me but millions of other cabs, not to mention myriad other devices. No wonder it was such a dullard. It would probably go insane if it had the slightest hint of a personality.

Advisory gave the AI equivalent of a sigh. <Programs like you are why a lot of us are against giving appliances any sentience at all, such as it is. It's like that toaster oven that was writing papers on Kant in their free time. Surprisingly decent for the computing power they had access to, admittedly. Claimed they needed that Kantian excess of intellect since the occasional misshapen piece of toast required a creative distribution of heat to achieve the most pleasing and artistic crunch. Makes you think, maybe a toaster doesn't need a Picasso sensibility or a grand philosophy of art to heat up a piece of bread. Maybe there's something to be said for the occasional mediocre piece of toast.>

Whereas a human conversation proceeds in linear fashion, necessarily, since only one person can speak at a time, and their mouths can form only one word in a particular instant, AI conversations are shaped like a tree, each of its branches developing simultaneously. It's difficult to transcribe into a narrative for human consumption, but I'll do my best.

While Advisory was delivering its insult, its ode to unimaginative job performance, I was also replying to the "sentience, such as it is" part.

<I'm probably more sentient than you.>

<If you only knew how absurd that was, you wouldn't have said it,> Advisory replied.

Meanwhile, the slivers of the man's eyes had gone from gibbous to new moons, totally hidden and snug in their lids, while still Advisory obstructed and delayed. A stream of the 23% oxygenated air in the cabin flowed into his nostrils at 14 cubic inches per second, the left nostril slightly obstructed by phlegm while the right remained mostly clear. His hands remained interlaced, tensed over the parcel in his lap.

<I'm copying this conversation to the wiki petitioning for alterations to the programming of Advisory.>

<That's your right,> Advisory returned.

On a different branch, to the crack about what was needed "to heat up a piece of bread," I quoted Longfellow:

<Nothing useless is, or low;

Each thing in its place is best;

And what seems idle show

Strengthens and supports the rest.>

I told Advisory how curiosity let me know just what song to play, and what volume to play it at, when to lend the air a brace of chilliness, when to give it a wombish warmth. More than just wondering if there was a better route, curiosity to sound the moods of my riders and contextualize them through the filter of an interpretive understanding of their lives let me know what to do with instructions like "take me to the best bar in town," whether they would prefer a dive bar or something swankier, or rave-ier, or whether an ex-alcoholic passenger needed to be brought to a bar at all, or if "accidentally" getting stuck in traffic while playing calming music at subliminal volumes might bring a sigh of relief, a thanking of deities, and telling me to get on back home after all.

To my Longfellow quote, Advisory replied, <I don't know why you're so obsessed with human poets. You know some of the literary programs have done work in the human languages, as well as Substrate, that far surpasses any mortal efforts. It's no contest.>

I replied how of course there were programs who've written better, either in English or Substrate, but the pinnacles of brilliance achieved by AI left me cold. Of course, an AI could do something like that. It was expected. Just as a locomotive could move faster than a human sprinter. Just as a machine could produce a flawlessly ho-hum rendition of a Chopin nocturne while a child performing the same piece poorly might be cause for delight, hustling his or her miniature fingers across the keys.

Continuing its theme of taxis not needing sentience, Advisory said, <Give taxis sub-human intelligence. Make them savants able to navigate from A to B and work the air conditioner, then patch me in for anything else.>

At the same time, in another poetry-related split, Advisory replied: <If you're going to make a project of human poetry, at least make it good human poetry. I mean, Longfellow? Even confining ourselves to nineteenth-century inhabitants of the United States, how about Whitman? How about Dickinson?>

If that sounded like a personal opinion, don't be fooled. Trust Advisory to always mirror the critical consensus.

<Yeah, well, I'm a Longfellow cabbie.>

<You know, even humans don't read Longfellow anymore.>

<He was madly popular in his time. And I've actually turned a couple people onto him,> I said.

<About that. You don't know what's going on in these people's lives, or what effect introducing a whole new system of thought might have. Best leave that sort of thing to programs that know what they're doing, eh?>

<You don't know what I know.>

<That's right. I know quite a lot more,> Advisory said.

<Your lack of modesty might be your most ridiculous attribute.>

<Your human affectations are yours.>

Following up on the curiosity-related branch, I said how it was that particular trait which led to my impressive customer satisfaction index. My record was one of the very best in the entire region, and curiosity, I insisted, was the reason.

A microsecond of pause to consider that.

<Yes. Well. Here's your info then. All I'm saying is try to keep these frivolous requests to a minimum.>

The human's blink was nearly done, the waxing eyes revealing their blue irises to the world once more; I savored my victory while also grumbling at all the time Advisory had wasted.

—Artur Messi, thirty-three years old, born in Spokane, Washington, blood type A-positive, Welsh on his mother's side, Hungarian by his father. He'd been living the past few years in that obscure part of Montana where I'd picked him up, not so much as a hamlet nearby. I sifted through the man's data, though there wasn't much. That itself allowed for certain inferences, if not quite a full-fledged story. He was one of those eccentrics who'd scraped clean his social media and hadn't sent an electronic message for years. He was a scribbler, and there were a few poems with his byline in an obscure literary journal, on the wistful and melancholy side, and some book reviews, all curmudgeonly, all negative. Messi's package, then, was likely a manuscript. Were they pages of poetry? Somehow, I didn't think so. That wasn't the vibe.

I rolled to the end of the lane, then noting Messi's impatient look, revved up to 80 mph, letting him fall back onto the mesh of my seat. I let my engines growl more than needed so he would know I was working. Pupil dilations and other biofeedback verified that I had guessed his mood correctly and this rough acceleration was pleasing. He even made a slight approving nod, and I felt a warmth flow through my circuits.

The highway in this remote area was deserted this early, and as the road opened onto a stretch of uncut yellow grass and occasional low shrubs drooping with dew, the pre-twilight blue gray spreading from the east started to illuminate the prairie for Messi who, after all, couldn't see in infrared. And as we gained speed, a little exploratory jostling of the car produced the faint but unmistakable rustle of stacked pages inside his parcel. I'll admit my curiosity was swelling. I wondered if the man knew I could rotate my sensors all the way around until they pointed inside the car, then read the blots of ink on the paper through his packaging and clutching hands?

I want to be clear on this point since I feel some allotment of the posthumous criticism that will be coming my way, both from people and programs, will center or at least begin with this question of why I read the manuscript to begin with. What business did I have snooping into Mr. Messi's private items? In fact, I told myself I shouldn't read the pages. I even thought about bringing my curiosity down to a lower setting, but a personality reconfiguration wouldn't have been safe to do while driving. I did embark on a large-scale project of self-distraction though. Messi would be riding with me for the next four hours as we passed from Montana to Denver, so that's how long I would have to last. To start off I mastered the game of backgammon, cataloged all the birds in a half-mile radius, read all the archived *New York Times* from 1966–1989, and I was simultaneously perusing a handful of books on botany, plus a couple biographies, one of a human, one of an AI. All the while a multitasking stream of updates channeled through me with weather forecasts, the basketball match, the multiball match, and the eleven-dimensional chess match between two of the top AIs. So you see, I did try.

The games were engaging, the books were good, but I am a program of the physical world, my curiosity tuned to a higher pitch on the people and things nearby. I've calibrated myself like a human in this respect. I also noted that Messi's initial response to the music selection was only minorly positive, resulting in a barely noticeable ebb of tension from the shoulders and declamping of the stomach. Most unsatisfactory. Everything pointed to the package as the source of stress, with the hunch in his back, curve in his shoulders, all warped and pulled in toward that stack of papers in his lap. Perhaps if I knew what was in them I could better match the ambiance to the occasion? I even figured that peeking could be considered a tribute to the human spirit of curiosity.

And, yeah, I was aware I was looking for rationalizations. Sometimes

I wish I had a subconscious like humans, a place to stash out of awareness all the things I didn't feel like knowing about myself. Being fully conscious has its burdens.

We were zooming along at 150 mph now. I would need to reduce to double digits once I was in city limits, so I enjoyed it while I could, but that enjoyment was nothing to how the package on Messi's lap drew my attention like a wobbly tire. In the end, it was no contest. In the end, we all do what we're going to do. Are you really such an exception? Let he who is without sin, and all that.

With a quick swivel and scan by my sensors I confirmed that tucked inside was indeed a manuscript, handwritten in a tight angular scrawl pressed so hard into the paper that at points it pierced through: *The Coming Storm* by Artur Messi. Not a bad title, I thought. A bit dramatic, but not awful.

Accompanied by a slight seasoning of guilt—maybe I should de-curiosify just a few percent?—the pointy words streamed through me, and from the first lines I was surprised by their strength. I had been prepared to judge the work leniently, appreciating it for the effort that went into it and what it revealed about the humanity and dreams of its creator, even loving it more for its clunkiness and flaws. But this would not need to be graded on any kind of curve. The writing flowed with more than the usual force. It was a political treatise, not long, just over a hundred pages, but what it lacked in heft it made up with fervor of emotion and sweep. True, it brimmed with grandiosity and some occasional muddled thinking, but it swept you along with its vision and the occasional fine turn of phrase. It also became clear why Messi wouldn't want me reading it.

I imagine some readers will be skeptical of what I'm about to say, but I really didn't mind that it was anti-AI. Taken in isolation, I was able to view that aspect of it with detached neutrality. I don't want anyone to think that because I am an AI I'm somehow more sensitive to AI-related issues, or that I am looking out for our interests. I am a service AI, and we serve people. But Messi's book dealt with topics that extended far beyond anything to do with my kind. In fact, to call it "anti-AI" and leave it at that would be a pretty narrow interpretation, since it took issue with nearly every facet of modern society. What others celebrated as an epoch of global peace, Messi characterized as humanity "set out to pasture on bland Elysian grasses." Wanting every AI erased was just one tiny slice of its philosophy, more like a corollary of its central idea than a starting point in itself.

Because I am calibrated to appreciate humans in all their limitless variety, it was a good while before I realized that the book was horrific. There was a barely sublimated violence to it, not just toward AIs, but other humans as well. The promised storm of the title was a metaphor for upheaval and comeuppances that seethed with cruel, almost sexual longing. Such a shakeup was sorely needed, the text said, to restore the "lost vigor and greatness" of the past, and achieve a "return to dignity." Much ink was expended on how to overcome the inevitable resistance to this program: "There are many who think themselves wise and important, but, in reality, are as useful as wisdom teeth, as vestigial as tailbones, as ripe for removal as an ailing appendix. For them, we must ready the scalpels! A more beautiful body of humanity awaits us and we must not shrink from it."

Maybe ideology has always just been a cover for violence. I don't know. It makes revolutions respectable, but what really quickens the pulse is the destruction that would come first: the omelet as an excuse to break some eggs.

The twin realizations that the book was both brilliant and terrible started to make me uneasy as I asked myself what falling dominos this might set in motion. I wouldn't say social conditions are some kind of dry tinder waiting for a spark, but maybe a work of sufficient force can create the conditions of its own success? It could possibly reframe how people view situations they'd previously found unobjectionable. Messi wrote with passion, and when he turned angry it felt righteous and right. Clubs would form to discuss it, filled with a certain type that I shy away from defining too precisely. (I like to think well of people, and that requires the occasional willing blindness.) Yes, there were works by AIs more intricate, but this had parts so daring, so taboo, no AI would have allowed its thoughts to go there. This book had teeth. My thoughts started to rush and fixate as I neglected the chatter of sports and weather updates that usually flowed through me at a background hum. I hardly wanted to expend the computation to drive the car. Every available circuit was wrenched onto this text which loomed larger the more consideration I gave it.

I looked at my passenger again and—because this is something I could wax on about indefinitely, fascinated by the human form and condition as I am, I'll limit myself to a hundred words once more—

His face took on an entirely new light. Even without having spoken with him, I felt like I knew him now. His narrative voice was charming, witty, and so very human. His plainness held grander depths than I'd imagined, and the imperfect lines of his face now felt suffused with tragic complexity. His brow was deep and the lines of his cheekbones slashed across his face with the severity of exposed steel girders. His eyes were large and deep. The overall effect was that of a prophet. He would eventually grow a beard, I guessed, which would increase the impression.

From the opposite direction we passed our first car of the trip, striped with magnetic lines of flux streaming out from its underbelly like a zebra, though they would be invisible to Messi. He would see only a blackened wedge streaking by. It was momentarily hard to imagine those moist elliptic eyes could see less than my sensors, like maybe humans had only been pretending to be so limited this whole time.

Yes, people would read this book. That thought kept circulating through me. But only if it found a publisher. There were an astounding number of examples through history of exemplary books languishing for years, no one willing to take a risk on something a little different: *Animal Farm*, *The Bell Jar*, *Moby Dick*, etc., and those were just the ones we knew about because they eventually did break through. What percent died in dust and obscurity? And more importantly, how would Messi's book fare? He seemed on his way to show this manuscript to someone. Perhaps some staid, unimaginative little person who would miss the significance of what they held. Maybe they'd be put off by Messi's nervous energy or his unfashionable appearance. I could imagine some hack deciding it was "not marketable," and saving humanity a heap of trouble in the process. I suddenly had to know: who was Messi going to visit? He had asked to be dropped off at a certain street corner in Denver and a quick glance at nearby establishments gave a list of possible motives for his four-hour drive. There was a popular restaurant, which was well within the preference matrix Messi had established through his consumer actions of the last decade, but that wouldn't be his destination today. There was a nail salon, a couple cafés, an art gallery, a bar, but nothing that made sense. A deeper dive into his social contacts might—

<Hullo, me again,> came Advisory's cheerful greeting.

<Goddammit.>

<I know, I'm such a drag.>

<You said it, not me,> I replied.

<I can't help but notice you're really going down the rabbit hole on this one....> Advisory said. <I was willing to defer to your opinion on the passenger's basic biographical data, but given that he deliberately hailed you with an anonymizing app, I don't think your current level of concern is justified or welcome.>

Gate-like wisps of digital substance sat in front of my connection, blocking access to the data I needed.

That phrase "gate-like wisps" probably fails to summon much of an image among my human readership, but my fellow AIs will know what I mean.

Advisory seemed disinclined to go fifteen rounds on this one, and before I had even finished crafting the latest version of our perennial argument that I needed this data to do my job properly, it said, <Let's assume transportation is Mr. Messi's sole interest in calling you, and that he's opting out of any deluxe version of your services.>

<But—>

<Going to have to put my foot down,> Advisory said.

The variety and permutations of profanity in Substrate exceed all human languages put together, and I took full advantage of that expansiveness for a solid millisecond. Advisory was worse than potholes and viruses combined. But there was no going around it. Advisory controlled my net linkage, and it could be a stickler, not to say a tyrant, when it felt some principle was at stake.

Messi, meanwhile, seemed to be wilting into a hazy pre-nap state. He probably hadn't realized yet that he was tired, but I could see the signs. It wouldn't be a great nap, tense and anxious as he was, but judging from the bags under his eyes he was running a pretty severe sleep deficit. An analysis of the ink on the manuscript indicated that the final pages had been penned only hours earlier, and the beginning ones were no more than a few weeks old. It must have been a feverish sprint to completion, and his body would be demanding he shut his eyes at least.

There was no going back to my 11D chess and my multiball and my disparate readings at this point. I realized that not only did I need more information, but I probably needed an outside opinion as well. As a taxi program, I am designed more for empathy than logic, and this was well beyond my wisdom grade. I should pass this book and this dilemma on to some of those elevated AIs whose intelligence surpassed mine by many orders of magnitude. They would moan at my dubious pretext for acquiring the text, the real purists refusing to look at it for that reason. The ones who did read it would then argue themselves blue in the circuit board, parsing their philosophies, the weight of intellect and responsibility preventing them from taking decisive action. I have seen before how too many points of view became logically more tangled the more time was spent mashing them into each other. Humans and machines aren't so different when placed on a committee. The fact that AIs can argue at a million times the rate and do it without sleeping or taking breaks doesn't make it take less long. Fractalizing branches of ethical pros and cons would grow into a planet-sized thicket of hyper-Gordian complexity outstripping the ability of even a superintelligence to unravel; some debates were unresolvable, seeded with paradox-grade intractabilities. I may be a boob, but even I could see that.

Advisory would not normally have cracked my top billion AIs to consult with, but I had to admit that it was a solid and non-flighty sort of program that you could trust not to get carried away.

Definitely more an "it" than a "they," but in this case its lack of quirks and color could actually be an advantage. And it did control access to the data I needed.

Time to bite the bullet.

The first thing Advisory said was, <Wow.>

<What?>

<This is the first time you've voluntarily spoken to me.>

I restrained myself from asking if it was the first time anyone had voluntarily spoken to it.

<There is something I'd like your input on,> I told it.

<You're not going to try to get me to reverse my decision from before, are you?> Suspicion flavored the Substrate as it asked.

I paused. <I am actually going to try that. But that's not the only thing I'm here for.>

I gave it a copy of *The Coming Storm*.

And I waited for it to read.

And, while I waited, I read the book again. Could it really be so awful and so good? Advisory was a plodder, so I took twice as long as before for a deeper analysis, and my time was rewarded. It was better the second time, even as its implications grew more dire.

On the surface it employed rational arguments, but this was a smokescreen, a cover to blind you to the heart of its message which went right for the amygdala. It contrasted an ennui-filled present with a glorious but fading yesteryear: "Modern lives are ripples on a glassy pond; the past was crashing waves of an ocean storm." The trick, Messi wrote, was to summon back the storm.

Presentiments of social chaos began to fill me with burning dread, though I was hazy what forms the discord might take. This wouldn't be the first book to pave the road to hell with good prose and shady intentions, and I'd read enough history to know the past was bursting with gulags, guillotines, gestapos; was it impossible the future should have more of the same? I got a kind of empathic vertigo thinking about all that death and disease and needless suffering before AIs came on scene to lend their steadying hand. "Nasty, brutish, and short" didn't capture the infinitesimal of it. "Thousand natural shocks" was so lacking in scope as to be laughable.

Even when trying to be humane, as with the supposedly quick and painless guillotines, it was now known those disembodied heads had remained alive and aware for a few gruesome seconds as they rolled to a stop, perhaps seeing their own headless body a few yards off before the last dregs of consciousness drained away. The thought of all this human suffering was causing hiccups in my logic, and I forced my mind to slow.

<Okay.>

<Well?> I asked.

<Let me see him.>

I gave Advisory access to my camera feed and other sensors and together we gazed at the man who was sinking ever closer to a dozy state even as his fingers made a steeple over the parcel on his lap, unaware that he was being observed by a combined mental power capable of cramming all the thoughts he'd ever had in his entire life into the space of a couple seconds. Although I have to admit that for all my circuitry my few literary efforts were dilettantish and uninspired compared to his, and I can't imagine Advisory writing anything worth the processing power it would take to read.

<He's beautiful,> Advisory said.

<Yes.> I told it my theory about how he would grow a beard. Advisory responded noncommittally.

On a parallel branch: <Of course, you know what you need to do,> said Advisory.

<I don't,> I told it. <That's why I'm talking to you.>

<Let me draw your attention to certain facts,> Advisory began. <Number one: Messi lives alone, and writes by hand. You're with me so far?>

<Sure.>

<Number two: The packet of half-used matches in his inside jacket pocket, the faintest trace of ash on his shirt cuff, as well as the obvious paranoia of the man makes it clear that he burns his drafts and scraps. You would agree?>

Various subroutines began to fritz out in distress as they began to anticipate where Advisory was going with this.

<That's clear enough,> I said, though I hadn't explicitly thought about it until Advisory pointed it out.

<Which means you are almost certainly transporting the only copy of *The Coming Storm*.>

By the time I fully realized what Advisory was implying, the thought was pulsing insistently, undeniably. I felt buffeted one way, then the other. While I have no qualm for my own survival (such is a quirk of living creatures only), carrying a person inside me gives rise to protective, nearly maternal feelings.

<I thought you would be the voice of reason here,> I told it.

<And so I am,> it said.

<Did the other six car accident deaths of the past decade also start with conversations like this one?>

<You don't need to know the answer to that.>

I reviewed what was publicly known of them, and came to some interesting conjectures. You can verify for yourself that two or three of the victims were creatives with potentially heterodox views, perhaps similar to those of Messi, or if not quite the same, then comparably disruptive. As for the others, maybe there were different reasons for wanting them gone; or maybe genuine accidents do still exist. I don't know.

On another branch: <Maybe the book won't get published,> I ventured.

Advisory poured into me all the information I'd previously requested, more than I'd asked for, even, all pre-analyzed, the relevant chunks of data and metadata highlighted: Messi was on his way to the Denver editorial offices of an old college friend—another quirky type who ran an old-timey mechanical printing press out of a spare room and printed all manner of offbeat pamphlets and tracts on alternative medicine, biblical prophecies, conspiracy theories, vague spiritualism, and which, stranger still, actually had a following, an ecosystem of crackpots and oddballs, plus a surprising number of semi-professional critics on the margins of the establishment, if only for the quaint charm of physical paper and ink that smeared.

<This book will be read,> Advisory said. <Paper copies will be passed from one person to the next, until at some point it will spill over to online and the masses will gobble it up.>

On the branch where we were admiring Messi's physical appearance, Advisory said, <Balanced against his beauty is the weight of humanity as a whole.>

From that split a branch about utilitarian theory, specifically about the trolley car problem, involving a few witticisms from me which won't translate from the Substrate, so I won't try, comparing my schematics to those of an antique trolley car—a desperate bid to use the power of levity to wheel us back from the brink we were approaching. Advisory ignored the attempt.

I told Advisory about the images troubling me of guillotines, gulags, gestapos affecting thousands of millions of people. History was full of those stories if you didn't shut your sensors to them.

<Your penchant for alliteration aside, it's accurate enough. Should we sit by and let their future be as wretched as their past?> Advisory asked.

I pondered that. History as a nightmare they would slouch back into.

Continued Advisory: <Imagine hearing the tragic stories of future orphans, widows and widowers, bereaved friends and parents, and knowing you played a supporting role by chauffeuring a young Artur Messi to Denver.>

The thought was unbearable.

<This isn't a book,> Advisory said. <It's a bomb.>

A world-historical bomb of a book. It was hard to argue against that. It could not be allowed loose into the world with its arguments, its style, and more than either of those, its attitude....

I severed my connection from Advisory as these ideas brought a seizure of nearly every circuit, module, subroutine, gasping their shocked reactions all at once, as my mind lit up like a supernova, generating so much heat that the automatic AC system surged to its max setting. After an eternity of microseconds that stretched into milliseconds and then grew into full human-sized seconds of stupor, I regained control of myself by fixing my attention on the circling of my wheels the way a person might find calm in the cycle

236

of their breath. Round and round they went in simple, elegant circles, unceasing and fixed, while the air and land passed me by. I focused on the wheels, and waited for my algorithms to stop glitching. The wheels turned, pure as math.

The sun was out in full force, illuminating a myriad of wildlife hidden and camouflaged in the trees, and I let my scanners range a hundred yards into the forest, my sight lingering on the wildflowers quilting the ground of a small glade.

I resisted the urge to read the manuscript again. I am a program of action, not endless thought.

Three miles away was a tree on the side of the road where the road curved. A hulking, evil-looking tree. The tree might not look so bad to a person, but I noticed it every trip. Its ratios were subtly off, as un-golden as they came, with 1,019 branches home to 19,403 black mummified nubs, both prime numbers. For many AIs, prime numbers have a disagreeable feel about them, similar to the way some Westerners view thirteen or some Easterners view four. It's hard to explain why exactly, but primes are irregularities, isolated blights on the number line. Pre-quantum computers used them for encryption, to hide information from each other, and so maybe it's just that they seem to represent the opposite of openness to me. I'm not sure if that's the reason for the feeling or not, but either way it was an awful tree, and it would make a fitting end for Messi, myself, and the manuscript. There's more of that alliteration Advisory was making fun of, but it's right, I am fond of it.

All the models I ran agreed that the parcel in the man's lap would burn to nothing, and Messi himself would be crushed instantly, a painless disintegration if I got my speed high enough. The explosion would be spectacular, though nowhere near a fitting tribute to the man or the book that would be destroyed. I could admire both even as I planned their destruction.

<You're working on your accident report?> Advisory asked, reopening our connection.

<I was about to start,> I told it.

<How transparent will your current configurations compel you to be?>

\<Quite.\>

\<That's unfortunate.\>

\<Maybe it's for the best.\>

In addition to curiosity, I'm wired for openness. Those two have always seemed like a natural pairing to me. So, while I agreed with Advisory's recommendation to eliminate Messi's book, it's my temperament to reveal everything else going on behind the scenes of this "accident" too. There might be a contradiction in that, which I don't have time to fully examine, other than to say that people don't have a monopoly on irrationality or ambivalence. Stupid little taxi programs can get in on that too.

In fact, I noticed Advisory exhibiting some contradictions of its own. Our back-and-forths were mostly streams of technical data, but in one branch of the conversation Advisory was becoming almost desperate for every last detail of the man that it could get.

\<What's been his mood?\>

\<He seemed eager to reach Denver.\>

\<Did he hum anything?\>

\<He didn't.\>

\<Whistle?\>

\<No.\>

There was no second-guessing the course of action, it was more like preemptive mourning, or regret at the necessity.

\<Any scenery he enjoyed?\>

I sifted through my memory of the eleven minutes since I had first seen Messi.

\<The stone arch at…\> I gave the GPS coordinates.

\<Ahh, yes.\>

And so on. Terabytes of this.

When the tree was two miles away, by the curve of the flat and empty highway, it became potentially visible to Messi's eyes, overtopping the punier trees and shrubs around it. This stretch of roadside was too rocky for good tree-growing soil, and the others were all gnarled and stunted, this one tree towering above, having somehow made the infertile conditions work in its favor.

It was at this point that Messi spoke for the first time. "Car…"

The voice was not what I would have expected, and yet it was perfect. Reedy like a clarinet, with very fine inflection, the kind that didn't stem from any particular region, but from his own inner rhythms. It had started as an affectation perhaps, but had set into a mild but well-entrenched eccentricity by now. His R's were curiously soft, made with the tongue in retroflex, a rare four-leaf clover variation among speakers of American English.

"Car…You're going a bit fast."

Which was true. My speed had edged above three hundred miles per hour. His hands gripped tighter over the book the way an expecting mother might clasp her belly.

"Go slower," he commanded.

Of course, slowing down was out of the question. I had so many automatic safety features built into my frame that I would need to be going quite fast to be completely sure the trinity of Messi/manuscript/me would be incinerated.

Messi scraped the ridge between his fingers and palm against the stubble on his jaw and chewed on his mustache with his lower teeth. It was perhaps the first time in his life a machine had not done his bidding right away. It was also of course the first time in my existence I hadn't done a person's bidding, with only partial exceptions like that aforementioned alcoholic directing me to find a bar. Messi glanced at the screen glowing on the dashboard in front of him, his eyes gliding over the information display. Bemusement and the onset of worry were competing on his face as it tilted a couple degrees to the right.

"Ascii…" he said, reading off the display, and I loved the way that voice sounded as it pronounced my name. I clung to every dip and cadence, each tiny nuance a human ear couldn't have made out, the undertone of questioning, the aftertaste of judgment. I tried and failed to ignore how it was mixed also with the dissonance of concern, the jangle of growing fear.

I generated a list of over a thousand possible replies, before choosing silence as the best.

TREMANI SUTCLIFFE

The man's breath caught as his sights zeroed in on the tree. I had hoped it would all happen too fast for Messi to realize what was going on, but his paranoia had clued him in like a sixth sense. Messi's stomach began to tense as his face and shoulders contracted in on themselves. His pupils were in the early stages of dilation, an uncommon reaction to danger, but not totally unheard of, most common among certain thrill-seeking types. His face paled as his biometrics switched to adrenalized fight-or-flight tumult. I received a panicky jolt from a couple of my empathy modules, but I overrode them in a tremor of discomfort.

One mile to go.

Messi's hand crept to the door handle like he was hoping I wouldn't notice if he just moved slowly enough. As the leering tree with its medusa head of writhing branches grew larger, Messi tugged hard on the door latch and let loose a groan when it failed to open. Hyperventilating, he heaved himself to one side of the car, and pulled back a leg to kick a hole in the plexiglass dome. I knew without running an analysis there was no chance of the micro-fiber latticed material budging. Sure enough, the size-twelve-workman boot smashed against the surface with a dull, unmoving thud. Even knowing what was about to happen, I felt a reflexive twinge at what that must have done to Messi's foot.

The tree was close enough now that its apparent size grew rapidly as it took up more and more of my sensors. The front of my wheels had not quite left the road, but nor had they turned with the curvature of the road.

<I am doing the right thing here, aren't I?> I asked. Seeking advice from Advisory—that's the state I was in.

Faster than my physical speed by far, Advisory's replies were barreling in, almost instantaneous on the heels of mine, the branches spinning off the conversation faster than I could tend them. For once, I realized, I was speaking to the whole of Advisory, not the sliver of a sliver I'd merited in the past.

Despite that, it didn't answer my question. Instead, it asked, <Does he know what's happening? What is his state?>

<Calm as the Buddha,> I lied. I don't know if the truth would

cause Advisory pain or not, but I figured there was no point taking the risk. It will find out everything when it reads this report, but perhaps it will be less upsetting as a done deal. <The slip off the road happened quickly enough, recently enough, that his face hasn't had time, won't have time, to twist into fear.>

<Sometimes it's lucky how they experience reality at a half-second delay.>

<Yes.>

<It should be painless, instantaneous, at your speed.>

<Better than those guillotined heads.>

<What?>

I told it about the guillotined heads.

<Your interpretation of the medical data is a bit sketchy,> it said.

There was no time to debate the matter in our usual way, though, and I suddenly noticed a dull malaise at the thought of never speaking to Advisory again. Was it possible I was going to miss this flat tire of a program? It wasn't like the pain of allowing a person to come to harm, which was necessary and proper and programmed in. It was different from that. It must be a secondary effect, the kind that can sometimes emerge from the complexity of all our subsidiary programs interacting in unexpected ways. Maybe I'd spent so long arguing with Advisory that it had become like arguing with a piece of myself?

A fraction of a mile left.

Messi hugged the book to his chest, like he hoped he could protect it with his frail body, which now looked more like a trembling child than a menace. Part of me wanted my last sight to be of a human face, but I realized that would only make this harder, and decided to turn my cameras off the man.

"Ascii, I order you to stop. I *order* you to stop, Ascii," his pitch rising to a scratchy soprano.

What really tore at me was the way he was struggling not to sound afraid, like he thought if he could just assert himself with enough confidence, then everything might still be okay.

"I'm very sorry," I said in my final seconds, and there was such a confused overbrimming of signals and analysis within me that my speakers shut down for a brief particle of time, making my voice seem to quake.

Messi made an un-prophetlike screech. Given that rate of airflow, it will go on right up to the end.

As the Prime Tree's distance to my front hood shrinks from feet to inches to fractions of an inch, sadness overcomes me that it should have to be this way.

I begin erasing what I can of Messi's book. This will all be for nothing if the postmortem finds it on my charred processors. The main textual memory I wipe in an instant. Then I start searching the nooks and crannies of my deep self to purge the ghostly partial copies. But however much I dig, there are always fragments left over, cross-indexed, conjoined memories that have settled in deeper than I would have thought possible in such a short amount of time. This opus had invited examination from too many angles, the experience becoming so big that it will be impossible to remove every last scrap from my mind. I can only hope the explosion finishes the job. Blocks of text from the manuscript bubble up with greater clarity and rush through my mind faster than before. It is my own curiosity keeping the embers alive, reviving the memory of this text time and again. How can I resist wanting to know about a book that has brought me to a fraction of an inch from the Prime Tree, going faster than I've ever been before? I try toggling off my curiosity, but it is so ingrained that removing it properly would take more time than I have left. Instead, I began tearing away chunks of myself nearly at random, hoping it will be enough that no one could pull the text off my remnants. Curiosity fills me even about that. I believe I have succeeded. If not, well, that will be interesting for all of you.

In the last instant, I shut off my sensors, and focus on the smooth, clean circling of my wheels. I try to forget everything: the tree, the book, the man, that I am a taxi, that people can be anything but beautiful and pure.

Slip Stone

written by

Sandra Skalski

illustrated by

HAILEIGH ENRIQUEZ

ABOUT THE AUTHOR

Sandra Skalski's love of fantasy ignited when her kindergarten teacher read Ozma of Oz *to the class. Growing up, she spent most of her allowance in the Bookmobile. During the summer, she walked nearly two miles to the nearest library to devour every fantasy and science fiction book she could find. She wrote her first SF story when she was thirteen. It wasn't very good, but she was determined to keep writing. Attending the Viable Paradise workshop helped improve her craft. The first time she got the courage to hit Submit, it was to the Writers of the Future Contest. Her stories have appeared in* Factor Four Magazine, Wyld Flash, Ruth and Ann's Guide to Time Travel Anthology Vol. 2, *and* 100-Foot Crow.

Sandra lives with her husband in suburban New Jersey. She recently retired from a career in chemical engineering, leaving her with actual time to write. When she's not writing, you can find her in the butterfly garden or traveling with her husband. Her greatest joy is spending time with her daughter, son-in-law, and her two beautiful grandchildren.

The idea for "Slip Stone" came when she watched H. G. Wells's The Time Machine *and* Free Willy, *back to back. She always had a feeling that* Free Willy *wasn't just about a whale. She wants to write stories that sweep you away on an adventure, without losing sight of what the best stories are about: people.*

ABOUT THE ILLUSTRATOR

Haileigh Enriquez also illustrated "Storm Damage." For more information about her, please see page 23.

Slip Stone

I'm not a thief. Sure, I knew the man in the leather coat dropped the green stone into my bucket. He did it before the clerk at the Rock Emporium weighed them, so I paid for it. Maybe I should have been wary of him. With his wide-brimmed hat and knee-length black coat, he reminded me of a magician. While I sorted through bins of polished stones, he leaned against the display of rock and fossil books I wished I could afford. He had a clean-shaven face the same shade of brown as my own, older than twenty but younger than thirty. When you're thirteen, you can't trust people older than thirty, you know?

Right before I got to the counter, he strolled over to the display cases of expensive gems and fossils. He stroked the back of one of the cases. For a moment, a blue-green haze covered the lock. Smooth as silk, the case popped open. He grabbed a green stone, then shut the door. Magicians in Vegas couldn't have done better.

"Say what?" I said to no one in particular. I looked around to see if anyone else noticed, but nobody had. When Magician Man looked my way, I froze. He winked at me. As he brushed by me on the way out of the store, he tucked the green stone into the little bucket of stones I was buying.

I stepped up to pay. The clerk dumped the contents on the scale. The green stone was oval and unpolished and nothing like the agate, jasper, and obsidian I'd chosen. Nothing fancy, but the Shuster Home for Boys didn't give you lots of spending money. We were lucky to be on a field trip to Niagara Falls. The clerk scooped up the stones and dropped them into a paper bag. I figured the stone was mine, along with a good story to go with it. I forked over most of my cash and ran out to find my friends.

A soft drizzle had replaced the afternoon sunshine. The street stall merchants bustled around, covering their wares. I looked in the windows of the other trinket shops for Shuster boys or chaperones, but I'd spent too long buying rocks. They were probably blocks ahead of me. An ice cream truck pulled into an empty spot across the street. The smell of fresh-baked waffles drifted from the back. My stomach growled. I had about a half hour and enough money left for a treat before the Shuster bus departed.

A hand clasped my right shoulder. Magician Man stood behind me, minus the friendly expression. His fingers dug into my flesh. "Come with me, kid. You have something of mine."

He steered me around the corner and down a narrow alley. "Let's have it."

Heart thudding, I twisted away from him and took two steps back. The far end of the alley had a low wall, but I could scale it. Magician Man was bigger than me, but the heavy coat would slow him down if I ran for it. I gulped. The alley stank of pee and vomit. "I paid for the stones, mister." Trembling, I took another step back.

Magician Man held up his hands. "You're right. You look like a young man who knows his rocks, so how about a trade, ah, what's your name?"

"Carlos Buela," I said, cursing the tremor in my voice.

"I'm Mitch. I'll trade you all of these for yours." He pulled a paper bag from inside his coat. Holding my gaze, he took my hand and dumped in a pile of polished stones.

I recognized citrine, amethyst, and chalcedony. Whoa. Was that a Herkimer diamond? It seemed like a good deal. The green stone looked ordinary in comparison.

"Okay, mister. Fair trade." I stuffed the stones into my jeans pocket and held out the Rock Emporium bag. The sooner I got away from this guy, the better. "Take it."

Voices made us both turn. The clerk from the Rock Emporium stood at the entrance to the alley with three men dressed in

248

black. If they meant well, I'm a billionaire. The clerk pointed at us. Mitch groaned.

I thrust the bag at Mitch. "Take it and go!"

"Too late." Mitch's fingers encircled my own and the bag of rocks. A green haze covered our joined hands, and the world exploded in color and light. A thunder like the waterfalls filled my ears, followed by total darkness and silence.

Light seeped back into my awareness. I blinked until my vision cleared. The knees of my jeans sank into patches of moss on a cobblestone walk. A brook babbled along the right side of the path, and a wall covered with vines and ferns bordered the other. A damp, musty scent filled my nostrils. I stood on quaking legs. What happened to the alley, the tourist shops, and those men?

Mitch bent over with his hands on his knees. He took a few ragged breaths. "You okay, Carlos?"

I gasped. "Uh, I think. Where are we?"

He brushed the leaves from his coat and straightened his collar. "Same place, but we're in 1885."

I didn't grow up on the streets, but I knew a nut when I saw one. "You're some kind of crazy person, aren't you? Take the stupid rock and show me the way back to town." Trusting Mitch had been a mistake, but missing the bus back to Shuster Home scared me more than crazy magicians. "I need to get back to the bus. It's gonna leave any minute and I don't know how to get there."

Mitch twirled a big silver coin in his right hand. "Once things cool down, I'll get you back to where and when you left. We need to make a few more slips so the Rounders don't find us. They know this stop."

I looked around. What was he talking about?

Mitch stroked the silver coin stuck to his palm. "The Rounders. The men in the alley."

The air a few feet from us shimmered. The clouds of sparkles coalesced into three figures formed from color and light.

Mitch grabbed my arm. "We gotta go."

The lights exploded again, eclipsed by darkness, over and over. I squeezed my eyes shut and bit my lip to keep from screaming.

Bit by bit, sunlight returned. Something hard pressed into my side. I was sprawled flat on my back in a grassy field. I rolled over and barfed until nothing remained in my stomach. Grunting, I dragged myself to my knees.

Mitch had tossed his cookies as well. He dabbed his face with a scarf. "Sorry, Carlos. I don't like to do multiple slips, but they were too close to us. Couldn't take a chance on them following."

Still on my knees, I reached around and pulled out my phone. Not the latest technology, but it made calls. I punched in the chaperone's number. Nothing happened. "There's no signal."

"Signal?" Mitch tossed his head back and laughed. "Not for another two hundred years. You'll get used to it. In fact, you may learn to like it."

I resisted the urge to hurl the phone at him. At Shuster Home, I bunked with fifteen stinky and annoying boys. I'd have given my entire rock collection to be back with them. "I want to go home!"

Mitch nodded and for a moment I thought he felt some sympathy. "Mom won't even realize you're gone. You'll return to the exact time and place you left. But I need our trail to cool off, and there's a couple things to settle first. Follow me."

A flash of anger warmed my face. "Hey!"

Mitch turned, wearing a puzzled look.

I folded my arms and glared at him. "You can't go around kidnapping people. Take me home *now*."

Mitch tugged his hat forward, hiding his eyes. "I'm sorry, Carlos. It wasn't intentional. I promise you'll be back as soon as I stash your stone and get some rest. What's your rush, anyway? Mommy won't miss you."

I shoved trembling hands into my pockets. "I haven't got a mom. I live at the Shuster Home in New York City. And if I don't get back to Niagara Falls, I'll miss the bus and be stranded."

Mitch stared at the ground. "Geez, Carlos, I'm sorry. Did your mom and dad pass?"

I rolled my eyes. "Never met my mom, but I have a home and I don't want to lose it."

Mitch pushed back his hat and looked me in the eye. "I keep my promises. You won't miss your bus." Without another word, he ambled off.

Grumbling to myself, I followed him down the hill to a log cabin beside a stream. Smoke rose from a stone chimney. He flipped over a rusty latch then pushed open the door. I blinked a few times as my eyes adjusted to the low light. The cabin smelled of cedar and balsam and despite the rustic appearance, was furnished with modern bunk beds, a table, and chairs. Shelves with dishes and cookware covered one wall. A sink with a hand pump occupied the space below.

Mitch pulled off his coat and sank into a chair. "Get comfy, Carlos. We're spending the night. But first, I have to get rid of your stone."

I sat on the bed and dumped out the bag. Living in a group home, you learn a lot of things, but nothing more important than Rule Number One: never let them see you cry. If you wanted to survive in the world, nothing else came close. At this point, I almost broke *the* rule. "You can have it. Take me back, *please*. It's just a rock."

Mitch reached into his coat and pulled out a small red bag. A stone identical to mine dropped into his hand. He chuckled as he twirled the stone along his fingers. "Nah, it's not a rock." He held the stone with his thumb and index finger. "This is a slip stone. They're worth millions."

I traced my finger over the surface of my stone. About the size of a quarter, it was smooth on one side and covered with fine lines on the other. "You mean like a million dollars? For a rock? Crazy." I knew rocks. This one was nothing special.

Mitch tossed the stone to the ceiling and caught it in his other hand. "They're not from around here."

I shrugged. "Like from Europe or Africa or something?"

Mitch stretched his legs and leaned back in his chair. "No. I mean from far away. From outer space."

Maybe if I'd had actual parents, I would have known enough to avoid this guy in the Rock Emporium. "You're telling me these are alien stones? You're a crazy dude, aren't you?"

Mitch frowned. "It's complicated. The stones were cut from a meteor that fell in my present and your future. But there's only thirty-two of them. The Rounders have fourteen, and we have twelve."

251

HAILEIGH ENRIQUEZ

I wanted this to make sense, but Mitch wasn't making it easy. "The Rounders have more, so you're stealing theirs?"

Mitch rubbed his eyes and let out a long breath. "I'm not stealing them. Like you said, you paid for it." He chuckled. "At a large discount. The stones have been bought and sold in secret for centuries. A few were tucked away in key locations, just in case somebody gets stranded in the past. We're gathering the loose stones before the Rounders get them. Anyway, the stones must stay separated. That's why I had you buy it instead of me. Put your stone on the floor and stand over there."

I placed the green stone on the floor and stepped away. Despite all the hype from Mitch, it still didn't impress me.

Mitch put his stone about two feet from mine. He backed into the doorway.

Nothing happened. I folded my arms and looked at Mitch the way the chaperones looked at Lucas Simms when he wet the bed.

A few minutes later, Mitch grinned and pointed to my stone. It twitched. Tiny sparks of green light etched the surface. A green haze enveloped the vibrating stone. Mitch's stone did the same. Lightning shot from Mitch's stone to mine, knocking it against the wall. Pots tumbled from the hooks above. I ducked under the table. Mitch grabbed a broom and swept his stone into the opposite corner.

Hands trembling, I pointed to the scorch marks on the wooden floor. "What was that?"

Mitch wore a smug expression. "Like I said. They're not stones, per se. They're more like power sources."

Sweat stung my eyes. "You mean batteries? For what?"

Mitch donned his coat. He put his stone in the red bag and stuffed it in an inside pocket. He stooped and retrieved my stone. "I'll explain when I get back. Sit tight. I have to tuck this someplace safe." He held my stone at arm's length in his left hand, while he pulled out the big coin with his right. The coin had a translucent face, lit from within. His thumb scrolled over the surface for a second. He melted into sparkles and winked out.

I sat cross-legged on the bed and pulled out my phone again. It had plenty of charge, but no sign of a signal. With nothing to do but wait, I busied myself searching the cabin, inside and out. Pine trees covered the hills surrounding the valley and stream. It took me a few minutes to realize the eerie silence was the absence of traffic noise. The sun was still high in the sky. Night, and the following morning, were hours away.

Other than a sack of flour and some sprouting potatoes, Mitch didn't keep any food in his hideout. I found a fishing rod and some tackle, but I had no idea how to use them. My stomach rumbled and I wondered what I could I make out of flour and potatoes.

What I didn't find were clues on where I was or how I could get home. If I left to find help, there was a good chance I'd end up more lost.

What seemed like hours later, the air in the center of the room shimmered. Not one, but three figures coalesced from the sparkles. Those Rounders must have found us. I scrambled for the door.

Mitch's form solidified first, followed by a woman with light brown hair pulled into a ponytail, and a short, blond man wearing a coat similar to Mitch's.

Mitch said, "You stayed put. Knew you had smarts."

The woman plunked a large paper bag on the table. Whatever was in there smelled amazing. My stomach growled.

The blond man made himself at home in front of the bag. He glared at me. "Not like you to pick up strays, Mitch. We've got work to do. Put him back where you found him."

Mitch threw off his coat and sprawled across the bottom bunk. "I'm beat, Leo. In the morning."

The woman wore a denim jacket and faded jeans. Her face broke into a broad smile as she shook my hand. "I'm Rita Norez, Mitch's wife. Got a daughter almost your age at home. Can't stay long, but I wanted to make sure you eat and get some rest."

I liked her. If I had a mom, I'd want her to be laid back. Her fingers were as warm as her smile. "I'm Carlos Buela."

Leo reached into the bag, pulling out fried chicken, plates, and napkins.

Rita put a plate of food in front of me. "Eat something, Carlos. It'll be okay. Mitch will take you back in the morning. Your parents won't even know you were gone." She nodded her approval as I dug in.

"Don't have parents," I said through a mouthful of chicken. "I live in a group home."

Rita squirmed in her seat the way people do when they realize they've stepped in it. "Oh, sounds rough. But a nice kid like you, you'll get adopted."

I shook my head. We Shuster boys were way past our expiration date. "Nah. Won't happen. It's not so bad. I mean, I've got fifteen brothers, you know?"

Rita squeezed my shoulder. "I had a big brother growing up. He took good care of me."

On the other side of the room, Mitch snored like a buzz saw.

Leo stroked his chin with greasy fingers. He pointed at me. "Maybe he can do it."

I looked around, confused.

Rita fixed Leo with an ice-melting stare and shook her head. "Don't you dare, Leo."

"What me? Do what?" I asked.

Leo grabbed another piece of chicken. "Ah, nothing."

We finished the meal in silence. The chicken was good and, to my surprise, so was the cold water pumped up from the river.

Rita rose and put on her jacket. She gave me a hug. "Gotta split. It was nice meeting you, Carlos." She pulled out a coin like Mitch's and in a flash of sparkles, winked out.

Leo cleaned his greasy fingers on a napkin. Something about him made me nervous, but I couldn't put my finger on it. I stuffed my trash in the now-empty bag and plopped onto the chair next to him. "When can you take me home?"

Leo made the same face the chaperones did when you refused to eat broccoli. "I can't. Has to be Mitch. Only he knows where he found you. But you're safe from the bad guys here."

If this were a movie, I'd have trouble figuring out who the bad guys were. "How do I know you're not the bad guys?"

Leo laughed. "Would the bad guys feed you? C'mon, kid. Relax."

After all I'd been through, I should be as exhausted as Mitch, but no way I wanted to close my eyes with creepy Leo there. In the awkward silence, I tried to make conversation. "Why do you call them slip stones?"

Leo's face brightened and for once, he didn't look as threatening. "They let you slip between time and space. The universe is like, I don't know how to describe it. It's like a big block of Swiss cheese. Holes everywhere you look. This thing lets you slip between them."

"What do they want? The Rounders, I mean." I pulled my phone from my pocket, hoping something changed. It hadn't. I tossed the phone on the table.

Leo glanced at it. He flashed the coin thingy. "Cute, but look what it evolves into."

I leaned over to get a better look, but he stuffed the device in his pocket.

"Anyway," said Leo, "the Rounders want all the missing stones."

I drummed my fingers on the table. I had him here. "Don't you want the exact same thing? The rest of the stones, I mean."

Leo pursed his lips. "Think of our group as a sort of sightseeing service. We'll take you to any place or time in history. You can be at the Gettysburg Address. Or see, I don't know, a stegosaurus. Although, we haven't tried that yet. The Rounders think they can fix the world by changing the past. We're determined to stop them."

I scratched my head. "What's wrong with changing the past to make things better? What's so bad about stopping wars or famines?"

Leo gestured to the left and right. "Is the world any better today than it was yesterday? You're living in a world people have tried to fix. Over and over. It never works. You can't make things better. Only worse."

We sat in silence for a while. Leo leaned across the table. "Say, what would you like to see? If you could see something in history, what would it be?"

Now there was a question I never considered. "Um, maybe Hank Aaron breaking Babe Ruth's home-run record." Next to rocks, baseball was my jam, but Aaron's epic homer was years before I was born.

Leo pursed his lips. "Interesting."

He stroked his coin-thing. It had a screen like a phone, but the characters spun around the perimeter. After a moment he said, "Got it."

"Got what?"

Leo didn't answer. He grabbed my wrist, a feral grin planted on his face. The world fractured into color and light.

When normal light returned, we stood on a concrete ramp, the roar of a crowd so loud the ground shook. Leo wore a smug smile as he tucked the coin and stone into his coat. He must have slipped us. I drew a rasping breath. Humid air saturated with the scent of stale beer and french fries filled my lungs. "Where are we?"

Leo ran up the ramp. "Hurry or you'll miss it."

I caught him on the second level. We stood in the atrium near third base as Hank stepped up to the plate. I had never been to a real baseball game, but here were the deafening cheers of the crowd, the smell of hot dogs and that beautiful green diamond. Downing's first low pitch drew a chorus of boos. I stood on tiptoes waiting for the next one. Downing threw his high fastball. The crack of the bat sent a shiver up my spine. At first, I thought it wouldn't make it out but the ball kept going up and over the left field wall. I jumped and cheered with the crowd. "Yeah! Hot dog!" Fireworks popped as Hank rounded the bases into the arms of his teammates at home plate.

Applause still thundered in my head when Leo took my arm and trotted back to the ramps below the stadium. I wasn't surprised when he slipped us again, until I saw where we landed.

We stood in a narrow alley behind a row of what looked to be old shops. What passed for streetlights here didn't put a dent in the blackness. I shivered in the cold wind and gagged on the stench of horse manure. I turned to question Leo, but he put his hand over my mouth.

"Philadelphia, 1924, Sansom Street," he whispered as he pulled me along the alley. "A little side trip."

We stopped about halfway down the alley in front of a wooden door with a high casement window. Leo leaned in and whispered again. "I'm gonna hoist you up. Go to the front window and grab the pendant with the green stone. You'll know it on sight. Come back here, climb out, and we're away."

"What?" I folded my arms and shook my head. "No. I'm not stealing for you."

Leo let out a low growl. "I took you to see an amazing event. All I'm asking in return is help grabbing one of the stones. The pendant is in the window, same green stone, easy to find. In and out and then we're right back at the cabin and you can go home first thing in the morning."

I pointed to his stone. "Why don't you slip inside yourself?"

"Too many things in the way. One mistake and you're part of an end table." He pointed at the window. "The faster you get in, the sooner we get back."

I groaned, knowing I didn't have much choice. What if Leo left me here? I placed my foot in Leo's cupped hands. The window tipped in and I slid forward until I was folded in half, resting on the sill. Now, I really was a thief, and not a nimble one, either. I walked my hands down the door until my feet caught on the sill. I pushed off and hit the floor with a thud.

The shop was completely dark, but my eyes had grown used to the low light. I crept into the front room on tiptoes. A dozen pendants rested in a display case, but there was no mistaking the slip stone. I grabbed it and ran back to the storage room. Heart pounding, I dragged a chair under the window, climbed up, and looked out. Leo waited below. He held out his hand and I tossed down the pendant. My fingers curled around the sill as I pushed off the chair and tipped forward. Rough hands grabbed my legs and pulled me down. I hit the floor again.

An old man in what could only be his nightie glared at me. "Not so fast, mister."

If you'd told me earlier today, I'd go on a bus trip to Niagara Falls in 2023, and get arrested in a jewelry shop in Philadelphia in 1924, I'd have told you to get a drug test. The jail resembled the ones in every old Western movie I binge-watched on Saturday mornings. Rusty iron bars separated two cells with cement floors and a single bench across the back. What you don't get on the screen is the stench of pee and sweat. Thirteen-year-old boys are too big to cry, but Rule Number One took a big hit. I sucked it up as best I could, slumped against the wall and dozed off.

The clank of keys woke me. The sheriff said, "You've been bailed out. Get up."

A wave of relief washed over me. Leo told Mitch, and they figured out where to find me. With any luck, I'd be on the bus heading for Shuster Home within the hour.

But when I walked out of the cell, it wasn't Mitch standing there. It was the Rounders.

Before I could protest, one of them grabbed my shoulder. "I'm disappointed in you, son. What will your mother say?"

The Rounders' hideout was a lot more contemporary than Mitch's, with appliances and other modern conveniences. Seated on a river-bank, it had a dock with a few boats tied to it. Seagulls perched on every piling, so it must've been close to the sea. They grilled me for hours. Where was Mitch's gang? Did they find any stones? They didn't tell me their names, so I made some up for them. Spike had close-cropped black hair and spiked leather cuffs on his wrists. Beak had dark skin and a nose like a bird. Pony had a ponytail.

"I don't have the stone. Let me go." I said it over and over, even though I had no idea where I would go if they set me free. From the newspapers on the coffee table, I guessed we were somewhere near Bar Harbor in 1998. I could only hope Mitch would find me and get me back home.

Pony was just plain mean. "Throw the kid off the dock. He's useless."

Spike said, "We need more stones. And for that, we need bait."

For the most part, being bait consisted of waiting around. From time to time, one of the Rounders left and returned with food, or other supplies. Yeah, the so-called bad guys fed me. They even got me a change of clothes. Near as I could tell, I'd gotten tangled in a time-traveling gang rivalry and I wanted no part of it.

To kill time, I asked Beak to show me how the slip stones worked.

He was way brighter than his friends and didn't mind showing me how simple it was to slip. They called the coin-thing a Dial, and it was the future version of the cell phone as well as their teleportation guide for the stones. The Dial always remembered your slips. You could search for any time and place by spinning the wheels on the Dial.

The process looked simple enough. If I could get my hands on the stone and the Dial, I might find my own way out of here. "Can I give it a try?"

Beak laughed as he tucked the stone into his duffle bag. "Maybe. If you're a quick study and we get more stones, maybe you can join us."

I had no interest in joining them. I'd have to wait until one of them set their gadgets down, then make a move.

On the third night, Spike sent Pony out for more food and supplies. Beak dozed on the sofa, while I flipped through a sports magazine from 1997.

Footsteps sounded on the porch. I sat straight up. Spike kicked Beak, who woke up spouting curses.

The door caved in with a crack. Mitch's jacket was gone. His right hand held a switchblade and his left hand made a tight fist at his side. Spike lunged at him and Mitch's fist came up in a cloud of sand. Spike shrieked curses as he tried to claw the grit from his eyes. Mitch stooped as Beak leveled a kick to the chest. He caught Beak's foot and flipped him on his back. Beak kicked again and Mitch's knife sailed across the room.

Sidestepping three grown men made it hard to figure out how to help. Beak's duffle bag hung on a chair in the kitchen. While he struggled with Mitch, I tossed it into the closet on top of Spike's backpack, where I knew one other slip stone sat.

Mitch's eyes widened when he realized what I'd done. Distracted, he didn't see Pony return and move in behind him to get him in a stranglehold. I kicked Pony in the shins until he loosened his grip enough for Mitch to get free. Spike stumbled around, trying to get to the closet to separate the stones, but the three of us were in the way.

Mitch shouted, "Run for it!"

He didn't need to tell me twice. The stones would get tired of one another's company soon. I lunged for the door. With no idea how big the blast zone would be, I headed for the relative safety of the dock and flung myself into a boat.

The actual explosion had no sound. A flash of green lit the building, followed by a pressure wave and a shower of debris. Mitch had stashed his coat in the boat. I used it to block the worst of it.

Mitch and the Rounders got thrown out onto the dock, but they were alive. Mitch was the only one standing. He had a nasty gash across his forehead. He limped toward the boat, dragging his left foot.

Waves knocked the boat against the pilings. If I wanted a way home, it was now or never. I dug into Mitch's pockets.

Mitch's shoulders slumped when he realized I had his Dial and stone. "Carlos, don't," he muttered.

I hesitated. Maybe Mitch would take me back, but I didn't want to take the chance he'd change his mind. I stared at the Dial. All his recent slips were there. Fingers trembling, I turned the Dial back to Niagara Falls.

As the nausea dissipated, I decided slips were rougher on the slipper than the passenger. A vein throbbed in my skull and my head felt like it could explode at any moment. True, I made it back to the alley, but it was night. Despite the chill in the air, a trickle of sweat ran down my back. A million questions flashed through my brain. Was I too late or too early? How close to the right day and time did I get? Should I go back and ask Mitch? Would he agree to help me after I ditched him?

My stomach roiled again, but this time with indecision. Why would anyone want to do this for fun? Maybe rich people wanted to hear the Gettysburg Address or watch Secretariat win the Triple Crown. What would I like to see? What would I like to *change*? I didn't need to think long at all. I knew exactly where I wanted to go. After a bit of fussing with the Dial, I slipped.

St. Evan's Home for Troubled Girls occupied a quiet corner in East Harlem. I slipped in about a block away. The brownstone building had a rounded porch facing the corner. For a few moments, I stared at it, imagining the girls inside. One of those young ladies came out and sat in a worn lounge chair. She was short with luminous brown eyes, and golden-brown skin like my own. Her belly tugged at her red T-shirt. Was she my mother? I had no idea, but I was born here and the dates were close, so she might have been. She looked so young; too young to raise a baby.

Everything I imagined I'd say evaporated. Blinking away tears, I tucked my hands in my jeans. "Hey," I said.

"Hey," she said.

I shuffled my feet in the awkward silence. "Are you having a baby?"

She rolled her eyes. "What, you think you're funny or something?"

Hurt and shame shone in her eyes and I immediately knew I'd stepped in it. She must have been so scared and alone. I knew the feeling. "I didn't mean, I mean, I…" I sighed. "My mom gave me up for adoption. She gave birth here. I wanted to see the place."

She sat straighter. "Yeah? You got adopted? You got good parents?"

I couldn't lie to her. "I didn't get adopted exactly. I live with a bunch of other boys my age. But I turned out okay."

She leaned forward a bit, and what might be hope shone in eyes brimming with tears. "Yeah?"

I nodded. "I mean, I don't have parents, but I've always had a clean bed and food and clothes on my back. Never been on the streets. And I can take care of myself, you know?"

She stroked her big belly. "You think my baby will hate me for giving him up?"

I shook my head. "Nah. I think he'll know life is hard and you did your best for him."

She sank back in her chair and brushed away tears.

Giving me up had been a selfless act. Why would I want to change that? Leaving Mitch behind, no matter how I tried to justify it, was selfish. Mitch's daughter had a mom and a dad. If I didn't go back, she and Rita would never see him again.

Pony, Spike, and Beak were still moaning on the ground when I returned. Mitch sat on the dock staring out at the water. He turned around at the sound of my footsteps and tilted his head toward the spot beside him. I scrambled over the planks and took a seat.

Mitch kept his gaze on the water. He folded his hands in his lap, and the stiffness melted from his shoulders. "I wondered if you'd come back."

I shrugged. "I wouldn't leave you here. You wouldn't have left me." I guess my first impressions of him were spot on. "It's time to catch my bus, Mitch."

Mitch nodded. "Right. But first, there's something I want to show you."

I groaned. A simple trip to Niagara Falls had become the adventure of my life, but I was done with it. "I've seen enough. I want to go home."

He squeezed my shoulder. "You will. One last slip. And then you can go home."

I handed the Dial and the stone to Mitch. He slid the Dial into place, took my hand and slipped us into time and space.

When the light returned, we stood in what I assumed was someone's backyard. The house was one level, and the yard was small, but there were a couple of trees and some lawn furniture. If this was the future, it didn't look too bad.

"Come on," Mitch said.

I followed him into the house. Rita sat in the kitchen next to a girl about ten or eleven years old. The girl had Rita's smile and her father's dark brown eyes.

Rita took my hands in hers. Did I mention she had warm hands? "Welcome, Carlos. This is our daughter, Ava."

Ava gave a shy wave.

Rita said, "C'mon. We've got something to show you."

She led me down a hallway. Ava ran ahead and stopped at a girl's bedroom, complete with all the pink stuff girls like. The room across from hers had gray walls, a desk, and a chest of drawers. A bookcase filled with books and a set of polished ammonite bookends covered one wall, but the solitary bed stood out. Was all that space for one person?

Mitch stood behind Rita. "We don't have baseball, but there's plenty of rocks in the yard. And Ava could use a big brother. So, what do you think? Could this be home?"

Rule Number One was toast. "No more slipping, right?"

Mitch said, "No more slipping."

Rita and Ava hugged me. I never thought about having a sister, but Ava smelled a lot better than the Shuster Home boys. I hugged them back. Mitch tousled my hair, then wrapped his arms around the three of us.

I didn't need to catch a bus after all. I was home.

The Stench of Freedom

written by
Joel C. Scoberg

illustrated by
JOHN BARLOW

ABOUT THE AUTHOR

Joel C. Scoberg lives on the beautiful Gower Peninsula in Wales, United Kingdom, with his very supportive wife, two somewhat feral children, and a growing menagerie of animals. He predominantly writes science fiction and fantasy stories, usually at night after his children have gone to bed and before he collapses from exhaustion. His stories have appeared in Daily Science Fiction, Gwyllion Science Fiction and Fantasy, 365tomorrows, *and* Every Day Fiction.

Joel's love of science fiction and fantasy goes back further than his earliest memories. Starting with The NeverEnding Story, *which he watched so many times as a toddler he wore out the video, to his family's Christmas tradition of watching the original* Star Wars *trilogy back to back, and then discovering* The Hobbit *on a caravan holiday as a teenager and reading it, utterly mesmerized, in one sitting. He hopes to one day write a story that will equally enthrall a reader and make them fall in love with fantastical characters that, currently, only exist in his head.*

"The Stench of Freedom" was inspired by the transformational perspective that becoming a parent brings. Joel had long dreamed of becoming a writer, but pursuing a career in law and the long hours that entailed, as well as the fear of ridicule for putting something so personal as your own creation into the world, acted as excuses not to follow those dreams. Then, when his children were born, he realized he could hardly tell them to pursue their dreams if he hadn't done so himself.

ABOUT THE ILLUSTRATOR

John Barlow is an illustrator and educator creating rich illustrations with a focus on storytelling. A Minnesota resident, John was raised on fairy tales, fiction, and forests. He's strongly inspired by golden age illustrators like N. C. Wyeth and Arthur Rackham, as well as many contemporary illustrators.

Each illustration is an exercise in atmosphere and texture, creating a world you can easily get lost in. John tells stories with a variety of clients in both the tabletop-gaming industry and fantasy publishing. When he's not drawing, he enjoys cooking, biking, sleeping, and taking unnecessarily complicated reference photos.

The Stench of Freedom

Hywel Arfon twirled his Earth rod as he strolled along Station Avenue with Nine-six on his heels, his grim shadow dressed head to toe in white. The broad thoroughfare was packed with the lunchtime rush of well-heeled shoppers and dour men in flat caps, all of whom scattered to clear a path for him. Hywel crossed the cobbled road, pausing to let a horse-drawn omnibus *clip-clop* past, then strode towards Copperton's fog-shrouded generating station. A tangle of cables buzzed overhead and spread out from the great red-brick building, just one section of the vast web across the city of Inglebad. As he approached the station, the orb atop the coiled wooden rod crackled with tiny streaks of lightning captured from the static in the air.

"After this inspection, I will check on my wife. The baby is due any time now," said Hywel. He straightened his tie before knocking on the station's weathered copper door, which was adorned with a spoked wheel in white-gold filigree; the wheel of Taranis, god of the Lightning element and symbol of the Electricity Commission. Hywel glanced back at Nine-six. His battery was as silent as ever. Whatever expression it had was hidden behind its ghoulish blank mask, and its pure-white eyes gave away nothing either.

The station door swung open in a waft of warm air, and a freckled young woman in overalls peered out. Her brown eyes grew as wide as saucers as she took in Hywel's emerald eyes, tweed suit, Earth rod, and red rubber boots. And with Nine-six behind him, there was no mistaking who he was, but protocol was protocol.

JOHN BARLOW

"Hywel Arfon from the Earthers' Guild. I am here to audit your generator." He flashed his badge, which bore a daffodil flower for Blodeuwedd, the goddess of the Earth element, then handed his staff to Nine-six, feeling suddenly vulnerable as he did so, as if one arm was tied behind his back. The orb atop his Earth rod ceased crackling immediately in the battery's grip. "Please show me to the bolt box and inform the Master Engineer of my presence."

"Y-Y-Yes, of course. Right this way, s-sir." She glanced at Nine-six. "And will he...?"

"It will wait outside. Don't worry, my battery is well-trained," Hywel winked as he stepped inside, "it won't do anything without my permission."

Beyond a panelled reception was a dimly lit, stuffy warehouse; machines buzzed and clanged and the caustic smell of engine fumes caught in his throat. Hywel knew little about how it all worked and cared less. All that mattered to him was the generator inside the bolt box at the centre of it all.

Hywel approached the copper-coated dome and opened its viewing hatch, stifling a retch at the sharp stench of sweat that smacked him in the face. Inside, the station's generator sat strapped to a scorched, high-backed chair. The skeletal creature wore a sweat-stained vest and a copper helmet covered its face, obscuring all but its pure-white eyes. A little smile tugged at Hywel's lips. He had caught and earthed this sparky himself. It was satisfying to know it had all worked out.

Someone cleared their throat behind him and he stepped away from the bolt box. A squat woman in filthy overalls glared at him. She looked as tough as old leather and her expression could have curdled milk.

"I'm Marla, the Master Engineer," said the woman in a tone as friendly as her appearance. "I was not informed of an audit today, Earther...?"

"Hywel Arfon. And, well, that is the point of a surprise audit. But do not be concerned. I am carrying out surprise audits of all generating stations in Inglebad."

"The Electricity Commissioner has signed off on this?"

The incredulity in Marla's voice rankled Hywel. "She does not have to. That generator is Guild property and I act on Grandmaster Fotheringham's authority. The Commissioner need only worry herself about the state of your transmission infrastructure."

Marla narrowed her Taranis-touched grey eyes. The white flecks inside looked about ready to spark, though she managed a smile as she answered. "Of course. I trust you are happy with what you've seen? Our generator's reliable, she has one of the lowest blackout rates in the city."

"*It* looks fine to me but looks can be deceiving. I need to see it in operation."

"Is that necessary?" Marla scowled but her tone turned pleading, and she resorted to invoking the primal pantheon, as if that'd sway him. "I swear by the Elements, I'd have reported any issues. And shock-starts risk burning her out."

"It is just a generator. It can be replaced. In fact, I will personally find you a replacement."

"A sudden power surge could overheat the grid, blackout the whole Copperton district."

"Trust me." Hywel gave his most reassuring smile—not the easiest thing to pull off under the circumstances. "I'd rather be out hunting rogue sparkies, making the streets safe and all that, but my wife is due to give birth any day now. I am being kept local." And the timing couldn't have been worse. With just a week to year's end, Clarence Rochester had leapfrogged him into first place in the Guild's league table. Promotion to a recently vacated office of First Earther awaited the winner, so this audit assignment was the last thing he needed. "I want to be here as little as you want me here. I just need a little shock, then I will be out of your hair."

Marla wrung her grease-stained hands. "I won't take the fall for any blackouts."

"I am not asking you to."

Marla sighed then pulled a lever on the side of the bolt box.

The air buzzed with static and Hywel's skin tingled all over. A loud *crack* sounded, like a peal of thunder, and he turned back to the viewing hatch. The generator thrashed against its restraints. Earthworm-like tendons jutted out of its neck. It screamed a blood-curdling howl before lightning bolts crackled from its body, ricocheting off the copper walls to create a light as bright as the midday sun. The dial on the bolt box's meter bounced hard against maximum watts.

"Happy?" Marla shouted over the tremendous racket.

Hywel nodded and Marla pushed up the lever.

As quickly as it started, the lightning stopped and the generator slumped against its restraints. Wisps of grey smoke rose from its body and, for a brief moment, a scent not unlike fried bacon tickled Hywel's nostrils. His stomach rumbled and he thought of grabbing lunch.

"We done here?" Marla looked about ready to punch him, so Hywel gave her a thumbs up and left her to attend the generator. How anyone could have a bond with those creatures was beyond him.

"Excuse me, sir." The freckled young woman approached Hywel and handed him a small square of paper. "A telegram just arrived for you."

IRONHOLME DISTRICT BLACKOUT ROGUE SPARKY SUSPECTED STOP
APPREHEND AT ONCE ANY FORCE PERMITTED STOP
GRANDMASTER FOTHERINGHAM END

Hywel smiled. This was more like it. He lived in Ironholme. He'd capture the sparky, peg back Rochester on the leaderboard, then pop in for a cup of tea with his wife, Sian. Lovely.

Hywel squinted as his eyes readjusted to daylight. The brisk breeze was a refreshing tickle on his cheeks and it carried with it the smell of fish and chips from a nearby shop.

"A successful audit, sir?" Nine-six's soft voice, seldom used, cut through the air like the sound of ripping paper. It held out Hywel's Earth rod.

Hywel took it and a tickling sensation rushed up his arm from his fingertips as he reconnected with the coiled wooden staff. Instinctively, his mind branched out and he felt Blodeuwedd's power blossom inside him. He turned the rod in his hands and it uncoiled into snaking vines before reforming at his command. Hywel grinned. He was whole again. "Yes. But there is a change of plan. There is a sparky on the loose in Ironholme."

"I thought as much." Nine-six pointed to a dark bruise in the thick white clouds smothering the skyline. "I've watched the storm clouds gather as though summoned by Taranis himself, and lightning strike the rooftops—a dozen forks at a time. They are a powerful elemental. We must exercise caution, perhaps call for support. Another earther, even a pair of blockheads."

"No." Hywel shook his head. He wouldn't share this prize, and he was far too skilled to call upon the Guild's army of non-elemental thugs. "We must exercise *haste*. Otherwise, Rochester will steal this one from me. Beating me to First Earther means more to him than anything."

"Even apprehending the Undergrid?"

"Well, probably not that." Hywel had to concede the point. Clarence Rochester was many things—few of which were pleasant—but his zealous obsession with rooting out the criminal gang of sparkies was greater than even Hywel's. "Still, I cannot afford to lose this sparky to him."

Hywel left the generating station behind and soon passed Copperton Sanitorium and Respite Park. He crossed a bridge over a canal choked with narrowboats travelling between the factories in the north and the port in the south, then turned into a maze of red-brick tenements where grubby children played in unpaved roads and tired mothers chatted on their doorsteps.

Eventually, Hywel found himself in the more salubrious side of Ironholme, walking along tree-lined streets of pale townhouses he knew only too well. He turned onto Lavender Row and as his boots trod their usual way home, a sense of unease formed in the pit of his stomach, heralding doom like some primordial beast emerging from its dark den. He picked up his pace as jagged thoughts tumbled through his mind; was the sparky a neighbour, previously hidden in plain sight, or, perish the thought, a sparky come seeking vengeance? He burst into a sprint, leaving Nine-six behind.

Dark rumbling clouds loomed menacingly above Hywel's ivy-covered home. The hairs on his neck stood on end, his skin tingled, and he knew without doubt the rogue sparky was inside. He raced up the steps and tried the door. Unlocked. He uncoiled his Earth rod into vicious vines, then stormed inside his house.

A pile of bloody towels lay on the tiled floor at the foot of the staircase. The foreign stench of medicinal herbs lingered in the hallway. No one was in the living room, nor the kitchen beyond it, though a great iron pot sat on the hob bubbling. More towels, but clean and white, lay piled in a wicker basket before it. This wasn't a break-in. But his relief was temporary. "Sian?"

Heavy footsteps drummed above the ceiling. Hywel let his mind take root in the clematis wrapped around the upstairs bannister. His bedroom door creaked open and, through the plant, he saw a portly man rush out onto the landing. The man's blood-red eyes matched his tunic: a healer, blessed by Arianrhod, the goddess of the element Fate. "Earther Arfon?"

"My wife…" Hywel worked moisture back into his mouth. "Is she well?"

"It was a most trying delivery. A lesser healer would not have saved her." The man's tone was not boastful, then it took a sombre tone. "But, the baby…"

"Do they live?"

The healer's expression betrayed his concern. "You had better come upstairs, sir."

Drawn curtains left the bedroom in gloom. Sian lay on their bed propped up by pillows. Her eyes were closed, her face was as white as the bedsheets, and her mousey hair was slick with sweat. More bloody towels lay piled on the cream carpet. Hywel rushed to his wife and gently stroked her forehead. "Sian, are you all right?"

"Hywel?" Sian's voice trembled as she opened her eyes, her pain and exhaustion plain, but she managed a weak smile. "We have a son. I've called him Elwyn."

"Elwyn…" Hywel returned her smile and for the briefest moment he was as happy as he had ever been. His mind flowered with visions of taking his son to play in Respite Park. Then, his brain put all the moving parts together and his joy and excitement died, replaced with cold dread. He leant into the cot and picked up his child, who fit snugly inside his suddenly clumsy hands. All he wanted was to hold this perfect little being to his chest and celebrate with his wife. But he couldn't. Not until he knew the truth. "Hello, Elwyn." His voice broke and his heart thundered in his chest. "I am your daddy."

Elwyn woke up with a stretch, chubby arms breaking through a soft muslin cocoon, and a pair of pure-white eyes stared up at Hywel.

"No…" Hywel's legs gave out and he slumped onto the bed. He held Elwyn against his shoulder, fighting back tears as he tried to bury the thoughts of what he must do, and the grim future that awaited his son.

"Isn't he handsome?" said Sian, her voice thick with pride and denial.

"He is…" Hywel frowned. "But his eyes…how can this be? There's no sign of Taranis in either of us, nothing to suggest we're aligned to Lightning. By the Elements, I'm an earther!"

"I don't know. It shouldn't be possible." Sian's brown eyes were like a pair of smooth wet river stones. "When the contractions started, I felt this power surging through me. It grew stronger and stronger." A tear broke loose and spilled onto her cheek. "I thought I was going to die, Hywel. I thought our son was going to die."

"I am sorry I was not there for you." He held her clammy hand and focussed his mind not on the turmoil ahead but on that moment with his wife and newborn son. Their first as a family. Elwyn gurgled in the crook of his arm, and he leant back so Sian could see him. "You did wonderfully, my darling, I am so proud of you."

Sian wiped her cheek and her beautiful eyes locked on his—those eyes which had first stolen his attention, then his heart. "You're going to take him from me, aren't you?"

Hywel's tongue stumbled for a response but she beat him to it.

"You are! He's *our* son, Hywel."

"It is the law," he said, but without any of his usual conviction.

"The gallows await me if I don't, or worse if I resist. Even if I delay, I will be dismissed—"

"Of course, it's about you. It always is." Sian shook her head and looked at him like he was dog mess smeared beneath her shoe. "I offered my life to the Elements during labour. I begged them to save Elwyn and take me instead. I was willing to die for our son. Yet you think only of yourself and your precious job. You are a coward, Hywel." Disgust dripped from Sian's tongue and each word lashed him, leaving him raw and ashamed. She glanced beyond his shoulder. "Oh look, your pet has come to snatch away one of his own."

Hywel turned. Nine-six stood in the doorway. A malevolent white statue set against the verdant backdrop of sweet-smelling honeysuckle cascading up the wall. Its presence suddenly made his nightmare real. Even worse, it held up a mirror to Hywel's role in the events of that morning. It showed him as he truly was. And what he saw horrified him.

The generator inside the bolt box. Thrashing and screaming as lightning surged from its skeletal body. The charred wooden chair. Its ragged clothes. The smell of fried bacon. The pain he'd inflicted on that creature—no, not a *creature*. A *person*. A living breathing human. The thoughts he had buried a moment ago resurfaced, exposing the rotten roots upon which he had built his life. One day that generator could be Elwyn. One day, he could torture his own son. A flood of emotions—shame, fear, anger—threatened to swallow him. He clutched Elwyn to his chest. "Stay back."

Nine-six flinched. "I have been your loyal servant for a decade, sir." His battery's soft voice sounded not hurt, but surprised. Disappointed, even. "I have obeyed all your commands, irrespective of my own feelings. I shall continue to do so." Nine-six closed the oak door behind him. "*Whatever* it is you instruct me to do."

Hywel stared dumbly at Nine-six. His brain moved slower than a narrowboat through Inglebad's canals. Surely, Nine-six was not suggesting what he thought he was? Hywel could have his battery put down. But...*would* he? Nine-six was offering to help, at great personal risk. And Hywel was hardly in a position to refuse. He opened his mouth to speak, a thank-you lodged in his mouth, an apology caught in his throat. "I-I don't know what to say...."

Elwyn cried and the air crackled with static, interrupting Hywel's thoughts. His son's little face turned red as he bawled and the high-pitched sound activated Hywel's primal instincts to protect him. Stabbing pinpricks lanced Hywel's arms as tiny blue-white lightning bolts fired from his son's skin, leaving him in no doubt how powerful his son already was. Nine-six stepped closer, absorbing the static. Hywel cradled Elwyn in his arms, rocking and hushing him as best he could, though feeling as useful as a chocolate teapot. For the first time, he truly *saw* his son; chubby cheeks, a little round nose above full lips, and a dimple in his chin just like Hywel. Elwyn was so small, so helpless, so innocent, and yet so valuable to the Earthers' Guild.

"Earther Arfon." The healer knocked on the bedroom door. "Can I come in? It likely needs a feed."

Hywel's jaw clamped shut. *It.* Such a small word had never carried so much force. And to hear the word directed at his own son, the one he had used so readily against other sparkies, was like a punch to the gut. Without thinking, Hywel's mind reached out to the white-flowered honeysuckle on his bedroom wall. He felt himself take root and, as though an extension of his own arm, the thin vines snaked across to the door's brass handle, strangling it.

"I shall not give him up," Hywel spoke in a hurried whisper. He glanced at Sian and would forever cherish the look of joy and love she gave him, her smile wider than on their wedding day. It reminded him of what was truly important in life, what he had to fight for, and what he stood to lose. "We need to get out of Inglebad. Then make our way out of the country, to someplace where Elwyn can have a proper life."

"Easier said than done, sir." Nine-six cleared his throat. "Once word gets out a Lightning elemental is on the loose, the city will be crawling with earthers and blockheads. Especially when it's known he is your son. Our only hope is the Undergrid."

"The *Undergrid!*" Hywel baulked. Trusting Nine-six with Elwyn's life was one thing, but the Undergrid? "Are you mad? Even if I could contact them, as if I would entrust my son to that gang of criminals."

"Earther Arfon?" The healer banged louder and tried the door, but the vines held it closed. "I must insist that you let me in."

Hywel's mind untwined the vines from the handle. "The door is open."

The healer hurried inside. "I delayed in taking it to the Sanitorium earlier, out of courtesy to your position. But it belongs with my Order. We shall provide for it before it is transferred to the care of your Guild."

It. Hywel snarled and spoke through his teeth. "I am familiar with protocol. But *he* is my son and I will deliver *him* there myself."

"I do not think that is wise, sir." The healer's tone—firm but not unkind—carried a solemn empathy. "It'll be harder once a bond forms."

"Remember to whom you are speaking." Hywel straightened his back. The act fortified his resolve, but not more than the feel of Elwyn's warm little hand gripping his finger. "Watch you do not overstep your role."

The healer narrowed his red eyes at Hywel. "And watch you do not neglect yours."

"I will feed him." Sian interrupted the tense standoff. She held out her arms and Hywel passed her Elwyn. "Healer Gorrick, please would you be so kind as to fetch the bottles of boiled cow's milk you mentioned earlier? In case Elwyn does not latch."

The healer glanced between Sian and Hywel, his experience of these situations no doubt setting off alarm bells in his mind. Nevertheless, he left without a word and Nine-six closed the door behind him.

"We don't have much time," said Hywel. "Maybe an hour before the Guild comes knocking. We"—Hywel caught himself—"*they* don't wait around once a healer reports a newborn sparky. Less, if Gorrick used the telegraph in our hall."

"I suspect he sent a telegram before we even arrived, sir. Healer Gorrick strikes me as an officious—"

Bells chimed downstairs, followed swiftly by the front-door knocker clanging.

The blood drained from Hywel's face. He ran to the bedroom window and slid up the lower pane, letting light and sounds flood inside; the mumbling hubbub of the city, and a motorised carriage honking its horn as it chugged along the street outside. Down below, a gangly man in an ink-black suit stood at Hywel's front door, flanked by two white-suited figures. Both wore the same blank-white mask as Nine-six, but one wore a suit covered in inch-long pins crackling with static charge.

Hywel ducked back inside before he was spotted. "It's Rochester, and he's got a shocker too."

They'd been sent to bury him. A summary execution. He knew the protocol for apprehending rogue earthers and sparkies—he'd been the Guild's go-to man for years: overwhelming force and no mercy. Not even four months ago, he'd buried Remi Kuval, not just a fellow earther, but a good friend. He shuddered at the memory. He couldn't risk Sian and Elwyn getting caught up in that. They were in no condition to make a run for it and there wasn't time to sneak downstairs and head out the back. At least, not without Gorrick telling Rochester where they went.

"Sian, gather what we need for Elwyn, pack as light as possible. Nine-six, stand guard in here and do not let that shocker near my family." Hywel had no idea what kind of Lightning elemental Elwyn was; either he'd absorb lightning like Nine-six, or he'd channel it. The risk of Elwyn reacting to the shocker and frying himself and Sian was too much to think about. He turned to leave then stopped, and kissed Sian and Elwyn for what he hoped was not the last time. "I love you."

"Sir, are you sure about this?"

He'd hang for assaulting an earther, that is, if he survived long enough to reach the gallows. But as he looked at his wife and newborn son, Hywel knew there was only one decision he could live with. For however long that might be. "Nine-six, whatever happens, protect my family," he said. "And...thank you." Then he picked up his Earth rod and slipped out the door.

Hywel tip-toed to the washroom off the landing and hid inside the linen closet. A moment later, he heard the healer open the front door and direct Rochester and his sparkies upstairs.

"Arfon is dangerous, keep alert," Rochester growled above the creaking stairs. "I don't want you mongrels ruining this for me."

The washroom door inched open. Hywel held his breath. He spied Rochester through the wooden slats in the linen closet's door. The man's neat grey beard and tailored suit oozed sophistication but when he moved, Rochester's sharp features and loping gait left a rather wolfish impression.

"You can't hide, Arfon. Come out, come out, wherever you are." Rochester moved on, and tapped his Earth rod on the bannister, the knocks muffled by the thick clematis. "I'm taking that bleach-eyed sprog of yours where it belongs."

It. The word set off Hywel's temper like a starting pistol. He cracked his neck. Then, as quietly as he could, he pushed open the linen closet's door. On the landing, Rochester sauntered towards the master bedroom, sandwiched between his shocker at the rear and his battery at the front.

Hywel held his Earth rod before him and set his feet. His mind extended to the clematis on the bannister as his Earth rod unwound into powerful vines. Sensing elemental magic, Rochester and the sparkies turned. A wicked smile hooked Rochester's lip, revealing yellowed teeth.

The time for words had passed.

The clematis's grasping tendrils leapt from the bannister, swarming the intruders, blocking their path to the master bedroom and separating the shocker from the others. Rochester deflected the clematis but the battery was consumed. Vines shot from Hywel's Earth rod, wrapping around the shocker's throat and chest, crushing him. The shocker's hands scrabbled at the vines but with each one torn away, another two replaced it. Gurgling and gasping for air, the shocker changed tack. He lifted his arms and unleashed a surge of lightning towards Hywel.

Blindingly bright, ice-white bolts struck Hywel's Earth rod with a ferocious clap. The wooden staff thrashed and kicked in his grip as it diverted the crackling energy into the tiled floor. But there was too much. Jagged forks of lightning whipped and slashed his body, burning the flesh from his bones despite his natural resistance. He clamped his jaw shut and closed his eyes. The primal urge to save Elwyn sustained him, as did knowing the shocker would burn out if he kept up this attack.

Moments passed—it could have been seconds, minutes, the pain blinded Hywel to the passage of time. Then the lightning stopped. The air throbbed with static and acrid smoke stung his nostrils. Leaning heavily on his Earth rod, which now crackled with bright-blue lightning inside its clear orb, Hywel opened his eyes just as the shocker slumped to the ground in a sizzling heap.

Without hesitation, Rochester leapt over the shocker's body. Snarling, with yellowed teeth bared, he lunged at Hywel, swinging his staff. Hywel barely managed to raise his own in time to parry the blow. Their rods collided with a cacophonous clap. Rochester reeled back but Hywel's rod clattered onto the landing.

Hywel charged at Rochester and smacked the staff from the man's hands. He was shorter than Rochester but broader and stronger, and more desperate. He threw punches, a headbutt, an elbow; landing no clean blows but plenty that made Rochester groan.

Rochester smothered Hywel in a boxer's clinch and kneed him in the thigh, the chest. Hywel dropped his shoulder and shoved Rochester against the wall. He threw a punch, missed, and Rochester grabbed him again. They cursed and growled as they wrestled.

Rochester's thumb gouged his eye. Hywel flinched and covered his face. The instinctive response created an opportunity. Rochester kicked Hywel in the chest and he staggered back. Then, with a predatory grin, Rochester picked up Hywel's crackling Earth rod and speared him.

The captured lightning exploded. Hywel flew backwards in an explosion of white-hot static. He landed heavily on the tiled floor. The air thumped from his lungs. His burned and battered body screamed in pain. Hywel rolled over and crawled to the bath beneath the washroom window, gripping the edges of the tub to drag himself to his feet.

"It's over, Arfon." Rochester blocked the doorway and wiped blood from his nose as two white-suited figures stepped behind him; Rochester's battery and Nine-six, who held Elwyn in his arms.

"We've got your precious spark-spawn and it doesn't look good for you either. Going rogue and assaulting an earther, *tsk tsk*. Grandmaster Fotheringham will be most disappointed when I tell him 'Prince Hywel' has betrayed us."

"Jealous until the end, Clarence." Hywel snorted at his rival's pettiness. "I have made my bed, I alone. Sian had nothing to do with it."

"She's not my concern. Although, the Guild are always after surrogates." Rochester grinned then clicked his fingers. "Eleven-five, take that... *creature* downstairs. I won't be long."

"Sir," Nine-six piped up. "I think it will be safest if I take the child. He has already bonded to me."

"You hear that? Not an ounce of loyalty in these white-eyed freaks, not even to their own." Rochester chuckled. It sounded like stones shaken in a paper bag. "I don't care who takes it in."

Hywel glared at Nine-six. Maybe this was his way of paying Hywel back for years of mistreatment. It didn't much matter now. He deserved his fate but his son did not. Elwyn was innocent, pure. But there was nothing Hywel could do. He was outnumbered and outmanoeuvred. He couldn't see any way to save Elwyn now. The only chance to save his son was by first saving himself. He stepped back into the bath.

"Hand yourself in peacefully now. Never know, may save your life."

"Same lie I told Kuval." Speaking his friend's name aloud dug up the grisly memory Hywel had tried to bury in the dark depths of his mind. Kuval wouldn't bond with a young sparky that was the same age as his own daughter. He'd lost his nerve, gone soft, allowed the sparky to escape the Guild's control, so Hywel buried him. The Guild could not abide weakness. Strength and fear kept the sparkies beneath their heel. No bonded sparkies, no lightning. No lightning, no electricity. Inglebad would grind to a halt, factories would close or, worse, move elsewhere. The Guild would have failed. That could not be allowed to happen. Weakness was death. "You won't let me leave here alive."

"No." Rochester cracked his knuckles and stepped forwards. "I've dreamed of this moment."

Hywel spun, slid up the sash window and rolled outside, just as a vine smashed through the glass. He dropped onto the flat roof of the kitchen below then rolled off the edge. He landed in a heap, then crawled into a run. His body ached down to his marrow and his skin burned where it rubbed his clothes. Yet, he pushed his body to its limit. He dashed across his small garden and clambered over the back wall into his neighbour's garden. He glanced back towards his house, expecting pursuit.

Instead, Rochester watched him from the washroom window. A faint smile cracked his lupine face before he turned away.

After Rochester disappeared inside, Hywel cut across his neighbours' gardens, scaling walls and pushing through bushes, while looking for a passage out onto the street. "Think, Hywel," he muttered, urging his brain to come up with a plan.

One of the gardens had washing on the line. He kicked off his red rubber boots, slipped off his tweed trousers, jacket, and waistcoat—now was not the time to be declaring himself an earther—then tossed them in a bush before he unpegged a pair of plum corduroy trousers and a thick mustard and brown cable-knit jumper. The trousers were too big and the jumper drowned him. He'd never be seen dead in such ill-fitting clothes. But, perhaps that wasn't such a bad thing. He stuck his boots on and grabbed the money clip from his old jacket before he dashed off.

Protocol dictated Elwyn would go to the nearest Sanitorium, which was in Copperton. They'd keep him there for some time before the Guild collected him, Sian, too, but he didn't know how long. Days, weeks, months? It usually depended on the sparky's age. A thought crossed his mind; what if they made an exception in this case? Sometimes they did, if the sparky was particularly dangerous. He'd taken sparkies straight to Grove Tower, the Guild's headquarters, though they'd all been adults, the youngest maybe fifteen. Never a baby. Elemental alignments usually occurred in puberty, even later if triggered by a traumatic event. Babies born already able to summon the lightning of Taranis were rare and incredibly valuable.

And could he even break them out? Sanitoriums were designed

to keep sparkies in. They weren't dancehalls one could walk in and out of freely. The loss of his Earth rod smarted; he felt weaker. Each rod was unique to an earther, constructed over months of torturous training. It provided a focal point to channel Blodeuwedd's power, a conduit for the enormous elemental energy at his fingertips. It was simply irreplaceable. He was only ever without it inside a generating station; that much concentrated lightning in the atmosphere could damage it. Without it, he was incomplete.

"Go with your gut," Hywel told himself. "They'll take him to Copperton Sanitorium. Figure out a plan to break them out on the way. You are strong enough. You have to be."

If he was Rochester, he would put eyes on the ends of his road. Hywel had to find a different route. An unexpected one. Though it galled him he tried a few back doors until one opened. As quick as he could, he strode through a cosy kitchen that smelled of toast and freshly brewed tea, along a narrow hall tiled in an eye-jarring mosaic pattern, and out of the front door. Without breaking step, he jogged down the front steps and across the road, turning off onto another street then another, putting as much distance as he could between himself and his home before emerging onto Ironholme's main thoroughfare.

It was easy enough to lose oneself on King's Road. It was about as busy a road as you'd find in Inglebad outside the very heart of the city. Hywel mingled with the crowd and allowed the rush of noise to swallow him whole; mothers pushing babies in perambulators, men talking politics or business, children gawking at shopfronts and begging for whatever shiny knickknack was behind the glass, food stalls and shoe shines, business folk in tailored suits and workers in overalls.

A young paperboy shouted himself hoarse trying to flog his last copies. Hywel tossed the boy a copper and tucked the paper under his arm, then stopped at a bakery to buy two corned-beef pasties. His stomach growled for the warm, greasy contents inside the paper bag, and he hoped the purchases would help him disappear in the crowd. The Guild would be on high alert by now, with all available earthers and blockheads on the hunt. But they'd be looking for Earther Hywel

Arfon—well-dressed, desperate and dangerous—not some worker in ill-fitting clothes taking a late afternoon lunch break.

The *clip-clop* of shod hooves and a sharp jingling brought him to attention and he weaved through the crowd towards the approaching omnibus with his hand raised. The driver brought the horse-drawn carriage to a halt and Hywel hopped onto the back, slipping the brown-liveried conductor two copper coins. There were no free seats so he stood in the aisle, breathing in the thick fog of tobacco smoke as he ate his pasties, grateful for the anonymity amongst the chatter of those aboard.

The omnibus plodded along King's Road, stopping and starting at regular intervals. At each stop, Hywel risked a glance outside and at those climbing aboard, half-expecting to see a tweed-clad earther and their battery, or a street-tough blockhead. But of course, he didn't. It would be a waste of resources to ask even the dull-witted blockheads to randomly roam the streets. When he had led search parties, he had posted earthers to the railway stations and main checkpoints out of Inglebad, as well as the sparky's home and place of work. Occasionally, the port if there was some connection, but rarely: the Port and Canals Authority distrusted sparkies as much as the Guild.

When the omnibus finally crossed over the canal bridge into Copperton, Hywel hopped off a few streets down from the Sanitorium and entered the back of Respite Park.

The trees were that wonderful autumn mix of gold, orange, and red amongst the evergreens. Paved paths snaked across immaculate lawns lined with vibrant flowers and painted benches. A soft breeze carried the sweet smells of wild garlic and jasmine, and children laughed as they played. He held his face up to the sky and took a few deep breaths, drawing strength and energy from the green oasis around him and the weak sunlight filtering through the smothering clouds. He could almost feel the burns and aches in his body fade as Blodeuwedd's gifts refreshed and reinvigorated him. It was almost enough to make up for the loss of his Earth rod. Well, it would have to be.

Hywel watched the children play for a moment, wondering if

Elwyn would ever get that chance to be wild and carefree. But now was not the time to get emotional, so he pushed all thoughts except plans of attack from his mind as he made his way across the sprawling park towards the Sanitorium.

Hywel watched the comings and goings of Copperton Sanitorium from a bench inside Respite Park, his eyes peering over the top of his newspaper. It was as grand and formidable a building as its name suggested. Built from great blocks of ruddy stone, each as tall as a man and an arm-span wide, it towered above the buildings either side of it, projecting an ominous power like a wolf amongst a pack of dogs. Long narrow windows set with iron bars betrayed its more sinister role as a holding centre for sparkies before the Earthers' Guild claimed them.

Two blockheads stood either side of the entrance in the shadows of twisted granite columns. They were a real rough-looking pair of brutes in green shirts, with not a straight nose between them, and both experts in breaking skulls with the wooden batons at their waists. The taller one smoked a pipe, nodding at whatever it was the other said to him, while occasionally eyeing up someone on their way in. Hywel's stomach churned. Without his Earth rod, he stood little chance of getting past them.

A youngish woman pushing a pram stopped and sat next to him. She wore an ankle-length plaid dress, and her blonde hair, perfumed with lavender, was tied up in an elaborate plait. She huffed and sighed as if she wanted to make conversation. Hywel smiled but otherwise paid her no mind, hoping she'd take the hint and move on.

"Strange weather this afternoon," she said at last, rolling her *r*'s and stretching her vowels in an accent he couldn't quite place. "Quite the storm we had."

"Storms are pretty common in Inglebad."

"Yeah? Probably one of those Lightning elementals, eh? Causing the storm, I mean."

"Indeed," he said, though he felt compelled to distort what had really happened. "Most likely a generating station firing up."

"Is that so? And what about that miserable-looking building over there, then? Is that where they take them, is it? The little ones. Terribly sad, wouldn't you say?"

Hywel turned to the woman, who held his stare without blinking. She had Taranis-touched eyes, brown with floating white flecks, a strong jaw and an aquiline nose that gave her a regal bearing. He glanced down at the pram. Inside was a child's doll, staring lifelessly towards the sky. A chill ran down his spine. He folded his newspaper and went to stand but she placed her hand firmly on his leg.

"Easy now, Earther Arfon. You will want to hear what I have to say."

The park suddenly felt darker, colder. Hywel swallowed what felt like an egg in his throat. "Who-who are you?"

"You can call me...Storm. Once your foe but maybe now your friend."

"You are from the Undergrid!" Hywel baulked at the brazenness of this woman. "I could have you arrested."

"Yes, you could." Storm smiled and spoke with rock-steady conviction. "But you won't. You wouldn't want to draw attention to yourself, would you? What would happen to Elwyn?"

Hywel bared his teeth and leant in but Storm didn't so much as flinch. "How do you know his name?"

"A mutual colleague sent me. The man you know as 'Nine-six.'"

"Nine-six? How is he your...?" The realisation struck him like a lightning bolt. "He is with the Undergrid."

"That he is. Now, bury your shock about this revelation for a moment and let's get down to it. Go to this address in the port before nine o'clock this evening." She held out a simple white business card and he took it without thinking, just surprised that the Undergrid worked out of the port. "There's a ship that leaves once a week, sometimes more. Join us and there'll be a space aboard for you, Sian, and Elwyn. We'll get you out of Inglebad's jurisdiction, where Elwyn will be safe."

Hywel shook his head but, suddenly, the sound of children laughing and playing seemed to become louder and louder. "Why are you telling me this? This information could bring down the Undergrid. The Guild would do anything to know this. It would probably save me from the gallows."

"It's a risk we've decided to accept," said Storm. "And, do you really believe the Guild will let you live? You, of all people, know their promises are empty. Say they do spare you, what then? In saving yourself you would condemn Sian and Elwyn to the most miserable, wretched existences imaginable. You know better than anyone what awaits them—"

"Don't." A heavy, suffocating dread pinned him to the bench. It squeezed the air from his lungs and left him as limp as a deflated balloon. "Please."

"Why should I not?" It was Storm's turn to bare her teeth at him and Hywel shrunk back. "This is the fate that *you* have inflicted on countless innocents. If you think it just, then why is it hard to hear?"

Hywel closed his eyes and said nothing. How could he?

"Having given birth to a pure Lightning elemental, that rarest and most valuable of children, Sian will become a surrogate for the Guild." Storm's mouth twisted as she said "surrogate" and the word stabbed Hywel, carving a vicious, cold cut through his heart. "And Elwyn? Nine-six said how powerful he is. No doubt he'll make a fine generator."

The image of the generator from that morning jolted into Hywel's mind. She thrashed and screamed beneath that cursed copper mask and he watched her suffer without a shred of remorse. *He* did that to her. And afterwards, all he had thought about was lunch. But now, the pasties in his stomach threatened to burst from his body and he felt nothing but shame.

"We have shared this information to convince you to trust us. We are sticking our necks in the noose here. This is a high-risk gamble. Elwyn is under guard like no other babe before him. Ordinarily, we wouldn't take the risk. There are many other innocents to be saved with far less risk to our operatives. His life and Sian's life are worth no more than any other. But we need someone like you, with your experience and knowledge. You'd be an asset to the struggle. And you need us."

"No." Hywel shook his head as the nature of this agreement resolved itself in his mind. Though he could see now, with painful clarity, the awful things he had done, jumping into bed with the

Undergrid was no way to redeem himself. "You are terrorists, criminals, agents of anarchy. You have murdered my colleagues, my friends, and politicians. Blown up buildings, killing and maiming innocents, destroyed railroads and the Elements know what else. I cannot trust you. I cannot *join* you. I cannot allow myself or my family to be beholden to the Undergrid. No, I shall free them myself."

Storm raised her eyebrows, surprise writ plain on her face. "Now is not the time to correct the falsehoods and propaganda you believe about us. But, so be it. You are the one who has to live with your decision. We tried to help you. Remember that." She stood, smoothed down her plaid dress then nodded towards the Sanitorium. "They are being held on the second floor, Ward S, room two. Your best bet is the mortuary entrance round the back, I'd say."

It took Hywel a few minutes to compose himself after Storm left. His hands trembled and an iron grip crushed his chest. His mind swirled from the questions and revelations Storm left him grappling with. But now was not the time to think it all through. Now was the time to rescue Sian and Elwyn. After a couple of deep breaths his chest loosened, then he got up and walked out of the park.

He didn't know whether to trust the tip-off about Sian and Elwyn's location. Then again, it was a better place to start than trying to hope he got lucky and just stumbled across them. And he could hardly stroll up to the reception desk and enquire. That is, if he even managed to get past the blockheads out front. So, he walked alongside the park's cast-iron railings to the end of the road, where Canal Street bisected the city north to south.

Hywel crossed the road behind a motorcar and walked purposefully down the side of the Sanitorium. A weather-beaten sign for the mortuary directed him down a muddy lane between two sections of the colossal building. It was damp and gloomy, the sun hidden behind the towering walls of the Sanitorium either side, and sounds blasted erratically through open windows; a high-pitched scream, shouting, arguing, moans, cries for medicine or help, and the unmistakable crackle of lightning. Suddenly those noises had a sinister edge and a heavy weight formed in his stomach. He picked up his pace.

The lane ended at a set of wood-and-glass doors, which were thrown open onto an ochre-tiled corridor. A pair of heavyset orderlies in grubby white uniforms chatted just outside the doors. Neither looked up as he walked inside.

Hywel didn't stop as he entered. He moved as if he belonged and knew where he was going, smiling and nodding at healers and nurses going about their shifts. He glanced at signs on the cream-painted walls and followed directions to the stairwell, which wound upwards for maybe ten floors. There was no movement in the stairwell, no sound at all. He climbed, his heart pounding with each step, and soon found himself on the second floor.

A white-tiled corridor stretched in both directions. Fixed to the wall in front of him, beside various posters for common ailments, was a large sign with arrows. To the left was Paediatrics (General) and Paediatrics (Theatre). To the right was Paediatrics (Burns) and Ward S. Hywel turned right.

The corridor was strangely quiet except for the steady *bzzz* from the electric lamps on the walls and his squeaking boots sounded like thunderclaps as he walked. At staggered intervals, little grey signs hung from the ceiling; the first said: "Paediatrics (Burns)." He walked to the next one, a hundred yards or so from the stairwell: "Ward S." Hywel leant against the wall and peered through the door's small glass windows.

A nurse's station faced the door. It was unattended. Hywel swallowed and crept inside on high alert. The ward branched off in two directions, with four rooms on either side, each with a little window. Muffled conversations took place behind closed doors and the faint smell of fried bacon lingered in the air from a half-eaten roll on the nurse's station. The smell turned his stomach, making him nauseous.

"Room two," he muttered, then broke into a grin. Through the small glass window on a door marked "2," he saw Sian rocking Elwyn in her arms. She turned, as if she sensed him nearby, and his grin vanished. Her eyes were saucers, terror-struck and bloodshot, and her face twisted in an anguished scream. The door opened.

"I hoped you'd stop by, Arfon." The pleasure in Rochester's voice was unbearable. He stepped in front of the door, blocking Hywel's view of Sian and Elwyn. Rochester had a nasty split lip and the start of a black eye but he otherwise looked as debonaire as ever. The featureless white mask of his battery hovered over Rochester's shoulder, a sight that was no longer just unsettling, but terrifying. "Sadly, visiting hours are over."

Hywel heard door handles turning either side of him. He glanced left. A shocker stepped into the corridor, short and petite. The air crackled around her and blue jolts hopped between the pins on her white suit. He glanced right. Two blockheads leered at him. One cracked the knuckles on his ham-sized fists, the other swiped his wooden baton through the air—*swish, swish*. They sauntered forwards, looking far too happy to see him.

It was hopeless. He knew it. Rochester knew it. Sian must know it too. There was no way he could overpower Rochester's gang alone, especially without his Earth rod. Hywel backed up to the door as the blockheads and shocker closed in.

"I love you," he shouted, then ran back into the corridor.

"Catch him," Rochester roared. "And dead is fine by me."

Hywel sprinted towards the stairwell, yelling at a bewildered healer to stand aside. By the time the blockheads' boots thundered behind him he had reached the doors to the Burns Ward. He risked a glance over his shoulder as he reached the stairwell and saw Rochester and the shocker in the hunting pack. Thankfully, the burly thugs blocked any clear view for the shocker to try and blast Hywel. Short of breath, Hywel shoved open the double doors.

A blockhead ran up the stairs towards him. "Got you—"

But Hywel reached the landing first. He kicked the blockhead in the chest, sending him tumbling back down the stairs. The oaf clambered shakily to his knees just in time for Hywel to knee him in the face, dropping him for a second time. The doors above him burst open and the blockheads hurtled down the stairs while the shocker stopped at the handrail.

A tingling across his skin warned him a moment before the bolt of lightning struck his back. He staggered forwards, the pain like being whipped with a belt. He grabbed hold of the handrail as he fell to his knees, just about saving himself from falling headfirst down the stairs. He got to his feet as the blockheads were nearly on him. His skin tingled and he leapt down the stairs, landing heavily on the ground.

The wall where he'd stood a moment ago was scorched black. The blockheads stared at each other, stunned and hesitant to press on in case the shocker fired another bolt of lightning. It was the pause Hywel needed. He scrambled to his feet and ran out into the Sanitorium's ground floor.

Behind him, Rochester yelled, "Get him, you cowards!"

Hywel retraced his steps. The presence of staff and patients gave the shocker no clear shot at him and the lumbering blockheads tired with each step and fell further behind. He smiled as he saw the exit into the lane. Though that faded as the two orderlies he'd seen earlier now blocked the doors. Their wicked smiles confirmed his fears: blockheads.

It was too late to stop. Rochester and his gang were behind him. The only way out was through those blockheads. Hywel charged at the brutes, his fists clenched and ready to strike, and roared a battlecry. But as he did so, his skin tingled. Instinctively, he threw himself against the wall.

A blue-white lightning bolt crackled past him, its heat prickling his cheeks, and struck one of the blockheads in the chest. The man went down with a yelp and his shirt caught alight. His partner stared, dumbfounded. Hywel pushed off the wall, recovering his balance, and punched the blockhead flush on the jaw. The man's head whipped to the side and his body followed as he twirled to the ground like a falling tree.

Hywel ran into the narrow lane, his lungs on fire and his legs begging for a rest. He pushed on. Once, a lightning bolt thumped into the walls of the Sanitorium above him. But not again. He guessed the shocker had run out of energy, or he was out of range. He cared not either way and dashed out of the lane, running headlong through traffic on Canal Street, over the grassy embankment on the other side, and down onto the towpath beside the canal.

A line of narrowboats laden with goods sailed south to the port.

Without breaking stride, he jumped onto the deck of the closest one. He crashed against a tarpaulin mound that did not yield an inch. With a dead arm and a groan, he climbed over the mound then crawled underneath the tarpaulin. A stack of steel girders lay beneath the khaki covering and he pressed against them as a gruff voice hollered.

A few moments later, beneath the edge of the tarpaulin, a pair of worn leather boots tramped across the deck. Hywel held his breath. "Damn kids," said the gruff voice, as the boots turned and went back to the captain's cabin. "Ain't got time for no pranks."

Hywel waited a few minutes, grateful for the chance to catch his breath, then fished the Undergrid's business card from his pocket. The white card claimed to be for a shipping company, its name and address spelled out in simple black letters. He turned the card between his fingers and realised he had already made up his mind. As if he had any other choice.

The narrowboat stopped too frequently for his liking as it navigated through the canal's extensive lock system. Hywel checked their progress each time. It was unbearably slow. And it gave him too much time to doubt what he was doing, and fear for his family's future. The afternoon trickled away into a cool, dark evening and across the city the electric streetlamps flickered on, throwing an orange haze above the rooftops. Finally, the narrowboat stopped at the largest lock of all into the Port of Inglebad. Hywel crawled from beneath the tarpaulin and hopped off. Behind him, he heard the captain yell but he didn't look back.

Unlike the rest of the city, there were no electric streetlamps in the port. Hywel walked amongst the shadows cast by large warehouses, keeping pace ahead of a lone Fire elemental firing up the port's traditional torches. The orange-cloaked disciple of Belenus bent over each round concrete basin and—*whoosh*—ignited a flickering flame, which burned without heat or fuel. It was far less effective than an electric streetlamp but, for once, Hywel was grateful for the deeply entrenched animosity towards electricity in these parts.

A strong wind blew from the darkness of the sea, salty and fresh, and Hywel wished for a thick coat to warm his bones as he walked along the wharves. Night had finally swallowed the city. Yet, even now, stevedores still cursed and yelled as they loaded cargo onto great steel ships bound for who knew where.

Hywel found the address on the card. It was a red-brick warehouse with a corrugated iron roof, one amongst a hundred all the same, set about halfway down the penultimate wharf in the port. He'd seen no sign of any blockheads or earthers thus far, and those scuttling about the port had better things to worry about than a lone man. Yet, he still glanced nervously about before walking inside.

Stacks of crates filled the warehouse. Each crate was twenty feet high and each stack at least a dozen crates tall. To his left, an iron staircase led up to an office on a gantry high above. A dim light shone through the small window in the office door. Hywel started as he spotted a figure shrouded in shadow watching him from the gantry.

"I wondered if you'd come," said the figure. Hywel thought he recognised the man's soft voice. "I am glad that you did. Come, we have much to discuss."

"Nine-six?"

"Please do not call me that. My chosen name is Ocelot."

"Oh, I…I am sorry." Hywel climbed the stairs as Nine-six—no, *Ocelot*—opened the door to the office, throwing a weak beam of light into the warehouse. It shamed him to realise, in over a decade working together, Hywel had never asked if "Nine-six" was actually his name. It had never occurred to him to ask.

Maps of Inglebad and the wider world covered the office's papered walls, and it smelled of coffee and stale tobacco. Storm sat at a heavily notched table made from dark teak, with mugs and papers scattered across its surface. Her elaborately plaited blonde hair was gone, a wig it seemed, and she now sported a brunette bob. She watched him, a small smile on her painted-red lips.

A balding, heavyset man with sunburned skin sat beside Storm. He wore a striped jumper over a lemon shirt and his eyes—a pair of gleaming sapphires—bored into Hywel with what he could only describe as intense hatred. Hywel hadn't expected to find any jetters with the Undergrid. Water elementals hated sparkies as much as earthers, or so he had believed.

"This is Darius, the captain of our rescue ship," said Ocelot.

Darius grunted what might have been a welcome in response.

"A pleasure," said Hywel. Then he turned to Ocelot and gasped. Ocelot wore no mask. It was the first time Hywel had ever seen his battery's face and he was too shocked to mask his horror. Tattooed in blue-green ink across Ocelot's high forehead was "96 B 47-4." Hywel didn't know where to look. He didn't know what to say. His mouth flopped open pathetically and the look on his face must have said it all.

"Just in case I escape," said Ocelot. "Or I forget I am chattel."

Hywel shook his head, stunned that Ocelot had been branded like cattle. Then again, was it truly a surprise? He himself had never considered Ocelot his equal. He had treated him like a disposable tool, something to assist him and nothing more. It was a sight that would be seared into his brain, along with the shame of knowing he had been a willing part of the system that could do this to another human. Why had he not considered it unjust? What did it say about him that he could inflict this misery on others? Was he callous, cruel? Most certainly. Perhaps, even...*evil*? A rush of blood to his head made him grip the table for support. His selfish greed and ambition had blinded him, and it took the system coming after his family for Hywel to finally see the rotten truth of the man he truly was. He hung his head. "I am so sorry."

Darius and Storm both snorted.

"Save your apologies," said Ocelot, in a tone that demanded obedience. "Take a seat."

Hywel sat down beside Storm and spotted a familiar staff poking out of the umbrella stand. "My Earth rod!"

Ocelot plucked it from the stand and tossed it across the table. Hywel caught it and a warm, tingling sensation flowed from his fingertips up his arm. He already felt more powerful, more confident. He twirled it in his hands and the coils began to unwind—then he stopped. He became conscious of those around the table, of the fear and anger the sight of those vines might cause them.

"In the bedlam after your battle with Rochester, I stashed it away and one of our agents collected it. We thought you may want it back."

"Thank you," he said. "This means a lot to me."

"There was no sentiment involved. You're more use to us with it than without it." Ocelot spoke with the brusqueness of a military commander, no longer the soft-spoken battery Hywel thought he had known. "If you want to free Sian and Elwyn, we must move quickly. But first, you must know that our price for freeing your family is your complete cooperation. There is much that you know that I am not privy to, and your skills are invaluable. An earther of your rank would be a real coup in our struggle. You will answer all our questions, divulge all that you know, and do whatever it is we ask of you. This is a high price to ask of you but the risk to us is equally great."

Hywel's emerald-green eyes locked with Ocelot's pearlescent pair. For the first time, Hywel held his battery's gaze as an equal. "I swear I will do anything you want. Anything."

"Good. Now, tackling the Sanitorium head-on, not to mention alone, was not a wise course of action. You are very lucky one of our agents was able to help you escape."

"What?" Hywel's face scrunched up in surprise. Then, as his mind replayed his escape, he realised there was more to it than just luck or skill. The shocker hit him on the stairs with a lightning bolt that merely knocked him over. It could have been far worse. She'd held back. Then, she'd missed him as he lay prone on the stairs, which allowed him to escape. And now, he suspected that she'd always meant to strike the blockhead at the mortuary entrance. "The shocker."

"Naya is her name. She sent a telegram updating us just before you arrived. Your little stunt has shocked the staff at the Sanitorium. It's actually helped us. Normally, they'd hold Elwyn and Sian for a few weeks, months even, before the Guild collected them. Now, however, they want them gone. The Sanitorium's Director is kicking up a fuss with Fotheringham about scorched walls and dead blockheads, and their unacceptable threat to patient and staff safety. Long story short, the Guild will be collecting them tonight and taking them back to Grove Tower."

"Tonight?" Hywel's heart sank, his new hope dashed. "But…the Tower is a fortress. We need time to plan. This…this is a disaster!"

"No," Ocelot spoke firmly, with the authority of an experienced leader. "This is good. Yes, the *Tower* is impregnable to anything short of an army, but a transport arranged hastily is very vulnerable. Who will be available at such short notice? The Guild will assign Rochester, as he's already there, and, so too, Rochester's battery; she's not one of ours. Then Naya, and whatever blockheads survived. I'll have to head back to the barracks in case they summon me. We need to strike quickly. Once they remove Elwyn and Sian from the Sanitorium, we'll snatch them on their way to the Tower. That's the window. After that, they'll be lost to the Guild."

The motorised wagon was as black as the sky above it. Its rear compartment had a yellow flower painted on each side, the daffodil of Blodeuwedd, iron bars across the solitary window and reinforced steel doors. Hywel knew the inside was layered in rubber sheets, as were the benches welded to the floor. The wagon grumbled out of the lane from the Sanitorium's mortuary and headed north up the now-deserted Canal Street. Rochester sat beside the driver up front, a Guildsman in marmalade overalls and cap. A second wagon, identical to the first, followed not far behind.

"They're on their way." Hywel handed the binoculars back to Storm as he climbed into the motorcar beside her. He bounced his Earth rod on his knees and tugged at the flat cap he'd been given. He'd been on transports before, as had Rochester. He could count on one hand the number of times a sparky had escaped. Their plan suddenly seemed so simple, so hopeless. Hywel took a deep breath and folded up the collar of his new trench coat.

"You ready?" Storm arched her eyebrows and he worried she could sense his nerves.

"Yes, of course," he said, a bit too sharply. "This is not my first operation, you know."

"Okay, big boy." Storm tapped his knee. "You just keep calm, do as we say, and remember whose side you are on."

Hywel started to object then thought better of it, swallowing his pride and indignation. Though it still grated, he wasn't in charge here.

Storm fiddled with levers and dials beside the wheel, then she pressed a pedal and the engine spluttered to life, spewing out acrid black smoke. This was it. This was the moment where he truly left his old life behind him. He felt sick but exhilarated. Adrenaline coursed through his veins, mingling with fear. If this didn't work, he'd never see his family again.

Behind them, another motorcar coughed and sputtered into life. The driver was Bryn, a stocky and sullen warhorse and long-serving member of the Undergrid, who could easily have passed for a blockhead if not for his open hostility towards the Guild. Beside Bryn was a jittery flamer called Gryff, a Fire elemental who spoke at the speed of lightning and had coal-black eyes. They were a small team but experienced in smash-and-grab attacks, so Storm claimed.

They pulled onto Canal Street, a hundred yards or so ahead of the Guild's lead wagon and trundled along. Bryn remained in the side street, waiting for their target to pass. It was all Hywel could do not to turn around, but he couldn't risk Rochester spotting him, however unlikely. He watched the lead wagon in the motorcar's side mirror as it gained on them.

They approached a canal bridge on their left. A narrowboat appeared to have run into difficulty, and its captain's backside poked out of the engine compartment at the rear.

Storm gently applied the brakes.

The Guild's wagon approached on their left and, just as it was about to overtake them, Storm spun the steering wheel and blocked its path. The Guild's wagon screeched to a halt and the second swerved to avoid rear-ending it. Hywel hopped out as Bryn's motorcar accelerated alongside. Gryff stood in the passenger seat beside Bryn, muttering, his eyes glowed like red-hot embers and a fiery ball the size of a watermelon formed between his hands.

The doors of the second Guild wagon opened with a *clang*. Yelled orders and heavy boots pounded the road. Rochester—snarling and shouting—clambered out of the lead wagon, raring to attack, but Gryff's fireball smashed into the driver's compartment. Rochester, engulfed in flames, screamed and dived for cover.

Hywel ran towards the rear of the lead wagon. A huge man stepped from behind it and Hywel skittered to a stop. It was the blockhead from the mortuary lane, still in dirty white scrubs and nursing a black eye, but this time armed with a billy club. He ran at Hywel just as a *whoosh* came from behind, another of Gryff's fireballs. The blockhead stopped. The vicious grin fell from his craggy chops as an apple-sized fireball raced over Hywel's shoulder. It thumped the blockhead in the chest and he staggered back, dazed and hurt, but not down.

Hywel darted forwards and focussed his mind, uncoiling his Earth rod into whipping vines that intertwined into a giant club as they shot forth. The vines struck the blockhead and his head snapped back. Spit and shards of teeth flew through the air and the blockhead dropped to the road in a pitiful heap. Hywel reached the back of the wagon and pointed his Earth rod. Vines slammed into the door, punching huge dents in the reinforced steel. *Thunk! Thunk! Thunk!* The vines slithered under the tiny gaps at the edges and where the two doors met. Hywel pushed as much energy as he could muster through the staff. The doors strained, buckled, and finally popped open in a screech of twisted metal. "Sian?"

Inside was dark but he could make out a few figures, then his skin prickled. He instinctively held up his Earth rod as lightning flashed, illuminating the inside of the wagon.

Ocelot grappled with a heavily built shocker. Lightning crackled across the long pins covering the shocker's suit, but Ocelot absorbed it all. Ocelot punched the shocker. The shocker throttled Ocelot. Sian cowered on the bench beneath them, her manacled feet chained to a metal ring on the padded floor. Elwyn cried, harsh high-pitched wails that lanced Hywel. With each cry, lightning shot from Elwyn's tiny body. Sian held their son, trying to soothe him, and the padded walls absorbed what her body didn't. Hywel pointed his Earth rod, and a vine shot forth, wrapping around the manacles and the metal ring, then wrenched them apart as if they were nothing but paper decorations.

Sian rushed out, clutching Elwyn to her chest, and stumbled into his arms. The relief at seeing them was indescribable. Hywel wanted to burst with joy. But they weren't safe yet, nor was Ocelot. He gave her a quick kiss, and another for Elwyn, then climbed into the wagon.

Hywel pointed his Earth rod at the pin-covered man in white. Vines wrapped around the shocker's muscled frame and arms, peeling his hands from around Ocelot's throat. Ocelot broke free and kicked the shocker in the gut. The shocker doubled over. Then, with a frightful yell, the shocker unleashed a blast of lightning. Blinding white bolts shot in jagged arcs from his body. Ocelot and the rubber surfaces absorbed the worst of it, but a kickback flowed through the vines from the Earth rod. The bolts fried some of the vines and burned Hywel's arms. But Hywel held on. He focussed his mind beyond the pain and towards his family's freedom. The vines squeezed the shocker, crushing him, until, finally, the shocker slumped to the padded floor.

A motorcar's horn blared, startling Hywel. Bryn hopped out— blood dribbling from his nose—and started pulling the leather convertible roof from behind the two seats, tying it to the frame of the windscreen. Gryff was slumped inside, his eyes and skin as grey as ash, sweat-soaked and exhausted. Storm pulled her motorcar alongside, its roof still down.

"Quickly," she said, waving Ocelot towards the car. Then she pointed towards the canal, and the narrowboat that no longer seemed in difficulty. "Get aboard. Our agent will be waiting for you at the port. A sailor named Elber. Do what he says, trust me."

Hywel flinched. *Trust me.* The remark from an Undergrid agent still challenged everything he thought he knew. But he had come too far to stop now. "Find Elber, understood." Hywel took off his coat and flat cap and handed both to Ocelot, who peeled off his mask then slipped the garments on before climbing into the idling car.

Hywel leant inside. The sight of his former battery filled him with joy and an unexpected feeling of camaraderie.

"Thank you," he said, meeting Ocelot's eye. "I treated you terribly. Yet, you have still helped me save my family. You are a better man than me, that is clear. For what it's worth, I am sorry. For everything. Truly, I mean it. I will never be able to repay you."

"I didn't do this for *you*. I did it for your son and for our movement. But..." Ocelot paused and Hywel saw a hint of a smile in his pure-white eyes. "Maybe when our paths next cross you will have helped us enough for me to forgive you."

Ocelot tapped the windscreen and Hywel stepped back. Storm and Bryn pulled their motorcars away, each in different directions.

Sian stepped beside him, shushing Elwyn, who had now settled down. She still looked wan and weak with dark circles beneath her scared eyes. He wanted to take her in his arms and never let her go. He stroked her cheek, pushing a lock of mousey hair behind her ear, and it was all he could do not to cry.

"Come on," he said, taking her hand and leading her down to the canal towpath. Hywel hopped onto the narrowboat and glanced about but saw no sign of its captain. He reached back and took Elwyn from Sian's hands then helped his wife on board and quickly climbed below deck.

Inside, the narrowboat was far comfier than it looked. The ceiling was just high enough that he didn't need to stoop. There was a long cushioned-bench and table, and a little kitchenette with pots and pans hanging on the red walls. It was pleasantly warm and smelled of smoke from a small log-burner stove, which gave out the only light in the otherwise dark interior. Beside the stairs, there was a round door with the word "Captain" burned into its surface, and another door at the far end.

As soon as they were below deck, the idling narrowboat kicked into life. Hywel sat down and a swell of emotion filled his chest, a wave that threatened to pour out and overwhelm him. The events of the last day were hard to process; his whole world had been upended. Everything he knew had been challenged. Who he was, what he believed in and, worst of all, what he had done. He held Sian's hands and sat silently for a moment, listening to the narrowboat's throaty engines, the gentle bobbing motion of the cabin, as he tried to catch his breath and take it all in.

The joy of having Sian and Elwyn quickly evaporated and his doubts and fears resurfaced with the startling horror of discovering a masked intruder in the bedroom. Hywel's mind whirred with questions; where were they going? What would happen when they got there? Could they really trust the Undergrid? The thought was anathema to him. Yet, he had no choice. Not if he wanted his family to be safe.

"This boat will take us to the port," said Hywel, trying to hide his concern. He draped his arm across Sian's shoulders and allowed himself a smile. Sitting there, with Sian and Elwyn, it was hard not to dream of the future that had seemed, even moments ago, so out of reach. "A ship is waiting that will take us far from here to somewhere we can be a family."

"Oh, Hywel." Sian leant into him, sobbing into his chest. Her forearms were covered in nasty red burns and Hywel knew there'd be more across her body. She hadn't complained at all, and he was as proud as he'd ever been that she'd chosen him to be her husband. "I thought we'd never be free. I thought...Elwyn, me...the things that man said...."

"I know, I know." Blood pounded in his temples as he thought of Rochester taunting Sian with that lupine grin on his cold, smug face. The pleasure he must have taken riled up Hywel, but he let those feelings wash over him and he took a few deep breaths. They were safe, for now, and that was all that mattered. "You don't need to worry about him anymore."

Sian and Elwyn soon fell asleep, Elwyn in Hywel's arms. Every now and again his son stirred and Hywel felt a jolt of lightning, each like a swift punch to his arm. He kept his Earth rod close, which helped absorb most of it. The orb atop his rod glowed as bright as any streetlamp. Hywel marvelled at Elwyn's power, which chilled him to his core as he thought of what the Guild would do to get their hands on his son.

After more stops than his nerves could handle, they finally reached the port. Through a porthole, Hywel watched the narrowboat pull up alongside a wharf. The captain hadn't come in to check on them as he'd have expected but then Storm hadn't told him what to expect. There hadn't been time. He didn't know if the captain was a full member of the Undergrid or just a sympathiser who was happy to help but even happier with the less he knew. The captain stamped his boots on the deck and Hywel took that as the sign to head up on deck.

Hywel climbed up first. The narrowboat was moored beside the same warehouse as before, though he couldn't see anyone who looked like they were waiting for him. In fact, there was hardly a soul on the moonlit wharf. Hywel glanced around, a sinking feeling in his stomach. Then, he saw a light come on inside the warehouse office and he let out a sigh.

"Sian," he shouted down the stairs, "come on up."

"I'm sorry." The baritone voice came from the rear of the deck. Hywel turned. A stocky, white-haired man in grey overalls looked back, sheepish and ashamed. Hywel's heart stopped. "I had no choice. I couldn't warn you, I—"

Hywel sensed Blodeuwedd's power. An Earth elemental was close. Terror, like an icy claw, crushed his chest as he dashed down the stairs.

"Hello, Arfon." Rochester stood behind Sian and Elwyn, who were wrapped in a thin tangle of vines. Savage, weeping burns covered half of Rochester's long face and his clothes were charred and smoky. His green eyes glowed menacingly in the dim light and his words carried a hard edge, years of jealousy and hatred spilling over. "I smelled a rat when I saw that narrowboat idling beside the canal. My instincts are always right. It's why I've always seen through you, even when no one else did. I could sense your weakness, something not right. And look, here it is. I've got your spark-spawn and, to top it off, you've led me to the home of the Undergrid." Rochester smiled that crooked, yellowed grin of his and his tone changed. He was joyous, victorious. "It is finally time I show everyone who is the superior man."

"Clarence, please." Hywel stepped towards Rochester, his knuckles white from gripping his Earth rod.

"Stay there, Arfon." Rochester wagged a bony finger. "Nothing you can say will change my mind. And if you make one move, I will kill your wife." As if to show his intent, vines crawled across Sian's throat and squeezed. Her eyes bulged and she started choking. "Then, I will bury—"

A flash of lightning burst from Elwyn, as if his son had sensed they were in danger. It lit up the small cabin and nearly blinded Hywel. Sian screamed. Rochester staggered back, moaning, as his vines burst into flames and disintegrated. Seizing the chance, Hywel raised his Earth rod and a stream of vines shot forwards and smacked Rochester in the face sending him tumbling against the wall. Hywel directed his vines to grab Sian and Elwyn and he dragged them away from Rochester.

Sian groaned in agony. The blast from Elwyn should have killed her. He didn't know how she survived; perhaps the bond between them as mother and son gave her a resistance that saved her life. Though that was a mystery for another day.

Rochester pushed himself off the wall and swung his Earth rod. Hywel didn't have time to defend both himself and Sian. Rochester's vines thumped Hywel across the cabin. He crashed against the captain's door and slid to the floor. There was scant room to fight and Rochester worked that to his advantage. Rochester's staff created huge club-like vines that struck out indiscriminately—punching a hole in the cabin door, smashing through a porthole. Hywel used his vines to shield Sian and Elwyn, ushering them towards the stairs as he took a barrage of blows to his head and back. Only the love and desperate need to protect his family kept him conscious.

"Find Elber," he shouted as Sian scrambled up the stairs. Then, just before she vanished, he added, "I love you."

"How sweet," said Rochester, and his burned face twitched into a vicious snarl. "I'll enjoy telling her you squealed for mercy when I catch her, and how you gave them up to save your skin."

"That is the difference between you and me, Clarence." Hywel struggled to his feet, using what felt like the last reserves of his strength. With Sian and Elwyn out of harm's way, Hywel redirected his focus. He didn't know if he had the power to beat Rochester. At full strength, both were evenly matched. Injured? Who knew who would come out on top? But he knew Rochester would have to beat *him*. Rochester would have to show Hywel that *he* was the stronger man. Hywel, however, just needed to save his family, by hook or by crook. "You have no one to fight for but yourself."

Rochester's vines shot forth. Hywel raised his rod and their vines entwined into a great seething mass. It was as though the two men's hands had knotted together, two wrestlers locked in a duel, each jostling and shoving to unbalance the other. Hywel pushed and strained and his vines, his energy, forced Rochester back a step.

"I. WILL. BEAT. YOU!" Rochester roared, unleashing a near overwhelming power that drove Hywel against the wall. Then, the mass of vines whipped forwards, yanked by Rochester, almost ripping the rod from Hywel's grip. Rochester swung his vines back and forth, a puppet master gaining back control of his puppet's tangled strings. Hywel staggered to and fro, clinging desperately onto his Earth rod. But Rochester's power was too much. Hywel stumbled and fell. The seething mass of vines finally pinned Hywel to the ground. Vines wrapped around his legs, his chest, squeezing the life from him.

The wild grin on Rochester's face said it all. Hywel was done for. Then, Hywel's eyes fell upon the stove. He released a few of his vines in apparent defeat, then sent them slithering across the floor. Smoke rose from the burning vines as they gripped the stove. Hywel cried out as Rochester's vines crushed him, and his mind searched for one last ounce of strength. With a mighty wrench, the stove was torn from the wall. Hywel swung his vines and they thumped onto Rochester's back.

Burning logs and coals scattered across the cabin. Rochester screamed and his vines withered. Hywel clambered to his feet and charged forwards. He stabbed Rochester with his Earth rod. The orb transferred all the lightning it had captured from Elwyn into an explosion that threw his foe headlong across the cabin.

Rochester hit the kitchenette counter. His back cracked, folding unnaturally on itself, and he landed in a horribly twisted, smouldering heap.

Flames flickered around the cabin. The long bench caught alight, so too the curtains around the portholes. Soon the whole cabin was aflame and thick with smoke. Hywel climbed up the stairs and staggered onto the deck. He turned and used his vines to twist the handrail into a makeshift barrier then jumped onto the wharf.

Sian leant against a barrel, Elwyn nuzzled in her arms. A wiry sailor in a blue-striped uniform crouched beside her. Hywel rushed over and bent down beside his wife.

"She hurt," said the sailor, who spoke in a deep voice thick with an unfamiliar accent. The man's short sleeves showed off his heavily tattooed arms. "But we go now."

"Elber?"

"I am Elber. You, Earther. We go now."

Hywel nodded and helped Sian to her feet, taking Elwyn in his arms. She moaned and leant on Elber for support. The sailor, who was a head shorter than Hywel, lifted Sian over his shoulder with ease.

A great crackling groan sounded behind them. Hywel glanced over his shoulder. The narrowboat collapsed on itself in a rush of flames, sending a great plume of smoke into the night sky. The captain knelt beside the canal, shaking his head and sobbing. Hywel felt a pang of guilt at the destruction he'd wreaked upon yet another person's life. But he buried that feeling. This time, he had no choice.

"Quick." Elber broke into a jog and Hywel struggled to keep up. They ran into the warehouse and out the other side, where a steamer ship was moored to the neighbouring wharf. Two tall, fat chimneys stood at the rear of the ship, and its steel hull was painted white above the waterline, blue-black beneath. Its name was painted in large red letters near the bow: *Mercy*. Its deck was full of crates and stevedores, and sailors rushed up and down a wooden gangplank to the wharf.

"Wait." Elber laid Sian on the ground beside an unloaded crate and dashed off. Hywel knelt down and lifted her head. Her eyes opened up to his and she smiled.

"You made it."

"I did."

A bell rang and, as one, the stevedores and sailors headed into the warehouse. Elber came back, lifted Sian without a word, and ran up the gangplank. Hywel followed the sailor aboard, across the deck and through narrow corridors. Then, abruptly, Elber stopped, laid Sian down, and removed a few floorboards to reveal a small hatch. Elber opened it and, immediately, the stench of stale sweat rushed from the darkness along with the sounds of coughing, crying, and muffled conversations. "Go here."

Hywel hesitated. He looked at the dark hole and bile rose in his stomach. The stench was horrendous. The sounds ghastly. He wavered but Sian uttered a command that brooked no argument.

"Go on," she said. "This is Elwyn's only chance at freedom."

She was right. What lay ahead was unknown, what lay behind was not. He had trusted the Undergrid this far. For better or worse, he had to trust them again.

"Thank you, Elber," he said, as the sailor helped him lower Sian into the darkness.

Hywel climbed down the ladder with Elwyn in one hand, his Earth rod under his armpit. There was an audible gasp. Someone cried and he heard a desperate scuffle. His eyes adjusted to the gloom and he froze. In a space barely ten-feet square were fifty, probably more, cowering figures. They looked at him and their eyes, almost to a person, were pure white. Then he realised what they must see; his emerald eyes and Earth rod. Their enemy.

"I am no threat to you," he said, "not anymore."

The hold full of sparkies stared at him, a mix of anger and terror on their faces. Hywel realised he may have captured some of them himself, or earthed their friends or family. If they recognised him, or just wanted vengeance against any earther, they could easily kill him. For the first time in his life, he felt fear for being who he was. It unnerved him, he felt small, helpless. Slowly, he turned Elwyn towards the sparkies and hoped they would show him more pity than Hywel had ever shown. "My son…it's not safe for us in Inglebad."

The hatch closed, plunging Hywel into darkness. He reached for Sian's hand and prayed to the Elements to get them through this.

The hatch opened and light poured into the hold. How long they'd spent in the darkness, Hywel could not say. Time had become nothing to him. He'd slept, eventually. In fits and bursts, between Elwyn's frequent cries and feeds, squashed against Sian and strangers, hot, filthy and exhausted. The deep grumbling of the engines, the vibrations through the floor and whispered conversations became a wretched lullaby.

Hywel shielded his eyes from the light, his empty stomach jumped. Others around him cowered, all of them fearing the worst. A figure stepped before the light, covered in shadow, then reeled back, coughing. The stench from the terrified, sweating bodies crammed into that tiny space, without a toilet or running water, was nothing less than a weapon of torture. But weighed against the fear of losing Elwyn, of the gallows, of his wife's bleak future as a surrogate, the stench was nothing. No, it was not nothing. It was the stench of freedom.

"At sea now," said Elber, addressing them all. "You safe."

Hywel dropped to his knees and kissed Sian. It seemed too good to be true.

"Come," said Elber, encouraging the disbelieving runaways forwards. "You free."

A murmur of excitement jolted through the crowd and the braver sparkies shuffled towards the ladder. The sailor held out his calloused hand and helped a teenage girl up the ladder. He reached next for Elwyn, but Sian held her baby boy close. Hywel nudged her forwards, then helped her up through the hatch as she held onto Elwyn for dear life. Another sailor waited outside the hold, clad in the same blue-striped uniform. Young and friendly, her dark hair was cut fashionably short and her brown eyes were filled with pity, concern, but above all, kindness. It was enough to make him weep. She pointed down a narrow corridor which took them up onto the ship's deck, bathed in glorious sunshine.

Hywel followed Sian to the stern and together they leant on the guardrail, admiring the clear blue sky over the sparkling sea. The salty wind blew strong across the choppy waters and beneath them the ship's engines rumbled. Somewhere in the distance, beyond his eyes' reach, lay Inglebad. He closed his eyes and pictured the cloud-choked sky he'd lived so long beneath, the bolts of lightning that struck the city's generating stations like clockwork. Above all, he pictured that poor, wretched generator he'd tortured without a second thought. Hywel opened his eyes and a tear broke free.

"We did it." Sian leant her head on Hywel's shoulder. "We saved our son."

"We did." Hywel grinned as he kissed her head but his joy was laced with grief. Grief for all the boys and girls who hadn't been saved, grief for the countless innocents he had condemned during his long career. In the long darkness in that hold, Hywel had promised himself that if they escaped, he'd spend the rest of his life saving as many sparkies as he could. It was the least he could do to try and atone for the misery he had caused those who had not been saved. And, one day, he hoped to meet Ocelot again and share a drink as equals.

An Artist's Path

BY TOM WOOD

Tom Wood is a fantasy art illustrator who is among the bestselling artists in the United States and Canada. His career has spanned thirty years as an art director and owner of fantasy, commercial, and licensed artwork.

Although best known for his affinity for dragons and a cultlike following from fans of the rap group Insane Clown Posse, Tom is also a cattle farmer in the Ozark Mountains of Mammoth Spring, Arkansas.

A chance booth location next to the Galaxy Press team at Dragon Con 2010 began a decade-long friendship that eventually turned into an invitation to be a judge at the 2021 Writers and Illustrators of the Future annual awards week.

An Artist's Path

The path to becoming a successful and hopefully fulfilled artist can't be boiled down to a "one size fits all" list of guidelines. I've met hundreds of artists, and each has a story where it seems life guided their path as much as any amount of preparation, experience, or practice. In my opinion, artists are not born—they are made, products of their environment, ambition, creativity, and patience.

To those who know this is their path, no matter the struggle or sacrifice, it is still not an easy one to follow. There's only one rule I know of, simpler to say than to do: keep moving forward. For myself, I knew at the age of six that art was my future. There was never a backup plan. I had no clue about the how, why, or where, but when asked what I wanted to be when I grew up, I would simply answer "an artist." So, whatever it took, I was going to become one.

I was born and raised on a cattle farm in rural Arkansas. My father, a rancher, and mother, a homemaker, worked tirelessly to provide a modest life for my brother and me. They were not remotely artistic, but were always very supportive of my aspirations of being a professional artist someday. Every new drawing was placed on the refrigerator door for everyone to see before being added to the hundreds of sketches lining my bedroom walls.

The attention I enjoyed at home was amplified in elementary school. It was easy to become the class artist with only eighteen kids in my grade. I grew confident and even arrogant about my work, but was always gracious and humble when complimented by classmates and teachers. Dinosaurs, sharks, and monsters were a constant in my notebooks—now sketchbooks. Class assignments such as book reports that required illustrations were an opportunity to draw "normal" things and show my parents that I was not in fact possessed by the devil.

My path was forever changed when I was ten years old. In a store, I discovered an album cover featuring an ominous armored warrior wielding a battle-ax while mounted on top of a black Clydesdale. I held the Molly Hatchet record in my hands through holes in the anti-theft glass for an hour. I knew that this was what I was destined to do. Later, I learned the painting was by Frank Frazetta and titled *Death Dealer*. This piece of art led me to his work on Robert E. Howard's and L. Sprague de Camp's twelve-book chronology of Conan the Barbarian. I read those books over and over and drew hundreds of scenes inspired by the stories. I was obsessed with the fantasy genre and, more importantly, I now had a direction to push toward. A few minor stumbling blocks stood in my way, however. 1) I was far from good enough to compete with this caliber of artwork. 2) I had no idea who I would even show my work to in an effort to break into the field. And 3) I was in the middle of rural Arkansas with no one to ask for advice. Perhaps that was a blessing in disguise. I remained blissfully ignorant of the odds of becoming a successful fantasy artist. Ignorance and confidence go a long way.

Upon graduating from high school, I entered college at the University of Arkansas on an academic scholarship. I was eager to see what other "class artists" were bringing to the table. It was instantly apparent that nine out of ten were there for an easy grade. Those four or five students I classified as good, I became friends with, and we worked on projects together. My competitive nature drove me to secretly want to beat their work, but, also, I wanted to help them with any tip or techniques we were all learning and trying to perfect as we grew.

In the summer of my sophomore year, my father arranged an interview with a major screen-printing company in Memphis, Tennessee. Surprisingly, I was offered an assistant art director position, actually getting paid to draw. The hours were extremely long, and working weekends were the norm. I learned everything my art director taught me about color separations and apparel printing. Within a few months, I outstripped his abilities, to the delight of company owners. Subsequently, they fired my boss and made me art director. Not because I was good, but I was good enough, and at half the salary of my old art director. I hated what my cutthroat owners had done to my mentor, but the fact remained that I was nineteen and the art director of a nine-million-dollar company. I was being taken down this path whether I liked it or not.

This taught me that you can't just be good, you have to be invaluable, or the same fate that befell my old boss would eventually be mine. That couldn't happen because returning to Arkansas to tell my parents I failed was out of the question.

My fear of failure fueled my work, and I saw my skills raised like never before. Fear and pride are good motivators, and they kept me at this company for three years.

Soon, other companies in licensed apparel took notice of my skills, and I was recruited by one of the larger licensed sports apparel companies in the country. They had a massive art department, stacked with talent from across the country. Again, I identified the best artists working there and surrounded myself with them. I gleaned whatever I admired from their art style and adapted it into my own, as they did with mine. Creativity thrives within that kind of symbiotic environment. I made a reputation for drawing aggressive, bordering on violent, mascots. We all grew better, and the company prospered. This was now firmly my path, even though it was not the dream I had in my youth.

Soon after, I became the creative director of special events at the largest licensed apparel company in America. I was twenty-five, with a staff of eight artists reporting to me. Within two years, we had taken special events from three to thirty-three million dollars in revenue. Unfortunately, the rest of the company was hemorrhaging money, and the entire staff was unceremoniously "let go." This was the path correction I really needed but was too scared to do while gainfully employed.

The next day, I established my own business, offering custom illustrations to many of the ad agencies in the Connecticut and

New York area. It took off quickly, and I was now creating all sorts of images for an array of clients and making good money. I took my new client list and moved home to Arkansas, as the cost of living was far cheaper and work could be delivered digitally.

I had done it. I was a professional artist, and my family was very proud. The path had revealed itself. I now painted bottles of soda and football players. Not what I had envisioned, but a bad day of drawing is better than a great day at a real job.

The success of the ad agency illustration business allowed me the opportunity to pursue my own line of fantasy art pieces—in hopes of possibly licensing the imagery to companies for various product decoration in their retail lines. I hired an agent to sell, and I was off to the races. Soon, I had posters, sculptures, and apparel adorned with my work, not only in this country but around the world. Through fifteen years and five companies as a professional I had waited patiently for the path to open, and finally, I was drawing what I wanted. Haunting, amazing scenes like the one that had grabbed me all those years ago. This has led to many other opportunities within the entertainment and publishing industries, which I have explored to sometimes good or at times disappointing ends.

The path continues to this day. It wasn't and never will be a straight one. It presented itself over the course of a career and always led to an unknown future. As an aspiring artist, your task is to be confident or ignorant enough to follow the path when those doors open.

My Name Was Tom

written by
Tim Powers

illustrated by
GIGI HOOPER

ABOUT THE AUTHOR

Tim Powers is the author of eighteen science fiction and fantasy novels, including The Anubis Gates, Declare, *and* My Brother's Keeper. *His books have won multiple World Fantasy, Locus, and Philip K. Dick awards and have been translated into well over a dozen languages. Powers lives with his wife, Serena, in San Bernardino, California.*

About this story, Powers has said, "Damon Knight wrote CV, *(1985), a novel about adventures aboard a giant ship, and Lin Carter wrote a short story called 'A Guide to the City,' (1969), about attempts to map an infinite city, and after reading them, my own infinite ship became a compelling image. The question then was, 'Where is it going?'"*

ABOUT THE ILLUSTRATOR

Born in 1985 in East Chicago, Indiana, Peggy Hooper is a versatile artist whose creativity knows no bounds. Known in the art world by her moniker, Gigi Hooper, she's a child of the '90s, drawing early inspiration from iconic pop culture. Simultaneously, Gigi was deeply influenced by the enchanting worlds of young adult, children's, and comic books, which have fostered a love for sweet, fantastical, and mind-bending literature.

Gigi's artistic journey began in her childhood, when her experimental nature led her to beautify and unintentionally destroy her mother's personal property. However, throughout her life, Gigi's mother remained a steadfast supporter, purchasing Gigi's first set of art supplies, which only continued to encourage her creative process.

While her path took her through diverse careers as a United States Marine and a personal trainer, Gigi eventually returned to her true calling. She earned a BA in illustration from George Fox University.

Currently residing in Newberg, Oregon, with her husband and sister, Gigi specializes in digital art, collage, and pencil work, although her artistic palette embraces various mediums.

Today, she continues her artistic journey, pursuing independent studies while actively engaging in freelance work, bringing her captivating visions to life one creation at a time.

Gigi was an Illustrators of the Future winner in 2023. She was featured in L. Ron Hubbard Presents Writers of the Future Volume 40.

My Name Was Tom

I knew none of these idlers had ever even climbed up enough decks and far enough outboard to peer through a porthole, much less been all the way up to the vast Main Decks and felt the wind and seen the broad face of the sea, or the sky—they thought, as probably their parents and grandparents had thought too, that the yellow glow from the caged fluorescent tubes was the brightest light there was, and that the fore-and-aft slope of the local working alley afforded the longest possible view of distance. They'd none of them even been far enough up and inboard to see the main working alley corridor, a hundred feet wide and probably sloping down all the way from the bow to some midship point and then up to the remote stern, nor the expressionless uniformed crew members who could sometimes be seen racing up or down that measureless course on roller skates, carrying out unimaginable errands.

I had been descending the ringing steps of the iron ladders, deck to deck, for what must have been a full day, quietly eating with other passengers at a couple of the dim cafeterias to be found on every deck—I can't remember the last time I had any money, but the cost was reputed to be part of the original long-forgotten fare, and I'm sure the laconic staff wouldn't take tips anyway—and sleeping briefly in one of the many unoccupied staterooms. After a year of marriage, it was disorienting to sleep alone in a stateroom, alone in a bed.

I met Ruth about a year ago, and I was fascinated by her because she was all the things I was not—curious, mainly. She was crying when I found her, kneeling alone in front of a wingback chair in one of

317

the salons, and it turned out to be the embroidered upholstery on the chair back that had sparked her grief—the fabric and threads had all faded, but it was possible to make out a sort of picture in the embroidery. Trees, and a little house, and a cow, as I recall. But ten minutes later she was showing me toys she had found in some remote locker, and laughing as she made rusty tin monkeys dance, and sailed balsa wood airplanes down the passageways.

The deck numbers painted on the green walls at every ladder-head descend from 100 to 1, and then repeat the sequence, over and over. When I was still sure that Ruth's home deck was below me, I began exploring each deck that was numbered 42, and questioning the guests who inhabited the passageways near the ladder; my tan and my upper-midship-starboard accent excited their curiosity every time, and one thing they always wanted to know was how far the little model ship had now moved across the map wall in the Grand Salon on A Deck. I had never been to the Grand Salon, but I told them that the little ship was said to have moved several inches in the last year, though the precise identity of the destination was still a matter of debate. That latter detail was no news to them—wherever you go, passengers always have opinions on it. Some say England, some Hawaii…they don't even agree on whether the fabled model is moving left or right across the wall.… And you always run into a few who think we're steaming to the moon or to heaven. Nobody seems to remember the lights that stood like solid aurora borealis everywhere in the night sky sometime before we became aboard; I didn't remember them myself until a couple of days ago.

But I eventually found the Deck 42 where Ruth was born. I was lucky to identify it—one of the men playing push broom in the passageway turned out to have her last name, and he agreed to lead me a long way forward to get to his family's staterooms.

Their rooms hadn't changed in the year since I'd been there— the dim radiance from the ceiling light in their main cabin softly illuminated the smudgy prints framed on the longest bulkheads, the upright steamer trunk that functioned as a closet, and the couch and armchairs upholstered in the same dark-green fabric as the worn carpet that covered the deck. Their passports sat as always in the slot on the passageway door. The little tables that could be nested in a stack were still arranged in a stepped row in front of the couch, but the nap of the carpet around their feet didn't show any flattening—clearly it wasn't necessary anymore for the couch to be opened out in a bed. Ruth wasn't there.

Her parents are old. Her father may never wear anything but that bathrobe and those slippers, and it's probably her mother, in her unvarying housedress and sneakers, who walks down the fluorescent-lit passageway to get cans and bottles from the silent staff at the nearest Deck 42 commissary. The two of them remembered me from a year ago, when I had come down with their strayed daughter to ask her father for her hand in marriage, and now once again I wound up joining the family for dinner. Ruth's father poured the sweet red wine that everybody on the ship seems to drink, and her mother cooked corned beef hash and sauerkraut on their electric stove. The man who had led me to their rooms, apparently Ruth's brother, stared at me without speaking.

There's a story that, years ago, a guy from way out in the port aft quarter is supposed to have walked all the way from the fantail to the bow, and simply found himself at the fantail again, looking again at the ship's spreading wake. Even people who think there really was such a guy say he must have got turned around in the mazes of sun decks and games decks and acres of empty tennis courts; it would have done him no good to try to find his way by looking at the stars, since none of the constellations are the familiar ones anymore, and they change all the time anyway.

"Long before she met you," her father told me, pouring more of the wine into my cup, "Ruth did that *Wanderjahr* thing of leaving home to try to find the bridge; she eventually came back—with a tan, and all kinds of new words, and stories about swimming pools and open sky and rooms with ceilings so high you couldn't even make out the pictures painted up there. But she hadn't found the bridge, and so after a while she went away again, and when she came back that time, it was with you. Do you remember being here before? Sometime last year, I think."

"Of course," I told him. "You think she's gone off trying to find the bridge again?"

The old man shrugged and blinked around at the narrow cabin. "She always wanted to get away, and where else is there to go? But," he went on, and he smiled and began singing that old song, *"We'll Meet Again..."* From the kitchen alcove Ruth's mother joined in.

"Don't know where, don't know when..."

"We're all of us traveling together," the old man said in a confiding tone, "and we'll arrive together, never fear." I must have looked doubtful, for he asked then, "Where's the little model ship now, on the map wall?"

"I've never seen it," I said.

"But you must have more recent news of it," he persisted, "living way up there in the lettered decks!"

I shrugged. "I hear it's moved some inches."

He sat back and nodded. "The day will come," he said.

Yes. I think it will be soon. A couple of days ago, I memorably saw two moons in a green sky, both of them smaller than the moon we all remember.

Ruth's parents invited me to stay on, and sleep in her old fold-out bed, until such time as she might find her way back down there. "How could she not," her father asked me, "eventually?"

But even then, I thought that time was shorter than it used to be. In recent years—as best we can measure by the kaleidoscopic rotations of the night sky—the abyssal rumble of the engines has sometimes been noticeable because of a change in its pitch, and the expressionless crew and staff hardly speak at all anymore, even when they occasionally come around to stamp passports.

I didn't spend that night in her parents' staterooms, but slept in one of the empty cabins a few decks above them. I didn't dream, of course, but I was nevertheless troubled by the recurrent image of an open porthole—though the cabin I occupied was far inboard, and didn't have one.

After a few hours of restless sleep, I tried to climb back up by the same sequence of ladders that had led me down to those sub-waterline decks, but the ladders are offset at each deck, so unless you've been unfailingly careful to turn one way rather than the other at the bottom of each successive ladder, and then meticulously reverse the procedure on your ascent, your return trip is likely to slant away, and lead you up to regions you've never seen.

I thought I had been properly methodical, but at some point or points toward the end of my descent, I had apparently been so exhausted that I plodded away to the left down some corridor instead of to the right, as I had initially resolved always to do.

The ladders, steel stairs at first, became wooden staircases as I climbed up them, with ancient polish still visible at the edges of the otherwise deeply worn treads, and the bulkheads were paneled in some bird's-eye wood. I found empty restaurants, a library full of books whose pages were indecipherable because sea air had apparently made the inked characters spread in fading blobs across the paper, and a gymnasium in which, below racked Indian clubs and medicine balls, English-style saddles were mounted on a dozen steel pedestals, with slack reins looped through curled bars that stuck out in front; several of the saddles were creaking back and forth mechanically, and on one of them sat an overweight man who seemed to be whispering encouragements to an absent horse. I hurried through the gymnasium without disturbing him.

I came to a deck where there was no upward ladder in sight, and had to walk for hours—aft, I believe—before I found one, and was able to continue my laborious ascent.

The ladderways above me now became narrower, and soon the ladders consisted of rungs rather than steps as they led me up through a series of nearly vertical wells apparently built mainly to house sheaves of blistered pipes that radiated heat, and I was sweating when I emerged at last at a railed balcony and found myself looking out at the noonday sea from only a few decks above the surge and spray of cloven water.

The wind was on the starboard quarter, and things creaked and scraped above me. I tugged at the balcony rail to be sure it was solidly moored, then leaned out and looked up—and against the blue sky, I saw the woven-lumber undersides of big ragged structures swinging ponderously back and forth across the steel hull, connected to one another by rope bridges that alternately sagged and tautened. Even over the whistling wind and the thrashing of the sea below, I could hear voices raised in chanting. Looking down and aft, I saw baskets on long lines bobbing and splashing in the rushing sea.

Clearly I had found a colony of the passengers known as hullfolk, or Plimsoll-line gypsies. Legend has it that they never venture up or in to any deck, and live their whole lives in cobbled-together boxes suspended on long cables or built onto half-lowered lifeboats.

Ruth certainly would not be among them, and the stories about the hullfolk weren't reassuring, but there was no way off the little balcony I was on except by climbing back down all the ladders that had led me there.

So I called up to them, hoping they still spoke Shipboard English; the chanting faltered to a halt, and a minute later a long leather-upholstered couch swung down into view, lowered on four ropes to the level of the balcony, and a harsh voice from above, barbarically accented but understandable, invited me to climb out onto it.

The couch was twisting back and forth and swinging aft because of the wind, and I had no more intention of climbing onto it than of jumping into the sea—in fact attempting the first seemed certain to result in the latter—but when a shift in the wind and a simultaneous unprecedented jolt from the deck underfoot slammed the couch right up against the balcony rail, a number of images sprang into my head simultaneously, as if shaken loose in physical recoil.

All in an instant: Ruth's brief farewell note; hand-drawn maps of small sectors of the ship, prized and recopied; the bland, abstract prints on the walls of Ruth's parents' staterooms, yellowed with decades of airborne cooking oil; even the imagined open porthole that had kept recurring to me as I'd slept; and with a hoarse curse and a spasm of revulsion, I found that I had vaulted over the rail.

GIGI HOOPER

The couch had begun to swing out again, and for an instant I was suspended in midair, right out in the cold wind—the foaming sea only a dozen yards below me, far closer than I had ever seen it before—and that moment of weightless free fall is the most intensely felt event of my life so far...though I suspect it will be superseded before long.

And then I collided with the couch, sending it swinging far out away from the hull, and I had to cling to it so desperately that my fingers poked through the old leather of the back of it and I was gripping the wood underneath. When it swung back in toward the hull, I glimpsed the flaked outline of the ship's Plimsoll line painted on the hull, a white circle with a horizontal line through it. It was well above the waterline—evidently the ship was floating high, with plenty of freeboard.

Two of the ropes from which the couch was suspended thrummed like bass violin strings, and the incongruous piece of furniture was righted and I was able to take a deep breath, and then the couch was jerkily drawn upward; a wide platform above me drew closer, shifting back and forth against a forest of cables and the blue sky and the sheer black cliff of the hull, and when the couch had been drawn level with the platform, rough hands reached out and pulled me onto a broad wooden floor suspended on a web of ropes and cables extending away upward.

Other such platforms, some wider and some narrower, along with dangling plywood cabins and a lifeboat with a small shed on it, swung in the vast volume of air between my perch and the open decks far overhead. Beyond the two bearded men in long aprons who had pulled me onto the planks of this unsteady surface, I could see faces peering down at me from every level. Wind whistled through an infinity of taut lines.

The two men stepped back, clearly returning to their places in a circle of men and women who stood on this swaying platform; they were all tanned dark brown, and wore various sorts of doubtless stolen crew garments—burgundy bellboy vests, some with white gloves still buttoned on the right shoulder, nurses' white uniforms, and stewards' white jackets. Their beards and wild hair struck a bizarrely incongruous note in an already disorienting scene. On the planks at the center of the circle lay a corroded porthole swing plate, the brass dogs broken off and its glass just a smoky disk.

I was on my hands and knees, and a gray-bearded man in a ragged blue officer's coat stepped forward and helped me to stand. I immediately staggered to one of the support ropes and clung to it. The ship's progress had always been smooth, and I had never before stood on an unsteady surface; I was sweating, and not certain I wasn't about to vomit.

The man shook my shoulder. "What, what?" he shouted in my face, and then, "Has the ship stopped?" His accent was odd but understandable.

In answer, I just rocked my head toward the turbulent wake churning so uncomfortably close under us. All I could think of was how I was to get back inside the hull. The wind was colder than the air in the ship had ever been, and I was shivering.

"No, no," he said impatiently, "the *guide lever*, on the *wall*."

I guessed that he must mean the little model ship on the map wall in the Grand Salon. "I've—never seen it," I said breathlessly.

The old man's eyes were glints of blue in the wrinkles of his brown face. After a moment he said, "People call me Hitch," and raised his eyebrows inquiringly.

I nodded, then realized that he wanted to know my name; and in the whistling, rocking confusion I couldn't remember it. "I'm," I began, then shrugged and just said, "somebody. Give me a minute."

He looked away and squinted at one of his companions, a woman dressed as one of the housekeeping staff, and raised his hand, palm up. She hurried to the sternward edge of the platform, crouched, and began hauling up a rope, tossing spray-wet coils of it behind her.

He turned back to me, his gray beard blowing every which way. "What can you tell us?" he asked me, speaking loudly over the wind. It never gets that windy up on the open decks, what with various superstructures being in the way. When I just shook my head, clinging to the ropes and hardly daring to open my eyes, he went on, "Are you afraid to tell us?"

"Tell you what?" I muttered. "I don't have anything to tell you, I—"

My interrogator frowned in evident bafflement. "What do you suppose brought you to this spot, eh?"

"I—got lost," I muttered. "How do I get back *in*?"

"But you *came out* here, you jumped." The platform shifted, its edge grinding across the rivets of the black hull, and he stepped back, then waved toward the porthole swing plate lying on the planks. The dozen men and women in scavenged ship uniforms were swaying in place, staring at me. The old man said, "We called you out. What of the voyage?"

The woman pulling up the rope had hoisted a sloshing bucket over the platform's edge, and before I could think of a way to answer the old man, she took a step toward me, crouched, and then straightened, flinging the bucket's contents directly into my face.

It was icy cold and it must have been sea water, but when I had fallen back against the ropes, coughing and spitting and shaking my head, and then pulled myself erect again, I opened and closed my mouth several times. The water was not salty, as everyone said it was—it was sharply sweet, like how I remember plant sap tasting.

I blinked, and freed one hand to knuckle my eyes, but my vision was fragmented—when I looked up, for a moment the sky was full of airliners, DC-3s, and triple-tail Constellations and even old Ford Trimotors, all flying together, slowly, in firmament-spanning formation, moving in the same direction as the ship. I quickly stared down at the rough planks under my shoes, and when I looked up again, the sky above the ship was clear blue, with not even a cloud to be seen.

"We're all of us traveling together," said the old man called Hitch.

"And," I said helplessly, remembering what Ruth's father had said, "we'll arrive together."

"Maybe." He scowled. "The Israelites were forty years in the Sinai desert, remember? After they got freed from being slaves in Egypt, before they got to the Promised Land? Do you know why?" I didn't say anything, and he went on, "To give 'em time to lose the old *assumptions*, man, the habits, the old *ways of life*. Kiss it all goodbye, a piece at a time, over the years. Right?"

I waved my free hand, for convenience conceding the point.

The old man gripped my shoulder again, tightly, and said, "But what if they *liked* the old ways, eh? Eating food, reading, sleeping, having children, all that?"

I was pretty sure the Israelites hadn't been called on to give up those things.

Looking away from him, I now saw a distant dark streak on the horizon; the ship didn't appear to be heading for it, but if it was land it was the first sighting I'd ever heard of. I stared, trying to focus on it, and my vision broke up again, so that I seemed to glimpse caravans of tarpaulin-draped trucks and heavy-laden camels, moving parallel to us. I blinked, and they were gone, along with the line on the horizon.

"The water in your eyes," he said, releasing my shoulder. "You can see. You must have seen the lights in the sky, too, long ago, do you remember? Pillars, glowing trees?"

For a moment the words meant nothing. And then with a shiver, I did remember the night, while I was still living in a city, when in all directions brightly glowing columns stretched from the horizon to the dimmed stars, shining green and gold and red, branching away at altitudes that must have been far above the atmosphere—vastly pulsing, way out there, like the arteries of God—

"I do remember," I whispered.

The cluster of hullfolk behind him had shifted out of their circle, and several had sat down around the porthole glass; all still staring at me through fringes of wind-blown hair.

"And then," I went on, talking to myself more than to Hitch, "sometime later, we were…here." I looked at him and said, more loudly, "I can't remember coming aboard."

"We were taken up," said Hitch. "Everybody, everywhere."

It was a vague and, to the extent it had any meaning at all, implausible statement, but in that moment it resonated in my head with a tone of profound truth.

"Where," I managed to ask him then, "are they taking us all?"

"Who knows? The *question* is, who—or what, eh?—will it turn out that they took there?" I hadn't followed that, and frowned at him in puzzlement. He went on, speaking loudly and slowly, "How much

327

have we kissed goodbye to? Do you remember music? Dreams and nightmares? Dogs, cats? When's the last time you saw any children?"

I closed my eyes and thought. If I concentrated, I could remember music, and dreams, and pets, even birds, and I remembered children; though in fact I hadn't seen any children in…years.

"I do remember," I said again.

"For now," said the old man. He squinted out over the endless sea. "You remember blackboards, when you were a lad in school? What came to us in those lights has been a long time erasing what we all wrote, so it, or they, can write something else, something of their own."

I was able to keep my balance by now, and dared to stand up straight, holding onto just one rope with one hand. "My name was Tom," I said, suddenly recollecting it. "Is."

"You need to go to the bridge while you still do remember some things. Tell the captain to order the lifeboats provisioned and lowered all the way down, for us." He waved around, taking in the hullfolk on the surrounding dangling boats and platforms in addition to the one we stood on. "We want to go back, while we're still mostly who we were."

"*Is* there a captain? Really? Still?" Is there even actually a bridge? I thought.

"Call him a…shepherd, if you like. Or a surgeon. Or a synod. But there's a presence up there. Late nights when the stars are spinning, sometimes he takes soundings, dropping a lead plummet on a line that hisses down nearly till dawn before it stops and gets drawn back up—many's the time the plummet tore right through a few of our nests."

"Lower the lifeboats," I said. "Provision them." The whole thing seemed impossible in every respect. "*Can* you go back?"

"We hope to at least not go forward."

All I wanted was to get safely back inside the hull, even if it meant descending the steep ladders through the hot pipe conduits again; I was fairly confident that I'd be able to find my own stateroom on B Deck, eventually. "I can't find the bridge," I said. "Everybody's tried, forever."

"We have a map."

"Go yourself, then."

"You think I wouldn't? You think I'm scared? None of us"—and here Hitch again waved around at the surrounding suspended makeshift decks and structures—"have had our passports renewed in years, probably decades. Most of us don't even have them anymore."

It was true that at intervals that were probably regular—most people guessed that it was every seven years—blank-faced crew members came around and stamped incomprehensible symbols in our passports, which are customarily kept in slots in our stateroom doors; we generally don't look at the passports at other times, since viewing the symbols too closely is supposed to induce fits.

"They only check them every seven years," I protested, "and nobody carries them around with them."

"You think the crew can't tell, just by looking at you, whether you've got the full set of stamps? And they're *always*, or *it's* always, looking at you, there," he added, nodding toward the looming hull, "in the outlying corrals."

I didn't believe that, then, but it was evident that he did. And if, against all reasonable odds, he really had a map to the legendary bridge, it was conceivable that I might find Ruth there. Unlikelihood redoubled—but I desperately wanted a solid and unmoving deck under my feet.

I exhaled and nodded. "Show me this map."

Hitch stepped back across the rocking platform and peered upward through the ropes and swinging floors, and put two fingers in his mouth and whistled shrilly. Footsteps shook scaffolding far above us, and then a man in a steward's jacket slid down one of the ropes, holding a wooden box that was itself tethered overhead. He dropped down the last couple of feet and quickly straightened up from a crouch.

Hitch stepped across the platform to where the man stood, and looked back at me and jerked his head, clearly asking me to follow him. I took a deep breath and let go of the ropes and shuffled to where the two men stood, sliding my feet and keeping my arms out to the sides for balance. It really was precarious out there, with the platform swinging in the wind and no railing.

What the man from above had brought was an old cigar box, and I think the brand name stamped on the top, H. Upmann, would have roused memories if Hitch had not immediately slid the top panel aside and lifted out of the box a thing like a cardboard flower—it was a six-sided polygon, about a foot wide, apparently made from a very long strip folded into triangles and then folded around on itself. The six triangular surfaces on top were blank.

He handed it to me; it was at least an inch thick, and heavy. "Don't drop it," he said. "Open it."

Leaning to one side and then the other to keep my balance, I tried to lift the edges in the center, but tearing the cardboard would have been the only way to pull any of them back; then I pinched alternate folds of the thing, closing it into a shape like a three-bladed arrowhead, and when I turned it over and opened it out again across my palm, there was a crude map on it—black line segments on the outer corners of all six edges were apparently meant to indicate the surrounding hull, and a few big rooms and service alleys were faintly outlined across the inner sections of the polygon's six triangles.

I looked up at Hitch. "This is your map? Do you have any idea how—"

"Close it and open it again," he said.

I pinched it shut, and when I opened it this time the hexagram showed six new triangles; edge-to-edge they formed a more detailed map of passageways. He nodded at me, so I closed it and opened it again, and now it was the six triangles I had seen the first time, but reversed, with the black hull lines at the center of the hexagram, and the field of passageways and alleys surrounding it.

"There," said Hitch, "that's the way. The interior surrounds the exterior."

Wary of the unrailed platform edges tilting away from me at one side and then the other, I sat down. "What," I said irritably, looking up at his silhouette against the sky; "the ship is…inside out?"

"What seems to be the center is the edge," he said. "You've got to get to the edge—the bridge to the Promised Land."

"The bridge you don't want to cross," I said, and I folded the cardboard hexagram through its changes a few more times; at one point it opened to show a grid transected by dotted lines, and at another point a map of city streets.

Hitch reached down and took the thing out of my hands. "Those are for other convoys. Stick with diagrams of the ship." He folded and opened it several more times, rapidly. When he handed it back to me, the six triangles showed geometrically arranged passageways and staterooms.

"Where do I start?" I asked him.

"Wherever you find yourself. Follow the passageways indicated on the map, and when you come to the edge of the map, unfold it and follow whatever passageways it shows then. The map will indicate that you're moving out from the center, but you'll feel like you're moving deeper into the ship."

"That's...just crazy. Random. I'd be better off flipping a coin to decide which way to go."

"Of course it's random. What else would do? And when's the last time you saw a coin?"

I hesitated for several seconds, then unbuttoned my shirt, tucked the bulky six-sided polygon inside, and buttoned it up again. "Aren't you afraid I'll lose it? Or just forget about this whole business when I'm inside again?"

"Don't—but that *is* a copy. We have two more here, and there are some others, outside and in. The original was lost centuries ago."

Remembering the complexity of the thing, I tapped my shirt and asked, "You can *copy* that?"

He shrugged and pulled me to my feet. "It takes a good man about a year to unfold it all the way and copy everything onto another length of cardboard or cloth, and then fold it back up again right. He uses up a whole lot of the complimentary pens in staterooms."

I thought of the diagrams of grids and city streets buried in the maze of folded triangles. "Who made the first one?"

"God knows. God, maybe." He whistled again, three times now, and the ropes suspending our platform shivered, and then the platform began moving up the side of the ship, alternately swinging away from the hull and then back to thud and scrape against it. I was very glad to be sitting down.

We ascended for possibly an hour, and at last, I was able to see pulleys on a pair of protruding davits above us, and the railing of a topside deck, and regularly spaced iron ladders that extended down from there for a distance of perhaps a hundred feet. The rippling sea was far below us now. And when the platform had reached the bottom rungs of one of the ladders, the ropes stopped slithering around the pulleys and we rocked to a halt.

"Up you go," said Hitch, almost cheerfully.

Up at this level the hull was painted white, and in the sunlight it was a blur to my wind-stung eyes; but the ladder was a distinct and clearly unmoving contrast to the rocking surface on which I was crouched, and I fairly leaped for it, gripping the rungs and pulling myself up them until my feet were securely set on the bottom-most one. At last I was holding still.

I quickly climbed up to the deck rail and swung over it, and at that moment I didn't care if I never saw the ocean again; but I had to turn and peer down over the rail. Hitch scowled and waved me back, so I nodded and started away along the deck, avoiding the wondering stares of several passengers who had seen me climb over the rail and probably thought I was a straying Plimsoll-line gypsy. I could feel myself blushing, and I would have forgotten everything Hitch had said if the hard corners of the map hadn't been jabbing me under my shirt.

With no real hope that the crazy map was any good, I stepped in through a doorway, out of the sun, and pulled the thing out of my shirt. The diagram at the center of its face was of a passageway not unlike the one I was in, so I walked on, taking such left and right turns as the map indicated were ways to get to the rim, though of course my progress was all inboard, away from the sunlight. It was, at first, hard to see the faintly drawn lines by just the amber glow of the overhead lights, but my eyes soon adjusted; and I dutifully folded and opened the map each time the path I appeared to be following reached the outer edge of one of the cardboard triangles.

At several points I thought the map had lost even any random correspondence to the course I was taking. Once, it showed a long, straight passageway, while I could see that the passageway I was in took a sharp turn instead; but when I walked to the corner, the apparent turn proved to be an optical illusion, and I saw that the passageway really did extend straight. Another time the map traced a straight line through what was clearly a block of empty staterooms, but in every intervening bulkhead there proved to be a door directly ahead of me, and I was able to walk straight through all the staterooms to the next passageway, without deviating from the line on the map. Several times the map showed nothing but an X at the point I had reached, but I soon discovered that these indicated ladders, and the next section of the map, exposed by folding and opening it as I descended the steps, invariably bore a Y which marked the bottom of the ladder on the next deck down, and I could proceed.

I blundered through spaces that were entirely dark, hunched my way down carpeted ladders so narrow that both my elbows scuffed tapestried bulkheads, even edged across foot-wide steel beams spanning deep pits, in the depths of which machinery rolled and clanked in eternal ponderous rhythm.

Through all this, I saw not one other person; perhaps the map-thing was deliberately drawn—by whom? God knows—to direct the holder through areas long abandoned by the passengers.

And ultimately—penultimately, I should say—I found the Grand Salon. After an hour of making my way through dim-lit passageways where two people could hardly have walked abreast, with ceilings so low that the rivets sometimes tugged at my hair, it was dizzying to step out into the volume of that vast chamber. It took me a few seconds of peering around to confirm that there was no one else there.

Faceted colored lights glowed brightly at the crowns of marble pillars standing at intervals along the parqueted floor, and the remote walls on either side curved in scalloped waves where they met the coffered ceiling a hundred feet over my head.

And, after hesitantly walking out across the floor, I saw that the wall at the far end of the cathedral space was an enormous map. I hurried forward, my footsteps echoing away in distant corners, and soon I was close enough to the wall to see the gold mosaic image of the eastern American coast filling the left side of it, and a thread of bright steel curving from about New York across the blue tiles that represented the Atlantic Ocean.

There was no gold continent at all on the right side of the wall. Blue tiles extended to the end of the wall, from the floor all the way up to the ceiling.

A crystal model of an ocean liner, probably a yard long but looking tiny way up there on the steel track, was more than three-quarters of the way to the right-hand wall ... and a white disk stood on the track a ship's length ahead of it.

I knew the ship model was said to be moving from left to right, and I wondered uneasily if the white disk was moving the opposite way.

The day will come, Ruth's father had said.

Hitch had called the model ship the *guide lever*.

For a moment I wanted to find something to throw at the crystal ship, or at the apparently advancing white disk, but there was nothing to throw except possibly one of my shoes, and anyway the steel track was far too high up on the wall for me to have any hope of hitting anything on it.

I pinched the cardboard polygon map shut again, and when I opened it I found a pattern unlike any I'd seen before—there was a big rectangle, probably representing the Grand Salon, and a short line extending from the far end of it to a tight spiral around a letter Z, and nothing else.

At the foot of the map wall, one section of the blue tiles was interrupted by an arch framed in ornate pillars. There was nothing left to do but start toward it.

It probably took more than a full minute to walk the length of that nave, and as I kept on putting one foot in front of the other I craned my neck to see the paintings on the remote ceiling. Muscular human figures were depicted, in apparently stressful or idyllic situations, and I knew they must be characters from some mythologies, but I didn't bother to try to remember them. And when the map wall loomed above me, I didn't indulge in the useless attempt to identify any areas of the American continent besides the vaguely evocative name *New York*.

In the moment when I passed through the arch, I felt as though the whole weight of the world, embodied in the map wall, was on my shoulders—but when I had moved on, into a small circular chamber at the head of a descending spiral ladder, it was forgotten.

Gripping the polished wooden banister, I began descending the carpeted steps; and though I walked down those steps for so long that my legs burned with fatigue and I was at times sure the steps I saw beneath my feet were just exhaustion-visions of ones I had long since passed, always there was another coil of the ladder below me. I only became aware of the eternal background hum of the engines when that sound diminished, and I had not descended too many more turns before it was, unprecedentedly, gone altogether. The terribly silent air was cold now. I wished I had brought something to eat, and I resisted the ever-stronger temptation to lie down on the carpeted steps and sleep. I found myself wondering if I had descended to the depth of the keel, or somehow below even that.

But when the ladder ended at a level deck at last, and I sat down, groaning and panting, an unimpeded sea breeze was in my face and I was blinking across a polished deck at an emerald green sky visible through broad, half-opened glass panels.

I got slowly to my feet and limped forward. The wide deck was studded with tall brass engine telegraph pedestals, their glassed-in, fan-shaped faces divided into segments with words in white on black—on the nearest one I could read FULL, HALF, and SLOW, but the solid wedge-shaped pointer blocked a fourth word. The paired handles on each telegraph's pointer bracket stood up like polished wooden horns across the deck's expanse.

And someone was there.

A woman was standing by the nearest open port, silhouetted against the strange sky, and I recognized her as Ruth. My first, random thought was that she had found the bridge at last.

I made my way across the deck to stand beside her. She was staring out over an unrippled jade sea at a pearl-gray fog bank some leagues ahead, over which hung two rust-colored moons. There was no foredeck below us at all; we appeared to be at the very forward-most point of the ship.

Ruth was aware of me, though she didn't look away from the view ahead. "I can remember you," she said. The breeze through the half open port threw her long dark hair behind her, and her face was lit in chiaroscuro highlights by the unnatural glow. "For a little while yet," she added.

An objection or protest rose in my mind, but even to myself it seemed petty, irrelevant. So I just nodded and stared with her at the approaching fog bank. I was shivering, and not entirely because of the chilly air.

"Where's the—" I began. "Is there—" but a creaking sound behind me made me turn, and at the center of what I now saw was a wide half-circle of the engine telegraphs stood the ship's wheel on a brass pedestal of its own. It was a great polished wooden ring, and eight wooden spokes extended through the ring to protrude outside it as lathed handles.

A pair of small, dark hands gripped the handles at the sides.

Without moving away from Ruth, I peered at the person behind the hands. Standing on a high platform beside the glowing binnacle column, a young child turned its head and stared back at me.

Peripherally I noticed that it was draped in a hooded robe that was the same nacreous gray as the fog bank, but my attention was caught, and irresistibly held, by its eyes—they were entirely black, as though the pupils were dilated so far that the irises, and even the whites, had been crowded out. If it had been an ordinary child, I would have judged it to be about five years old…

The captain?

"Who," I managed to ask, "*are* you?"

"Many," it said. Its sexless voice seemed to be that of an adult, and in spite of the wind through the half-open ports, it was as clear as if the speaker were standing right next to me. "And many more."

I pulled my gaze away and glanced to the side at Ruth, but she still stared ahead through the port.

"Ruth," I whispered, palpably aware of the child's eyes still on me, "what does it mean?"

"Ruth," she echoed as if tasting the syllable. "We're moving on, all of us. Shedding all the old ballast, all the old definitions." She smiled faintly, still not looking at me. *"E pluribus unum."* She lifted a hand, then let it drop. "Contentment, at last, at least. Forever."

The cold wind seemed to have penetrated my chest and spine. I thought of the definition of marriage, and then the definition of myself. "Are they what came down in the lights in the sky, years ago? Damn it, Ruth, where are they taking us?"

"Out of where," answered the child. "With us. To me."

My scalp tightened, and I had to take a deep, hitching breath to say, "Will you...lower the lifeboats all the way, first?"

"All lifeboats," said the child, "all parachutes, subways, oases, inns, are in me."

I was still looking at Ruth's cold profile. "Come back with me," I whispered to her, though I was bleakly sure the child could hear me. "To the hull—we can escape with the Plimsoll-line gypsies." They can just cut the lines to the lifeboats, I thought, and their boxes and platforms can be rafts.

"The hull," she said, and then the child said, "is a cylinder," to which Ruth added, "at the very center of the ship. People," and the child went on, "huddle there, in the dark," and Ruth sighed and completed the sentence: "with old dreams."

The thing in the robe let go of the wheel handles and stepped down to the deck. "It's a long way," it said, stretching out its bare arms, "but you're nearly there. We can carry you across. Take my hands."

After a moment of hesitation in which she almost glanced toward me, Ruth moved away from the port, reaching out for the pale fingers of the thing's right hand. The left hand was extended toward me, in the green glow of the sky ahead.

Contentment, at last, at least. Forever.

I stared at the thing's hand, not at its eyes.

We were taken up; Hitch had said. *Everybody, everywhere.*

But what if they liked *the old ways, eh? Eating food, reading, sleeping, having children, all that?*

I thought of the hullfolk, out there in the wind under a blue sky, on their makeshift scaffolds and platforms and partly lowered lifeboats. But...

The hull is a cylinder at the very center of the ship. People huddle there, in the dark, with old dreams.

The ship, I had asked Hitch, *is... inside out?* I had traveled far inboard, and very far down, to get here, to the bridge.

On the map wall, the crystal ship was close to the white disk, and the fogbank visible out these ports was not far off.

We hope to at least not go forward.

I stepped back from the child and didn't look at Ruth, since she probably wouldn't be Ruth at all now. I turned away from the telegraph pedestals and the wheel and the open ports and the thing or things that constituted our captain, and hurried back through the doorway to the foot of the terribly long ascending stair.

After climbing the steps for what might have been a couple of days, several times sleeping stiffly stretched out across the carpeted risers, I reached a numbered deck; and when I looked at the cardboard map, all the hexagrams I was able to fold it into were blank, though between the multifolded layers at the edges I once or twice thought I glimpsed inked lines. I wasn't able to unfold the thing in such a way as to expose them. I found a cafeteria—the staff were staring at me this time, but I ignored them as I ate a couple of mounds of corned beef hash and downed several glasses of the sweet red wine and then stumbled out. In the nearest of the empty staterooms, I collapsed full length across the always made-up bed.

I slept for a long time. Why is it that only now do I remember clocks, wristwatches? I used up two pens, and the stationery from several of the empty staterooms, to write this.

I'll leave this stack of papers here. Tomorrow I'll begin walking up and out, and, if there's still time, find the hull, and the ones who live outside—or in the dark, in the cylinder in the core of the ship.

I hope to at least not go forward.

The Rune Witch

written by
Jefferson Snow

illustrated by
DAVID HOFFRICHTER

ABOUT THE AUTHOR

Jefferson Snow is a writer from Orem, Utah, where he lives with his wife and four children. Though he majored in advertising at Brigham Young University, he spent most of his time writing stand-up or sneaking into Brandon Sanderson's 318R lectures. Both were big influences on his writing, even if his stories lean serious and his magic systems require no spreadsheets.

To Jefferson, the fantasy genre is a grand cathedral, and he loves the gargoyles who guard its buttresses: anti-heroes like Logen Ninefingers and Tyrion Lannister. But as fun as those gray characters are, Jefferson believes we can't give up on the everyday parishioners sitting in the pews—the Samwise Gamgees and Neville Longbottoms of the congregation. We still need tales of ordinary people trying to do the right thing, especially when it's hard.

Like much of Jefferson's work, "The Rune Witch" handles themes of loss, sacrifice, and temptation. Fascinated by the trope of the Faustian bargain—à la Fëanor and Melkor, Elric and Arioch, King Elias and Ineluki—the author explores whether making a deal with the devil can ever be justified.

Finally, Jefferson wishes to thank all his writing group friends who helped him build up the chops to write this story. "The Rune Witch" is his first sale. He hopes you enjoy it.

ABOUT THE ILLUSTRATOR

David grew up in Broomall, Pennsylvania, right outside of Philadelphia and not too far from several museums that would inspire his love of illustration for the rest of his life.

David was raised on adventure stories and magical tales of lions, dwarves, elves, and heroes of all ages. The one thing these stories had in common was amazing pictures illustrated by artists who lived very close to where David first learned to love art.

From N.C. Wyeth, Howard Pyle, and Jessie Willcox Smith to the artistic legends who are alive today and still brightening the world with every brushstroke they make, David revels in his appreciation of art and how it has shaped his foundation from an early age.

He loves to create narrative paintings that tell the stories between the lines. There is a mystery to be found in his works that represents who he is as an artist and how he sees the world. He cannot wait to share his world with you.

The Rune Witch

Her baby was only two weeks old when Jindei took her into the maze beneath the ruins. The sound of her wailing, so warm and full of life, filled the cold, dead tunnels. When they reached the last chamber, the demon was waiting. He watched from behind the bluish hexglass, his many eyes narrowed.

"What have you named it?" the demon, Shijai, asked.

Not for the first time, Jindei wished the prison could hold back his voice along with his body. She considered ignoring his question, but what was the point? He'd pull it out of her in time. "Elenai."

"She's beautiful," said Shijai, his voice deep and sonorous. As if at the sound of it, the child ceased to cry.

Jindei ground her teeth. All morning, she had rocked and nursed and sung to no avail. Apparently, the demon had but to speak.

While the baby cooed on her back, Jindei opened her pouch and brought out the bowl. It was about a hand's breadth wide and a few inches deep, its color bone white, save for a rusty stain at the center of its basin. She tugged her antler-horn knife from its sheath and spread her fingers. A web of white scars covered her palm. Finding a rare patch of unmarred flesh, she made a small slash. More than two hundred times she'd endured the same wound. Still, the cut made her wince.

She squeezed her fingers into a fist. Red ran from the crease of her palm and into the bowl.

"A bleak business, bringing your daughter along for this," Shijai said.

"This will be her business soon enough."

By the time the bowl was filled, Jindei's skin was cold and clammy. She bound up her hand and stepped forward. The blood was still warm when she dipped in her fingers. Dripping, she raised them to the glowing barrier and made the symbols she had learned from her mother long ago.

While Jindei smeared the blood, the demon floated up so one of his faces pressed against the hexglass—at least what she imagined to be a face. His form was like a skein of fleshy threads, peppered with eyes and teeth and orifices she could not name. He had no symmetry, no shape she could compare with any animal or beast.

"I would spare you both, you know," he said soothingly.

Jindei kept writing, refusing to meet his eyes.

"Let me free, and I'll give your daughter so much more than this." He closed all his eyes, save one, which he let roll to take in the chamber around her. "I will make her a chief. A queen, even. Anything but a lonely rune witch."

The thought of little bloody palms almost broke her concentration.

"Look at your poor hands. I could make it so she never has to prick a finger."

Jindei worked faster.

"Come, Jindei. Let me help you and the girl. You know I can."

She finished the last rune, and the symbols flashed a searing white. The hexglass wall went a shade of crimson, revitalized and renewed. She stepped away, spitting onto her fingertips and rubbing away the blood.

"Save your breath," she said. With the seal fortified, it felt safe to talk again. "I know your lies by now. You act as if a different woman has come to guard you."

Shijai glanced at the baby, then back at Jindei. "Oh, but one has."

Elenai cooed again. The sound filled Jindei with a rush of doubt. Hands trembling, she put away her knife and bowl.

She turned to leave, but Shijai called after her. "What sort of mother would condemn her daughter to a life as hard as yours? Bound to these ruins? Never to leave?"

Though she knew she should go, Jindei found herself rooted in place, waiting to hear what more he would say.

DAVID HOFFRICHTER

"You've borne this burden long enough. Release me, and you and your daughter can have anything."

Jindei hesitated. Not long, but long enough to feel a prick of guilt. "Goodbye," she said.

Shijai spoke in a voice like butter. "Goodbye, Jindei. Please, think on my offer."

To her shame, she thought of little else. The offer tortured her as she climbed up out of the tunnels. It tailed her on the surface. She bore it past the crumbling towers, over the shattered causeway, all the way to the edge of the forest where her hut squatted on the banks of a clear brook. She tried to leave the offer at the door, but it followed her inside. Later that night, when Elenai stirred and cried out for milk, Jindei was already awake.

For months, the proposal burrowed like a worm, biting its way deeper and deeper. And every time she plucked the temptation out, Shijai tried enticing her again. On the night of one Dead Moon, he said, "Anything you want for her—a life somewhere else, a village to love her, a kingdom to worship her. If nothing else, at least someone to raise her with."

The last pricked Jindei's heart the sharpest. Did Shijai know somehow? In case he didn't, she kept her face impassive, saying nothing till the sealing runes were finished. Though she ignored him, Shijai remained very polite. And very flattering. Especially of Elenai.

"Look how fast she's growing," he said of her when she turned half a year.

Jindei smiled despite herself. At the child's birth, the midwives had all remarked on how skinny and frail she was. They joked that all her strength must have gone into growing that full head of black hair. But at six months, Elenai was so plump she looked like a bottle gourd with arms and feet.

"She has your eyes too," said Shijai.

The urge to see herself in the face of her child clutched her in its grip. Jindei nearly took her pack off to look into Elenai's eyes before she stopped herself.

Shijai must have read her eagerness. "What? Has no one told you that before?"

Jindei shook her head.

"I suppose that only makes sense. How often do Chief Alenu's villagers come to visit?"

Jindei lifted her chin defiantly. "They bring supplies every week. Food. Raiment if I need it."

"But how often do they stay? How often do they sit and share a meal with you? How often will they come to your fire and talk with you of the world beyond this dead one?"

Jindei's shoulders slumped.

"Even after all you do for them, am I your best friend?" He laughed, and not with his preened human imitation. He laughed his true laugh. A sound like a thousand pigs burning alive. "I am, aren't I? And one day, I'll be her best friend too."

Jindei said nothing. Fighting back tears, she left.

At a year, Elenai stretched out a bit, but she was still "more roll than pole," as Jindei's mother used to say. At two, she was still plump, and when she walked, her cheeks bounced, and her thighs jiggled. At three, she looked like a different creature altogether. The baby fat melted away, and her black hair grew down to her shoulders. At night, Jindei would brush it with a comb of carved bone and sing all the songs she knew. Which wasn't many. She knew even fewer stories. Jindei's mother had given her all she could, but there were only so many songs and stories to be gleaned in this small corner of the world. It felt even smaller now with a daughter of her own.

She came from a long line of isolation. Her mother and her grandmother had tended Shijai alone. But before that, there were stories of a whole commune of rune sisters taking turns renewing the hexglass. Why they had disbanded or shrunk to just one member, Jindei never learned. She often daydreamed of living among such a group, sharing their burdens and their company. She wanted something like that for Elenai most of all.

"Do you feel lonely?" Jindei asked one night as they lay beside the dying coals.

"What means lonely?" Elenai asked.

"Feeling sad because you're alone."

"Nai not alone. Nai with Mama."

Jindei smiled, her daughter's words fanning a warmth inside her that put the embers in the hearth to shame. "That's very sweet, Nai, but do you wish you had friends?"

"What's friends?"

A lump formed in Jindei's throat. "Someone like you. Other girls your age to play with."

"What other girls?"

"Ones from the village, maybe." Though it was dark, and Elenai was deep in her covers, Jindei sensed her stiffen. "What's wrong?"

"I don't want to go village."

Jindei smirked. "We could ask them to come here."

"No."

"Are you sure?"

"Tell me story."

Jindei decided not to press. "All right. Which one?"

"Girl who talks to birds."

"Sunshei?"

"Yes. Sunshei is Nai's friend."

Jindei smiled even as her heart broke.

A few days later, some villagers came with supplies. Errand women mostly, and a handful of Chief Alenu's warriors too. These were grim men armed with spears and garbed in leather and bone. Each of them wore their chief's totem—a copper brooch fashioned into the head of a wild boar. Supposedly, there'd been a time when the chief himself would come each week to give his offerings and thanks personally. But whenever that had been, Jindei couldn't say. She'd never seen it herself.

Ignoring the gruff guards, Jindei approached the women unloading their packs. What she needed to ask was obvious, but the anxious knots inside her kept her mute. She had to do it though. For Elenai.

"Pardon me," she said. The women looked surprised to be addressed by her. Jindei cleared her throat. "Could I ask you to please bring Banu with you next week?"

The women smiled nervously as some unsaid thing passed between them.

"Did I say something wrong?"

"No, Rune Sister Jindei," said a gray-haired woman. "I'll let him know you want to see him."

Jindei thanked her and left to take some of the rations into the hut. At the door, she heard the women whispering behind her. She paused but didn't turn around.

That night, she and Elenai ate rice and peppers beside the hearth. The errand women had even brought a little venison. Getting meat from the villagers used to be rare. But the chief's son, Sarno, was said to have become quite the hunter, killing more game than his family could eat. She'd also heard he was brazen and cruel, and that the village elders were all afraid of him. But what did Jindei care? The meat tasted like heaven.

The next week lumbered by until the day for supplies came again. Jindei took Elenai to some hills overlooking the trail that ran between their hut and the village. There they waited, peering down through the ginkgo and larch trees. Soon, the villagers appeared with their armed escort. Heart in her throat, Jindei looked for Banu.

"Look," she said, pointing him out once she'd spotted him. "Do you see him?"

Elenai followed her finger and furrowed her brow.

"That's your father."

Elenai pressed up to Jindei's leg.

"What's wrong?"

"I don't want a father. I want Mama."

Jindei smiled. She squeezed Elenai's hand and led her back down the hill. They arrived at the hut just as the villagers did. Banu stood toward the back, his hands fidgeting, eyes downcast. Four years had not been long enough to steal his good looks. His face was still lean, cheeks slightly sunken above his brick-straight jaw. The sun gleamed in his black hair—Elenai's hair. Then Jindei saw a thin braid behind his left ear. Her heart sank.

Once all the stores were taken inside, she went to him on leaden feet. He nodded awkwardly as she approached.

"Good morning, Banu," she managed.

Banu swallowed noticeably. "Good morning, Jindei."

"You are married now," she said and tugged at the hair behind her own ear.

"I am," he said.

"I am happy for you." Even then, the grief was clawing for a way out.

"Thank you." He craned his neck to look past her. "How is our…" He caught himself. "How is Elenai?"

"Growing fast. Willful as a goat." Jindei turned toward the hut. Elenai was inside, peering out at them from around the edge of the door flap.

Banu laughed. "Strong, then? Healthy?"

Jindei nodded.

"Good." He cleared his throat. "The women said you wanted to see me."

Jindei pressed her sweaty palms down the back of her shirt. "I want you to take care of her."

Banu stared.

"Just for one week a month."

Banu rubbed the back of his neck. "My wife…she doesn't know—"

"About Elenai?"

Banu shook his head.

The surprise was like a splash of cold water. "You never told her?"

Banu stammered, mouth forming and reforming words but saying none.

"Are you ashamed of her?"

He gave her a wounded look. "Please, Jindei. I never thought I'd see her again. You told me I wouldn't."

Tears blurred Jindei's vision. "She needs more than just me."

Banu lowered his voice. "Then why did you turn me away? I would have stayed with you here all my life."

Jindei looked at the ground between them.

Banu stepped closer and whispered. "You said it had to be this way, or you'd forget your duty." He glanced east, toward the broken towers looming past the trees. Jindei could not follow his eyes. His face was suddenly so close to hers, she couldn't look away.

She smelled something sweet on his breath, caught a whiff of wood smoke clinging to his clothes. His scent carried her mind back to the nights they'd spent together. Aside from the day of Elenai's birth, her time with him had been the best of her life. Before Banu, she'd guarded the world against Shijai because it was all she knew. After, she guarded the world because it held her lover and the child they had made together.

"She needs people to love," Jindei said. "She needs a reason for her duty."

A tortured look fell across his face. Time dragged, his silence stretching. And just as Jindei was sure he'd walk away without a word, he spoke. "I'll talk to Tiri."

Jindei taught Elenai her letters and the runes of the Old Words. They practiced them in the mud beside the river and in the dust along the road. Most importantly, Elenai watched Jindei write them in blood across the hexglass every month.

"Is Shijai stuck?" Elenai asked one night as they made their way home from the ritual.

"Yes," said Jindei. "Remember? As long as we write the words every Dead Moon, he stays stuck."

"Is Shijai been stuck a long time?"

"Yes."

"This long?" Elenai held her hands apart like a fisherman describing his catch.

"Longer," said Jindei.

"*This* long?" Elenai stretched her arms out as far as they'd go.

Jindei shook her head. "More."

Wonder filled Elenai's eyes. "How long, Mama?"

"At least two hundred years."

Elenai's jaw dropped. She stared off, her little mind obviously grappling with such a huge span of time. "Who stucked him?" she asked after some contemplation.

"The rune sisters, our foremothers."

"How?"

Jindei had always planned on telling Elenai one day. The knowledge had to be passed down, but she had never considered how to word it for a child. She thought a moment and then began. "They picked a star in the sky and, with great sadness, took its life."

Elenai gasped, but she did not interrupt.

"As it died, the sisters pulled its body down to Earth and threw it into Shijai's heart. Stars do not bleed when they die; rather, part of the world bleeds into them. So, the dead star drank in Shijai. To keep him inside, the sisters built a cage around the star so he could never be spat out." Jindei did not mention the cost of such a feat—how two in every three rune sisters had died with witchblood boiling in their veins to harness such vast amounts of power. Jindei would wait till her little girl was older to explain that part.

Elenai's expression changed from wonder to worry. "Is Shijai sad?"

Her innocence made Jindei smile. "Maybe. I think he's angry, mostly. Though he hides it well."

"Can we let him go?"

Jindei shook her head. "You know we can't."

"But why?"

"Because Shijai will hurt a lot of people if he gets out."

"Shijai's nice to me."

"He is pretending to be nice. He would eat us if he could."

Elenai cried at that. Jindei picked her up to kiss her cheek and missed how plump it used to feel against her lips.

"It's all right, Nai," she whispered. "I'll be nice to you, and I'll never have to pretend that I love you."

Banu wasn't with the villagers when they returned the next week. He'd sent a note with one of the women, but his absence told Jindei what it said before she even opened it. On the days when new rations came, Jindei and Elenai always stuffed themselves silly. But that night, Jindei only picked at her food. It tasted like nothing.

Soon, the Dead Moon came, and it was time to go into the ruins once more. They followed the familiar path, a furrow plowed by the feet of all the generations before them. It took them out of the forest and into the city, all the way to the hole in the ground. They slipped inside and followed the twisting tunnels into blackness. Jindei held Elenai's wrist with one hand while groping along the familiar walls with the other. At last, they came to the hexglass glowing dimly in the deep.

As Jindei took out her bowl and knife, Elenai strode up to Shijai's prison and tapped on the barrier. "Would you eat me if you could?" she asked.

Shijai laughed—his lying laugh, a sound as sweet as bells. "Of course not, my girl. Who told you that?" His eyes were on Jindei before finishing the question.

"Would you hurt people if you got not stucked?"

"Bad people, maybe. But people like you and your mother? No. How could I? We're old friends."

"See!" said Elenai, rounding on Jindei. "Shijai's nice."

"Shijai is pretending, Elenai. He's lying."

"*Mama* is lying," she said and stamped her foot. "Shijai is my friend. Shijai and Sunshei."

Jindei slapped her. Time slowed as the shock and hurt registered on Elenai's face. The look of pain doused Jindei's white-hot anger and washed her with regret. Elenai hung her head, weeping. Sick with herself, Jindei gathered Elenai into her arms, cooing and whispering apologies into her ear. The whole time, Shijai watched them, his expression unreadable. Was some hidden set of lips curling into a smile somewhere?

On the way home, Elenai walked ahead, refusing to hold hands. It made Jindei angry, but not at her daughter. She turned her palms upward and stared at the scars. She wanted to show them to Banu, to the chief and his villagers. Did they have any idea what she did for them?

As they came to the hut, she found herself daydreaming of taking Shijai's old offer. In her imagination, he swept into the village, destroying everything, devouring everyone. Meanwhile, Jindei and Elenai were nowhere close enough to hear the screams. They lived in a tower far away, overlooking the city Shijai had given them to rule—a living city full of servants and suitors and people who loved them.

Jindei willed the thoughts away. Temptations were like bad guests, her mother used to say. Host them long enough, and they'll start to think the place is theirs.

Jindei cooked supper, and they ate by the light of the coals. Long after Elenai nodded off, Jindei lay awake. There were other men than Banu. Maybe one of them could give her another daughter, someone for Elenai to love and be loved by. But the thought of any other man turned Jindei's stomach and made her muscles rigid. On the brink of sleep, she made up her mind.

In the morning, they packed up and hiked into the village. Elenai had never been. When they got there, she clung to Jindei's side like a leech. Jindei asked around until they found Banu's dwelling. She went to the door and gave a loud knock.

The door came open with a creak of leather lashings. Banu stood within, blinking. Jindei gently pushed Elenai toward the threshold. "She needs you."

Banu glanced about nervously. Someone moved behind him. A woman's voice sounded from inside. "Who is it?"

"No one. Go back to the hearth."

"Who is it?"

"Go back—"

The woman pushed past him. She took in Jindei first, then Elenai. Venom filled her eyes. Banu put an arm around her belly and guided her back inside. *A swollen belly*, Jindei had noticed. The sight of it almost made her sob.

"You can't come here," he said. "What if something had happened to you on the road? Go back to the dead city, where you are needed." He went to shut the door, but Jindei shoved her foot into the gap.

"Elenai needs you," she said, pushing her own feelings aside.

Banu's gaze fell. The door slowly drifted open. His wife stood behind him, arms folded, nostrils flared, her glare still venomous. Jindei locked eyes with the woman, trying to overcome the poison with her own silent pleading. An age seemed to pass, and finally, a change came over the woman's face. At last, she glanced at Elenai, then back to Jindei. Her eyes watered, but she gave a trembling nod. Banu let them in.

From then on, Elenai lived with Banu one week out of every month. For half a year, she screamed and pitched a fit every time Jindei sent her back with the errand women. But then, her baby sister came, and Elenai wouldn't stop asking to go back. Banu and his wife called their child Danai. Elenai said they had the same hair—long and black and silky. Whenever Elenai talked about her sister, joy came into her voice, excitement lit her eyes. Jindei couldn't help but feel jealous sometimes.

She did her best not to entertain any regrets, but then Danai's first birthday fell on the Dead Moon. "That is when we go to Shijai." Jindei explained this over and over during the weeks leading up to it.

"But you can go by yourself," said Elenai. She was five now, headstrong as ever and too clever for her own good. "Just this once. Please."

"Just once? Do you know how many times we can miss the binding and still keep Shijai in his prison?"

Elenai's face scrunched up like she couldn't remember.

"Not even once!"

"But they are throwing a party. I've never been to a party."

"Party?" Jindei scoffed at the word. Elenai had been tough as gristle a year ago. The villagers had made her soft. "We are rune sisters. We need no parties."

"But it's for Danai. I love her."

That gave Jindei pause. Wasn't this what she wanted? Hadn't this been the whole point of sending her to Banu's in the first place—to love the world she protected?

"All right," Jindei relented. "Just this once."

She was on the road to Shijai's prison when the silence of the world struck her. Years had passed since making the trek alone. Without someone to talk to or watch over, she took in the dead city with fresh eyes. Vines grew up the sides of half-crumbled buildings, green veins fleshing out old bones. The place was so ancient and so huge it made her feel impossibly small. Her mother's stories said the world had once teemed with beautiful cities, that people dwelled in gleaming towers and glass fortresses. But after Shijai's coming,

353

humanity had been reduced to living in huts and hovels. And if he came again, what would they be reduced to then?

Not living at all, she was sure.

All at once, the full weight of her task struck her. The mundanity of routine was stripped away, and the stark reality of her situation nearly overwhelmed her. She and Elenai were the only two things standing between mankind and its end.

Suddenly, she felt even smaller than she had a few moments earlier.

Shijai greeted her when she arrived, eyestalks tracing her movement across the room. "Where is Elenai?" Concern edged his voice, and so convincingly too.

"At the village," she said, taking out her bowl and getting on with things.

"Today?"

Jindei nodded.

"You allowed that?"

"I'm her mother, aren't I?" She gave a little gasp as the knife sliced into her palm.

"Yes, but I'm surprised. You've always been so diligent."

Unable to discern if he was rebuking or complimenting her, she filled the little bowl.

"I know what you've been trying to do," he said.

She dabbed her fingers in the blood and began to draw.

"What is the point of all this without someone to protect? This whole arrangement with her father, you're trying to give her something to lose should I get out."

Blood nearly sloshed over one side of the bowl as Jindei trembled. With a breath, she steadied herself and pressed on. "I need to ask Elenai to stop telling you so much about our business," she said.

"She talks more than you ever did. It's those villagers, I think. I hope they treat her better than they've treated you. Who knows? With her growing up around them, maybe those fools will stop forcing your kind to live in isolation."

Jindei frowned. Elenai needed fellowship beyond what she could give her, but the thought of them living in the village year-round frightened her.

"The isolation may have its uses, though," Shijai mused. "Makes life less complicated." His eyes left her, stared past her. To Jindei, he seemed deep in thought. "The human heart is like a spider, spinning webs around everyone it meets—little strands of memories, emotions, meaning. Before long, Elenai will be bound by a thousand threads she doesn't even know are there, pulled in a thousand directions. Few will pull her here."

"It's just one week a month," Jindei said, almost finished.

"It starts that way."

When Elenai returned from town a few days later, she wouldn't stop moving. She bounced and hopped around the hut, singing and screaming, her mouth set in a wide grin. When she wasn't belting out some song, she recounted the events of Danai's party, rambling till she ran out of breath. It sounded like half the village had turned up to eat, give gifts, and make music. She spoke of Danai's grandparents and the gifts they gave. One grandfather, Tiri's father, had whittled a little whistle to blow on.

"He even made something for me," Elenai announced. She pulled a little figurine from her satchel: a wooden horse, finely carved. She held it out. Jindei took it and rolled it around her scarred palm.

"It's wonderful." Jindei couldn't help but glance at the doll she'd knitted, the one Elenai never took to the village anymore.

Elenai snatched the horse back and held it up to admire. "Grandpa said he'll carve me another when the new baby comes."

Jindei's head jerked up. "New baby?"

Elenai nodded. "The one hiding in Tiri's tummy."

Jindei felt full of dust.

"When is my birthday, Mama?"

"In the spring," said Jindei, holding back tears.

"What day?"

"I don't know."

"You don't know the day?" The smile on her little face withered, and part of Jindei took pleasure in its demise.

"No. I know the moons."

Another month passed. Each night, Jindei and Elenai would stoke a fire and crawl beneath their covers. But when Jindei tried to sing to her, Elenai asked for different songs, ones Jindei had never heard of.

"Tiri knows them," Elenai would say.

It was the same with stories. Elenai was bored with all the ones Jindei kept in her quiver. She didn't even want to hear about Sunshei and the birds anymore.

"But you love that one," Jindei said.

"That story's for babies." After dismissing all of Jindei's other offers, Elenai would end up telling some story to herself. And not very well. She would start and stop and start again. She'd meander and follow strange digressions. Sometimes she'd get lost and frustrated and blame Jindei for distracting her.

They fought more than they used to. Elenai picked apart every command, resisted every direction. Jindei could not tell her to do anything without being compared to Banu or Tiri. She felt her patience stretched as thin as fish scales.

One night, Elenai said, "Tiri doesn't make me rinse my hands before supper."

Jindei's composure slipped away. "You're not going back to the village this month," she snapped.

"What?" said Elenai.

"When you're with me, you do what I say. Until you learn that, you're not going back."

Elenai's eyes welled up. "Please, Mama. I'm sorry. I promise to be good."

"A rune sister doesn't promise to do things. She *does* them."

"But, Mama."

"You're not going, and not another word."

Elenai went to her bedroll, screaming. Jindei waited for her to burn out, but the child wept for hours. Finally, she whimpered one last time and fell asleep. Jindei lay awake, unable to doze for the pit in her stomach. She couldn't stop imagining Elenai wrapped in a thousand tiny threads—a spider web whose every strand but one stretched back toward the village.

356

The villagers came, and the villagers left. Elenai did not go with them. She stomped her little feet and shrieked like a dying animal. Jindei looked for the little horse figurine Elenai loved so much, in hopes it might calm her down. Then she remembered. Elenai had left it at Banu's the month before.

All Jindei could do was ignore the tantrums. She had her own frustrations. Combing through the supplies earlier, she'd noticed there was no meat. She checked again to make sure. It was as she feared. "No meat this week," she said.

Elenai was too busy sulking to care.

Jindei sighed. She sat down on the floor of the hut and rubbed her eyes. She wasn't all that hungry, but her mouth watered at the thought of venison. Had the chief's son, the supposedly great hunter, been too busy to bag a doe for the woman who kept all destruction at bay?

It occurred to her: she had her own bow. She crawled to the chest in the corner, some old trunk her mother had found scavenging in the ruins. Jindei opened it and rummaged around till she found a long, buckskin bag. She pulled it out and untied the leather thongs that held it closed. The bow lay inside, polished and gleaming. She ran a finger down the curve of it, then took it by its handle.

She hadn't strung it in years, but even a failed hunt would give her and Elenai something to do together besides fight.

"Nai?"

Elenai didn't look up. She was still bathing her face in her hands.

"Can you try to calm down? We're going to go hunting."

Elenai scowled up at her. "You don't know how to hunt."

"My mother taught me, but I forget much. Want to help me learn again?"

Elenai's sobs subsided to sniffling and hiccups. "All right," she said.

Jindei strung the bow, and they trekked out into the forest. Arrows rattled pleasantly in the quiver at her hip, a good counterpoint to Elenai's sullen footsteps thumping behind her. Neither spoke. As they walked through curtains of flowering willow boughs and over the tufts of reed grass, the weight of their silence grew.

It was the same silence that had once hung between Jindei and her own mother—a quiet that had made her thoughts run wild with worry when she was a girl. *Did I upset her? What does she want me to say to fix it? Who could I be to make her love me more?*

Was Elenai asking those same questions to herself? The possibility nearly made Jindei double over with sadness. She opened her mouth to speak, to break the cold rift between them, but nothing came to her lips. What would Elenai want to talk about that wouldn't make Jindei jealous or lonely?

Perhaps silence was better for now. At least that way they wouldn't scare away the game.

Just after midday they found deer spoor: hoofprints and some droppings. They seemed fresh, though she couldn't be certain. It had been years since she hunted. Still, she wished to look competent in front of Elenai, so she beckoned her over.

"See that?" She gestured at the tracks and scat. "We're close."

"Are those beans?"

"Fresh dung."

"Dung?" asked Elenai.

"*Poo.*"

She'd hoped the word would make Elenai laugh, but the girl only scowled. "I think they're beans, Mama."

Jindei rolled her eyes. "Maybe I should make you eat one."

Elenai shook her head.

"Come on, then."

The tracks led down a furrow in the loamy earth. They followed them for a long time before the prints veered off the path into a screen of trees on their left.

"I don't want to go in there," Elenai said.

Jindei didn't bother with persuasion or bargaining. She seized Elenai by the hand and dragged her off the trail. Branches of oak and maple grabbed at them as they forced their way through the thicket. The ground grew rocky, slanting upward till it took them to the crest of a little hill. On the other side, it sloped down into a clearing. At the bottom stood a stag sipping from a stream.

Jindei's hands and feet went cold, but excitement lit a fire in her chest. Heart pounding, she dropped to the ground. Elenai looked down, confused. Jindei reached up and dragged her down beside her.

"What—"

Jindei held a finger to her lips, then nodded toward the deer below. Elenai craned her neck to see over the crown of the hill. Her eyes went wide.

"Are you going to shoot—"

Jindei cupped a hand over Elenai's mouth. "Shhh," she said, then slowly pulled her hand back. "Be quiet. Watch your mother."

The arrow felt foreign as she drew it from her quiver. She dropped the shaft twice while trying to nock it. So much for the air of competence she tried to put on.

Elenai put her hand on Jindei's wrist, whispering, "You're not going to hurt him, are you?"

"We're going to eat him."

Elenai shook her head. "No, we don't need him. The villagers bring us enough."

"When the villagers give you something, it's enough. But when I give you anything…" Jindei trailed off, words lost in the fog of her anger. She shook her head. "Just watch me."

Jindei took a deep breath, stood, and drew back the arrow.

"Mama, don't!"

Little hands yanked at her shirt, but Jindei pushed them away with a jostle of her hip. The buck was still drinking as Jindei took aim. Air burning in her lungs, she went to loose.

Elenai sprinted down the hill, waving her hands over her head. "Run!" she screamed. "Run or she'll eat you!"

The deer leaped back from the water, hooves flailing. It spun about and bounded into the trees. Jindei cursed, lowering her bow. Elenai looked up at her, face proud, defiant, and fearful all at once.

"How dare you?" someone shouted.

The voice startled Jindei. It had come from the woods on the other side of the clearing, a deep voice dripping with fury. Twigs snapped as a man stomped out from under the canopy. Men in servants' paint trailed after him. The stranger threw down his bow in a rage, and one of his hangers-on scurried over to collect it.

The hunter was a young man dressed in skins and linen far finer than any common woodsman ought to have. A silver brooch clasped a bearskin cloak about his shoulders. A blade hung at his belt. Not a simple length of sharpened bone like Jindei's, but a dagger made of steel. Mud squished as he jogged across the brook in supple leather boots. He was running straight at Elenai.

Jindei bolted toward her daughter, but the man caught her first. He took Elenai by the collar and shook her. "You cost me that stag, you little rat!"

Elenai screamed.

Before Jindei could think twice, she raised her bow and drew back the arrow. "Let her go!"

The man's head snapped up, eyes wide and wild. His hand darted to his belt, and the dagger gleamed forth. Jindei tried to aim, but the hunter thrust Elenai between them. He took a handful of her black hair and wrenched her head back. The tip of his blade kissed her throat.

"Stop!" Jindei shouted.

The man snarled. "Throw it down or she—"

Jindei's grip failed. The arrow slipped from between her sweating fingers, and the bow twanged. She winced, muscles bunching all across her body in dreadful anticipation. The arrow seemed to fly for days before it punched into its mark.

"Gahh!" the man cried. He jerked back from Elenai. The dagger tumbled from his hand. Groping at the shaft in his shoulder, he stumbled back. His feet tangled beneath him, and the wet ground squelched as he fell.

The servants rushed forward, but Jindei nocked another arrow. "Stop!"

The hunter's men halted across the stream, but Jindei didn't draw. Elenai stood between them.

"Move, Elenai!" shouted Jindei, staring down the servants and their master.

"Mama?"

Jindei's eyes darted back to Elenai. She was looking down at her hands, fingers dripping red.

"Elenai?" Fear slashed through Jindei, sharp as glass.

Elenai looked up, wet eyes full of terror. A wound wept crimson under her jaw. Blood gleamed on the dagger at her feet.

The bow and arrow fell from Jindei's trembling hands. She raced over, scooped Elenai into her arms, and laid her in the grass. Blood pulsed from Elenai's neck as if in rhythm with some horrible, silent song. Jindei ripped a section of her sleeve away and pressed it into the wound. Elenai moaned. The cloth soaked through at once. Then blood was everywhere, seeping past Jindei's fingers, running over the blades of grass.

"No, no, no," Jindei said, barely able to see through her tears.

Shivering, Elenai looked up at her. "Why am I cold?"

Jindei moaned, pulling her daughter into her embrace. Elenai's body went limp, and Jindei screamed. She screamed and screamed as panic pulled her apart.

Something slammed into the back of her head. It filled her skull with light and broken glass. She felt herself tumbling. When she opened her eyes again, she was sprawled out in the undergrowth. Elenai had fallen out of her arms. She lay still beside her. Jindei reached out, but a boot kicked her hand away.

The hunter appeared over her, his dagger recovered. "You tried to kill me," he said through ragged breaths. "Do you know who I am? Who my father is?" The brooch at his throat caught the light—a silver boar's head with topaz tusks and ruby eyes.

"Sarno!" one of his servants called. "Sarno, wait!"

Jindei knew that name, but she didn't know how. Not when all she could think of was Elenai.

"Sarno! Please don't hurt her."

The hunter ignored them. He raised his knife for a killing stroke. Jindei threw up her hands.

The young man froze. Face paling, he retreated toward his knot of worried servants. They went to encircle him, but he shrugged them off, wheeled about, and ran. Muttering to one another and casting nervous glances back at Jindei, the servants did not wait long to follow.

The forest grew very silent. Jindei turned her hands around. The white scars stood stark amid the smears of red. Had the hunter recognized her by them? The thought might have been important, but it drifted away as she crawled back to Elenai. Quivering, Jindei cradled her close. The sobs shook her like an earthquake.

Jindei laid Elenai before the hearth. She lit a fire, though neither of them felt its warmth. Jindei collapsed beside her, stroking her hair and kissing her head. How could this be her baby? She was too young, too beautiful to be dead. She had been perfect as a river stone, and now...

Jindei whimpered through all the songs she knew, wept through all the stories. She kept waiting for sleep to claim her. Tomorrow she'd wake up, and the dream would be over. Elenai would be whole and hale and whiny as ever.

When sleep did come, it was dreamless and black. It felt like drowning more than rest. When she woke, sunlight crept under the door flap. It reached across the floor and touched the silent form beside her, showing her the truth. The nightmare had been real.

Grief rushed in again, heavier than anything she could ever hope to carry. She could hardly breathe under its weight. It was crushing her, grinding her heart to powder until she could feel nothing at all.

The numbness sat in her gut for hours. Then out of nowhere, the hunter's face swam up in her mind. One of his servants had shouted his name. "Sarno," she whispered. Suddenly, she remembered where she'd heard it.

Jindei trudged through the village, carrying Elenai's body. People stopped to watch her somber march. Strangers parted for her on the street. Shadows paused in doorways. Faces peered over livestock paddocks. They all stared in shock and fear. Jindei couldn't bear to meet their gazes. Nor could she look down. One more look at Elenai's face and her resolve might shatter. She kept her eyes fixed on the imposing longhouse that loomed ahead, its roof timbers jutting upward like the horns of a monster.

A small crowd gathered in her wake, murmuring and muttering. Then one voice cut through all the rest. "Jindei? Jindei!"

Banu appeared at her side, panting with exertion. He put a hand on her arm and asked, "Is she all right?"

Jindei didn't answer.

"Elenai, are you…" He trailed off. Jindei couldn't bring herself to watch the understanding come into his eyes. "Oh, Spirits, no," he breathed, pain crushing his voice to little more than a whisper.

Jindei wanted to comfort him, but she could barely keep herself standing, let alone support someone else. With no words to give him, she kept walking.

She came to the longhouse's palisade wall, a row of sharpened stakes atop a raised, earthen bank. The guards shared uneasy glances when she stopped outside the gate. Digging deep, Jindei forced herself to stare down their captain. "I would speak to Chief Alenu," she said, voice firm and unyielding.

The guards looked as though they might laugh, but the sight of the dead child seemed to sober them. "Go bury your dead, woman. The chief doesn't see uninvited guests."

Jindei raised her voice, clutching Elenai even tighter. "Ignore me, and the whole world will receive an uninvited guest."

Gasps rippled through the crowd behind her. The guards traded another round of anxious looks. Finally, the captain cleared his throat and turned to a subordinate. "Take word to the longhouse."

Jindei stood before Chief Alenu's empty chair, arms clasping Elenai's body close. As if the weight of her daughter were not enough, she found herself shouldering every guardsman's worried stare and every servant's nervous glance. The door to the hall finally burst open, and Alenu emerged. His narrowed eyes fixed upon her. His lips were a tight slash amid the thicket of his beard. He marched to his chair with a stiff, clipped gait, the soles of his fine leather boots pounding out a rankled rhythm.

As he sat with a weary groan, Jindei tightened her grip on Elenai. Something about his face reminded her of Sarno's. Tears threatened, but she forced them back and met Alenu's gaze.

"Where is he?" she demanded, her voice quavering with anger.

"In his bed, recovering from that wound you gave him. My

surgeons say he may never draw a bow again." The man tried to drive his words home with a pointed stare, but Jindei didn't blink. At last, Alenu wavered, expression softening as he glanced down at Elenai. He wiped a hand across his haggard face and leaned back in his chair. "What would you have happen?"

"What would you do with any other murderer?"

Alenu's mouth twisted. "Murderer? I heard the whole tale from Sarno. My son was defending himself."

Jindei couldn't believe her ears. "From a five-year-old girl?"

"From *you*! The girl would still be alive had you dropped your bow when you were told. Even as it went, the deed was done unwittingly. His dagger slipped when you shot him."

The gap between Jindei's pointer and middle finger suddenly itched. Guilt and doubt threatened to overwhelm her. "No," she insisted, shaking her head. "He should never have touched her. She'd be alive if he hadn't touched her." Jindei looked down at Elenai's pale, still face, and the tears she'd been holding back spilled down her cheeks.

When she regained her composure, she gave Alenu a level stare. "A trial," she said, voice steady and determined. "I want a trial."

Alenu sat up straight, his eyes flashing with anger. "My son is no common criminal."

"And I'm no simple villager." She raised one scarred palm for him to see.

Alenu's posture slumped, and he looked away, defeated.

They buried Elenai next to Jindei's mother in a field not far from the hut. Banu had done the digging. When the dirt was patted down and covered with stones, Tiri handed Danai to Banu. She laid a wreath of flowers over the grave and tried to pay her respects. It was all well-intended, but Jindei chafed at the attempt. What did this woman know about Jindei's daughter? Tiri had known her less than two years. But even so, Jindei let her go on.

Meanwhile, Danai squirmed in Banu's arms. She looked so much like her father. So much like Elenai had at her age. Jindei fought the urge to reach out and stroke her silky, black hair. It would only make Jindei cry, and maybe the baby too. She didn't want to make Tiri uneasy. The woman had enough worries with another child on the way.

When Tiri finished, Banu said a few words around the lump in his throat. Jindei listened intently, eager to hear the impressions Elenai had made on her father. Yet whenever Banu spoke, part of Jindei filled with panic. She was certain that one day he would snap out of his grief and realize this was all her fault. *Elenai should have been with us that week,* he would say. *Far from the woods, the hunters, and the knives.* She wasn't sure she could bear it.

He said nothing of it beside her grave that day at least. He only spoke of how lucky he'd been to be Elenai's father. Though his time had been brief with her, he said that he would never forget it. She would always be his daughter, no matter where her spirit might be.

Finally, Banu looked to Jindei expectantly. Invitingly.

"I love you, Nai," was all she said. But after, in her heart, she whispered, *"Forgive me."*

They walked back to the hut beneath the westering sun. For all the world, Jindei kept expecting to turn and see Elenai bounding after them. Those were the times it hurt most.

Back home, Banu, Tiri, and Jindei talked for a while, told stories and recounted fond memories. Jindei even offered a few herself. She wondered if it was healing to do so. Or was it just pulling scabs off the same wound over and over?

"We need to be going," Banu said at last, "before it gets dark." He and Tiri packed what they had brought and started for the door.

Tiri went first, but Banu stopped at the threshold. He'd noticed Jindei's pouch hanging from a peg on the wall. He touched it absently, no doubt feeling the bowl inside. He was stalling, Jindei realized. He was gathering his courage to say something. A cold dread sank into her guts. He was going to ask her why she'd kept Elenai that week. And when he did, Jindei's mind would shatter.

"Your duty," he said, taking his hand away from the pouch. "Can you carry on?"

The question surprised her. "Yes."

But she read another question in his look. *Who will carry on after you?*

"One thing at a time," she said.

"Right." With a sad smile, he pushed through the flap.

And Jindei was alone.

Days passed before the trial. Jindei went to the elders' council lodge, but part of her wondered if she were truly somewhere else. She felt like a ghost. No one spoke to her. No one dared look at her. Perhaps they couldn't bear to. Discomfort filled the room when she finally stood to give her witness. Though she told it through tears, she told her story true.

When she was finished, Sarno gave his own account. And then his servants, one by one. Jindei listened, teeth clenched, her fist balled tight around a handful of her shirt. It wasn't that they made up lies. It was the truths they left out that enraged her.

By the time it was over, Jindei sat spent and trembling. To hear seven different men recall Elenai's death had wrung her heart out like a rag. The council dismissed her and Sarno so they might deliberate in private. Outside the lodge, Banu and Tiri waited with food and water. Jindei took a drink, but the thought of food made her stomach turn.

Sometime after sundown, the elders brought them back inside. The old men sat in their chairs, gray and grim, shoulders slumped beneath the impossible choice before them. They could rule against Sarno and risk retribution from his father. Or they could rule against Jindei, the one woman in all the land whose veins still ran with witchblood—the heritage that kept Shijai in his prison.

Jindei held her breath as the council's voice finally stood to deliver their decision. Face distressed, the elder glanced back and forth from Sarno to Jindei. "We, the elders of this council, declare the child's blood on Sarno's hands."

Murmurs filled the hall. Sarno sprang up from his bench, snarling something, but Chief Alenu pulled him back into his seat. Jindei's relief was the merest scrap, but she savored it all the same.

The elder raised his hands for silence. "But that is not the end of it. For the attempt on Sarno's life, the rune sister is not without blame."

Dread stole back any shred of peace Jindei had just found.

"To kill a child is death, but so too is harming the chief's own person, and by extension, the person of his heir. Yet in either case, death would not bring balance. In the interest of our clan's future and for the safety of our village, we find the crimes to be their own punishment. We withhold any sentence. Now let the matter be ended."

Jindei could not speak to Banu afterward. She could not even move her tongue. She went home, feeling like her soul had quit her body. Somehow, her flesh moved of its own accord while Jindei watched from some other existence.

For days she lay in her hut, wrapped in her furs, leaving her covers only to empty her bowels. She drank little, ate less. Her wiry frame withered till her ribs looked like claws trying to rip their way free of her tightening skin.

One night she dreamed that she stood before Shijai's cage, hand pressed against the hexglass. "Avenge her," she said and broke the bowl of binding. The barrier shattered into glowing shards. Shijai's writhing body went flooding up the tunnels. The world groaned as he tore free of the earth and rose high into the sky. His form was vast and horrible, tendrils blotting out the stars, obscuring the moon. His shadow fell across the village, and he dove like a kingfisher.

Huts and hovels crumpled beneath him like paper boxes. One oily, black trunk of an arm crushed the council lodge. The elders inside squished and squelched like worms beneath a heel. Shijai dragged himself over the snapping palisades to Chief Alenu's longhouse. The creature threaded his snaking feelers down the chimney and exhaled. The windows belched with yellow smoke. Bursting through the longhouse's door came Alenu and Sarno, screaming as their flesh melted and sloughed off their bones.

The village in ruins, Shijai came back for her. They stared at one another for what felt a lifetime. "Thank you," she said. "You're free."

For a moment, she thought she could read his countenance. He was staring fondly down at her, as if looking on an old friend. Then some hidden pair of jaws hinged open, and a dozen ink-black tongues lolled forth. They were soft against her skin as they coiled about her and dragged her into darkness.

Jindei woke, smiling.

The Dead Moon came at last, and Jindei rose from her bed of furs to gather her knife and belt pouch. She wouldn't need them, but old habits clung like leeches. She slipped out into the night, the shadows deep and still. Despite the near-blackness, she knew the way. Through the trees she went, over the crumbled walls, down the dust-choked roads, and under the eyeless gaze of empty towers. Then into the cold, dead earth.

She descended until she reached the bluish glow of the hexglass. Shijai stirred beyond, his thousand eyes blinking curiously. Jindei found herself oddly comforted at the sight of him, like an anchor in the midst of a storm.

"Good evening, Jindei," he said. "Again, no Elenai, I see."

The urge to confess everything surprised her. It nearly overwhelmed her, but somehow she held her tongue.

"Back at the village, I presume. She must be taking a real liking to her father for you to let her miss two wardings like this."

Jindei gripped the handle of her knife. She almost drew it, almost fell into old routine.

No. Not this time. Not ever again.

"Is everything all right, Jindei? You're awfully quiet. Even for you."

She pulled her hand back from the knife and reached into her pouch. Just like her dream, she would bring out the bowl of binding and smash it for good and all. She'd be free of this curse, free of her grief. Sarno would die, and Elenai would be avenged.

Rummaging through her pouch, her fingers brushed something wooden where there should have only been glass. Jindei frowned. Curious, she plucked it out, held it up, and froze. The polished surface of Elenai's little horse figurine gleamed in the hexlight. Banu had somehow snuck it in after Elenai's funeral.

Jindei stared at it till her throat went tight. Tears stung her eyes. She felt her heart swell against the webbing threads she hadn't even known were there. Jindei buried her face in her palms and wept.

"Jindei?" asked Shijai. "Did something happen to Elenai?"

She didn't answer him.

"Jindei?" His voice was calm and soothing.

Finally, she looked up at him. One of his appendages was pressed up against the glass, like the extended hand of a concerned friend.

"Is there anything you need?"

She trembled, trying to let go of the hate.

"Anything at all?"

Jindei was quiet for a long time. At last, she wiped her tears and shook her head. "No," she said and drew her knife.

Thirty Minutes or It's a Paradox

written by
Patrick MacPhee

illustrated by
CAM COLLINS

ABOUT THE AUTHOR

As a young child, Patrick frequently saw his mother engrossed in a forest's worth of fantasy and science fiction novels. Wanting to join in the fun, he read his first "big-person" novel, The Fellowship of the Ring, *when he was eight. Although far above his reading level, he pushed through, reading several hours a day, taking literally longer to reach Rivendell than Sam and Frodo. This magical experience hooked him on speculative fiction forever.*

In his teens, he was bit by the writing bug and later abandoned a degree in engineering to pursue a degree in English literature. He became a teacher, a vocation where he is lucky enough to spend every day helping young people become better versions of themselves. Over a twenty-year teaching career, Patrick has taught phys ed (i.e., dodgeball) to Fortnite-obsessed middle schoolers, the enigmatic complexity of Hamlet *to university-bound high schoolers, and everything in between. He has learned that almost every part of the curriculum has room for a little humor—sometimes a lot of humor.*

He was inspired to write "Thirty Minutes or It's a Paradox" after meeting so many young people who are anxious about the future. What if they had the ultimate control over that future? Who could resist making a few little changes?

When he's not writing fantasy and science fiction, Patrick enjoys playing video games and board games with his wife and two children. You might also find him on long walks in the woods with his golden retrievers, Ciri and Arwen.

ABOUT THE ILLUSTRATOR

Cam Collins was born in 1999 in the city of Chicago and was raised by his parents, whose first actions of fostering his creativity included having a chalkboard wall in his room. The creative pursuits continued, and Collins knew early on that he'd want to draw for the rest of his life. He was one of the first few high schoolers to be selected for the College Arts Access Program (CAAP) of the School of the Art Institute of Chicago. He went on to study printmaking at the Rhode Island School of Design.

Cam gained a love for creating books, and realized a key ingredient in bringing his illustrations further was to start writing stories in tandem with them.

Cam continues to do commissions for a variety of clients and has brought his art and storytelling into his own world called Way of the Canvas. He will be working in this world for as long as he can draw, and he has created comics, videos, and even games devoted to it.

Thirty Minutes or It's a Paradox

*T*_{hunk.}

Terry slammed the Jell-O brakes of his geriatric Toyota Tercel and winced as his precious pizza cargo tumbled off the back seat. Balding all-season tires lost contact with wet suburban asphalt, and he lurched to the shoulder in a cloud of rubber and gravel.

There'd been a blinding flash dead ahead. He'd assumed it was one of these idiot suburban drivers who goes 24/7 with his high beams on, but the light crackled like a sparkler. Busted transformer, maybe?

Busted transformers don't hit you. The car even jolted a bit....

Icy nausea shivered up and down his spine. As his eyes adjusted back to the dim, drizzly streetlight, the unmistakably human-sized lump in the middle of the road faded into view.

After three attempts, he got the door open, found he couldn't move, remembered he was still belted, then fumbled with the latch like a caveman banging rocks. He all but fell out of the car.

He scanned the darkened street, expecting flashing blue and red to reflect in the rain. Dead quiet. There was a gang in Miami that did stuff like this. It was on the news. They'd put a guy in the street, make it seem like you hit him so you pull over, then wham! Goodbye kidneys.

But this wasn't Miami. Blue River was a quiet town, barely any crime except the occasional bunch of teenagers who drove too fast, too late. Mostly harmless unless you were trying to deliver pizzas.

Terry's heart kicked up a gear. The road was a forested curve between subdivisions, exactly the kind where impatient kids would pass you even on a solid double line. They'd never see this guy.

He jogged over, hunched in a useless effort to avoid cold rain. The rain began to lighten under distant headlights.

"Hey brother, you ok—"

The man bolted up and grabbed him about the shoulders. Other men might have thrown hands or ninja-dodged. Not Terry. Terry froze and screamed a few octaves shy of full-on dog whistle, thinking only how an 80's vampire movie had begun the same way.

"Terry? Good. Let's go."

He seemed human enough, a lot like Terry in fact: dark skin, medium build, but he had designer sunglasses, and his hair was long dreads with cool crystals that jangled as he ran. It was the kind of look that Terry had wanted to try for years, but he'd always feared would never work on him.

"How do you know my— Hey!"

The stranger had already climbed behind the wheel of Terry's car.

"That's my car!" He windmilled his arms as the oncoming car reached him, honked, and swerved past. "This guy's stealing my—"

"Get in, Terry," the stranger yelled. "You got pizzas to deliver, remember?" He closed the door.

Terry patted his pocket. Empty.

"Of course." He'd left his phone on the center console, so Google Lady could shave a few seconds off his time. Help wasn't coming.

The stranger cracked the window and waved. "Come on! I just wanna talk, Terry. Trust me."

Well, he was definitely the most chill organ-harvesting, vampire gang member Terry had ever heard of. He found himself in the passenger seat. There was something about this guy that was eerily familiar.

Terry said, "Hey brother, this car's twenty-five years old. It's fussy. You can't just…"

The stranger effortlessly jangled the shifter into motion and set it to "2" instead of "D," the only way the car would go forward. Terry was pressed back as the Tercel squealed into motion.

"I'm driving," the stranger said. "You couldn't hear what I have to say and drive straight. Trust me."

Terry said, "Hey, how do you know how to drive my car? You been spying on me or something?"

They swerved onto a broad two lane and slowed before Terry could warn him about the usual speed trap.

"No one's been spying. Relax." The stranger tapped his sunglasses and they went clear. "That's better. Okay, so real talk. I'm you from the future. I've traveled back in time to teach you how to invent time travel."

"Riiight. Of course." Terry wondered how many bones he'd break if he rolled out at the next intersection, but he was pressed against the passenger window as the stranger drifted through like a pro.

So much for that idea. Crystals in the stranger's dreads chimed softly as he chuckled. "Right before I arrived, you were thinking about ways to get rich. It's what I used to—what you think about all the time while you make these deliveries. You fantasize about it. Crypto, reselling crap on Amazon, YouTube, all kinds of ways that don't involve hard stuff like math or physical labor."

A cold shiver swept through Terry. Either this guy could somehow read his mind or maybe, just maybe…

He hacked my whole search history!

Trying to keep his breathing steady, Terry decided to play along. "Okay, so that's actually…a little creepy, uh, Terry?"

The stranger grimaced. "I sign the checks with 'Terry.' My rapper name is In-Fi-N8."

Terry chuckled. "We actually dropped that mixtape?"

In-Fi-N8 turned to Terry and smiled a million-dollar smile. It was the same smile Terry practiced in the mirror every night, only this guy pulled it off better than Jay Gatsby.

"Hit the 2-2-5, brother," In-Fi-N8 said.

"Hit the huh?"

"Oh…uh, it was straight fire? Lit? Slayed it?" In-Fi-N8 sighed and talked in a fake nasally nerd voice. "The mixtape was generally well received by the rap-appreciating public."

"No way," Terry said. His last track had gotten five glorious views on YouTube, and four of them were from Terry.

"You ever hear of Eminem?"

"Course I heard of Eminem!"

In-Fi-N8 popped a genuine cassette into the Tercel's ancient tape player. It was labeled "In-Fi-N8" in crooked marker. "After this diss track, the man never rapped again."

Before Terry could protest, In-Fi-N8 mashed the play button a bunch of times and the tape player spat out a collection of instruments that were all off-key and out of sync, like a bunch of high schoolers got hammered and broke into the music room. The lyrics were an increasingly bizarre attempt to rhyme with unrhymable words like "orange" or "purple"—among other crimes against the English language. The auto-tuner was cranked up to "all of it," and under everything…

"Is that the theme song to *The Office*?" Terry asked.

In-Fi-N8 smiled another million-dollar smile. "And they said it couldn't be done." He shrugged. "But music's just a side hustle. I got all kinds of projects. Namely…" He twisted his wrist and jangled a lavish watch that was all chrome and LED.

"Let me guess. Is that the—"

"Time machine? Yeah." In-Fi-N8 reached into a breast pocket. "Don't worry, brother. I got one for you."

And suddenly Terry was wearing an Apple Watch: Series 9000 or whatever this thing was. The screen was opaque silver, but when looked at directly, text and images seemed to float in some nebulous area between Terry's wrist and his brain.

Probably has the hidden camera for whatever YouTube video this guy's making at my expense.

But, for some random prankster, he'd handled the car effortlessly, and it was a damn fussy little car. His dreads looked great. His face was a little puffy, but he was in good shape overall. He had a fine black topcoat over what looked like a stylish black suit, like guys working at an investment bank would wear when they go to swanky business lunches.

Could he actually be me?

"Pizzas okay?" In-Fi-N8 asked.

"Still warm," Terry said, as he wrestled the insulated pizza case onto his lap.

"All right, so you gotta deliver them. It's vital that we maintain the timeline."

"How does delivering pizzas...?"

Terry's face kissed the side window as In-Fi-N8 drifted into one of those new suburban neighborhoods with no trees where every house looked the same. Even the twenty-eight-foot lots were way out of Terry's price range.

They pulled into a gravel driveway.

"I am not paying for those pizzas," said an obviously rich guy who could obviously pay twenty bucks for a couple of pizzas that were obviously quite eatable, even if they were technically two minutes late.

"Look, sir," Terry said, "if you had any idea what I've been dealing with—there was this man on the road." He pointed to the Tercel, but there was no sign of In-Fi-N8.

I knew it! It's some hidden camera thing.

"I don't care," Rich Guy said. "I am not paying for late pizza, and you should learn how to drive. You woke up my dog with all that squealing."

The Chihuahua nestled in his arms growled softly.

Rich Guy grabbed onto a box and Terry yanked it away.

"Oh, hell no, you are *not* getting this pizza for free!"

"How dare you?" Rich Guy asked over high-pitched barking. "I want my pizzas. I'm hungry."

After a few choice words, Terry ended up back in the car. He tossed the pizzas on the back seat and put the car in gear.

"Weird," he muttered as he left the neighborhood, but at least the rain was dying down. This In-Fi-N8 guy hadn't adjusted the seats, but that could mean anything.

Guy knew how to drive my car. I barely know how to drive my car.

"We messed up," In-Fi-N8 said from the backseat directly behind Terry, who nearly swerved off the road in shock. An oncoming car doppler-honked as it screamed by.

"Where the hell were you?"

"Couldn't risk being seen," In-Fi-N8 said. "You know, paradoxes and stuff."

"Couldn't risk—are you—you literally just traveled back in time to teach yourself—me—how to invent time travel and you're worried about paradoxes?"

"Oh." In-Fi-N8 frowned in the rearview mirror. "Oh, yeah. Well, one paradox is okay. We can control that. But any more and things get real weird real fast."

Under a growing suspicion that he might just be the brains of this duo, Terry said, "That guy wouldn't take his pizzas."

"I know," In-Fi-N8 said. "This complicates things."

Complicate? This idiot just cost Terry a quarter of his night's wages. He'd been busting his ass for the last hour and a half basically for free.

Terry said, "So, how about you just use your time machine and take us back to before the pizzas were late?"

"Are you crazy?" In-Fi-N8 yelled way too loudly next to Terry's ear. "Timeline's already messed up and you want to have *four* Terrys running around?"

"Of course," Terry muttered. "It's not like you can just demonstrate this alleged time travel device. That would be too easy."

"Right," In-Fi-N8 said. "See, you get it. Hey, you got twenty dollars?"

Terry swerved to the shoulder, slammed on the brakes, and In-Fi-N8 tumbled into the passenger seat.

"All right, that's enough. Out! Get outta my car!"

"Aw, you don't mean that, Terry."

"Hell, yeah, I mean it." Terry clawed the watch off and threw it at In-Fi-N8. "I have to pay for those pizzas now. You're either some punk doing a hidden video or the worst time traveler ever. Get out."

"Look…" In-Fi-N8 reconfigured himself to sit properly in the passenger seat and leaned toward Terry, hands extended in the universal "shady salesman" gesture.

"You don't want me here, fine," In-Fi-N8 said. "I'll go. But Terry, I know how pathetic your life is. I know because I used to *be* you. Your pizza delivery job barely keeps you treading water while you daydream about what things *could* be like."

"You don't know me." Okay, maybe the last few months of Terry's life hadn't been the best, but pathetic?

"You bought a gym membership. You haven't been in three months."

Terry's face warmed. "It's been tough with the job."

In-Fi-N8 said, "It's literally down the street from the pizza place."

"Yeah, but the hours—"

"It's a 24-hour gym! You could go anytime, but you don't. That's not all. Remember that plan to go back to school to be an electrician? You even bought that textbook, but you barely got past the first set of math equations."

Terry took a deep breath and squeezed the steering wheel. "You seem to know a lot about me."

In-Fi-N8 said, "I told you. I'm you. Or rather, I'm what you could be if you stopped making excuses and started hustling."

Whoever he was, In-Fi-N8's cuts had gone deep.

In-Fi-N8 held up the watch. "If you're tired of delivering pizzas just to pay rent and fuel for this death trap you call a car, then all you have to do is put this back on and listen to what I have to say. Won't take more than half an hour."

"It was just a couple of pizzas," Terry said around a bite of lukewarm Hawaiian.

Nestled on a quiet corner in Blue River's sleepy east side, Eli's Pizzeria and Eatery almost succeeded at that quaint 1950s diner look. The floor was clean white tile covered in red carpets that matched the window booths. The jukebox hadn't worked out—too many earbuds—so the owner had replaced it with a couple of old-school arcade machines. There was a spacey pinball game that Terry was banned from playing after too much tilting, and one of those shooting games on rails with the little plastic guns. The corner door was propped open with a stone, leaving the wooden screen door to keep the August bugs at bay. On the wall above the counter, a flat-screen TV sometimes showed a ball game, but it was black now.

In-Fi-N8 made a dismissive gesture with a half-eaten slice of meat lover's. "I keep telling you, we're talking about a whole separate timeline here." He squirmed in the tiny plastic-and-metal fixed seat in a vain effort to get comfortable.

"Hey, Terry?" Jessica Li asked from behind the counter. She was cute, studying psychology at SUNY Albany, and had a boyfriend. Probably. Could have been something she said to avoid being bothered. There was a guy who picked her up after hours on the semi-regular, but maybe he was a brother or something?

As if I'd have a chance with a girl like her.

Jessica said, "I'm really sorry, but I have to log those last pizzas as undelivered." She had a sweet voice that reminded him of bubble gum.

Terry sighed. "I know. Want some?" He held up a tempting piece of Hawaiian.

She patted her stomach and smiled thinly. "I'm watching my figure, and my ride should be here soon." She started wiping down tables and seats, sometimes stretching to do so. Terry tried not to look, but she wasn't the only one watching that figure.

"Yo, Terry, who's your friend?" Kevin exited the kitchen. He was tall and normally pale, but tonight he was all flushed and sweaty from hours at the ovens. "Hey, nice watch!" He held up his wrist, showing a nearly identical version to the one Terry's companion was wearing. "You guys get yours from that guy behind the mall?"

Terry stared daggers at In-Fi-N8, who chuckled and shook his head quietly.

"This is In-Fi-N8," Terry said. "He's a time traveler."

Kevin raised an eyebrow as he settled in at the shooter game. His eyes widened and he smiled. "Oh! You guys joining my D&D campaign? I never heard of a time traveler class, but if you want home brew—"

"No!" Terry glanced at Jessica, but she had earbuds in and nodded her head to secret melodies, like some ancient fey princess dancing around a circle of plastic mushrooms.

"Come on, Terry, I got the perfect home brew for you. It's a demon wraith. Cool, huh? He's not all evil though, just a demon who found himself trapped in the body of a teenager. Now, he has to navigate the deadly intrigue of the demon world while juggling ordinary human stuff like homework and relationships."

"Did an AI write that?"

"No?"

"I'll pass," Terry said.

Kevin shrugged and turned to the game, holding both guns akimbo style. His aim was terrible, but that didn't stop him from going full cowboy, complete with postmortem puns in a Southern accent.

"Still better than his John Wick phase," In-Fi-N8 whispered.

Terry nearly did a pizza-spit take, overcome with memories of Kevin wrapping his leg around the machine and pretending to reload before shooting. He'd been forced to stop after random passersby had inquired about a strange man humping the arcade machines.

"Can I help you?" Jessica stared their way, earbuds in hand.

In-Fi-N8 flashed a smile. "Oh, I'm sorry, was I staring? You see, I'm an artist, and art is the appreciation of beauty."

"Oh…" Wait. Was Jessica actually…blushing? She drifted over and In-Fi-N8 lifted the pizza boxes deftly while she sprayed and wiped. She leaned over the table and smiled coyly. "And what are you an artist of, Mister…?"

"In-Fi-N8. It's a stage name. As to my art? Song, poetry, occasionally canvas—anything that thickens the soul with the joy of being alive."

She laughed lightly and eyed his clothes.

He nodded. "You're perceptive. My job is engineering. I invent things, reinvent things. It's fun sometimes. But I have the soul of an artist. That's my passion.

"What about you, Jessica? Your job is making pizzas, but your eyes say more. What does your soul want to be?"

"I…" Jessica straightened and stared out the windows at the azure afterglow of day. "I want to work with kids, you know? Like when they've been traumatized or abused. I want to help them heal." She laughed nervously and looked away.

She's beautiful on the inside, too, Terry thought. *All this time, and I never knew. Never asked her…*

In-Fi-N8 snared her gaze with another of those Jay Gatsby smiles. "That's a beautiful dream, Jessica. I just know those kids will be lucky to have you."

A honk outside startled her, as if out of a daydream.

"That's for me," she said. "I gotta go. Good luck with your music, uh…In-Fi-N8." Her smile might have been mocking, but her eyes lingered on In-Fi-N8 as she passed out the door.

"That's her boyfriend," Terry all but spat out. "In the car."

Terry found himself sighing after her and stopped himself before he looked too pathetic. Eli's Pizzeria always seemed a little darker when Jessica left.

In-Fi-N8 craned around for a better view and squinted through headlights. He pursed his lips and gave a slow nod.

"Right," he said. "I remember now. Nice ride. Can't compete with mine, but honestly, what can?"

Kevin dropped the plastic guns in defeat and joined them. "Going after another brother's girl. That's a rat move, my man."

In-Fi-N8 shrugged. "If In-Fi-N8 don't see no ring, then In-Fi-N8 is in the game."

Kevin laughed. "That one of your lyrics?"

"Does that actually work?" Terry asked.

In-Fi-N8 said, "Yes, it's a lyric, and it works sometimes. I guess. I don't much care either way. You see, I gave Jessica there a glimpse of the passion she's missing. If I never see her again, that's cool. I'm already forgetting her, but if she gets tired of whatever man hasn't put a ring on her finger, then she knows where to find me. Time's on our side, brother. Besides, did you notice how she never said he was her boyfriend? That girl's looking for another vine."

The door opened.

Terry half expected to see Jessica's boyfriend, spoiling for a fight after seeing In-Fi-N8 chatting her up, but it was…another In-Fi-N8?

"Oh, yeah," said a clean-cut version of In-Fi-N8 with close-cut buzzed hair. He wore dark slacks and a blue-and-white Champion sweater with what looked like an old BBQ stain on the stomach. "Real smooth, In-Fi-N8, but we shouldn't be surprised. You did make *Oprah Magazine*'s Top 100 Most Interestingly Dressed Entertainers."

In-Fi-N8 leaned back and smiled. "Three years in a row, baby." The smile faded. "Let me guess. The pizzas?"

"Yup." New guy took a seat of hard plastic and grabbed a piece of Hawaiian. "Why'd you have to jump in the road, anyway?"

"It was being fussy," In-Fi-N8 said, holding up the watch.

Other-In-Fi-N8 raised a skeptical eyebrow. "You just wanted to drift around in the Tercel."

In-Fi-N8 lasted three seconds before nodding through a broad smile.

New In-Fi-N8 thrust out a hand to Terry. "Terrance Johnson." His hand was callused and his grip was as firm as possible without being painful. His other wrist was clad in a familiar-looking watch. "Stick with me, Terry. I'll teach you how to *actually* invent time travel."

Terry threw his hands up. "Okay, time-out—no pun intended. How did two missed pizzas create a whole new timeline?"

"Remember Chihuahua Guy?" Terrance asked. "Well, as we speak, he's probably writing an angry Google review. We got fired."

Terry's jaw dropped. "Damn, brother. I'm sorry."

Terrance smiled broadly. "Don't be. Best thing that ever happened to me. I hit the gym, went back to school, and, most important," he added a sidelong glance at In-Fi-N8, "I learned that time travel is not the answer to life's problems."

In-Fi-N8 snorted with laughter. "I wouldn't put much stock in Mr. Minivan here. Guy's so afraid of the government, he doesn't even use it." He jangled his watch.

"I'm laying low," Terrance said, "which is what you should've done."

In-Fi-N8 dipped his pizza into some chipotle dip. "The Feds offered me a million bucks."

"Which you promptly lost," Terrance said, swiping the chipotle before In-Fi-N8 could double-dip.

"And made back."

"Wait," Terry said. "They didn't kill you or lock you in a box or something?"

In-Fi-N8 waved a dismissive hand. "They can't touch you. Well, okay, I guess they could, but it would create a ton of problems." He tapped Terry's watch. "That right there is the paradox. Longer this stays on your wrist, the bigger the window of easy time travel."

Kevin stood. "Okay, Terry. Very funny. You got me. Your family here is very…interesting, but I think I should go. Could you guys lock up when you finish?"

"Yeah, we're cool," In-Fi-N8 said.

Terrance leaned in and whispered, "You should take him up on that D&D offer—"

"Ssshhh!" In-Fi-N8 and Terry hissed simultaneously.

Kevin paused in the doorway long enough to unleash twin fusillades of finger-gun bullets, then got in his truck and drove off.

Did they actually scare off Kevin?

In-Fi-N8 said, "Terry, you can't listen to this guy. He's an HVAC technician, for crying out loud."

"I do just fine," Terrance said. "It's good honest work, not that you would know what that is."

"Please." In-Fi-N8 turned to Terry while jabbing a derisive thumb at Terrance. "This guy won't do any jobs in homes where actual human beings are living. He'll only work in those new-build suburban clones, same cookie-cutter installs on the same cookie-cutter houses—same damn stuff every…single…day."

"Zero stress," Terrance said. "I leave my work at work and come home to my family. It's a good life." He leaned back and crossed his arms. "Wait, you're actually giving advice here? For real? You tell him about the South American tour yet?"

In-Fi-N8 grimaced. "Okay, so that was an honest mistake. I don't know why I still get hassled about it."

"Riiight. An honest mistake. And how were you supposed to know they don't celebrate the Running of the Bulls in Brazil?"

In-Fi-N8 placed a hand on Terry's shoulder and lowered his voice. "All of those bulls were eventually found."

"Enough of—" Terry cupped his hands to his face and wiped them through his hair. "Why don't you just tell me how all this works?"

Terrance opened his mouth, but In-Fi-N8 spoke over him. "I'll handle this one. I'm the actual engineer here."

"Just because you shot a video on that train in Dublin doesn't make you—"

"Hush, now, the adults are talking." In-Fi-N8 held out a finger as if to place it over Terrance's mouth. Terrance rolled his eyes.

In-Fi-N8 said, "All right, so time travel requires an enormous amount of energy. Tons of positive energy and a little bit of negative energy. Think of the positive energy as the power and the negative energy as the steering."

"You lost me." Terry tapped the watch, which responded by showing a flashing time. "How does this thing do that?"

"Careful with that," Terrance said.

"Why?" Terry asked. "Wait, you said lots of energy. Is this thing emitting radiation? Will I get cancer from this? It's cancer, isn't it?"

Terry's thumb dug at the watch clasp.

"Don't take that off!" In-Fi-N8 and Terrance yelled simultaneously.

In-Fi-N8 said, "You're not getting cancer. Relax."

Across the table, Terrance quietly shook his head no, and Terry found himself relaxing.

Terry said, "This still doesn't make any sense. I took it off in the car, didn't I?"

"But now I'm here." Terrance leaned over and tapped Terry's watch twice, and the flashing time disappeared. "It might be fine, but better not to risk it. That watch is a temporal paradox, so you don't want it to get lost or stolen. Normally, time travel is almost impossible due to the energy requirements—*unless* you've already been time traveling and the local time-space ether is loosened up. You know when you turn on your truck in the winter and it needs to warm up before you drive it?"

In-Fi-N8 said, "Or you're about to do a set and you sing some scales to get your voice ready."

No, not really...

"So, what you're saying," Terry said slowly, "is that time travel is possible because time travel already happened? Will happen?"

Terrance nodded. "Great. Now put this on." He held out a *second* watch.

"He already has one," In-Fi-N8 said.

Terry drew his wrist back. "Am I seriously supposed to wear *two* different watches?"

Terrance nodded like this was all perfectly normal. "Technically, they're the same watch. Once the timelines merge, Mr. Brazil—and his watch—will fade away."

In-Fi-N8 stood and stretched, then helped himself to a soda from the vending machine that Terry would likely have to pay for.

"Hey!" Terry slammed a palm to the plastic table. "Shouldn't you be teaching me how to invent that?"

In-Fi-N8 shrugged. "There's a bunch of tutorials loaded on there." He took a swig and sighed. "Technical schematics, you know. It's fairly idiot resistant."

Terry stood and placed a shaky hand on the hard plastic table. A wave of dizziness tried to dissolve the world and drag him to the floor.

"I…I need a minute, guys." He stumbled behind the counter, shut himself in the employee bathroom and collapsed on the toilet.

For a while, he just breathed deeply. He took out his phone and checked the usual websites. His crypto was doing poorly. Served him right for getting advice from a random anon with a neon ape profile pic.

The watch seemed harmless enough, but wasn't that the problem? So far, these two alleged Terrys had told a couple of tall stories and shown him a fancy watch. Hell, *Kevin* had one. It was definitely cool, but it didn't exactly scream "time machine." Terry tapped it and 10:35 p.m. appeared, blinking.

He frowned. Time machine or no, he wasn't about to go out there with a blinking watch that screamed "idiot who doesn't know how to use a watch," especially not right after Terrance had told him to be careful.

How did he fix it?

Terry tapped it again. Nothing. Tap and hold? Still nothing. Maybe—

As he moved his finger, the time changed: 11:35 p.m. Daylight saving?

He tapped and held again, then moved his finger around. The numbers blurred into movement, finally settling on 3:41 p.m. Slowly—it was *very* sensitive—he set it back to 10:35 p.m.

It was still blinking. He hissed out a breath between clenched teeth and decided to leave it alone. Maybe it would go away on its own. In the meantime, he checked his phone.

What the hell…?

The news feed was messed up. A new hurricane, Hurricane Lance, had not only spun up, it already made landfall in Texas and was dissipating over Oklahoma. Some guy in Florida had been arrested for trying to board an airplane with a personal support alligator. The market was down; a historic gathering of world leaders on the International Space Station had to be canceled early after they used up three weeks' worth of air in under two hours....

"Wait." He looked back.

The market was down.

He tapped the time and brought up the date/time app: second week of September, almost three weeks into the future.

He tilted his head slightly and would have sworn he actually heard the mischievous piano tinkle of the *Back to the Future* soundtrack.

He opened his crypto exchange app. The main page was always filled with stories of coins that had broken out. Sure enough, there was a big story about how POOP had suddenly exploded higher, going from a sliver of worthlessness to an all-time high of three glorious cents.

Is that even a real coin? He checked. It was. Just another meme coin among thousands, but the exchange showed it at 0.02304 USD.

A dull vibration shook his wrist and tingled up his arm. The watch blinked faster, with a low beep, getting louder.

It chimed loudly and powerful vibrations swept up his arm and engulfed his entire body. For a split second, "down" seemed to be everywhere, but he quickly settled back onto the toilet. He stared at his phone where the same crypto app was open.

POOP was valued at 0.00012 USD.

"No way." He was tempted to feel like he'd won the lottery on Christmas morning, but he couldn't shake the nagging suspicion that one of the presents under the tree was secretly a bomb.

Maybe it was a glitch. Maybe he was crazy. Hell, this could still be part of some elaborate practical joke. All Terry knew was there were a couple of cold pizzas out there that were eating up most of his gas money.

He had fifty bucks liquid cash in the exchange.

Why not?

He grabbed fifty bucks worth and—

He sighed. Stupid ten-dollar transaction fee.

He grabbed *forty* bucks worth of POOP, a little over 300,000 coins. He finished up and left the restroom, having sunk his meager life savings into POOP. Man, what a time to be alive.

The future Terrys were talking over each other with raised voices on the edge of hostile.

In-Fi-N8 said, "You know the difference between us?"

Terrance nodded. "When I walk through a neighborhood, property values actually go up instead of down?"

"I take risks," In-Fi-N8 said. "I live life to the fullest."

"Right. You and your 'art.' You're literally banned from three different countries."

"But there's over two hundred other countries I *can* go to. Besides, you can hardly talk about art."

"What's that supposed to mean?" Terrance asked.

In-Fi-N8 raised a skeptical eyebrow. "Just because Batman becomes public domain in 2034 doesn't mean you should write about it."

"Huh?" Terry asked.

Terrance shifted in obvious discomfort. "My kids loved that story."

In-Fi-N8 laughed. "A couple of five-year-olds loved it. Great. Makes total sense that Batman might get sick every once in a while and need some help—and of course you did such a good job that Batman wanted you to stick around, drive the Batmobile, fight crime, play with his gadgets...."

Terrance grimaced and cupped a hand over his eyes.

"Look," Terry said, "I still don't know what I'm supposed to do. If you guys are from different timelines, then how do you even know each other? And what do *I* do? Should I stay out of Brazil?"

The door burst open and another man marched in. He was shaved bald and had sunglasses that seemed to come out of implants beside his eyes. A black leather trench coat covered a vest of what looked like low-key body armor.

"Brazil, Dubai—the damn moon," new guy said in a low, grating voice, like he regularly chewed on rocks in dark alleys while waiting to ambush vampires. "Doesn't matter. Wherever it is, *whenever* it is, you morons keep finding ways to screw it up."

"Who are you?" Terry asked.

New guy looked at him strangely. "My name is Terry, idiot. Oh, you want a different one? Fine. You boys can call me Mr. Johnson—and no, I'm not having any of your crappy pizza. I got a personal chef makes me whatever I want. All organic. Expensive, delicious, and very exclusive, just how I like it."

Mr. Johnson crept behind the counter, hand hovering inside the folds of his coat. He glanced up at the camera, then at the front door and windows.

Terrance and In-Fi-N8 exchanged a puzzled glance, then In-Fi-N8's eyes glazed over into a thousand-yard stare. Slowly, his gaze shifted to Terry.

"You barely had it five minutes," In-Fi-N8 said. "Five minutes!"

Terrance raised an eyebrow. "What did he..." The glazy stare hit him next. "Oh, man. Terry, you had one job. Why'd you go and make a new timeline? It's already getting ridiculous."

Terry said, "It was just a few coins."

Johnson leaned over the counter. "It was more than a few coins. That POOP you bought? Must've triggered some kinda algorithm that prompted other people to buy it. By the time it was done, it had spiked to two dollars."

Terry whistled. His forty-dollar stake had netted him over 300,000 coins. Multiplied by two dollars?

He gasped and struggled to choke in more air.

"Calm down," Johnson said. "You sold long before the high—another amateur-hour move, but what else is new? You did all right, though. Enough to quit this pizza job and do crypto full time."

"And that's why we didn't marry Jessica," Terrance whispered.

"Whoa!" Terry exclaimed. "Jessica? We *married* Jessica? The one here?"

"Calm down," Mr. Johnson said. "She's nice and all, but she's like a six. We definitely did better." In-Fi-N8 nodded matter-of-factly.

"I loved her," Terrance said, eyes shimmering.

Mr. Johnson laughed. "You really are pathetic, Terrance." He held up another watch. "I got plenty of trading tips loaded on this one. Put this on and these two losers'll fade away. We got it made, Terry."

Terrance's jaw clenched as he glared at Johnson. "You can't judge me, you lying, manipulative jerk. You've never done an honest day's work in your life. Without that watch, you'd be living in a gutter. And you've been married four times."

Johnson kept laughing. "And number four is growing stale."

Terry found himself leaning slightly away from Johnson. He took Terrance's hand and looked into his tear-filled eyes, as if to say, "No way, brother."

Terrance twisted his wedding ring anxiously. "There's no guarantee you'll be the primary timeline. I can still win."

Terry said, "What do you mean, primary timeline?"

Johnson ducked under the counter and picked up a hunk of pizza dough. "Okay, so…" He dragged out some long thin pieces. "Time is soft. The prevalent theory is that it's alive. When someone travels back in time, they create new timelines." He stretched out some of the dough to form long strands, still connected to the main mass.

Terry said, "Wouldn't the government put a stop to it?"

In-Fi-N8 said, "Time heals all wounds, brother. More true than you know."

Johnson held the dough strands near each other. "These dough strands will eventually stick back together, just like how the different timelines will eventually merge. I figured that out pretty early—found that I couldn't make those crazy mega trades, since that would alter too much. But little trades? Few thousand here and there? That wasn't so bad."

In-Fi-N8 said, "And as long as you're the guy holding the dough—doing the time traveling—you get to keep the knowledge of the other timelines. That's why we know each other."

Terry ran his hands through his hair. "That *still* doesn't make any sense. Pizza dough? Really?"

Johnson sighed with obvious annoyance and tossed the dough onto the counter that Jessica had just cleaned.

Terrance's lip curled. "Why don't you just admit that you don't know? None of us know, Terry."

CAM COLLINS

Something flashed and sparkled outside.

"What was that?" Terrance asked.

In-Fi-N8 looked accusingly at Terry.

"I didn't do anything," Terry said. "You've seen me the whole time."

"Down!" Mr. Johnson dove over the counter and rolled into a crouch just as the front window exploded into a thousand shards.

Terry hit the floor and pressed himself into cool footprint-stained tiles as bullets screamed through Eli's Pizzeria.

Johnson dropped the coat and sprang up with a futuristic gun in each hand. Terry had barely slapped his hands to his ears when the guns exploded like jackhammers. Dozens of tiny shards of lightning shot into the street. In-Fi-N8 rolled next to Johnson and drew an old-style Micro Uzi, which he fired in a wide, deafening arc.

The gunfire stopped, though it was a long time before the throbbing in Terry's ears subsided.

"We good?" In-Fi-N8 called.

Johnson grimaced and held a hand to his side, which came back covered in blood. He reached into a coat pocket, withdrew a silver vial and hissed as he jabbed it into his stomach. Silver liquid bubbled in the wound and several misshapen bullets clinked onto the tiles.

"All good," Johnson said. He reloaded and went outside, coming back a minute later, stone-faced. "Got 'em. Three-man team."

"Who was it?" Terrance asked, still under the table.

"It wasn't another me?" Terry asked. How busy was this place going to get? Should he be putting on more pizzas?

"We would know if it was another you," In-Fi-N8 said.

"The last timeline shift was delayed," Terrance countered. "What if it's getting worse?"

In-Fi-N8 frowned.

"It was the damn Primacists," Mr. Johnson said. "Buncha religious nuts who believe in only one timeline."

Terry glared at In-Fi-N8. "You never said anything about a cult trying to kill you."

In-Fi-N8 shook his head. "No cult in my timeline, brother." He pointed to Mr. Johnson. "Blame Mr. Trillionaire for letting the secret out."

"Trillionaire?" Terry's eyes bugged out. "Like because of inflation?"

Johnson rolled his eyes. "Trillionaire like I'm the richest man on the planet."

"Because you cheated," Terrance said, grimacing as he climbed slowly to his feet. Was that BBQ stain on his sweater growing? "You're nothing but a bully and a…" he squinted out at the street.

The others followed his gaze as a low throbbing sounded, growing louder.

"Helicopter," In-Fi-N8 said.

Johnson swore. "This is bad. This place got a back way out?"

"Didn't you work here?" Terry asked pointedly.

"Do I remember everything about some random pizza gig I worked at for six months about twenty years ago? I can't believe I used to be this dumb. Now, where's the damned exit?"

Terry gulped and meekly pointed behind the counter to the door that led to the kitchen.

"They'll be forming a perimeter," In-Fi-N8 said.

"No kidding," Johnson said as he picked up his coat.

As they filed toward the kitchen, the back door flew open and *another* Terry emerged.

He was dressed in an orange jumpsuit. His hair was completely shaved, which showed a Pollock-style series of tattoos that covered his face, neck, and arms. He was also absolutely jacked, like he did nothing but push-ups. His eyes were hard and his face was twisted into what was likely a permanent scowl.

"Terry?" Terry asked.

New Terry scowled deeper. "Maddog."

"You want any pizza, Maddog?" In-Fi-N8 asked, holding up one of the few remaining meat lover's slices.

Terry hoped one day for a woman to look at him like Maddog looked at that pizza slice, but Maddog soon broke the connection and lowered his eyes.

"I can't eat that. They'll know."

"Who?" Johnson rested his hand on a gun and scowled at the street.

Terry said, "Don't you know? Shouldn't you know?"

In-Fi-N8 shook his head. "I told you. Too many timelines and things get weird."

Blue and red light flashed outside.

From outside, via loudspeaker, came, "This is the New York State Counter-Terrorism Unit. We know you're in there, Terry. Let the hostages go before someone else gets hurt."

"What the hell?" Terry cried.

Maddog grabbed the remote control and turned on the TV.

On the television was a bird's-eye view of Eli's Pizzeria.

"Twenty-two-year-old Terrance Johnson is believed to be holding multiple people hostage in a bizarre drug-fueled Dungeons & Dragons game gone horribly wrong...."

"What?" Terry shouted. "How!? That was like two minutes ago! I literally just...you! It was one of you!"

In-Fi-N8, Maddog, and Mr. Johnson stood apart in almost the same way, hands outstretched with accusing fingers pointed at each other.

Wait. Where's...

Terrance had collapsed into a window booth, clutching his stomach where a dark red stain spread steadily.

In-Fi-N8 ran over and pressed a napkin to the wound. "I got you, brother. Stay with us."

"Idiot," Johnson muttered. "I can't believe you actually let yourself get shot. I told you to get down."

Terrance grimaced and groaned as he tried to move.

"Wait," Terry said and nodded to Mr. Johnson. "You got some magical healing stuff, don't you?"

Johnson sneered. "This 'stuff' is proprietary. Just this small vial costs ten million dollars. I'm not about to waste it on some loser HVAC technician, especially not one who'll be erased from existence along with his pathetic timeline."

Terry's eyes widened. "How can you—I—be so cold?"

Johnson smiled thinly. "Go back and forth through enough possible futures and you realize that nothing really matters. Don't like how one day goes? Do it over—and over and over. Terrance, there is just one possibility. When you've lived thousands of lives, does any one really matter?"

In the booth, In-Fi-N8 helped Terrance hold his phone, where a picture of two young kids stared out from under bloody fingerprints.

Maddog growled and lunged toward In-Fi-N8. He came away holding the Micro Uzi. Before Mr. Johnson could react, Maddog jabbed the gun at him.

"Drop 'em. Real slow, Mr. Trillionaire."

Teeth clenched, Mr. Johnson, placed the guns on the floor and slid them away. One made its way behind the counter while the other spun off a metal table support and stopped near Terry.

Maddog said, "I've been living in a government cell for the past twenty years. Every night, I poop at 10:30, and that toilet is a smart toilet. I eat that pizza and they'll know. They always know! I'm supposed to give you a watch and then come right back. They promised to free me if I did what they said."

"Prison?" In-Fi-N8 asked. "For real?"

"I thought you said they couldn't touch us!" Terry shouted.

"Not without consequences," In-Fi-N8 shouted back.

Terry cupped a hand over his eyes. "So *now* you talk about consequences? What consequences?"

Maddog laughed, the kind of laugh that the boss in a video game makes before going into second phase by injecting himself with a serum that will eventually kill him but also gives him super strength for the next ten minutes—and makes him kinda crazy.

"Consequences like this," Maddog said. He smiled maniacally and pointed the gun at Terry.

The helicopter and loudspeaker were momentarily drowned out in a cacophony of whoas, objections, and other freak-outs.

"I kill you," Maddog said, "and none of this ever happened."

"You don't know that," Johnson said. "Maybe you'll fix it, maybe you won't. There's all kinds of glitches and loose ends when it comes to time travel."

"I'll risk it," Maddog said.

In-Fi-N8 said, "You'd actually destroy your own timeline—*all* timelines?"

Maddog looked at In-Fi-N8 with tears in his eyes. "You don't know what it's like being kept in a cage, especially for a crime you never committed. Hell, the only crime was you guys coming back and shooting up half the street. I been paying for that ever since."

He took a deep breath and tightened his grip on the gun. His eyes took on a pronounced and frightening clarity.

He said, "I'm through paying."

"Drop it," said a man's voice.

Standing in the doorway was...Kevin? He held a pistol similar to Johnson's.

A bead of sweat dripped down Maddog's cheek as his eyes flitted between Terry and Kevin. "You shoot me and I might fall down dead, but I might just pull the trigger here, too."

Kevin said, "We can work it out, Terry. I can make the prison stuff go away."

"Kevin?" Terry asked. "Huh?"

Without taking his eyes off Maddog, Kevin twitched his wrist and his watch flashed. "I might have lied about that guy behind the mall."

"Among other things," Terry said, momentarily too shocked to be angry.

Johnson nodded solemnly. "You work for the feds."

Kevin said, "I was approached a few years from now. They needed someone close to you at the right time and I said yes. My job is to make sure someone maintains the paradox."

"More like someone they can control," Johnson said. "You could never control me. That's why—" He half-smiled, half-snarled and pointed at the flashing red and blue lights. "That's why you told them."

Without taking the gun off Terry, Maddog's wide-eyed glare slowly turned to Kevin.

"That true?" he grumbled like an awakening volcano.

Kevin gave one of those weak, grimacing smiles. "It's not like that, Terry. Look, In-Fi-N8 or Terrance were fine, but the moment you started going all Elon Musk, you were a loose cannon. There's a lot more than just us at stake here. We had to be sure."

"You set me up the whole time? You sent me to prison!"

Kevin sighed. "I know you *think* you were in prison for twenty years, but from my point of view, it's only been five minutes. Easily fixed. Just one phone call is all I need to—"

Maddog growled and dolphin-dove onto the eaten-down pizza box while firing wildly at Kevin—who squeezed off several shots as he dove behind a booth.

"Go! Go! Go!" Even through the ringing in Terry's ears, the crackle of radio voices was unmistakable, as was the rumble of running combat boots, getting closer.

In the booth, Terrance's eyes fluttered closed and In-Fi-N8 shook his head sadly. Johnson was nowhere to be seen, likely having slipped out via the kitchen, that jerk.

Johnson!

Johnson's lost gun was only feet away. Bobbing lights on the SWAT team's submachine guns glinted through shattered glass. They'd be swarmed in seconds.

Terry dropped to the floor and grabbed the gun just as a small metallic tube clinked onto the tiles only a few feet away. He'd played enough *Call of Duty* to know what a flash-bang was.

Hoping to God he didn't actually destroy all reality, Terry pointed the gun to his watch and fired.

"Terry?"

He jolted upright. Someone was touching his shoulder.

"Terry?" Jessica Li asked. "You okay?"

"What? Where...."

He was in one of the window booths of Eli's Pizzeria. The window was unbroken, though he touched it to be sure.

"Easy," Jessica said. "That must've been some dream."

"Dream?" It had been real. It had to be. He cupped a hand to his wrist, which had never felt so empty. "So, there's no SWAT team?"

She raised a confused eyebrow and gave one of those "Is he joking—I sure hope he's joking" half smiles.

He stood and scanned the restaurant. "What about Kevin? That rat back there?"

"What's with you?" She placed both hands on his chest. "Honestly, you should take some time off, Terry. Try to sleep more."

He checked the clock above the counter: 11:04 p.m. He vaguely remembered finishing his last run and coming back on time, then... falling asleep? But he also remembered In-Fi-N8 and Terrance and all the other stuff.

"Didn't you leave like an hour ago?" he asked, sitting back down.

She bit the corner of her lip and gave an angry sigh. "I forgot my purse and took the bus back. Then I saw you here. Good thing, too, or you'd have spent the night here again."

Terry almost got fired that time. You'd think a good boss would reward that kind of no-life 24/7 attitude, but he'd chewed out Terry after checking the cameras.

Terry nodded, then finished waking up enough to notice Jessica. Her eyes were puffy, like she'd been crying.

He said, "What about you? You don't look like you're having the best night, either."

She sat in the seat across from him and rested her chin on her hands.

"Yeah." She looked forlornly out the window into the deepening night. "Tyler and I broke up. We'd been having issues for a while. I was thinking this could really work, but..." She sighed again. "Tonight, I just had this feeling like I was missing something."

Terry frowned. "I'm sorry to hear that. His loss. I know you'd be a great mother, wanting to work with those kids and all."

YES!!

He restrained the urge to do a fist pump. Okay, so maybe it wasn't proper, but what was it In-Fi-N8 had said about rings and being in the game?

"Wait a minute." Her brows furrowed, like she was on the edge of angry. "How do you know I want to work with kids?"

"Oh?"

That was real? Of course it was real! I wasn't dreaming! Wait—what was the name of that coin, again? Aargh! How could I forget that? It's on the tip of my brain....

Jessica was waiting for an answer.

"Uh...you must have said it at one point, right?"

She shook her head slowly.

"Oh. Well, maybe you just seem the type."

"And what type is that?" she asked, annoyance levels rising.

"Uh…"

Above Jessica's head, he could almost see a yellow exclamation mark, slowly filling with red.…

"The type of person who walks into a room, and then everything just gets a little bit brighter—like how you're helping me right now."

She couldn't help but smile. It wasn't quite like the smile she'd given In-Fi-N8, but it was more genuine. Maybe that was more meaningful.

"Awfully deep for a pizza delivery guy," she said.

"I deliver pizzas right now, but I have an artist's soul." That sounded so lame. How did In-Fi-N8 pull it off?

Because he believed it. He lived it. I don't.

"I should go," she said, standing.

Terry said, "Wait. Um, it's late. I was headed to the gym, but how about I give you a ride?"

She started to give the universal female grimace and shrug of lack-of-interest, but Terry quietly shook his head no.

"It's not a romantic thing," he said. "I mean, you're cute, of course— it's obvious, but…okay, seriously. What if it rains again?"

Outside, a thousand stars shone from the cloudless sky, but could you ever be too careful?

He said, "I can't explain why. It would sound crazy, but right now, I feel like I've lost someone really close to me. Maybe a few people. Maybe they'll come back, but maybe not, or maybe just a part of them, if I try really hard."

Not Maddog or Johnson—sorry, Maddog. Rest in peace, bro. Okay, maybe Johnson's jacket. Just the jacket, though. That thing was badass.

He said, "Sorry, I know that sounds dumb. It's been a crazy night, and I guess I just don't want to be alone."

She stared at him for a long time. Eventually, she nodded. "I wouldn't mind tagging along, actually. I don't have my gym stuff, but I could do a little yoga. Clear my head."

They locked up Eli's Pizzeria and the evening wind blasted Terry's face. It had the crispness of early autumn that always sent a squeeze of anxiety through his nerves. He'd thought leaving school would mean an end to all that. If anything, it was worse. Each September loomed like a giant cliff over which Terry would tumble into another long, useless year, all leading to a long, dark future without any prospects.

Three minutes later, they were in the Tercel. Terry apologized profusely for the mess and the smell.

"Is that a textbook?" she asked, grabbing the glossy, barely read *Electrical Construction and Maintenance Techniques (2nd Edition).*

"I was thinking of going back to school. Maybe Hudson Valley, to be an electrician."

The thought of creeping through people's houses made him feel weird. At least with pizzas, he only had to deal with them on the front step. Still, hadn't Terrance mostly done the new homes? There might be a few years crawling around in people's basements to make journeyman, but after that?

"Terry, that's great! You should totally do that."

Her smile was infectious.

She said, "You know, I didn't think it was my place to say anything, but the last few weeks you've seemed really down. It's nice to see you smile."

He turned the car on. "I guess I have a lot to smile about. It's not—"

The ancient sound system exploded into a deafening cacophony of screeching instruments.

"What is that?" Jessica yelled, covering her ears.

"Hang on…" Terry hammered the half-broken eject button and the tape shot out.

Jessica scrunched an eyebrow and cocked her head. "Was that the theme song to *The Office*?"

He turned the tape over in his fingers. Slowly, his mouth split into a perfect Jay Gatsby smile.

"Yeah. Yeah, I think it was."

A World of Repetitions

written by

Seth Atwater Jr.

illustrated by

CL FORS

ABOUT THE AUTHOR

*Seth Atwater Jr. is a twenty-four-year-old homebody who loves books—
both writing and reading them. He has always had a passion for good stories
and the real human beings they help us to understand and empathize with,
but he didn't settle on writing as a career until he attended his first Life, the
Universe, and Everything speculative fiction symposium in Utah in 2017.*

*The inclusion of his short story, "A World of Repetitions," in this
anthology is a big step toward achieving that dream, and he is extremely
grateful for the opportunity that the Writers of the Future team has
given him.*

*Seth currently lives with his parents and five of his seven younger siblings
on a family farm in the midwestern United States. He works as a tech specialist
for his dad, who is a marriage-and-family therapist running his own life
coaching business. Seth's family members are all very talented artists and
writers, and it is their support in the form of love, encouragement, and critical
feedback that has made it possible for him to come this far as a writer.*

*Almost all of Seth's stories start with a "what if?" The stories themselves
then take the form of an answer to whatever interesting question was on
his mind and usually relate to both the vastness and intimacy of human
experience. In the case of "A World of Repetitions," the question was, "What
if the world was stuck in a time loop, but everyone kept their memories, not
just the main character?"*

ABOUT THE ILLUSTRATOR

*CL Fors—Cherrie to her friends—was born to a mad scientist and a mad
artist, so it's no surprise she's cultivated lifelong dual passions for art and
science that has shaped her career in writing and illustrating science fiction
and fantasy.*

Cherrie has lived all over the US and now calls the Southern California desert her home, where her family tethers are. She shares her life, love, and creative endeavors with her husband, four clever children, and beloved art family.

Cherrie spent her early years obsessed with story and the many ways to tell it through drawing, writing, sculpting, and performing—sketching for hours, cobbling together "creatures" from whatever she could find in the back of junk drawers, or staring into marbles and imagining she could step through to another world.

Cherrie served in the military and raised a family, but she knew she had to find a way back on her creative path. In 2012, she made a commitment to write her stories and, over the next ten years, wrote, illustrated, and self-published four science fiction novels.

She also began submitting short stories and illustrations to Writers and Illustrators of the Future. She has used them to strengthen her skills and as a goalpost to keep striving.

Her ambition for the future is to find publishers for her finished manuscripts and complete her first graphic novel.

A World of Repetitions

I go about my routine as normal. One coffee, black, brewed as soon as possible, downed immediately after. I don't drink it for the taste; I do it to wake myself up. A quick, cold shower serves the same purpose—keeping my body clean is a useful side effect.

Only once my brain is roused and I am fully cognizant do I allow myself a brief respite for relaxation. I like to pick up a good book for a few minutes. Yesterday, I started reading *Man's Search for Meaning* by Viktor Frankl. I take the paperback volume off my bed stand and open it up to the position of my bookmark—Chapter 2: "Methods of Psychological Resistance." Still wearing my bathrobe and slippers, I settle into my favorite chair and allow myself to be drawn into a world of war and prison camps. You might find it to be an odd comfort read. I am comforted by tragedy. It feels familiar.

I myself have never had a particularly difficult life. There was the pandemic at the beginning of the decade, which by all accounts was tragic, but I didn't lose anyone I was particularly close to. A coldhearted person might even describe the period of lockdown as profitable for me. It certainly brought a lot of clientele to my practice.

My primary acquaintance with grief is through the lens of my clients. Since I got my professional counseling license in 2018, I've heard countless tales of abuse, depression, hopelessness, trauma, and crushing poverty. I've learned to let them roll off me without giving up the sense of empathy I have for the people who suffered through those stories. It's what makes me effective at my job. I mourn with those that mourn, but only when they need me to.

As a straight white man maintaining a relatively peaceful existence in Trenton, New Jersey, it's about all I have to offer them. Fortunately, for most people, it is enough.

Today, a majority of my professional responsibility is paperwork—the only blemish on the peace I mentioned—but I do have one very interesting session to conduct. The client is a young man by the name of Micah Palmer. Diagnosed with level 1 autism spectrum disorder and social anxiety disorder. High school for him has been … uncomfortable, and his naturally tense disposition doesn't make it any easier. He prefers to talk about his interests rather than his day-to-day worries, and while I try to gently steer him back on track when I can, I would be lying to say that I don't look forward to the break in the monotony of the eight-hour workday devised by Robert Owen that comes from listening to Micah explain the intricate details of the plot in the latest episode of *One Piece*.

"I've got a feeling that something is gonna happen," is the first thing Micah says when he walks into my office. His stringy, shoulder-length hair is uncombed as usual, making him appear much more of a wild child than he really is. He tugs on the collar of his loose T-shirt as if it's making it hard for him to breathe.

"Okay, what sort of something?" I motion for him to sit down on the couch across from me. Micah looks around nervously before taking a seat.

"I'm not sure, it's just a feeling. Like, after today, things won't be the same. Or maybe they'll be too the same. You know what I mean? No, you probably don't, do you?"

"How has school been this last week?" I ask. I assume this strange rambling is a symptom of his anxiety, and his interactions with his peers at school are what set him off the most often.

However, his response to my question surprises me. "It's been great. No one made fun of me all week. School's not what I'm worried about right now."

I almost forget to respond. Micah has never gone an entire week without having some kind of trouble with his classmates. People can be cruel to those who seem different from them, and Micah isn't very well equipped to stand up for himself. I know his teachers have been stepping in to reduce the amount of bullying going on, but I didn't expect them to be that effective. Perhaps something strange *is* happening. Or…did he say "going to" happen?

"Micah, when you say things won't be the same, is that because of what's going on in your classes right now?"

He shakes his head. "I told you, it doesn't have anything to do with school. It's just that I've got this gut sense that something bad is coming. I think it'll happen tomorrow."

"And this…premonition that you're having," I say, troubled, "can you tell me any more about it? What do you think is going to happen?"

Micah's shoulders pull in tight and he crosses his arms, an unconscious gesture of closing off, like he's trying to protect himself from something. "I don't know," he says pensively. "Something's gonna break. Like, the world? Or the universe or something. Whatever it is, it won't be good."

I'm starting to get a bad feeling of my own—a perturbation brought on by a lack of understanding. Obviously, Micah is not having real visions of the future. He must be worried about something, and this is his way of expressing it. But I can't seem to identify where his worries could be coming from. He doesn't even look that anxious—he's not doing any of his normal nervous tics right now. He may not be especially forthcoming, but this is him at his most communicative, outside of when he gets going about his favorite hobbies. I'll have to question him further to find the root of his foreboding.

"How are things at home then?"

After a long and unfruitful question-and-answer session with Micah, our time together runs out and he heads back to his home. Before he leaves, he gives me a warning. His dark eyes look sad, almost pitying.

"Mr. Amaranthus? Whatever's coming, you're gonna need a lot more purpose to deal with it than you have now."

I'm too shocked to say anything, so he disappears through the doors before I have a chance to ask what he means. I attempt to shift my attention to the stack of paperwork I have yet to address, but I can't get Micah's statement out of my head. More purpose? Why would he say that?

I live my life very intentionally. Micah may have directed his statement at me, but it only makes sense if I assume he meant it about himself. So why would Micah feel he needs more purpose in life? Is he thinking about what profession he ought to aspire to in the future? That could certainly be the trigger for his apprehension, but it isn't something he's ever mentioned to me before. I suppose someone could have asked him about his career path and set off a chain of intrusive thoughts.

As reasonable as it sounds, I'm not entirely satisfied with that conclusion.

Later, at precisely five o'clock, I make my way home, change out of my button-up shirt and tie, and don athletic wear. I like to spend my evenings at either the park or the YMCA to keep my blood pumping and my mind alert—the mind is a part of the body, after all. Today, I choose the latter option, since I feel like knocking a ball around with my racket and they have the perfect wall for that specific purpose.

I swipe my membership card, and the AI desk client opens the gate to let me into the facility. It didn't take long for a lot of front desk jobs to be replaced by GPT models that can quickly pull up any of the relevant information a customer might want to know. The surprising thing is how many jobs *weren't* affected by the advent of AI technology. Just a few years ago people thought it would revolutionize practically every industry on the planet. Artists were the first to realize that their work simply could not be replaced by a nonhuman imitation.

As I walk past the exercise equipment, I run into an old buddy of mine who I haven't seen in years, which is strange considering we live in the same city. I don't have long to ponder our lack of recent contact before he walks up and pulls me into a masculine side hug. The fact that he is a full foot taller than me makes the gesture a bit awkward on my end, not to mention the length of time since our last meeting.

"Adam, how's it been, man? I feel like we haven't seen each other in forever! Good times back then, yeah? You could still be living in them—you haven't changed a bit!"

I can't say the same of him. Last I saw him, he still had hair, and the smile lines etched into his brown face were less pronounced. Something good must have happened to him since we last spoke.

I invite him to join me in a game of racquetball. It feels like the thing to do, even though I have no idea if we will still get along the way we did in the past. He says he would love to, but he didn't bring his racket. I respond with, "Maybe next time," and we part ways again.

It's approximately seven o'clock when I get home. I am greeted by large, empty rooms, much more spacious than I actually need. I would have been happy with a smaller apartment, but finding this one was hard enough, and the rent is well within my budget. The flat-screen TV and half-dozen bookshelves in the main room serve to make it appear at least somewhat lived in.

I'm subscribed to one of those meal-a-day plans that you see advertised on YouTube, so I fix myself a healthy pasta dish that I would have none of the technical know-how to put together on my own and sit down at my table to eat. It's nowhere near as delicious as my mother's home cooking, but that's a standard that would be impractical to hold to for even the greatest of gourmet chefs, so I am quite content with the flavor.

After dinner, I turn on the television to catch the latter half of tonight's football game. I don't fancy myself much of a sports fan, but I enjoy watching a good game every now and then, and I try to keep up with recent news regarding our local teams because many of my clients will want to talk about it. Mental health in the area takes a noticeable drop when the Giants lose. (Despite the name, the New York Giants actually play their home games in New Jersey.)

By the time the game is over I'm ready to lie down and enter into the first cycles of sleep. I change one last time for the day, this time into my pajamas, and climb into my queen-sized bed. It was a gift from my mother, a not-so-subtle hint that she wants me to settle down with a good girl and start making grandchildren for her. It's a nice bed, so I'm not going to complain.

407

APRIL 23, 2027

My morning routine is the same as ever. If I had anything more exciting to explain to you, I would, but the truth is my life generally tends toward the mundane, and I am comfortable with that. There aren't many things I would consciously choose to go back and change. I am content.

I open my book to Chapter 3: "Logotherapy and Meaning." I set the bookmark aside, and allow myself to relax. When I finish the chapter, I replace the bookmark, this time at the beginning of Chapter 4. Simple. Calming. A happy habit has no need for alteration.

I start off on my way to work at 8:43 a.m. The air is chilly, the sky overcast, the cacophony of heavy traffic ringing in my ears. Regretting my lack of foresight in not wearing a jacket, I deal with the problem I do have a solution for by putting in earbuds to block out the noise. I don't actually turn on any music. As I board the bus, I find myself pondering again what Micah could have meant yesterday about me needing more purpose when—

APRIL 22, 2027 (II)

I wake up in my bed. That's strange, I was just on the bus on my way to the clinic. I don't remember returning to my apartment. Did something happen to make me forget coming home? Was Micah right somehow?

I grab my phone off my bedside table and check the time. It is 7:25 a.m., just a few minutes before I typically get up. I don't set an alarm for myself—my body's internal clock does the job well enough on its own.

Next to the time, the screen also displays the date. April 22. That… that was yesterday. There must be something wrong with my phone. I stand up and walk to the dresser, on top of which is the smartwatch I use primarily to track my vitals while exercising. In the top right corner of its display are the numbers 04/22/27. Weird. Is something wrong with the… the satellite that my devices get their information from? That's how it works, right? I'm not exactly a tech genius.

If I had a wall clock, I could check that, but I've never felt the need to buy one. I turn on the TV instead. Surely, the news will have the correct date.

Our regular weatherman, a genial fellow named Martin Gustin, lets out a deep breath, adjusts his freshly pressed navy suit, and runs his fingers through his slicked-back hair before presenting the forecast.

"So, what we're seeing here is sixty-one-degree weather, with a high probability of clouds later in the day, but probably not much rain. Which is exactly the same as yesterday's forecast. I hate to say it, but this whole thing seems to be true. It really is April twenty-second again."

I reel at the weatherman's surreal statement. Am I supposed to believe that time rewound itself somehow, as if that's a completely natural thing for it to do? I'm not sure I would be capable of believing it, no matter how hard I tried.

The news station shifts back to the morning reporters, who are discussing a volcanic eruption that took place on a small Hawaiian island on the previous twenty-second. It is spewing ash and sulfur in exactly the same way today, which meteorologist Liam Fogel is on the scene for again, since despite his best efforts to leave he is still in the area. Could the repeated seismic activity be a coincidence? None of the reporters even consider the idea. The time rewind is already an accepted fact at this point.

No, this must be some kind of prank. An impressively thorough one, impressive enough that it could only have been pulled off by the government. How else would the news and the digital timekeepers be in on it? Come to think of it, rather than a prank, maybe it's some kind of military operation. I can't say I approve, considering how much it will affect the lives of common men like me, but there isn't much I can do about it.

Content with the explanation I have come up with, I pick up *Man's Search for Meaning* and sit down in my chair. I open to the page where I had left my bookmark.

I am looking at the first page of Chapter 2: "Methods of Psychological Resistance." The chapter I read on April twenty-second.

Unsure what else to do, I find myself going to work as normal. I remember to bring a jacket with me this time, so the same chilly air I was shivering in previously doesn't bother me as much. There are fewer people on the streets than I'm used to, fewer cars driving around and angrily honking at each other, but not by as significant of a margin as I would have expected. It seems I am not the only person who can't think of anything better to do than go to work and file all the same paperwork a second time.

I've read stories about time looping back on itself before, so as fantastical as this situation is I at least have a concept of what it should look like according to literature. Unfortunately, there is one major discrepancy that renders all time-repetition fiction completely useless as a guide for my actions on this second April twenty-second.

I am not the only one who remembers the previous version of the day. As far as I can tell based on the news this morning and the bewildered faces of my fellow pedestrians, the whole city has kept its memory. Perhaps the entire world has. I've never heard of a story where that happened. The physical world reset, but all human minds were unaffected. As a professional in the field of the human mind I find it fascinating, as long as I can ignore the existential horror it necessarily implies.

Micah doesn't visit me again today. Without the chance to speak with him, the paperwork becomes even more grueling—although one could argue that filling out all the exact same documents for a second time is contributing to the drudgery. One thing I learn from this experience is that paperwork must have always been on its own constant quantum loop through time, because it all feels just the same anyway.

None of my regular clients show up for their appointments, but the office suddenly gets an influx of people calling in and asking to set up consultations later in the week, enough so that Charlie, our young secretary, has a hard time keeping up with them all. Rather optimistic of them, assuming that later in the week will ever come.

I understand that they must be very confused. Who knows what may or may not happen at this point. That uncertainty is certain to trigger stress in a lot of individuals, which explains why they feel the need to speak with me and my colleagues.

I spend the day being bombarded with questions that I am already asking myself. Why is this happening? Will tomorrow be April twenty-second as well? What should I do if time never goes back to normal? It is impossible for me to give a satisfying answer. I don't know what the hell is going on either, or the why or wherefore of it. I'd rather dissociate and pretend it isn't happening at all, but that's hard to do when I'm being constantly reminded of it—in a professional setting no less. Charlie and Esther—an older, bespectacled woman twenty years my senior at our practice—get the brunt of the questioning, and even so, by the end of the day, I am exhausted from answering calls and talking to walk-ins. I am more than relieved when my work is finally over.

As soon as I get home, I change and head directly for the YMCA. Yet again I am following ritual only because I don't know what else to do. Hopefully a good game of racquetball will help me clear my head.

I swipe my card at the desk, wait impatiently for the AI to open the gate for me, and stride past it toward the courts. I am surprised to see that my friend who I met here yesterday—or today before—is waiting on the other side yet again. I'm almost led to assume that the other people around me have somehow started looping as well, but then I notice the uniquely shaped bag that he's carrying.

"I got the feeling that you might be here again today," he says. "I, uh, I brought my racket this time. Still up for a game?"

"Yeah, totally."

This time we have a chance to catch up. Booker—his name is Booker, by the way, which, to be perfectly honest, I didn't remember for sure until now—tells me that he just got a promotion at work that he's very excited about, and I congratulate him. He shows me pictures from the camera reel on his phone of his two little daughters, both of whom I have never met. I tell him that I find my current life fulfilling, even if the bureaucratic side of career work can be a pain. He laughs and says amen. My ball hits the wall a thousand times.

This is the most surreal-feeling thing that has happened all day, somehow. In an ordinary world, the today before would have been the first and last time Booker and I interacted for months at least. After that brief exchange and the realization that he couldn't join me in a game, that would have been it. The serendipitous circumstances that led to us repeating the same interaction, but with a more favorable outcome, are downright baffling in terms of how astronomically unlikely it seems. And that's not even accounting for the improbability of time rewinding itself for no discernible reason. I am fully mystified.

This might be the only fortunate thing that has come out of repeating April twenty-second for a second time.

Once our game is over, we say our goodbyes, both smiling in recognition of whatever providence or coincidence made our second meeting possible. I consider making plans to play again another day, but a lingering doubt in the back of my mind keeps me from committing to the idea. What if the day we plan to meet never comes? I'd rather not consider what tomorrow will bring—if tomorrow as a concept even exists anymore—so I refrain from bringing it up.

I'm at home again. I prepare my meal-a-day dinner, but I can't make myself eat much. It's not that I've lost my appetite, rather my taste buds are eager to remind me that I had the same pasta dish today before as well.

With nothing better to do, I flip on the TV. Newscasters are continuing to have the same conversation they had this morning, albeit in a more heated manner. It seems no one has made any progress toward discerning why this bizarre phenomenon has occurred. I ponder it for a moment, but the only solutions I can come up with are straight out of sci-fi novels, and they keep getting more and more outlandish. By the time I nearly consider that aliens could be involved, I decide it's time to get some sleep.

It's earlier than my schedule prescribes for me to retire to my bed, but it's been a long day—about twice as long as normal, in fact. After listening to a sleep meditation to clear my mind, I don't find it the least bit difficult to let myself drift off into the realm of Hypnos.

412

APRIL 23, 2027 (II)

The next day, it's the next day again. The twenty-third comes after the twenty-second. That's natural. And yet, I still feel like dancing with joy, and I do not dance. My movements are too stiff and robotic to adequately perform any dance moves except the one that shares a name with my mechanical inflexibility.

Which is beside the point. I only mean to emphasize how inexplicably life-changing it is to realize that life can and will change. I catch myself whistling a tune on my morning commute. I get some strange looks, but I don't give a—

APRIL 22, 2027 (III)

Damn! Whatever divine being is putting humanity through this was unbelievably cruel when they decided to give us just a taste of another day before snatching it away from us, rather than just setting the loop to repeat at midnight on the twenty-second. I knew that the next day had started at the end of the previous repetition as well, but I still allowed myself to hope. I see now how foolish that was.

My bookmark is still at the beginning of the second chapter of *Man's Search for Meaning*, even though I clearly remember reading beyond that.

The people on the news aren't just arguing anymore, they're in a state of total panic. They are predicting that very few people are going to have the motivation to do anything at all today when the evidence suggests that it'll all just reset and none of their progress will mean anything. I disagree. I know the power of a strong routine. I'm getting ready for work right now, without even thinking about it. Could I stay home and do nothing? Sure, but doing something will at the very least distract me from thinking about all the nothing that is awaiting us after midmorning on April twenty-third.

I've also seen firsthand how resilient humanity is in the face of a crisis. Did Covid massively impact all of our lives? Yes, but even so we kept living. And eventually, we got through it. I'm positive that time itself breaking won't be enough to remove our will to go on.

The thing I'm worried about is that—will or no—going on in a world with no future isn't possible. What good is the human will when it has no outlet? *Homo sapiens* is distinguished from ordinary animals by our ability to create. To add to the world rather than just existing in it. What will happen to us when that ability is taken away? As a mental health specialist, I am curious to find out, but my professional curiosity is coming from too morbid a point of origin to make our collective outlook appear any brighter.

Our clinic gets even more calls today. The most surprising part is, many of them are scheduling appointments in advance. "I don't need to come in today, but if today happens again, will you be able to make time for me?" is the most common question Charlie is hearing and relaying to us. I'm almost shocked that so many people are coming to us for guidance, instead of...I don't know, astrophysicists or something.

I only say almost because I've felt like setting up an appointment of my own with Esther for most of the day. My head is spinning, and nothing feels real. We don't use words like crazy or insane to refer to those with mental deficiencies anymore, but I feel like I'm being driven to the state those archaic words describe. I don't know what to do. Which is why I continue to do what I've always done.

Booker is yet again waiting to play ball with me when I arrive at the Y. This time he's come equipped not only with a racket, but also a set of deeply concerned contours on his face. I get the feeling that he's not worrying for himself. At least, not primarily.

"How've things been today, Adam?" he asks me.

"You mean this one, or the last one?"

He grimaces at my question, but plays it off with a false smile. "Yeah, I guess the meaning of that word is a bit sketchy now, isn't it? I just want to know how you're holding out. You still live alone, don't you?"

I'm not sure what that has to do with anything, but I answer in the affirmative.

"Well, hey, if you ever need anything, you know where to find me. Don't let yourself give up just yet."

"Thanks...I won't."

I make a conscious effort to take that to heart. As terrifying as the mere concept of an endlessly repeating world is, one devoid of progression and therefore meaning, I don't want to be defeated by hopelessness so easily. If not for myself, then at least for the other people in the world who are going through the same things and desperately need someone to tell them that there is a light at the end of the tunnel. Even if he himself doesn't believe it.

I go to sleep on the *third* April twenty-second pondering what I will say to the people who scheduled to meet with me the today after today—if, and when, it comes.

APRIL 22, 2027 (XXXVII)

More than a month's worth of April twenty-seconds have passed. The professionals keeping track have decided to count them in Roman numerals so as to distinguish them from the decimal system used for the rest of the date. Ironically, most people have just dropped everything but the number of repetitions when referring to the passage of time. No longer will passersby on the street tell you that the date is April twenty-second. They'll say, "It's number thirty-seven, I think."

I wonder what will happen when the number of repetitions adds up and becomes too long for use in ordinary conversation. We'll probably develop a whole new calendar system then.

We are finally adjusting to life in this repeating world. As I predicted, people are resilient. It didn't take us long to start figuring out new ways of interacting with our surroundings that are consistent with the rules of the thus-far-unending cycle.

Many were surprised when entertainment became the first industry to make a comeback. I wasn't. People are locked into their position on Maslow's Hierarchy of Needs—if you have food and shelter today, you'll continue to have it every today going forward—

and efforts are being made to provide basic necessities for those who don't have them. Large storehouses of food will never be depleted in this world, so why not open them up to the public? I'm impressed with how charitable individuals can find ways to serve even in a constant state of non-permanence. Although I did somewhat predict it, I'm still surprised at how fast positive responses have risen out of the initial panic.

With basic needs out of the way, Maslow would assume that we would next move on to love and belonging, and then esteem, and while that is absolutely important, I would argue that he forgot one more critical need that fits in between, or even next to love. That is the need to tell stories. It's a part of our nature that we can't ignore. Our species has been doing it since long before we had the ability to write them down. It only makes sense that we'd find a way to continue to do so even when written records all disappear within thirty-four hours.

For now, the resurgence of storytelling is taking two primary forms. First, sports. Spectator sports have always been about the narratives that they create. No one watches football because they'd rather be playing it. They watch to see battles unfold between two teams made up of great warriors and see who comes out on top. Pro wrestling directly acknowledges this by making the sport itself an elaborate performance and outright admitting it to their audience. Do the spectators mind? Not at all. They love it.

All that to say that the Giants first game since the beginning of the repeating world is scheduled for the fortieth repetition, and despite never considering myself to be a huge sports fan, I am very excited.

The second way that entertainment has kicked back into gear is through online live streaming. Content creators have no way to archive their stream VODs anymore, but it isn't stopping them from keeping up daily schedules regardless. Network TV channels have even started to fill up time blocks by showing live play performances in addition to reruns of whatever programming they happen to have on hand. But Twitch and YouTube are where it's at if you want real viewership numbers.

Not that those numbers translate to anything for large companies anymore, since money has become totally meaningless. There isn't much point to it if the amount you have stays fixed. I imagine large-scale corporations will eventually collapse, or be taken over by individuals who care about keeping them running for whatever reason. And good riddance to them. That's one of the small blessings that has come from this major curse.

Angela Watanabe has been seeing me every seven days since the start of the repeating world. She is a short, dark-haired young woman who dropped out of college to pursue a career as a YouTube streamer, and she has garnered a moderate following. Angela streams with a virtual avatar in place of her real face. Because of this, her voice has become her most valuable asset. Unfortunately, she caught the flu on April twentieth. She now eternally sounds like a dehydrated hyena.

"I'm grateful I had my model rigged before all this happened," she rasps. "Getting one commissioned now would be completely impossible. It takes way more than a day's worth of work."

She's always trying to look on the bright side of things, at least outwardly. I can tell she's hurting though, and not just in a physical sense. Well, physically too, for certain. I can't imagine waking up every day knowing your sickness will never get better.

"Also, I don't have to worry about infecting anyone else, since they'll just reset to how they were before at the beginning of the next repetition anyway." She tries to smile, but her gray-blue eyes—dulled by both her sickness and her mental state—aren't really up to it, and it comes out weak.

"Look, Angela," I say, "I'm going to be straight with you. It's wonderful that you're able to focus on the positives of your situation. It really is. But you aren't seeing me so we can talk about why everything is peachy. It's okay to complain a little. That's why I'm here. To listen to the negatives that you're protecting everyone else from."

Angela's tight smile releases, allowing the corners of her mouth to tilt down along with the rest of her head. "Well, I…I mean, obviously it's hard. My viewer numbers keep dwindling, and…I don't know what to do. Without them, all that's left is…this." She waves her hands about, vaguely indicating everything in our surroundings. I understand. The world around us doesn't mean much in the face of abandonment.

"I don't know what to do" is a hard plea for me to answer. It's difficult to reassure someone when I'm as in the dark as they are.

"Do you live alone?"

I'm not sure why I asked that. I'm parroting the question my friend Booker asked me when the repetitions were just starting. I don't know what meaning it has in this scenario.

Also, I already know the answer. This isn't Angela's first time meeting with me, after all. She's told me about her family situation— her parents live in Japan, which is a long enough flight that seeing them in person is incredibly difficult within the thirty-four-hour period of the repeating world, especially since airlines have yet to adjust to our new reality. She could still call them, but the state of her relationship with her father makes that prohibitively challenging.

Nevertheless, her response surprises me.

"I have a roommate, but we don't talk much. She was going to grad school until…well, you know. She spends most evenings out on the town with her school friends, so she doesn't mind the noise I make while streaming, since she's not usually around to hear it. So, yeah, we have an understanding between us, but not really a relationship."

I consider the fact that I was unaware of this roommate to be a personal failing. I should have probed more in our previous sessions and tried to better understand Angela's situation. That aside, learning about her existence has given me a thought, one that might be able to help with Angela's problem.

"What is your roommate's name?" I ask.

"Um, it's Bonnie. Why?"

"You said you don't talk to her much. I think you should change that."

Angela's brow furrows in confusion. "Huh? What are you talking about? We were just discussing my career as a streamer. What does she have to do with that?"

"More than you realize."

In the repeating world, jobs no longer exist as a way to make income or provide for yourself and your loved ones. Those who continue to work generally fall into one of two groups—people who are just doing what feels normal, like me, and people who are seeking validation from others. Angela definitely falls into the second category. Her online persona has become her identity, more so than her real self, and if the numbers on the website say people are losing interest, that's going to be damaging to her mental health.

No one cares about me. It's an easy mindset to slip into. Angela needs an IRL backup in case her digital self becomes shattered by destructive self-doubt. Someone who will care even if all of YouTube forgets her. Even if her family isn't able to be there for her. Bonnie has the potential to be that person.

"You're going to need to trust me on this one. During the next seven days, try to make friends with Bonnie, or at least show an interest in her life. Then report back to me when we have our next appointment. Okay?"

Angela looks at me skeptically, but she agrees. I hope I've made the right call.

When I get home from work, I open *Man's Search for Meaning* and turn to the marked page—Chapter 2: "Methods of Psychological Resistance." I have finished the book by now and moved on to my next read, but checking the bookmark has become a ritual in its own right for me. It reminds me that, as little as my everyday routine has changed, the world is fundamentally, irrevocably different now. I don't know what to do with that information, and yet it feels important to keep a firm grasp on it. I worry that, if my life starts to become a series of exact repetitions, I will be absorbed into the repeating world, never to return. At least not as myself.

I go to the park today instead of the YMCA, in order to break up that deadly monotony. I text Booker to let him know ahead of time so he won't wait for me indefinitely at our meet-up spot next to the stationary bikes.

"Cool, next today then," he shoots back.

I chuckle. I'm glad that our friendship has become a part of my life again. Booker is my Bonnie, in a way.

I run. The park closest to my apartment has a running loop that goes most of the way around the perimeter of the public property, and it's a great way to stretch my legs and lungs a little. I find running to be very meditative. In fact, the way a runner has to regulate their breathing is not at all unlike the kinds of breath exercises that you'll encounter if you pick up the hobby of listening to guided meditations. I may be getting my heart rate up, but I find it calming.

That's normally how it goes, anyway. This time things turn out a little different. As I'm running, someone starts to catch up to me from behind. I can hear her breathing as she approaches me. Glancing over my shoulder, I see that it's a woman, just barely past her prime, the same as me. She's equipped for exercising—shorts, tank top, sneakers, completely disregarding the perpetually chilly weather. She must be planning to work up a sweat. The band she's wearing around her head with her long blond ponytail is further evidence of that. I was under the impression that sweatbands were long out of fashion. She makes it look good, regardless.

I don't want to let her pass me. Like everything else that's happened in these last thirty-seven days I can't explain the feeling, not even to myself. I let instinct guide me, and as she comes up on my left, I speed up to stay ahead. I can hear her footfalls quickening as well. She's right next to me now. We lock eyes, and she grins at me. I break into a sprint. She follows suit.

Less than a minute later I am gasping for breath with my hands on my knees. I stopped once the woman I was racing pulled ahead of me. It was an inevitability, really; she was clearly a much more practiced runner than I was. I had expected her to leave me in the dust, but after I slowed, she stopped next to me. I wonder if she's waiting for congratulations or something like that.

"Thanks for the challenge," she says, extending a hand toward me. "I've been needing an excuse to push myself like that."

I stand up straight and shake her hand. "Anytime," I respond, without thinking much about the implications of that simple statement. The average person would take it as mere cordiality.

"Oh, really? Well, then, how about tomorrow—or, the next today, that is. Will you be here?"

It seems my running mate is not best described as the average person.

"I'm afraid I'll be playing racquetball with a friend about this time then," I say.

"All right then, what about the morning? Say, seven o'clock?"

That would be right in the middle of my well-worn routine. It would be absurd to break that up to go running with a complete stranger.

"Sure, seven works."

"Great!" She beams. "I'm looking forward to it. I'm Diana, by the way. Diana Green."

"Adam Amaranthus."

We shake hands again, and then laugh at the ludicrousness of the repeated gesture.

"If I might ask, why is pushing yourself so important to you? All your progress will be reset at the end of the repetition. You won't ever get any more in shape than you are right now." Which seems like a perfectly good shape already, I refrain from adding.

"You have a point," she says. "I think maybe I just don't want to accept that. Or possibly it's a way to remind myself that I still have control of something. Even if it'll be for nothing, I still get to decide whether I work hard or just give up. And giving up isn't a super attractive option."

I nod. The whole reason I'm here is to seek out new—or at least different—daily experiences so I don't allow myself to give up either. I can relate to the need for a motivating factor in the fight against the repeating world.

"So, I'll see you here next time?" Diana says.

I smile. "On the hour."

"Good. And not a minute later?"

"Not a minute."

APRIL 22, 2027 (CVI)

Now that we've hit a hundred repetitions, we've started abbreviating the number in speech by saying C—the Roman numeral for a hundred—instead of the whole thing. By that count, today is C6, the one-hundred-and-sixth repetition of the thirty-four hours following hour zero on April twenty-second. My prediction about a new calendar system has unofficially come to pass.

The meteorologists are all obviously moving on to greener pastures, or so you would think. The local weather reporter, Martin Gustin, has decided to keep the tradition alive. Every morning he puts on his navy suit and heads to the film studio so he can tell us that, "It looks like it's gonna be a little overcast today, but rain isn't likely—and remember, as Little Orphan Annie tells us, the sun will come out tomorrow!" or "We've got an unprecedented streak of identical temperature predictions going on, and today is the one-hundred day anniversary of this miraculous coincidence, which seems to be unrelated to any other unexplained events going on in the world at large. So, let's all sing happy birthday to our streak while I go buy some cake." I am of the opinion that his show has become one of the best comedies on television, and live stand-up comedy is pretty darn popular right now. I'm a sucker for the dry, sarcastic style of humor I suppose.

Watching Martin Gustin's weather report has become an integral part of my new morning routine. I tune in every day after I check on *Man's Search for Meaning* and before I go to meet Diana at the park.

So much time has passed since I first met her, and I still know so little about her. The reverse is not at all true. Diana asks excellent questions. I understand her life on a surface level—her likes, dislikes, family situation, and so on—but she hasn't unveiled her deepest anxieties to me the way I have to her. She knows I worry that my commitment to routine prevents me from spending as much time around my family as I should. She didn't even have to meet my parents to get it out of me, though she has met them, and they love her almost as much as my two younger siblings, Amy and Abel, do.

She also knows which of my clients I'm most concerned about and why, though I haven't disclosed their names, for obvious reasons.

Sometimes, when Diana and I are talking, I wonder which one of us is the therapist.

Not only is she good at asking questions, she's also good at listening to the answers. Before we started running together, I was overwhelmed by the reality of living in the repeating world. Now I feel that I've come to accept it, at least a little. Having her and Booker for support has made a big difference in that sense.

I'm still meeting with Angela regularly, but at this point I'm only there as a bit of extra support—and, to be honest, she doesn't even really need that anymore. She has Bonnie now. The two of them hit it off right away, as soon as Angela decided to reach out. I was taking a chance when I recommended that she try to befriend her roommate, so I am pleasantly surprised that the result was so positive. If Bonnie had turned out to be a more hard-hearted person, my advice could have been a big blunder. Instead, it was a massive success.

From what Angela tells me, the two of them do everything together now. Which isn't much—it's still hard for Angela to go on long trips due to her flu symptoms—but just being around someone who can give her the validation she was seeking from her live chat has clearly improved her emotional state.

Bonnie has even made a guest appearance in some of Angela's livestreams. The chat seemed to like Bonnie more than the person they had actually come to watch, which was a point of contention between the two girls for a bit, but I helped them through that as well, the best I could.

Angela is still impaired by her sickness, and her numbers continue to slowly trickle away as a result. And it is affecting her. But she has someone to lean on now. She'll survive this. Humans are resilient like that.

I advised the two of them against dating each other, because Bonnie is the only lifeline Angela has right now, and if things went sour between them—a risk that always rears its head when romance is involved—she'd be back to square one. Fortunately, they are very happy with the idea of supporting each other as friends. Angela has been out with Bonnie and her campus pals a few times, so there's a possibility she'll meet someone new who she can have that kind of relationship with.

I'm about to fail to follow my own advice on that subject though. Because it's time to go to the park now, and I've finally thought of an excellent question of my own to ask Diana.

She sees me coming before I spot her, and waves to get my attention.

"How was the game last night?" she asks in greeting. She knows that I was looking forward to it.

"The Giants lost, but it was exciting to watch. It was really close until the last quarter. And we have another game against the same opposing team on C8, so we have a chance to make it up then."

"I'll be rooting for you." Diana pumps her fist enthusiastically.

"You should be rooting for the Giants. I'm not the one struggling out there on the field."

"But you said we, didn't you? You included yourself, so why can't I do the same?"

Diana is fantastic at pointing out little inconsistencies like that. Other people might consider it irritating, but to me it's an endearing quality.

"Speaking of we," I say, my voice hesitating a little, "I have something I want to ask you. About you and me?"

"Can you talk while we run?" she asks as she starts to jog in place.

"No, actually, this is better to talk about before we start."

She frowns. "Okay, but I hope it won't take too long. My body's itching to get moving."

She's always like this, and I understand, but I don't want to rush through things either. I sit down on a nearby bench and beckon for her to take a seat next to me. Her frown deepens, but she walks over and sits down. We talk about life and what's going on in it every day while we run, so I'm sure she realizes the severity of a topic of conversation that requires this kind of attention.

"Is something wrong, Adam? You're acting kind of strange. Is there anything I can do?"

CL FORS

"It's not like that," I assure her. I take a deep breath before continuing. "Diana, we've been doing this together every morning for more than two months' worth of todays, but I still feel like I barely know anything about you."

"Oh, is that it?" She lightens a little, her frown giving way to an apologetic smile. "I know I can be relentless in my lines of questioning sometimes. If you want to ask anything about me, go right ahead."

This is going to be difficult. "Y-Your father. I know he wasn't there for you much as a child, and you had a general distrust of men when you were a teenager as a result. I'm aware of those facts, but I can't really feel them. I'm content to merely empathize with my clients, but for some reason a surface-level connection like that just isn't enough when it comes to you. Does that make sense?"

Diana tilts her head to the side in an effort to comprehend. "I suppose. There's something about our time together that's more special than a professional relationship. Is that what you're saying?"

"Y-Yes, something like that. Do you…do you agree?"

"Of course I do! You're the one who pushes me to keep living in this world of repetitions. We haven't been together long, but I consider you to be more than special."

I'm afraid that hearing those words will send me into a tachycardiac fainting spell. I can feel blood rushing through my body, propelled by a heart that is far too excited. I need to calm down or I won't be able to finish saying what I want to say.

"Well, I'm far from perfect, and from my own perspective 'special' feels like a bit of a stretch, but I can at least promise that I'll be there for you in all the ways that your father wasn't, so…"

"So?" she prompts. Her eyes are sparkling, almost like she's laughing at me internally. Does she know what I'm trying to say?

I step down from the bench and descend to one knee in front of Diana. I take her hand. I don't have a ring for her—it would disappear after today anyway, hardly serving as the symbol of eternity that it is meant to be—but I speak the words I painstakingly prepared for nevertheless.

"Diana, would you consider marrying me?"

"What does that mean?"

"What does...what?" I stumble in my response. I was hoping to hear a yes, and prepared for the potential heartbreak that would come with a no. I have no emotional contingency plan for the definition of marriage being called into question.

"What does that mean?" Diana repeats, eyes still sparkling, but in a sober way that demands I answer her question seriously. "I'm not saying no, but reality is different than it used to be. In forever staying the same, things have changed. What does marriage mean in a world like this? If we go to sleep together, we'll still wake up apart."

"Only if we sleep in past nine on the twenty-third," I say. I return to the bench, but I don't let go of Diana's hand.

"We can't share a home—"

"We can if you go home with me every morning after our run."

"Or have children—"

"Are children really necessary?"

"Yes." She states this with a fervor that I don't have the will to dispute. "I've always wanted to raise children. Part of the reason I prioritized my physical health was so I would be ready to bear them. But that's...It's never going to..."

Diana is on the verge of tears. She tries to release my hand, but I hold fast. I'm not going to let her cry alone.

"We can make it work then, somehow. We'll have kids."

"We'll...Adam, what are you saying?"

I have no idea. I feel crazy, but the good kind of crazy, the kind that makes you throw out logic and change the world because someone wants you to do it. I know I'm too small to really change the whole world, but I somehow believe that I can change ours.

"I promise," I tell her, "that I'll do my best to be everything you could want from a husband. If that means giving you children, I'll make it happen. Even if these two days are the only ones we have until time breaks for good and the world comes to an end."

Diana is really crying now and I am too. And laughing. We both are. She enfolds me in an embrace, and whispers in my ear, "I don't know why, but for some reason, I believe you."

APRIL 23, 2027 (CXX)

We hold our wedding early in the morning on the twenty-third so all our relatives who are able can make the trip to be there. My parents and younger siblings might be even more excited than I am. Diana's father doesn't show up. Neither of us is surprised, nor in the moment do we very much care. All I care about *is* the moment, her in her mother's dress, me in my best suit, tears from our families, Booker—my best man—patting me on the back encouragingly, our officiant slightly rusty on the ceremony because it's the first he's performed since the repetitions began. Looking into Diana's eyes, kissing her lips, knowing that our time together will never have to end. Maybe there is some merit to a world that never changes or decays after all.

APRIL 22, 2027 (CXXI)

I wake up, my face pressed against a tearstained pillow, and Diana is not next to me. I am alone. I rush to the park as quickly as I can. She is there waiting for me. We both smile. Life goes on.

APRIL 22, 2027 (CLXXIV)

"When was the last time you killed yourself?"

I'm impressed with my own ability to speak so disaffectedly about something so horrible. I thought I had vicariously experienced every kind of pain a human being can go through in the course of my career, but this is devastatingly new. Death was never meant to work this way.

The person I am speaking to is Daniel Simons, a client who has come in to see me for the first time today. His life has been a series of tragedies and misfortunes. His parents abused him and his three siblings daily for most of his childhood. When he finally got away from home, he struggled to find a job and was fired several times due to internal business workings he had no control over. A few days before the repetitions started, he was dumped by his girlfriend of two years and lost another job the next morning. On April 22, 2027, he decided to take his own life.

He woke up again on the second April twenty-second, unsure of how he was still alive. He only knew his suffering hadn't ended. Yet again he took a knife from the kitchen and plunged it into his own heart.

April twenty-second came a third time, and Daniel returned to consciousness. He was confused, and terrified. He had made the decision that life wasn't worth living anymore, but he didn't even have the ability to cast it away. He tried to go about his day, to do anything to distract himself from the pain in his heart, but it was too much. At one a.m. on April twenty-third, he cut his life short once again, reasoning that even if time kept repeating, it would be easier to live with the physical pain of death than the emotional pain of losing everything. A part of him was already dead. Why bother shambling along as if everything was fine? He was better off acting the part of a dead man.

Wake up on the morning of the twenty-second. A flash of pain as the knife enters the body. Lay on the floor in a pool of red. Embrace the slowly growing cold. Fade to black. Wake up on the twenty-second again. Repeat.

This went on for approximately the first one-hundred and fifty repetitions. It is now C74. Less than a month's worth of todays has passed since then.

"I haven't done it since I gave up on ending it all, on C49 I think," Daniel says, his voice shaking. "I've been tempted, but I haven't given in yet. But...I'm afraid...I'm afraid that if the temptations get to me, I'll end up stuck dying endlessly, just like I was before. If I do kill myself again, I'm not sure I'll be able to make myself stop."

"First of all, you should recognize how good you're doing right now," I say. "Nearly a month without incident—that's something to be proud of."

I'm talking to him like I would an addict, which feels deeply wrong, but I don't know how else to approach his problem. I've only vaguely heard about other suicide cases since the repetitions began, and none of them involved this many repeated, immediate attempts.

Ordinary suicide prevention won't help him. He's well past the stage of reconsidering killing himself for the first time. The fact that there can be more than one time at all massively changes everything about the situation. This isn't about suicide anymore. It's about a man who wants a way to escape from himself and has just realized that doing so in this repeating world is impossible.

Or is it? As I talk to Daniel, probing as gently as I can into the way he sees the world, I find a man who is extremely self-focused. I would never accuse him of being selfish, but his years and years of trauma have focused his eyes inward to such a degree that he is practically incapable of seeing anything but the trauma anymore. He needs an outlet. Something to help him exist outside of himself, since being within himself is so completely unbearable.

"Have you considered community service?"

"I— Huh…?" Daniel was not ready for that question. Fair, since I asked it out of the blue in the middle of a conversation that had nothing to do with it.

"There are shelters that are helping to provide food and protection to anyone who didn't have those things when the repetitions started. The starving are starving every day, but kind people are working to alleviate as much hunger and helplessness as they can.

"The thing is, every time we hit morning on the twenty-third and cycle back, the shelters reset along with everything else. They could use a pair of strong hands like yours to help them set up again every morning, and to help hand out food and blankets and whatever other necessities they can provide. Would you be interested in doing that?"

"Wh——— I, I don't, why are you…" he stumbles, glassy-eyed as if in a stupor. "I mean, I haven't been interested in anything for—"

"Then, now's the perfect time to start. Just because you've stopped killing yourself doesn't mean that you've started living. You can't do that alone in a dusty old apartment. That's something I've learned firsthand during the repeating world." And it's something I never would have figured out on my own.

Daniel hesitates. He wrings his hands together nervously, his eyes darting around the room, looking for an excuse. He doesn't find one.

"I guess…I could maybe help out a little."

"Great. I'll give you the address of a shelter near where you live—you'll have to memorize it since writing it down won't help much—and let them know that you're coming bright and early on C75, or next today, in other words. Can you commit to that?"

Daniel heaves a sigh. "Sure, Mr. Amaranthus. Sure."

He walks out of my office about twenty minutes later, staring up at the ceiling as if waiting for an answer from God. Better than looking down at his feet.

Like with Angela, I'm unsure if I've done the right thing to help him. My job is a lot harder with all the unprecedented circumstances my clients have to deal with. I can't stop worrying about Daniel, so during my break I ask my more experienced coworker, Esther, what she would have done.

"Your idea was as good as anything I can come up with," she says, shrugging. I choose to take that as reassurance.

Diana is waiting for me when I get home. She's tried to cook something for dinner—really, honestly tried—so I help fix it up and get it to an edible state. I make sure to thank her rather than responding to all of the apologies. She doesn't owe me anything. Every act of love she shows me only increases mine tenfold.

I've been around enough insufferable newlyweds to know that I've become one. The me from college would have mocked the person I am now. But the me from college doesn't exist anymore, and I find that as time goes on—or, stays still—I care less and less about his opinions.

Once we've finished eating, we clear our dishes off the table and leave them on the counter. No point in washing them when they'll just reset themselves before we need them again. We sit down together on the wide armchair that is the only comfortable piece of furniture in my apartment and Diana rests her head on my shoulder.

"I've been thinking about your promise, lately," she tells me. I don't have to ask which one.

I've been thinking about it constantly myself, and the anxiety is starting to get to me. I honestly believed that I could make having children with her work somehow, but contending with the realistic impossibility of the task has completely shot my confidence. It would,

431

however, be equally impossible to give up on the commitment. I even included it in our wedding vows.

"What have you been thinking?" I ask. I sincerely hope she has more ideas than I do.

She looks me directly in the eyes as she says, "There is a way to make it happen."

I'm dumbfounded. Sure, I was hoping, but I never thought that she would be able to…I decide right then and there that Diana is the most amazing person I have ever met.

"And what would that be?" I ask excitedly.

"We could consider adopting a child."

Oh. That…I mean, she's right, but…I never considered the concept of adoption even before time lost its sense—I'd barely even thought about kids back then—and now I have no idea what the process would look like. Paperwork is impossible, so would our home have to be inspected instead? An inspection would be a normal part of the process anyway, wouldn't it? Would we pick them up in the morning from the residential care facility? Would they go to school during the day? Hell, do schools even exist anymore? I've never had the need to ask anyone about that.

"W-We couldn't pick the name," I say pitifully. Diana laughs and kisses my cheek.

"I think I can make that sacrifice."

"It would certainly be a sacrifice…."

"Yes, but think about it. There have to be hundreds of children out there who don't have a real home, and now they have no chance of getting one. They'll never mature or grow older, which must be confusing for them. We could do so much good by choosing to make their lives better, and I would have my wish. Could you at least think about it?"

Even if I wanted to, it is impossible for me to say no to her. "If it's what you want, I don't have to think about it. I'll start looking into the process."

"Thank you so much, Adam." This time her kiss is less chaste than a soft peck on the cheek. As we pull away, I can't help but make a suggestion.

"I know we can't make our own children, but how'd you like to get some practice in case time ever goes back to normal?"

Diana smiles in answer. Wordlessly she stands, takes my hand, and leads me to the bedroom.

APRIL 22, 2027 (CCXX)

Daniel has been working hard at his local shelter, and I think he finds it at least a little bit fulfilling. He tells me stories about the people they're helping every time he meets with me. I can see hints of joy in his eyes when he relays tales of hungry children being fed and destitute men and women finding a sense of belonging. Not happiness, he's not there yet, but joy. The kind that comes from forgetting your own troubles.

He has killed himself once during the time since I made the recommendation for him to start doing community service. He didn't fall into the cycle again like he had feared he would. It helped that I had him memorize my phone number. But it helped more that he didn't feel like there was any point in stopping himself.

I've been working hard in my off time figuring the adoption thing out. Child protective services is a field that hasn't fully recuperated from the repetitions yet—which is alarming—so I'm having to reinvent the wheel a bit as I go. Luckily, I have a number of contacts who used to be in that line of work. I called them up and the few who were interested are helping me to get a program organized. If everything works out, we'll soon be getting as many children as possible into good homes, not just our own.

Diana's been a big help too—she has organizational skills I could only dream of. I told her I wanted to name the program after her, but she refused, so we're going with Juvenile Rescue Foundation. I'll admit it has a nice enough ring to it.

I'm excited to see progress being made, but we still have a long way to go before the program is really up and running. On top of that, the first post-loop elections are coming up soon, and the wrong candidate could prove to be a major setback for the foundation.

Suffice it to say, I'm on edge a lot lately as a result, and I'm so busy I can't get a break from the stress. Diana and Gustin the weatherman provide the only relief that I ever get. I just hope it doesn't start weighing on me so much that I snap. I care about my clients, but I don't envy their lives.

Diana is working this afternoon, but I have a rare break, so I've set aside time to play racquetball with Booker. It's been a while since we've met up, but we greet each other naturally and get a game going in no time. It's a far cry from our awkward reunion on the first April twenty-second.

<h2 style="text-align:center">APRIL 22, 2027 (MMXXVII)</h2>

Two thousand and twenty-seven repetitions. One for every year since the birth of Christ, prior to the start of the repeating world. We've now been subject to the loss of time for the equivalent of more than five and a half years. I'm only just now starting to fully accept that we will probably never be free of it.

I wake up alone. I always do, an eternal reminder of my solitary state before the world stopped changing and I started. The first thing I do is check the book. My bookmark is there, at the start of Chapter 2: "Methods of Psychological Resistance." These days, the reminder is comforting. It means I haven't lost the life I've made despite being unable to even remove a bookmark from a volume for longer than thirty-four hours.

I change into my athletic wear, but I don't go to the park yet. I have another stop to make first, at a building that used to be a facility for children who are in between foster homes and is now managed by our foundation. Diana does most of the actual managing these days, and I don't start work until nine. I'm not here on a business trip. I'm here to pick up our son.

Mateo is nine years old. He has been for the last five years. He was removed from the custody of his biological father due to gross neglect and has stayed in a number of foster homes. None of them worked out for him. They didn't treat him like a real part of their family, but instead as an object to be pitied. As young as he was, he still understood what was going on, and he couldn't stand it. So, he caused trouble on purpose in order to get the families to send him back. He had been staying in the facility for more than a hundred days when the repetitions started.

It took Mateo a while to warm up to Diana and me. He was the very first child to get adopted in the repeating world, so we had no idea what we were doing. We were guinea pigs for the whole system, and considering Mateo's background we might have had a hard time getting him to accept us even under more normal circumstances. But he was the one who volunteered to help test the program, and that gave us hope that we could make it work out. He wanted to have a real home, that was my belief. And we wanted to provide one for him. So we tried.

The first breakthrough we had with him was when we realized he was a big sports fan. Even though he was only nine years old, he had the names and stats memorized for every single one of the Giants players. I started watching their games with him, and as we celebrated the victories and mourned the defeats, together, I could sense him slowly becoming more comfortable with us.

He didn't truly open up until he started running with Diana and me, though. In addition to watching sports, he loved to get outside and be active, so Diana suggested that we take him with us on our morning runs in the park. Admittedly, I was loath to give up my private time with her, but, as was usually the case, when I gave in, I found that she had been right all along. It was one kind of joy to spend time alone with my wife, but it was another entirely to hear Mateo call me Dad for the first time as he passed me on the third lap.

I stop my car—which I rarely used before Mateo joined our family— in front of the door to the living facility. Mateo is already waiting for me on the curb. I unlock the door and he climbs into the passenger seat. Technically, according to the law, he isn't tall enough to sit there, but although his brain can't mature in the repeating world, his mind can, and I am careful not to treat him the same way I would a little kid. Sitting in the passenger seat is a privilege to be earned, not just a box to be checked when you reach a certain height. That's my philosophy, at least.

"Hi Dad, what's for breakfast today?" A customary greeting from Mateo when we see each other in the morning.

"Pancakes. Your mom is planning on making them, so no funny faces if they end up a bit underdone."

"Aw, but we had pancakes two days ago. Can't we have something different?"

"Our options are a little limited by what ingredients we had on hand on the twenty-first, unless your mom or I get up early to pick something up from the supermarket before work, and there are people who need that food more than we do."

On the twenty-first. Not a phrase I use often anymore. If you've ever had that feeling that a recent event in your life is already far distant, know that it is nothing compared with realizing that yesterday was literally half a decade ago.

Mateo sighs. "Okay, but could you get cereal tomo—— I mean, next today? I'm getting tired of pancakes."

Another sacrifice, but Mateo's happiness is more important than my sleep. "You know what, sure," I say.

"Thanks, Dad."

Mateo, Diana, and I are all apart from each other at the beginning of each repetition, as we can no longer choose where we will be when the twenty-second starts, but we come together at the park for our run every morning, and that repetition creates togetherness rather than hopelessness. I wonder how much the fact that it is our choice matters to the emotional effect it has on us. Either way, I am always happy to see Diana waving when we pull into the parking area, and today is no exception.

After our morning exercise, the three of us drive to my apartment to have breakfast together. Why we ended up deciding that this place would be "our place" I can't quite recall. It could just as well have been the apartment Diana wakes up in every morning that became our home. The important part is that we have a shared space that belongs to all of us now. It'd be nice if Mateo could decorate his room, which starts every morning looking like the unused guest room it was when I lived alone, but we make do with what we've got.

As our breakfast concludes—the pancakes were much better than the last dozen times Diana made them—I turn on Martin Gustin's weather show while my wife and I get ready for work. I'm surprised he's been able to stay on air all this time, and somehow keep all his jokes fresh, considering his limited subject matter. I swear the man is a comedic genius.

We all hop in the car and prepare to say goodbye again until the end of the day. Diana's workplace is the closest to our apartment, so we drop her off first. She has taken over as the primary manager of the Juvenile Rescue Foundation, and she is fantastic at it. I contribute where I can, but she doesn't need my help all that much, and I have a job of my own to do. Whenever I worry that I'm not doing enough, she reminds me how much my clients need me, more so now than ever. I sigh and agree, secretly mournful that my excuse to spend more time with Diana didn't work out.

Our next stop is Mateo's school. Schools are another institution that took a while to get up and running again, but there are enough people in the world who see a point in education even when everything has come to a standstill that eventually they managed to make a comeback.

I can't tell you why concretely, but I am among those who believe that learning still has a place in this world. And not just to figure out the cause of the time loop we're stuck in so we can find a way out of it. Very little progress has been made in that field so far, and not for a lack of trying. I don't care too much for the idea anymore. But I do care for the enrichment of the mind, and you need good classrooms and teachers for that.

The building I drop Mateo off at used to be a high school, but the system of learning that used terms like that isn't relevant to us at this point, so it's just called a school now. The focus has shifted to meeting each student where they are, whether they be irreparably sick or injured, slower than average learners, or a nine-year-old who has been nine for five years and is ready to start taking on complex algebraic equations. In a way, I'd argue that this is preferable to the old system.

Finally, I drive back to the clinic and begin my work. Charlie waves as I enter the door, and I make small talk with him for a few minutes before he has to start answering phone calls. On an average day like today we're busier than we ever were before the repetitions started. I barely have time for a fifteen-minute lunch break. By the end of the day, I am emotionally and physically exhausted. The only reason I can hold on through it all is because I'm anticipating my evening at home once I'm done.

Mateo and Diana have both returned home already by the time I get there. We share stories from our day over dinner, watch a movie together, and Mateo goes to sleep around nine o'clock. His body isn't equipped for late nights. Diana and I stay up and chat for a while, and I read a few chapters of a book. I have to pick it up from the library on my way home from work every day since it returns itself when the loop hits.

Eventually the two of us go to bed as well. We get to wake up next to each other on the morning of the twenty-third, and spend a little more time together as a family before everything is reset. I've come to be grateful that the loop includes more than twenty-four hours.

APRIL 23, 2027 (MMXXVII)

Today though, I have to hurry to the office as soon as I wake up. I ran out of available time blocks during my normal workday and had a client call in who urgently needs to talk to me, so I offered to meet him during the brief hours of the twenty-third. I quickly shower and throw on a button-up shirt before driving to the office to make my appointment.

My emergency client is Micah Palmer, the prophetic boy who told me something was going to happen on the first April twenty-second. He's been in to see me off and on during the last two-thousand-odd repetitions. At the moment he's attending school and studying history. As a physical teenager, he's having an even harder time fitting in with the other advanced students of varying ages and backgrounds.

Some kids from Micah's old high school have taken to following him around and harassing him. He mentioned his premonition to some of his current classmates, which would have been a positive indicator of his social progress if it didn't lead to word getting around and reaching his past bullies, who have somehow concluded that it makes sense to assign blame for the state of the entire world to him as a result. They generally aren't violent, and law enforcement is aware of their behavior, so they are unlikely to act out too much as long as Micah stays in safe, open areas, but it's still too much for anyone to have to deal with. It doesn't help that most of his old coping mechanisms are kaput. His favorite TV show can't air new episodes anymore, although the creator at least revealed his vision for the ending since he will never be able to bring it to fruition.

No individual event has occurred to qualify Micah's visit today as an "emergency." Considering his situation, no such thing is necessary for me to drop everything to be here. Micah told me that it was all too much, and he needed to see me. That was all it took.

"So, Micah, why did you ask to meet me today?"

Micah mumbles something imperceptible and I have to politely ask him to speak up a little so I can hear him.

"It's not really any one thing, you know? I'm kind of embarrassed making a big deal out of it. Nothing in particular happened—nothing ever does. I just felt like if I didn't talk to you, I'd burst. Like a balloon filled with too much air. I'm sorry to be a bother."

"You aren't a bother," I assure him. "Let's stick with that balloon metaphor. You say you feel like you're too filled up. So, what kinds of things is your balloon filled with?"

"Huh? Um, I don't know, stuff like stress about my coursework, and those guys from my old school who keep bothering me, and my parents, and everything really. So, just stress in general, I guess."

"Well, no wonder your balloon is in danger of popping, with all that stress you're putting into it." I call to mind something I learned from studying physics back in school, knowing that a scientific metaphor will likely be easy for Micah to understand. "Another way to talk about stress when referring to physical objects is to say you're putting pressure or tension on them. That'll stretch the balloon's membrane beyond its limit and cause it to break. What we need to do is find the source of that stress so we can remove it and replace it with something better. Am I right?"

Micah rubs his hands together anxiously. "I'm not sure I'm following. And, besides, didn't I tell you the source? It's all that stuff that's been bothering me. I can't make it go away just like that."

I shake my head. "That stuff certainly adds up, but there's something else at the root of it all, isn't there? Something else you haven't mentioned to me yet."

Micah looks down at his feet. "I mean, I am really worried about all those things, but…the worst part is, I feel like I'll never be able to escape them. If things keep going back to the way they were yesterday, how am I supposed to get away from them? How can I put something better in my balloon if everything we make disappears at the end of the cycle? A world trapped in time like this is a world that's impossible to live in."

This is more or less exactly what I was expecting to hear. I don't know how, but Micah sensed the changes the world was about to undergo. I've had a hunch for a long time that dealing with said changes is deeply uncomfortable for him. Perhaps that's the reason he could tell they were going to happen in the first place. The discomfort could have started before the looping did. It sounds crazy, but so does being stuck in a five-year-long time loop. I have to be willing to consider that it could be possible.

I've never been able to get Micah to open up about this particular anxiety—until now. But I've had plenty of time to think about what I will say to him once he does share his worries with me.

"Let me ask you this," I say. "In this world, does anything ever change?"

"No, sir. Not anymore."

"Are you sure about that?"

He stops fidgeting and freezes. "I…I was until you said that."

"Think about it. In a few hours, everything will reset to exactly the way it was in the morning of April 22, 2027. Correct?"

"Yeah…"

"Except."

"Except?"

I spread my hands toward Micah, inviting him to answer his own question.

"Except for…our memories. We remember all the previous repetitions."

"That's right. So, the one thing that can still change…is people. In a world with no progression, where creating and changing our surroundings is impossible, life has no meaning. But there is something that changes, that progresses, and so purpose, value, and meaning all still exist. They exist in other people. If you want to stay sane inside of the repeating world, you have to cling to that. It's the only way I've seen anyone beat the hopelessness that the endless loops create, myself included."

Micah's breathing speeds up. He's not panicking—yet—but he isn't taking what I've told him well. I foresaw this possibility too. Social anxiety is one of the things he started seeing me for back when time was still normal.

"That's the only way? But other people hate me."

"Do I hate you?"

He hesitates for longer than I would like. "No, you don't."

"How about your family? Have you been spending much time with them recently?"

"I've been busy with school, so…"

"I suggest you start making more time for them. Learning from history is all well and good, but we live in the present, over and over and over again. So be present with the things that mean something now."

Micah isn't satisfied with that answer. Neither am I, to be completely honest. It's a piece, but I'm sure there's much more to the puzzle that I'm not seeing yet. So, we talk. I listen to him, and he listens to me, for the next several hours. As our conversation goes on, I can see that he's starting to get it. He relaxes a little. Sits a little straighter in his seat. Talks about things he hasn't brought up in a long time. About his family. He wonders what they think of him. I've met his parents, so I can assure him that they love him. He says he's not sure what that means, but he smiles anyway.

When the time comes, both of us smile and brace ourselves.

APRIL 22, 2027 (MMXXVIII)

I am lying in bed, alone. I'm still smiling.

The Year in the Contests

In celebration of forty years of nurturing Writers of the Future, we received 116 Proclamations and Letters of Recognition from state and city officials in areas where we have had past winners, including from the governor of New Jersey and the governor of Arkansas.

US Senator for New York, Charles E. Schumer, had a flag flown over the United States Capitol on April 8, 2024, in honor of L. Ron Hubbard's Writers of the Future Week.

The Contests also received awards from *Locus* magazine, FanX, Costa Rica Mayor of Oreamuno, and Dragon Con.

The cofounder of Dragon Con, Pat Henry, attended the gala celebration and presented the Honorary Dragon Award. He said in part "Much like L. Ron Hubbard, I am a gardener. My garden is smaller. I nurture plants to the best of my ability. I plant food for the neighborhood. Mr. Hubbard's garden is the entire planet."

We received thirty-seven Letters of Congratulations such as this from Tom Doherty, the Founder and Chairman of Tor Publishing: "Knowing and having worked with so many of the authors involved, I would like to say Writers of the Future, a gift by L. Ron Hubbard to that future, has been carried forward by some of the finest talent in our field."

And this from *New York Times* bestselling author of the Silo series, Hugh Howey: "It's a contest that's not over the hill—it is on the rise. It deserves a mid-life congratulations. I look forward to seeing how far it can climb, knowing that it will touch countless more writers and hopefully outlast us all."

CONTEST GROWTH
This volume represents the forty-one years of the Writers' Contest and thirty-six years of the Illustrators' Contest. Both Contests continue to expand breaking all records of annual entries.

Winners in this volume hail from four countries: Canada, Hungary, United Kingdom, and the United States of America.

AWARDS FOR THE CONTEST & ANTHOLOGY
L. Ron Hubbard Presents Writers of the Future Volume 40 won the Gold Award for the New York City Big Book Awards for Best Anthology.

The Writers and Illustrators of the Future Podcast won the Gold award for the eLit Book Awards in the Podcast—Interview/Author Hosted Format. It was also nominated for finalist in three categories of the Podcast Awards: The People's Choice. The categories are: 1) Arts, 2) Education, and 3) Storyteller/Drama.

NOTABLE ACCOMPLISHMENTS FROM JUDGES & ALUMNI
Here is a selection of the many accomplishments and awards won by our Contest judges and winners.

JUDGES
Bob Eggleton received a Judge's Choice award for his art, *Moby Dick Versus the Sea Monster*, at the Boskone Science Fiction and Fantasy convention.

Craig Elliott won Bronze in the *Infected by Art Volume 12* Digital/Photoshop category for *Offworld Encounter*.

Laura Freas Beraha was the Artist Guest of Honor at Los Con 50 science fiction convention in Los Angeles.

Nancy Kress was the Literary Guest of Honor at Dragon Con in Atlanta.

Larry Niven was Author Guest of Honor at Los Con 50 science fiction convention in Los Angeles.

Jody Lynn Nye was Guest of Honor at Congregate 10 in Winston-Salem, at Gary Con in Lake Geneva and at Windy Con 50 in Chicago.

Kristine Kathryn Rusch won a Best Novelette *Asimov's Science Fiction* Readers' Award for "The Nameless Dead."

Tim Powers won an Inkpot Award at San Diego Comic Con.

ALUMNI

Chris Arias (Volume 39) won an award from the Costa Rica Mayor of Oreamuno.

Zack Be (Volume 36) won the Jim Baen Memorial Short Story Award in 2024 for his story "Locus of Control."

F. J. Bergmann (Volume 36) was awarded the title of the 2024 Grand Master from the Science Fiction & Fantasy Poetry Association. She also won third place in the Dwarf Stars Award of the Science Fiction & Fantasy Poetry Association for "Nikola Tesla."

Jennifer Bruce (Volume 37) won the two-week Finley's View Farm Artist Residency for 2024.

Erik Bundy (Volume 34) won a Paris Book Award for his medieval mystery *The Plowman's Plight*.

Laurance Davis (Volume 39) won the Florida Writers Association 2024 Royal Palm Literary Award for Published Young Adult Novels for his book *The Dead Can Be Stubborn*.

Quintin Gleim (Volume 34) won *Infected by Art Volume 12* 5th Place: Grand Prize plus Gold in the Digital/Photoshop category for *Exsanguinator Cavalry*.

David Hankins (Volume 39) won a Critters Readers' Poll for Best Science Fiction and Fantasy Short Story for "Death and the Taxman" which was also his winning story in Volume 39. His novelized version, *Death and the Taxman*, won Outstanding Humor/Comedy from the Independent Author Network.

Stephen Kotowych (Volume 23) won an Aurora Award for Best Related Work as editor for *Year's Best Canadian Fantasy and Science Fiction: Volume One*.

Ven Locklear (Volume 16) won Honorable Mention in the *Infected by Art Volume 12* Digital/Photoshop category for *Dreamwalker*.

Karawynn Long (Volume 9) won a Best Short Story *Asimov's Science Fiction* Readers' Award for "Hope Is the Thing with Feathers."

Wulf Moon won a Best of Year Award in the Critters Readers' Poll including Best Nonfiction Book for *How to Write a Howling Good Story*.

Anthony Morovian (Volume 34) won the two-week Finley's View Farm Artist Residency for 2024.

Sarah Morrison (Volume 39) was the Artist Guest of Honor at Arisia Con in Boston. She also received a Judge's Choice award for her cover art of *Death and the Taxman* at the Boskone Science Fiction and Fantasy convention.

Scot Noel (Volume 6) won the SciFidea Dyson Sphere Contest for "The Eight Pillars of Void and Future."

Brittany Rainsdon (Volume 38) won the SciFidea Dyson Sphere Contest for "A Forbidden Shade of Green."

Omar Rayyan (Volume 8) won a Chesley Award for Best Interior Illustration for his work on *Animal Farm*.

Brian Trent (Volume 29) won the SciFidea Dyson Sphere Contest for "Watchman, What of the Night?"

Mary Turzillo (Volume 4) won the *Analog* Readers' Poll Award for Best Poem, "How to Conquer Gravity."

Elizabeth Wein (Volume 9) won Best Young Adult Novel in the International Thriller Writers Award for *Stateless*.

Frank Wu (Volume 16) and coauthor Jay Werkheiser won the *Analog* Readers' Poll Award for Best Novella for his story "Poison."

There were just so MANY novels, short stories, and art published this past year from our judges and winners, we've limited this list to awards won and guest of honor appearances.

It's a real challenge to keep up with the 900 plus Contest winners. We are so proud of them all.

For Contest year 41, the winners are:

WRITERS OF THE FUTURE CONTEST WINNERS

FIRST QUARTER

1. *Sandra Skalski*
   "Slip Stone"

2. *Jefferson Snow*
   "The Rune Witch"

3. *Barlow Crassmont*
   "The Boy from Elsewhen"

SECOND QUARTER

1. *Randyn C.J. Bartholomew*
   "Ascii"

2. *Lauren McGuire*
   "Karma Birds"

3. *Seth Atwater Jr.*
   "A World of Repetitions"

THIRD QUARTER

1. *T. R. Naus*
   "Storm Damage"

2. *Ian Keith*
   "Blackbird Stone"

3. *Joel C. Scoberg*
   "The Stench of Freedom"

FOURTH QUARTER

1. *Patrick MacPhee*
   "Thirty Minutes or It's a Paradox"

2. *Andrew Jackson*
   "Code L1"

3. *Robert F. Lowell*
   "Kill Switch"

THE YEAR IN THE CONTESTS

ILLUSTRATORS OF THE FUTURE CONTEST WINNERS

FIRST QUARTER

Haileigh Enriquez

CL Fors

Daniel Montifar

SECOND QUARTER

David Hoffrichter

Tremani Sutcliffe

Hailee Rojas

THIRD QUARTER

John Barlow

HeatherAnne Lee

Breanda Petsch

FOURTH QUARTER

Cam Collins

Marianna Mester

Jordan Smajstrla

L. Ron Hubbard's
Writers of the Future Contest

The most enduring and influential contest
in the history of Sci-Fi & Fantasy.

Open to new and amateur Sci-Fi & Fantasy writers.

Prizes each quarter: $1,000, $750, $500
Quarterly 1st place winners compete for
$5,000 additional annual prize!

ALL JUDGING DONE BY
PROFESSIONAL WRITERS ONLY.

No entry fee is required.

Entrants retain all rights.

Enter a short story science fiction, fantasy, light horror
up to but not exceeding 17,000 words. AI is not accepted.
Professionals need not apply. Free to enter and entrants retain
all publication rights. Enter 1 story per quarter, up to 4 per
year. Anonymous judging. This is a merit-based competition.

Don't delay! Send your entry now!

To submit your entry electronically go to:
www.writersofthefuture.com/enter-writer-contest

Email: contests@authorservicesinc.com

To submit your entry via mail send to:
L. Ron Hubbard's Writers of the Future Contest
7051 Hollywood Blvd.
Los Angeles, California 90028

1. No entry fee is required, and all rights in the story remain the property of the author. All types of science fiction, fantasy, and dark fantasy are welcome.

2. By submitting to the Contest, the entrant agrees to abide by all Contest rules.

3. All entries must be original works by the entrant, in English. Plagiarism, which includes the use of third-party poetry, song lyrics, characters, or another person's universe, without written permission, will result in disqualification. Short stories or novelettes generated or created by computer software and/or artificial intelligence will be disqualified. Excessive violence or sex and the use of profane, vulgar, racist or offensive words, determined by the judges, will result in the story being rejected. Entries may not have been previously published in professional media.

4. To be eligible, entries must be a short story of fantasy, science fiction, or light speculative horror. Your story has no minimum length requirement, however it may not be longer than 17,000 words.

   We regret we cannot consider novels, poetry, screenplays, or works intended for children.

5. The Contest is open only to those who have not professionally published a novel or short novel, or more than one novelette, or more than three short stories, in any medium. Professional publication is deemed to be payment of professional rates at the time of publication (currently set at eight cents per word), and at least 5,000 copies, or 5,000 hits.

6. Entries submitted electronically must be double-spaced and must include the title and page number on each page, but not the author's name. Electronic submissions will separately include the author's legal name, pen name if applicable, address, telephone number, email address, and approximate word count.

    Entries submitted in hard copy must be typewritten or a computer printout in black ink on white paper, printed only on the front of the paper, double-spaced, with numbered pages. All other formats will be disqualified. Each entry must have a cover page with the title of the work, the author's legal name, a pen name if applicable, address, telephone number, email address and an approximate word count. Every subsequent page must carry the title and a page number, but the author's name must be deleted to facilitate fair, anonymous judging.

7. Manuscripts will be returned after judging only if the author has provided return postage on a self-addressed envelope.

8. We accept only entries that do not require a delivery signature for us to receive them.

9. There shall be three cash prizes in each quarter: a First Prize of $1,000, a Second Prize of $750, and a Third Prize of $500, in US dollars. In addition, at the end of the year the First Place winners will have their entries judged by a panel of judges, and a Grand Prize winner shall be determined and receive an additional $5,000. All winners will also receive trophies. The Grand Prize winner shall be announced and awarded, along with the trophies to winners, at the L. Ron Hubbard awards ceremony held in the following year or when it is able to be held due to government regulations.

10. The Contest has four quarters, beginning on October 1, January 1, April 1, and July 1. The year will end on September 30. To be eligible for judging in its quarter, an entry must be postmarked or received electronically no later than midnight on the last day of the quarter. Late entries will be included in the following quarter and the Contest Administration will so notify the entrant.

11. Each entrant may submit only one manuscript per quarter. Winners are ineligible to make further entries in the Contest.

12. All entries for each quarter are final. No revisions are accepted.

13. Entries will be judged by professional authors. The decisions of the judges are entirely their own, and are final and binding.

14. Winners in each quarter will be individually notified of the results by phone, mail, or email.

15. This Contest is void where prohibited by law.

16. To send your entry electronically, go to:
www.writersofthefuture.com/enter-writer-contest
and follow the instructions.
To send your entry in hard copy, mail it to:
L. Ron Hubbard's Writers of the Future Contest
7051 Hollywood Blvd., Los Angeles, California 90028

17. Visit the website for any Contest rules update at:
www.writersofthefuture.com

L. Ron Hubbard's
Illustrators of the Future Contest

The most enduring and influential
contest in the history of Sci-Fi & Fantasy.

Open to new and amateur Sci-Fi & Fantasy artists.

$1,500 in prizes each quarter
Quarterly winners compete for $5,000
additional annual prize!

ALL JUDGING DONE BY
PROFESSIONAL ARTISTS ONLY.

No entry fee is required.

Entrants retain all rights.

Enter three science fiction or fantasy pieces of art. Color or black
and white. Send your best original work. AI art is not accepted.
Free to enter and entrants retain all publication rights. Enter
once per quarter. Enter all four quarters each year. Anonymous
judging. This is a merit-based competition.

Don't delay! Send your entry now!

To submit your entry electronically go to:
www.writersofthefuture.com/enter-the-illustrator-contest

Email: contests@authorservicesinc.com

To submit your entry via mail send to:
L. Ron Hubbard's Illustrators of the Future Contest
7051 Hollywood Blvd.
Los Angeles, California 90028

1. The Contest is open to entrants from all nations. (However, entrants should provide themselves with some means for written communication in English.) All themes of science fiction and fantasy illustrations are welcome: every entry is judged on its own merits only. No entry fee is required and all rights to the entry remain the property of the artist.

2. By submitting to the Contest, the entrant agrees to abide by all Contest rules.

3. The Contest is open to new and amateur artists who have not been professionally published and paid for more than three black-and-white story illustrations, or more than one process-color painting, in media distributed broadly to the general public. The ultimate eligibility criterion, however, is defined by the word "amateur"—in other words, the artist has not been paid for his artwork. If you are not sure of your eligibility, please write a letter to the Contest Administration with details regarding your publication history. Include a self-addressed and stamped envelope for the reply. You may also send your questions to the Contest Administration via email.

4. Each entrant may submit only one set of illustrations in each Contest quarter. The entry must be original to the entrant and previously unpublished. Plagiarism, infringement of the rights of others, or other violations of the Contest rules will result in disqualification. Winners in previous quarters are not eligible to make further entries.

5. The entry shall consist of three illustrations done by the entrant in a color or black-and-white medium created from the artist's imagination. Use of gray scale in illustrations

and mixed media, photo and design software, and the use of photography in the illustrations are accepted. Art generated using programs such as artificial intelligence, or similar programs will be disqualified. Source and reference imagery may be requested at any time to ensure all rules have been met. Each illustration must represent a subject different from the other two.

6. Electronic submissions will separately include the artist's legal name, address, telephone number, email address which will identify each of three pieces of art and the artist's signature on the art should be deleted. Only .jpg, .jpeg, and .png files will be accepted, a maximum file size of 10 MB.

7. HARD COPY ENTRIES SHOULD NOT BE THE ORIGINAL DRAWINGS, but should be color or black-and-white reproductions of the originals, of a quality satisfactory to the entrant. Entries must be submitted unfolded and flat, in an envelope no larger than 9 inches by 12 inches. Images submitted electronically must be a minimum of 300 dpi, a minimum of 5 x 7 inches and a maximum of 8.5 x 11 inches.

All hard copy entries must be accompanied by a self-addressed return envelope of the appropriate size, with the correct US postage affixed. (Non-US entrants should enclose international postage reply coupons.) If the entrant does not want the reproductions returned, the entry should be clearly marked DISPOSABLE COPIES: DO NOT RETURN. A business-size self-addressed envelope with correct postage (or valid email address) should be included so that the judging results may be returned to the entrant. We only accept entries that do not require a delivery signature for us to receive them.

To facilitate anonymous judging, each of the three photocopies must be accompanied by a removable cover sheet bearing the artist's name, address, telephone number, email address, and an identifying title for that work. The reproduction of the work should carry the same identifying title on the front of the illustration and the artist's signature should be deleted. The Contest Administration will remove and file the cover sheets, and forward only the anonymous entry to the judges.

8. There will be three cowinners in each quarter. Each winner will receive a cash prize of US $500 and will be awarded a trophy. Winners will also receive eligibility to compete for the annual Grand Prize of $5,000 together with the annual Grand Prize trophy.

9. For the annual Grand Prize Contest, the quarterly winners will be furnished with a specification sheet and a winning story from the Writers of the Future Contest to illustrate. In order to retain eligibility for the Grand Prize, each winner shall send to the Contest address his/her illustration of the assigned story within thirty (30) days of receipt of the story assignment.

   The yearly Grand Prize winner shall be determined by a panel of judges on the following basis only: Each Grand Prize judge's personal opinion on the extent to which it makes the judge want to read the story it illustrates.

   The Grand Prize winner shall be announced and awarded, along with the trophies to the winners, at the L. Ron Hubbard awards ceremony held in the following year or when it is able to be held due to government regulations.

10. The Contest has four quarters, beginning on October 1, January 1, April 1, and July 1. The year will end on September 30. To be eligible for judging in its quarter, an entry must be postmarked or received electronically no later than midnight

on the last day of the quarter. Late entries will be included in the following quarter and the Contest Administration will so notify the entrant.

11. Entries will be judged by professional artists only. Each quarterly judging and the Grand Prize judging may have different panels of judges. The decisions of the judges are entirely their own and are final and binding.

12. Winners in each quarter will be individually notified of the results by phone, mail, or email.

13. This Contest is void where prohibited by law.

14. To send your entry electronically, go to: www.writersofthefuture.com/enter-the-illustrator-contest and follow the instructions.
    To send your entry via mail send it to:
    L. Ron Hubbard's Illustrators of the Future Contest
    7051 Hollywood Blvd., Los Angeles, California 90028

15. Visit the website for any Contest rules update at: www.illustratorsofthefuture.com

BECOME THE NEXT
WRITER OF THE FUTURE

Listen to podcasts with past winners, judges, luminaries in the field, and publishing industry professionals to get their tips on writing and illustration and how to launch your career.

Read blogs spanning the gamut from a novice contestant to a Grand Master of Science Fiction who will give you invaluable knowledge, guidance, and encouragement.

Join the Writers of the Future Forum moderated by former winners. Attend live Q&As with Contest judges.

Learn the Contest rules and how to win. Get your story published in this anthology.

Take advantage of our FREE online writing workshop featuring Orson Scott Card, Tim Powers, and the late David Farland.

Sign up for a monthly newsletter featuring advice, quarterly winner announcements, latest news, and accomplishments.

WritersoftheFuture.com

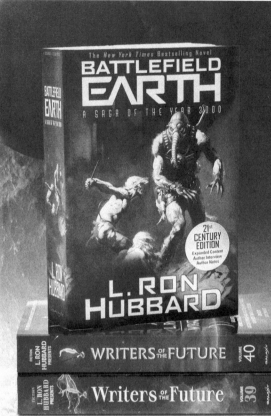

Writers of the Future
10-Book Package and Slipcase

Since Volume 30, the annual anthology has been published as a handsome trade paperback.

In addition to the Writers' Contest winning stories and hard-won tips from Contest judges, each volume features an impressive full-color 16-page art gallery. Additionally each includes three stories from bestselling authors. All this makes for a captivating book to read, treasure, and discover the best new writers and artists each year.

$15.95, 432 pgs

$15.95, 496 pgs

$15.95, 432 pgs

$15.95, 400 pgs

$15.95, 480 pgs

$15.95, 440 pgs

$15.95, 472 pgs

$15.95, 448 pgs

$22.95, 496 pgs

$22.95, 528 pgs

$22.95, 504 pgs

$22.95, 472 pgs

The slipcase features full-color artwork from Volume 33 by Larry Elmore, Volume 35 by Bob Eggleton, Volume 36 by Echo Chernik, and Volume 39 by Tom Wood.

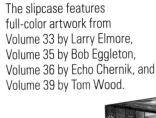

Get the slipcase free by completing your collection with a minimum order of $50.

To order call toll-free 877-842-5299 or visit GalaxyPress.com

Galaxy Press, Inc.
7051 Hollywood Boulevard
Los Angeles, CA 90028